DSB

The shining splendor of our Zebra Lovegram logo on the cover of this book reflects the glittering excellence of the story inside. Look for the Zebra Lovegram whenever you buy a historical romance. It's a trademark that guarantees the very best in quality and reading entertainment.

A TIME TO DREAM

"You are enough to make a man question his sanity," Shadow Hawk said. He sighed, and stroked her hair gently. "My love for you is so strong it frightens me."

He was standing so close to Aissa that she could see the subtle changes in his eyes as they darkened from blue to gray. She was aware of his height, of the scent of his skin. Impulsively she stepped closer, pressing her body against his. She lifted her mouth, kissing him deeply. She wanted him more than she wanted anything else in this world.

"You're full of surprises," Shadow Hawk whispered. "Sometimes I feel I'll go mad with desire for you."

"I've already gone mad," Aissa said, brushing his lips with hers.

"I've decided something," Shadow Hawk said. "I'll go to my people. I'll visit for a time, and then I'll come back."

Aissa nodded, trying to contain her fear. He had left her twice before.

"I will come back, Aissa," Shadow Hawk said. He looked at her, his expression one of the greatest love. "And when I do, we will be married. It is time, Aissa."

Aissa smiled, but her eyes filled with tears. She couldn't believe that after everything they'd been through they were finally going to be together. She laid her head against Shadow Hawk's chest and let him hold her. She had never felt so happy in her life. . . .

KAREN A. BALE

ZEBRA BOOKS
KENSINGTON PUBLISHING CORP.

To Hollie and Michael.
Thanks for all your support.

ZEBRA BOOKS

are published by

Kensington Publishing Corp.
475 Park Avenue South
New York, NY 10016

First Printing: March, 1993

Printed in the United States of America

Chapter One

Aissa smiled as her father and Shadow Hawk argued over their game of checkers, just as they had argued over beam and plank. It had taken them ten months to build this house after Ray Grimes had burnt down the house Aissa had grown up in. Aissa brushed the thought of Ray Grimes aside and looked around. There was work that still needed to be done, furniture that needed to be bought, and curtains that needed to be made for the windows. But at least it was home.

Aissa finished the last of the dishes and put them on the cupboard to dry. She walked over to the table and sat down, studying the game board. She tried not to smile. Her father had never learned that Shadow Hawk's instinctive grasp of strategy made him a formidable opponent even though he hadn't played the game long. Aissa covered her smile as Shadow Hawk took his black piece and jumped over five of Ben's men until he reached the other side of the board.

"I believe I won, Gerard."

"You didn't win," Ben replied, pushing the board away from him. "You cheated."

"I did not cheat. You were not paying attention."

"I always pay attention. You cheated. I saw you."

"You saw nothing, Gerard, except me taking your men."

"Ah," Ben said in frustration and slid away from the table and stood up. "I'm going on up to bed. I'm going to read that new book you got me, Aissa."

"Good night, Father."

Ben glared at Shadow Hawk. "We'll see who wins tomorrow night."

Aissa smiled as she watched her father leave the room and climb the stairs. She glanced at Shadow Hawk. He was dressed in buckskins and a blue work shirt. She looked at his hands as he picked up the checker pieces and the board. He had long, graceful-looking fingers. Aissa loved to watch him work. Whether he was swinging a hammer or using the fine bone needles his mother had given him, his hands were steady.

"What is it?" He looked up at her, his eyes more gray than blue in the soft light of the kerosene lamp.

Aissa reached out and touched his hand. "You're a handsome man."

Shadow Hawk tensed his mouth and pulled his hand away. "Why do you say such things?" He stood up and put the checkers away in the bookcase next to the fireplace.

Aissa walked over to him. "What's wrong? You haven't been yourself lately."

Shadow Hawk looked at her, nodding. "You're right, I haven't been myself. I have become a white man and I'm not sure if I like it."

Aissa turned away, aching but not surprised. She had always feared the day would come when he would have to return to his people. "Nothing is keeping you here, Shadow Hawk. You can leave at any time." She felt his hands on her shoulders, and she closed her eyes. She wanted him to touch her; she wanted him to make love to her. But she would not try to keep him that way. She pulled away and walked toward the door, grabbing her shawl from the hook next to it. She threw it around her shoulders and went outside, walking toward the garden. She had built a bench and carefully laid a rock trail around the primrose and iris she had planted. She sat down on the bench, breathing in the fresh night air. She heard Shadow Hawk walking toward her in the darkness. He was being noisy on purpose, Aissa knew. He didn't want to startle her.

"You are angry with me." He sat down next to her.

"No, I'm not angry. I'm just scared." She pulled her shawl closer around her, tightly gripping the ends.

"Just because I miss my people does not mean I want to leave you, Aissa."

She closed her eyes. Even his voice moved her and the feel of him so close to her was unsettling. "I understand if you want to go back to your people, Shadow Hawk. I felt the same way when I was in your camp."

"Yes, but both times you were in my camp you were a captive. It was different for you."

"Maybe it's not so different. You're here but you don't want to be here. I think you should go home if that's what you want." She tried to make her voice sound even and unemotional, but she hadn't succeeded. She felt his hand go up to her shoulder and grab her thick braid. He undid the ribbon, running his fingers through her long hair until it fell around her shoulders like a cape. He took the shawl from her clenched fingers and dropped it to the ground. He turned to her, straddling the bench, and reached out to run his fingers up underneath her hair along the back of her neck. He moved closer to her, pulling her against his chest. She didn't resist but welcomed the warmth and safety of his embrace.

"I miss my people, Aissa, it is true. But I only wish to visit them. That is all." He kissed the top of her head and wrapped his arms around her. "I do not want to live there again. This is my home now."

Aissa pushed him away and stood up. He called her name but she ignored him, hurrying from the garden toward the house. She didn't want it to be this way. She had seen what power they had over each other through their bodies, but she wondered if that was enough to make them happy. She was almost at the door when she heard him behind her and felt his arms go around her. Effortlessly, he lifted her up. "Don't, Shadow Hawk. If my father hears us—"

"Gerard is not stupid, Aissa. He knows how we feel about each other."

"But it's not right, it's just—" He kissed her into silence. She felt the familiar warmth begin to glow within her body. She wouldn't fight him; she couldn't. And he knew it.

Aissa laid her head on Shadow Hawk's shoulder as he carried her back past the garden and down the path to the pond. Overhead the stars twinkled in the black immensity of the sky. The air was heavy with the scent of summer clover. He set her into the soft grass while he stood over her, taking off his clothes. She could barely see him in the darkness but suddenly he was next to her and her mouth sought his eagerly, willingly. After an eternal kiss, he released her. She sat up as he unlaced her boots and pulled them off. Then she stood up, suddenly chilly and embarrassed. She began unbuttoning the bodice of her dress, determined to overcome her girlish shyness. She was a woman, after all, and she wanted this as much as he did. She shoved her dress from her arms and down over her legs. She was dressed only in her chemise. She tried to stand proudly but the truth was that as much as she loved Shadow Hawk and as much as she enjoyed the feeling when their bodies were together, it made her feel uncomfortable. More than that, it made her feel guilty. She had been with Shadow Hawk before yet he wasn't her husband. What did that make her?

"Aissa."

His voice was husky with desire. He pulled her gently down in the soft grass next to him, and she felt the warmth of his hand on her arm. He ran his fingers up until he touched her collarbone, then he traced a line along her neck to the tops of her breasts. He lowered the straps of the chemise. She closed her eyes as she felt his hand move to excite her, and Aissa delighted in the feeling, lost herself in it. Shadow Hawk slid the chemise up her bare thighs, and began rubbing, stroking. She felt his fingers stroke her gently, then urgently as she began to respond. His head moved to her breasts, kissing them, gently biting the nipples through the soft cotton material.

Aissa moaned softly and pulled him closer. "Don't stop," she pleaded, her voice sounding strange and urgent in the night.

"Aissa." Shadow Hawk whispered her name.

"Yes," she said, feeling his mouth cover hers. "Yes," she murmured again, as they sank together into the soft grass.

Suddenly she felt his lean body on top of her. He spread her legs apart and lifted her slightly until she felt him inside her. But he didn't begin the rhythm she ached to feel. He stayed still, unmoving, and Aissa didn't know what was wrong. All she knew was that her body was screaming out for him. Involuntarily, she raised her hips, bringing him deeper inside her.

"Do not move, Aissa."

"Shadow Hawk." She said his name, hardly recognizing her own voice. It was filled with desire and yearning. She was embarrassed but she didn't care. She wanted him to love her.

He held himself still inside her, holding her as close to him as she could possibly be. She could hear him breathing, feel the quick strength of his heartbeat. Every muscle in his body was tight, ready, but still he did not move. His breath quickened against her ear, yet somehow he controlled himself. Aissa fought the urge to cry out. At the moment she thought she would burst with desire, Shadow Hawk began to move. She threw her head back, unable to believe that anything could feel like this—so all-consuming, so overwhelming. Without quickening the rhythm, Shadow Hawk increased the force of his thrusts until Aissa could no longer tell where her body ended and his began.

Aissa opened her eyes to see the dusky silhouette of Shadow Hawk's face against the ink-dark sky. As her passion rose she reached out her hands and dug her fingers into the soft soil, still warm from the sun. She matched Shadow Hawk in intensity and strength. Somewhere in the corner of her mind, a voice was whispering that this was wrong, that until they were married, it was up to her to control her desire for him. But the whispering voice was lost in the insistent pleasure that washed over her, lifting her to heights she had never known before. She felt Shadow Hawk tensing and knew that he was close to the release of his own passion. His excitement ignited hers and an instant later, the flame of their love exploded. Aissa closed her eyes as tiny colored stars danced across her inner vision. For a moment, she had no life and no love apart from this. Later, when she opened her eyes, the stars had lost their color and she could again feel the soft grass against her back.

Although the moment of sheer ecstasy had passed, Shadow Hawk was still here in her arms, as real and as loving as anything she could imagine.

Shadow Hawk rode hard, leaning down over the paint's neck, letting the big stallion have his head. He felt a certain kind of strength when he rode, a certain kind of freedom that he never felt anywhere else. When the paint began to tire, Shadow Hawk leaned back, letting the animal drop back to a canter. A mile farther on, he pulled the paint back into a walk and patted his neck, speaking to him in a gentle tone. Across the meadow, Shadow Hawk could hear the gurgling of a stream. He walked the animal to the water and let him drink.

Shadow Hawk looked out at the distant mountains and he felt a peculiar ache, a certain longing. His people were there—his mother, his brother, his uncle, and his cousins—and he would probably never see them again. He had given up that life so he could be with Aissa.

He shook his head, thinking of the woman who so totally possessed him. He couldn't get her out of his mind. He had never experienced lovemaking with any woman like he had with Aissa the night before. He had never wanted any woman as much as he wanted her. He closed his eyes, thinking how sweet it had been to be inside her. The nicker of the stallion brought him out of his reverie. He shook his head, trying to clear his thoughts.

The house was almost finished now, and he knew that Aissa would want him to marry her. But was that what he really wanted? He sat on the paint as the animal walked lazily along the stream, grazing on the tall, green shoots of grass. Shadow Hawk wondered if he could live in the white man's world for the rest of his life and be content. Could he live in a white man's house, dress in a white man's clothes? He didn't know for sure. But in all this confusion there was one thing he knew for certain; Aissa could not live in his world. Her memories of the Apache camp were painful and ugly, and some of her pain had been his fault. He could never ask her to go back there. So his only choice was to live here among the whites.

The paint snorted impatiently and lifted its head, its nostrils flaring.

"What is it, boy?" Shadow Hawk patted the stallion reassuringly.

The paint tossed its head and snorted again, and Shadow Hawk looked down the valley, squinting his eyes against the sun. There was a figure, a lone figure, walking unsteadily, almost staggering. Shadow Hawk loosened the paint's reins and kneed the animal, urging it into a canter. As he got closer, Shadow Hawk could see by the long skirt that it was a woman. But something was terribly wrong with her. She walked with her arms hanging loosely at her sides, her uneven strides taking her from side to side. Shadow Hawk urged the stallion faster but the woman lurched sideways, falling into the hard dirt before he could reach her. Shadow Hawk pulled up and jumped off the paint, running toward the fallen woman, carrying his water bag with him. He turned her over and held the bag to her lips. She opened her eyes and gulped greedily at the water, trying to take it from Shadow Hawk's hand.

"Easy, do not drink too much."

"Please, I'm so thirsty," she pleaded.

"Take small sips. There." Shadow Hawk poured some of the water over the woman's face. For the first time, he saw that she was young, about the same age as Aissa. Her skin was burned from the sun and her lips were dry and blistered. He shielded her from the sun with his body, wondering what had happened to her and what would've become of her if he hadn't come along. She had been less than half a mile from where he had watered the paint and yet she would've almost certainly died from thirst. Her long hair was a deep brown with streaks of red and her eyes were a light green. And she had small freckles on her nose. Her body was womanly but she looked like a little girl.

"May I have more water? Please."

Shadow Hawk held the bag to her lips once more. "That is enough. You will be sick if you drink too much."

The woman closed her eyes and sagged against him.

Shadow Hawk lifted her into his arms and onto his horse, swinging up behind her. He walked the paint uphill to an oak tree with spreading branches. He dismounted and carried the woman with him, setting her gently down in the shade. He took off his bandanna, wet it from his water bag, and held it against her forehead. She mumbled something, but he couldn't understand her. As soon as he was sure she wouldn't pass out, he would take her back to the house. Aissa would know how to take care of her.

The girl opened her eyes. "Thank you." She attempted to sit up, but Shadow Hawk gently pushed her back down.

"Rest. You are weak."

"But my family. . . ." She struggled against him. "They're out there somewhere. I have to find them."

"I will look for them after I take you to the house."

The girl shook her head, her eyes wild. "I have to come with you. Please."

Shadow Hawk held her tightly. "You're not strong enough to go anywhere. I'll search for them. I promise you."

"They're all I have." She closed her eyes, and Shadow Hawk saw tears beading her lashes.

Shadow Hawk splashed her pallid face with more water and held the bag to her lips once more. "Drink," he said gently, supporting her with his arm. She held onto him and sat up, flinching and pressing one hand to her forehead.

"My head aches."

"You are not hurt, it is only the sun."

"I'm so worried about my family," she said frantically, looking down the valley. "They're back out on the desert."

Shadow Hawk hid his astonishment. That meant she had walked twenty or more miles. Or perhaps the sun had confused her thoughts. Either way, he had to distract her so that she would rest. "I will look for your family, I promise you," he reassured the young woman. Then he quickly changed the subject. "What is your name?"

"Christina. Christina Marley."

"I am Shadow Hawk."

"You're Indian?"

"Yes," he said simply.

"They told us in Wilsonville that this wasn't Indian country."

Shadow Hawk shrugged his shoulders and smiled. Like most settlers, Christina's family had been lied to. There were Apache everywhere. "It's a long story. I'm staying at the Gerard ranch. I will take you there as soon as you feel better."

"No, I won't be beholden to people I don't even know."

"You will like these people. They are good." Shadow Hawk lifted Christina into his arms. She didn't argue this time but rested her head against his shoulder. She weighed very little, and Shadow Hawk could feel her bones through the cloth of her dress as he lifted her onto the paint. He rode slowly, letting Christina doze. When he got close to the house, he slid off, pulling her gently into his arms again. He walked through the pasture and up to the house. It still amazed him, this huge, immovable lodge. He looked past the house. Aissa was working in the garden, her golden hair shining in the afternoon sunlight. He called her name and watched her turn. She dropped the hoe and ran to him, looking at Christina.

"Bring her into the house."

Shadow Hawk followed Aissa up the stairs. He laid Christina on the narrow cot in the small guest room Aissa had insisted upon. "I was riding down the valley toward the alkali flats and I found her wandering around. She says her family is out on the desert."

Aissa quickly brought some water and poured it into the bowl on the washstand and grabbed a cloth from the hook. She sat on the bed and dipped the cloth in the water, patting it gently over Christina's face and neck. "She's been out there awhile. Her face is blistered."

"I'm going to go look for her family."

"Be careful," Aissa said softly, the affection obvious in her tone.

Shadow Hawk leaned over and pressed his mouth against hers. "I will be back."

* * *

Shadow Hawk found the wagon before nightfall by following the woman's zigzagging trail back out into the desert. It was an old Conestoga-type wagon, heavy and graceless, stuck in the thick sand in the bottom of a dry wash. Two bodies, their throats slit, were lying close to the wagon. The woman had also been shot in the back. The man had been partially scalped. Shadow Hawk shook his head. Christina's parents would not be riding back to the ranch with him. He had expected as much, but it still made him sad for the girl.

He let the paint browse in the dry brush as he walked around the wagon. There were no mules or horses. The wagon had broken an axle and was leaning to one side. Things were scattered across the hot sand: clothing, pots and pans, a broken mirror, a Bible, with some of the pages torn out. Shadow Hawk dismounted, looking closer at the tracks in the soft sand. The wind had blown many of the tracks into shapeless depressions, but it was not hard to figure out what had happened.

Christina's father had stopped to fix the broken axle and couldn't finish it before dark. They had camped here; there was still the remains of a fire. While Christina's father had worked on the wagon, Christina and her mother had been cooking. There was a pot, emptied, that was thrown next to the fire. Shadow Hawk followed the tracks a little farther out of the camp and into the brush. The family had been ambushed, and it hadn't been by Apaches. The horses had been shod. There had been seven of them . . . or eight. Somehow, Christina had gotten away and her parents had been killed. Shadow Hawk looked around. There were empty shells by the wagon. Her father had used a rifle. Maybe he had enabled her to get away while he tried to fight the attackers off, or maybe Christina had been off to one side when the attack came and had remained hidden.

Shadow Hawk took off his shirt. He reached for the spade that hung on the side of the wagon and began to dig. These people had suffered indignity for too long already. He dug until he had a hole deep and wide enough for both bodies. He looked inside the wagon and found two blankets, wrapped the bodies, and gently placed them next to each other in the grave. Then he covered them up, making sure the dirt was securely packed over them. He looked around, wishing there were rocks to mark the grave and to protect it. He finally rolled one of the heavy water barrels from the wagon and placed it over the grave to ensure that the coyotes wouldn't dig. He looked at the wagon and thought of Christina's little-girl face, and her parents who now lay in the grave. "Take these people, Great Spirit, to the land beyond, so that they may know no more suffering."

Shadow Hawk put his shirt back on, thinking. He couldn't take the wagon back to the ranch without fixing the broken axle and bringing a team from the ranch to pull it, but perhaps there were some things of value he could take back for Christina. He climbed back into the wagon and looked around.

There was a trunk that was open, its hinges sprung. It had already been rummaged through. He took out the pieces of clothing, dishes, and books. There was a wooden box at the bottom. He opened it. It contained papers and dried flowers and other strange objects. A white woman's medicine bundle? Shadow Hawk suddenly felt as if he were intruding, offending the dead woman's spirit. He set the box down and looked around for clothes. Which dresses were Christina's? He held one up. It was faded and worn. He put it down and lifted another. The cloth was torn. He gave up. She could borrow some of Aissa's clothes.

There wasn't much here, Shadow Hawk realized. This family had had very little and what was theirs had now been brutally taken from them. He picked up the box and started to leave then he stopped. There was a heavy old chest standing askew, its drawers pulled out and sagging. On an impulse, Shadow Hawk pushed the chest aside. Underneath lay a cloth packet wrapped in string. He picked it up, not knowing what it was, but hoping it would be of some value to Christina since it had been hidden. He jumped down from the wagon and mounted the paint. He looked at the grave once more, nodded solemnly, and rode back to the ranch.

* * *

The group of men was loud and raucous. There were eight of them, men without homes or families or a reason to care. They'd already drunk enough whiskey and mescal to put most men under the table. There were Mexicans, half-breeds, and white men. Ray Grimes had picked them up in saloons and jails on his way west. He paid them for their loyalty.

Grimes sat apart from the men, and they had learned to leave him alone. He made it clear that he was superior to them and that they offended him most of the time. But there were times, too, when their cruelty amused him . . . and they knew it.

It had been more than a year since he had almost killed Aissa Gerard. She had only survived with the help of her Apache lover. Ray cleaned his nails with the point of his knife, thinking about Aissa. She had humiliated him, taken his land from him, and driven him away. And what was she really? He would make her pay for what she had done in ways she couldn't even imagine. He would finish what he had started a long time ago.

Aissa heard Christina's scream when she was halfway up the stairs with the breakfast tray. Poor Christina. She had awakened several times with nightmares. Aissa hurried toward the guest room but stopped at the doorway. Shadow Hawk was holding Christina in his arms, comforting her as she cried. Aissa was proud of the way he had handled the situation with Christina, but she also felt something else. It was strange watching the man she loved hold another woman in his arms.

Aissa walked into the room, setting the tray on the chair by the bed. "I've brought you something to eat, Christina." She watched as Christina pulled away from Shadow Hawk, wiping her tear-streaked face. She really was a very pretty girl, and her tentative smile was endearing. Aissa imagined losing her father the way Christina had lost her parents and she shivered. To shake off the feeling, Aissa busied herself, plumping up the pillows behind Christina. "Sit back. I'll put the tray on your lap."

"You're too kind, miss," Christina said.

"I'll come see you later, Christina," Shadow Hawk said as he left the room.

Aissa helped Christina get comfortable and set the tray on her lap. "Now, I want you to eat. You need to get your strength back."

"I don't know how I'll repay you."

"You don't have to repay us. You're welcome here as long as you want." Aissa took a deep breath. "I'm so sorry about your parents, Christina."

"Thank you," Christina replied, her voice shaking. "I don't know what I'll do now. I don't have an education like you, miss. I—"

Aissa took Christina's hand. "Don't worry yourself about such things now, Christina. You just rest and get well." Aissa walked out of the room and down the stairs. She went out onto the long, wide porch and leaned against the railing, taking a deep breath. She knew something of what Christina was feeling. She had thought her father was dead when she'd been taken captive by the Apaches. There was no worse feeling in the world than feeling that you were alone. She heard the door close behind her and she felt Shadow Hawk stand next to her.

"You are good to her," he said, his arm going around Aissa's shoulders.

"My heart aches for her. She's all alone in this world." She didn't resist when Shadow Hawk pulled her close to him. "I remember what it was like in the Apache camp when Teroz took me captive, and I thought my father was dead. And when I thought I had lost you, too. . . . I wanted to be dead."

"You will not lose me again, Aissa."

"I'm going to help her through this. I'm going to do anything I can to make it easier for her." She felt Shadow Hawk's hands on her shoulders. He turned her around to face him. His hand brushed her cheek, and she closed her eyes for a brief moment. There were times when she wished that she could live alone with him in some far-off place of their own making, a world where people did not stare at them—a world where people did not kill and hate.

"Your goodness shines in you, Aissa."

When his mouth touched hers, she reached out for him. "Sometimes I get so frightened. I don't ever want to be separated from you or my father again." She felt as if she were going to cry and she lowered her eyes, not wanting to show her weakness. He lifted her chin.

"What is wrong, Aissa? What is it?"

She shook her head. "I don't know. Just a feeling, I suppose."

"What feeling?"

"That something bad is going to happen again."

"Why do you say that? You are safe here."

"I have never been safe here, Shadow Hawk." She pulled away from him, walking the length of the porch. "I suppose that's what's frightening me; no one is ever safe. Just look at Christina."

Shadow Hawk came toward her. He took her hands in his, lifting them to his mouth and kissing them softly. "I can't argue with what you say, Aissa. There is much danger in the world. But if something were to happen to you again, I would do anything in my power to make sure you were safe. Do you believe me?"

"Yes." Aissa leaned back to look directly into his eyes. "But you couldn't protect me from Ray and you couldn't protect me from Teroz." She hesitated, her voice shaking. "You couldn't even protect me from yourself when you were so angry." She saw the hurt in his eyes and looked away. She hadn't wanted to bring up the past but she couldn't forget it. He had hurt her.

"Will you never let me forget what happened in the Apache camp?"

His voice was strong but not angry. Aissa looked up at him. "I love you, Shadow Hawk, and it still troubles me that you thought I would love someone else. I was a captive. I didn't want to be there. Yet still, you didn't trust me."

"And that is what all this is about?"

Aissa shook her head and looked at Shadow Hawk. "I don't know."

"Tell me, Aissa."

Aissa chewed nervously at her lower lip. "You and I are very different. I can't be happy in your world, and I'm not sure you can be happy in mine."

"So, you have decided this for me?"

"No, I . . ."

"Listen to me, Aissa." Shadow Hawk grasped Aissa's shoulders. "I left you once before and I almost lost you. I went back to my people without you. I was with my family but I was not happy there. I wanted to be with you. I still want to be with you."

Aissa looked away. "I sometimes think you feel obligated to stay here."

"For someone so smart, you can be very foolish." Shadow Hawk loosened his hold on Aissa and leaned against the railing, looking out at the distant mountains. "When my father died and my mother and my brother and I had to leave the Comanche camp and go to the Apache, I was very angry. I hated the Apache, I swore I would never like it there. But every day I learned something different about it and slowly I grew to like it. The same thing has happened here. You and your father have shown me things that I would never have known and I have grown to care for this land." Shadow Hawk reached out and wrapped his knuckles around the rough-hewn planks of the house. "I have even come to like living in this white man's lodge."

Aissa looked at Shadow Hawk. "I don't know . . ."

"What of the night we spent together? Do you remember what it was like when our bodies were as one?"

Aissa felt her cheeks burn and she looked down, trying to ignore Shadow Hawk's piercing gaze. "Don't talk about that here."

"Why not? Do you wish that it never happened?"

Aissa shook her head. "We shouldn't talk about it, that's all." She was almost whispering.

"Why, Aissa? Why?"

"Because we're not married." Embarrassed, she turned away from Shadow Hawk, walking down the porch steps. She started toward her garden but stopped when she heard Shadow Hawk's voice. He was almost shouting.

"Do you wish me to talk of that night right here?"

Aissa shook her head angrily, glancing up at her father's bedroom window. "No!" She hissed the word at him.

"Then where do you wish to talk about it?"

Aissa could tell by the look on Shadow Hawk's face that he wasn't going to stop. "Let's go to the garden." She led the way, stopping to pull some weeds when they reached the edge of the flower beds.

Shadow Hawk sat down on the bench, stretching his long legs out in front of him.

"Why are you talking about such things now?" Aissa asked.

"When should I talk about them?"

"I don't think we should talk about what happened."

"You just want me to forget what happened between us? Can you forget, Aissa?"

Aissa turned away, trying to hide the blush that spread over her cheeks. She would never forget what they had shared together. But the other night . . . the other night was something even more. There was an ache low in her belly whenever she thought of Shadow Hawk and the way he had made her feel.

"You did not answer me, Aissa. Can you forget what we have shared?"

Aissa turned. "I'll never forget what we shared, Shadow Hawk. But there has to be more than this for me and I don't think. . . ."

"You're talking about marriage."

"Yes."

"Why does marriage mean so much to you?"

"It's different with us, can't you see that? It's important for a woman to be married to a man before she—"

"Before they are together."

"Yes. And you and I have been together many times, Shadow Hawk. It makes me feel . . ." Aissa searched for a word that Shadow Hawk would understand. "It makes me feel unworthy."

Shadow Hawk shook his head impatiently. "You and I love each other. Is that not enough?"

"No, it isn't enough in the white world. It shouldn't seem so strange to you. The Apache marry."

"Yes, but for the ones who choose not to marry, there are other ways. . ." Shadow Hawk shrugged his shoulders.

"You mean there are certain women who share pleasure with men."

"Yes."

"And they are not married," Aissa said flatly.

"No."

Aissa nodded slightly, unable to hide her disappointment. "I suppose I am one of those women then. I share pleasure with you but that is all. I am not good enough for you to marry."

Shadow Hawk reached out for her but Aissa pulled away. "Don't. You're making me feel more ashamed."

"Aissa, listen to me."

"There is nothing else to say. I thought you and I would marry. I was wrong." Her eyes filled with tears. "I feel like a fool, but it's better to know now."

"I want to ask you something, Aissa. Give me an honest answer."

Aissa nodded, trying to maintain her composure.

"You say that marriage would make you feel like a worthy woman. Did you feel that way when you were married to Ray Grimes?"

Aissa closed her eyes, wondering why Shadow Hawk was trying to hurt her. "You know what I felt like when I was with him. I hated him and I hated myself."

"Then marriage will make no difference in how I feel about you. I love you, Aissa." He rubbed her cheek. "I cannot imagine sharing my life with anyone but you."

"Those are just words, Shadow Hawk."

"They are true words, Aissa. You are a part of me, just as I am a part of you." He put his hands on her face, forcing her to look at him. "When I am inside you, I feel whole."

Aissa looked up at Shadow Hawk, staring into his intense blue/gray eyes. He could speak of such things as if they were so ordinary. She could not. But she understood what he meant. She had never felt such completeness as she had when Shadow Hawk made love to her. Perhaps he was right, after all. Her marriage to Ray had caused her nothing but pain. If she didn't marry Shadow Hawk, at least they would be together. Perhaps that was the choice she had to make. She leaned forward, resting her head on his chest, letting him enfold her in his arms. This was the place she wanted to be. What did marriage matter as long as they were together?

Chapter Two

Christina knelt in the soft dirt by the pond, digging with her fingers. She pulled a cattail out of the mud and placed it in her apron along with the others she had found. She stood up and walked to the water's edge, washing her hands. She looked around. It was nice here, so clean and new. It wasn't like where she was from.

Her parents had moved from Tennessee to Kansas when she was just a young girl, hoping they could make a better life for themselves. But the land agents had misrepresented everything. All of the riverbottom land had been claimed years before. One by one, the Marleys had sold their possessions while they argued, trying to decide what to do. They had ended up squatting on a stretch of land that was almost unusable. They had tried to farm it but the land was unforgiving. And it wasn't only the land. It was the tornados, the wind, the snow.

They had lived in a small sod shack, and they had done the best they could. When her mother had become ill with the consumption, her father had decided it was time to move again. So they packed up what little they had and headed south.

Christina remembered the trip vividly: her mother's cough, the jarring of the wagon, her father's worried eyes. But their spirits picked up as the weather grew warmer and for the first time, Christina dared to hope that their lives might get better. Her father talked of getting a job in one of the towns doing anything he could, and her mother talked of getting work as a seamstress when her cough improved. Christina talked of going to school to learn how to read and write.

All that changed the night those horrible men rode into their camp. Christina and her parents had been sitting around the campfire, talking, making plans, when they heard horses. Her father had gotten the rifle and told Christina and her mother to hide underneath the wagon. Peeking out from between the planks, Christina watched frozen in terror. Men rode into the ring of firelight from every direction. She would never forget their faces, unshaven and distorted with senseless cruelty.

Her mother had forced her up underneath the wagon, into a compartment that had once held the original owner's valuables. She tucked her skirt between her legs and squeezed herself into the narrow space, her arms and legs shaking. Her mother had whispered fiercely in her ear, begging her not to move. She had obeyed. When one of the men dragged her mother out from underneath the wagon, Christina had wanted to kill him, to leap from her hiding place and tear at his eyes, but she didn't. She didn't move. She had heard her mother's cries and her father's anguished pleading. There was a shot and then there was nothing. The men rummaged through the wagon, kicking dust into her eyes through the floorboards. Christina heard them ride away, but her terror and her grief kept her hidden for hours. Finally, so chilled and stiff that her limbs ached, Christina wriggled free and dropped to the ground. Her throat was so dry that she could not swallow and she lay still with her eyes closed, unable to cry, unwilling to see what the men had done.

Eventually, she had fallen asleep and when she awoke, it was morning. Slowly, she got up and walked to her parents' bodies. They were both bloody, awful to look at. Christina had stared at them, and then, in a daze of grief and hopelessness, she had wandered off into the desert. She hadn't been looking for help, she had only wanted to die. But Shadow Hawk had found her.

Christina sat down, reaching into the water to wash the tears from her face. It was still hard for her to believe that her parents were gone and she was all alone. She couldn't stay at the Gerard ranch forever, but what could she do? She had no education and no real experience in anything except dirt farming and hard work. She let out a deep, shuddering breath and sat down, grabbing one of the cattail roots from her apron. She dipped it into the water and washed it off then began to chew on it. This was a nice place, much better than Kansas. Her parents would have liked it. She felt a movement on the ground and turned. Hoofbeats. Her body tensed. What if it wasn't one of the Gerards? But her alarm quickly subsided when she saw Shadow Hawk's large paint. He rode up, slipping off the horse and walking to her. She dropped the cattail onto the ground and smiled, self-consciously brushing back strands of hair from her face.

"Why are you out here all alone?" Shadow Hawk sat down next to her.

"I decided to take a walk. Then I started seeing plants that I'm familiar with and I picked them." Christina knew she was rattling on, that her voice was too shrill, but he made her nervous. "I wound up by the pond. It's nice here, don't you think?"

"Yes, it is."

"I don't believe I ever thanked you rightly for saving my life."

"You thanked me."

"No," Christina shook her head. "Not in the way I should have. I'll be leaving before long. I mean, I don't expect. . . ." Christina thought of her parents and lowered her eyes, wishing that they had known some sort of peace in their lives before they had died. Her eyes flooded and she found she could not finish what she had been trying to say.

"You're welcome here for as long as you want,

Christina. Do not feel that you have to leave."

"I can't be staying here forever."

"Don't be in such a hurry. Take this time and heal yourself."

Christina nodded. "Why aren't you with your people?"

Shadow Hawk smiled. "Do you always ask what's on your mind?"

Christina shrugged. "I guess I do."

"I'm here because I've chosen to stay here with Aissa and her father."

"Do you have family?"

"Yes, I have a family, but I have not seen them for a long time."

"Don't you miss them?"

"Yes, I miss them very much sometimes."

"Then why don't you go see them? Anything can happen, you know. Look what happened to my parents."

"It's different for me, Christina. I have made my choice to stay here."

"But you can still visit your family, can't you?" Christina realized after she spoke that she had gone too far. His face looked strained. "I'm sorry, Shadow Hawk. It's no business of mine what you do or don't do."

"It's all right."

"It's just that I would give anything to see my parents right now. It's probably hard for you to understand that."

"No, I can understand very well. I lost my father many years ago, and there are days I would rather speak to him than to anyone."

"You do know how I feel then."

"Yes, I understand how you miss your parents." Shadow Hawk shrugged his shoulders. Christina watched him pick a slender stem of grass. "I have been thinking of my family lately."

"Well, I know it's none of my business, but I'd go see them before too long if I were you." She had hoped that he would smile again but he did not.

"My mother and brother are gone anyway. Perhaps I will visit in awhile, when they have returned."

"Are you and Aissa going to get married?"

Shadow Hawk's stern face became almost fierce-looking. "I don't know."

Christina was so flustered that she grinned at him and blundered on. "But I can tell you love her."

"Yes, I love her very much." Some of the anger in Shadow Hawk's face softened when he spoke, and Christina hurried to fill the uncomfortable silence.

"She's really pretty. I bet every man that sees her likes her."

"And you're wondering why she'd settle for an Apache?"

Christina grimaced. "I didn't mean that. Why don't you take her with you to see your family? I'm sure they'd like to meet her."

"No, that would not be a good idea."

"Why not?"

"Do you never stop asking questions?" Shadow Hawk's voice was tense.

"I'm sorry, I just can't seem to stop myself. My pa always used to say that I could irritate the stink right out of a skunk."

Shadow Hawk laughed agreeably.

"It's none of my business. I just have a natural curiosity." Christina fiddled with the hem of her skirt. The last thing she wanted to do was offend this man who had been so kind to her. "It's just unusual that a white woman . . . I mean, how did you two—"

Shadow Hawk leaned toward her, grasping her forearm and holding her so that she had to look directly into his eyes. "I will tell you the story once and only once, and then I will tolerate no more questions." He released her arm, and Christina sat back. "Aissa was taken captive by my people when she was a young girl. I helped her to escape. I think I knew even then that I loved her. Our lives kept touching in odd ways, often when one of us needed help. Even so, I would probably have stayed with my people, but one of my enemies took Aissa captive and brought her to our camp. She escaped with the help of my cousin."

"Why didn't you help her?"

"That is another long story and one that really is not your business. The important thing is that Aissa and I are together now."

"You love her very much. I can tell by the sound of your voice." Christina smiled shyly, lowering her eyes: "I hope someday some man will talk about me the way you talk about Aissa."

"The man who falls in love with you must be prepared to answer many questions, Christina."

Christina laughed. "You're a nice man. I was always afraid of Indians before I met you."

"And I was afraid of whites before I met Aissa and her father."

Christina stood up, brushing the dirt from her skirt. "It's funny how things work sometimes, isn't it?"

Shadow Hawk stood next to her. "Do you want a ride back to the house?"

"No, I'll walk. I like walking around here. It's so pretty."

"Do you wish to go back to your wagon, Christina? Are there things that you want that I did not bring back to the house?"

Christina shook her head. "I don't think I want to go back out there. You brought me everything that was important."

"You are sure?"

"Yes." Christina shivered inwardly at the idea of ever seeing that place again. Her parents were buried there and maybe she should visit their grave, but she knew that they would understand how hard it would be for her. Impulsively, Christina reached for Shadow Hawk's hand, squeezing it firmly. "Thank you again. I wouldn't be alive if it were not for you." She was surprised when Shadow Hawk put his arms around her and held her. It was a nice feeling.

"I'll walk back with you," Shadow Hawk said, leading the paint.

Christina gathered her skirt, walking beside him, feeling awkward. She had never seen such a tall man in her life. Her pa had only been a few inches taller than her, and she wasn't very tall. And Shadow Hawk had a real handsome face, not like the hard, mean-looking Indians in the picture books she and her ma had sometimes looked at. He didn't look like any Indian she had ever seen hanging around the towns either.

Shadow Hawk caught her staring and smiled. "Aissa tells me you're a good student."

"I've already learned the alphabet, and I can spell some words. I can't wait until I learn how to read."

"You will learn quickly enough. Aissa is a good teacher."

"As soon as I learn how to read and write, I'm going to help Aissa and the regular teacher at the schoolhouse."

"You already help out enough here on the ranch, Christina."

Christina nodded silently but she didn't really agree with Shadow Hawk. How could he know how hard it was for her to live with these people and keep accepting their kindness? She had never had much in life but her parents had instilled in her a fierce sense of pride. One way or another, she would find a way to pay back the Gerards for everything they had done for her.

Aissa watched Christina, Shadow Hawk, and her father as they played cards. When Christina laughed, she lit up the room. She was seventeen years old but she seemed much younger. Aissa had already grown quite fond of her.

"Are you all ready for a break?" Aissa took the cake to the table.

"Why don't you let me help, Aissa?" Before Aissa could say anything, Christina had gotten up and hurried into the kitchen. A moment later, she was back carrying plates and forks. Aissa poured coffee for everyone and took the cups to the table while Christina quickly followed with the cream and sugar. As Aissa cut slices of the chocolate cake, she glanced up to find Shadow Hawk staring at her. They had spent little time together since their talk. Shadow Hawk had been preoccupied with Christina. The girl followed him like a puppy as he went about his chores on the ranch. Aissa had spent time with Christina, too, teaching her how to read and write. The young woman was a nice distraction for all of them, but Aissa knew that she was using her as a good excuse not to talk to Shadow Hawk. And now there was that unsettling silence between them. She had caused it, she supposed, by mentioning marriage to him. Maybe she was growing up, thinking like a woman now, instead of like an impulsive girl.

"Good cake, darlin'," Ben said.

"Thank you, Father." Aissa sat down in a chair next to Shadow Hawk.

"Is there anything you can't do, Aissa?" Christina asked, her eyes wide with admiration.

"There are many things I can't do, Christina. Many." She glanced briefly at Shadow Hawk before taking a sip of her coffee. His mouth was curved into a slight smile.

"Well, it seems to me you can do anything."

"My daughter is an extremely capable young woman, that's for sure," Ben agreed. He took a generous bite of cake and set his fork down. "That new teacher's lucky she's helping out. Aissa's the best teacher those kids ever had."

"Didn't you used to be the regular teacher, Aissa?" Christina asked.

Aissa carefully avoided Shadow Hawk's eyes. "A lot of things have happened over the last year or so. I didn't think I could devote my full time and energy to the children."

"Well, I know what a good teacher you are. I think it's a shame the children won't have you."

"Thank you," Aissa said softly. "More cake, anyone?"

"No, I'm all filled up. I think I'll go on up and finish that book," Ben said, standing up. "It's getting real exciting now."

"I'm glad," Aissa said, smiling at her father. She stood up, kissed Ben on the cheek, then cleared the table. Immediately, Christina jumped up. Aissa put her hand on Christina's shoulder and gently pushed her back down. "Sit still. I'll tell you if I need help."

Shadow Hawk followed Aissa into the kitchen. "I want to talk to you."

Aissa glanced back at the table. "Not now."

"Don't make excuses, Aissa. I want to talk to you tonight."

Aissa nodded wearily as Shadow Hawk left the kitchen. More talk wouldn't help. She pulled the kettle of hot water from the stove and put the dishes into the wash basin. She scrubbed at them, then dried them, running the cloth back and forth across the delicate china until the plates shone like mirrors. She put them away slowly, still stalling. She could hear Christina's laughter from the next room. Aissa looked around. The sideboards were clean; every bit of mess was cleaned up. If she stayed in here any longer, it would become obvious that she was avoiding Shadow Hawk. Aissa hesitated in the doorway.

Christina and Shadow Hawk were attempting to toss cards into one of Ben's hats. This time Christina was the teacher. She was adept at sailing the cards, and Shadow Hawk had no idea what to do. Christina had a fit of giggles as Shadow Hawk's card sailed past the hat and hit the wall. Aissa smiled as she took off her apron and put it on the cupboard. She walked into the living room.

"You seem to be very good at this, Christina," Aissa said, sitting down in the rocking chair that was next to the large couch.

"My pa and I used to play it all the time, especially when we were traveling."

"This is a silly game," Shadow Hawk said impatiently, throwing his last card. This time it landed a few feet short of the hat. "There is no point to this."

"Of course there's a point," Christina said, picking up the cards. "The point is to get as many cards as you can into the hat. The person who gets the most in there wins."

"So there is no point," Shadow Hawk said again, "because you win nothing."

"That's not true. You win. It's fun to win."

"You're absolutely right, Christina," Aissa said, glaring at Shadow Hawk. "If all games were pointless then why would we play them?"

"I did not say all games were pointless but many of the white man's games. . . ." Shadow Hawk gestured disdainfully.

"Oh, you don't think this game can compare with the gambling games your people play? I have seen the men sit there gambling away things they have either made or traded for, just because they want to see how the bones will fall. You think that game has a point to it?" Aissa's voice was rising, and she couldn't stop it. What was wrong with her?

"It gives the game more excitement when you risk losing something," Shadow Hawk said flatly.

Aissa laughed harshly, remembering the worst of the gamblers in the Apache camp. "You think it's exciting when a man gambles away his own wife?" She shook her head in disgust. "A man who does that shows no respect for his wife or himself."

"It really doesn't matter much," Christina said, trying to intervene. "It's just a silly old game anyway." She placed the cards on the table in front of the couch, then looked at them, her eyes moving uneasily back and forth between their faces. "I think I'll head on up to bed now. Good night."

"Good night, Christina," Aissa said, barely taking her eyes from Shadow Hawk's face.

"Good night," Shadow Hawk said brusquely. He held Aissa's eyes as Christina left the room and went upstairs. "Why are you so angry? I'm not like the men in my camp. I would never risk losing you."

Aissa stood up and paced back and forth across the room. "But you almost did lose me. You weren't here when Ray Grimes forced me to marry him, and you weren't here when

Teroz took me captive. You were with your people. Maybe that's where you belong."

"I never wanted to leave you, you know that."

"But you did. And then when Teroz brought me to your camp, you did nothing to help me. Instead, you had already married Paloma."

"That's all in the past, Aissa."

"But I can never forget it, not any of it." Aissa turned away, hoping he would just leave her alone. She was surprised and uncomfortable with her own anger. She had been happy and content for the last year just having Shadow Hawk with her. What had happened to make her change her mind?

"All right then, I'll marry you."

Aissa whirled around, her anger flaring. "Don't do anything you don't want to do." Aissa hesitated. "I know you don't want to marry me." She watched as Shadow Hawk's eyes changed. They darkened, hiding his emotions.

"So, you know my thoughts now? You can speak for me?"

"You already said that it wasn't necessary for us to be married."

"But it is necessary for you, isn't it, Aissa?"

"Maybe it is. Maybe I want to be your wife instead of just your woman."

"Then I will marry you."

"No!" Aissa fought to keep her voice from quivering. "You have to want it, too, Shadow Hawk, or we won't have a chance together." She tried to turn away but he stopped her, his hands on her shoulders.

"Is it not enough that I have given up my people to be with you? Is that not enough?"

Aissa stared into Shadow Hawk's eyes and for the first time, she saw the pain there. It startled her. She had expected to see anger or impatience. "I'm sorry." She lowered her head, covering her face with her hand. "You're not bound to me in any way. You can leave whenever you wish."

"Is that what you want, Aissa? Do you want me to leave?"

"I want you to be happy and I don't think you're happy here." She tried to keep her voice even, to control the tears that would only make him feel like he had to stay. She didn't want to keep him that way, but she was also afraid that he would say he wanted to go. Instead, he took one of her hands. He held it to his mouth and kissed her palm.

"I do not want to leave you, Aissa. I love you. I understand why you might not believe me. I have given you reason to doubt me in the past."

"But your family—"

"I will visit my family, but I want to stay here with you." He put his hands on her waist, pulling her close to him. "You are my life, Aissa."

"No—" She protested as his mouth covered hers. He had more power over her than Ray Grimes had ever had and sometimes it frightened her. As his kiss deepened, she felt the familiar, helpless warmth engulf her. Was this the way it would always be between them? Or was it really just a physical union boasting nothing else? In spite of her desire for him, she pulled away. "No, not here. Not anymore." She expected his angry protest, but there was none. Instead, he kissed her gently and nodded.

"All right. There will be time enough later."

Aissa was puzzled. "What do you mean?"

"When we are married, we can make love whenever we wish."

Aissa felt herself blush.

"Good night, Aissa."

Aissa slowly climbed the stairs to her room, looking back once to see Shadow Hawk watching her. She wanted to believe that he loved her enough to marry her. She was not trying to hurt or anger him, she was only trying to protect herself.

Aissa held her books and papers in one arm as she walked down the narrow dirt road toward home. She liked walking back to the ranch after her morning sessions at the schoolhouse. It gave her time to herself and it gave her time to think.

How was it possible that her life could've changed so much? It had all been so simple once. When she was a little girl, it had seemed to her that her father had always been Agua Prieta's sheriff . . . and that he always would be. But that had all changed because of Ray Grimes. Aissa clenched her fists. He had caused more misery in her life than any human being should be allowed to cause another. It was hardly a Christian thought, but she hoped he was dead.

Aissa shifted her books to her other arm and shook her head to rid herself of thoughts of Ray Grimes. If he wasn't dead, at least he had left Agua Prieta—and was leaving them alone. Things were all right now. She knew her father missed being sheriff but at least Joe kept him in touch with things. After all his years as her father's deputy, Joe was running the sheriff's office on his own and doing a good job of it. He was also a good friend to her and her father.

As always, her mind turned to Shadow Hawk. Since the night she had refused to make love to him, they had not spoken again about getting married. She couldn't tell what he was thinking. Every day he got up at dawn and helped her father mend fences or move cattle from one part of the ranch to another. He seemed fairly content with his life on the ranch, but only time would tell. Aissa was determined not to push him one way or the other.

Aissa stopped for a moment and picked a wildflower that grew beside the road. It made her smile. It looked so bright and untamed. It reminded her of Christina. Aissa shook her head when she thought of the girl. In barely three months, Christina was writing third and fourth form lessons and reading at a higher level than that. She helped with all the chores around the house, as well as anything that needed doing outside. She had seemed uneducated and backward at first, but Aissa soon discovered a real depth to Christina. She observed everything around her, and she didn't seem to forget a thing. She had turned out to be a good cook, using many of the wild roots and herbs that grew around the ranch. She played cards and checkers with Ben, and even badgered him to go for walks with her. She even had something in common with Shadow Hawk—she could hunt.

One day, all on her own, Christina had set snares around the pond and had come home with three rabbits. She had proceeded to expertly gut and skin the carcasses and had made a delicious stew. Aissa smiled when she thought of Christina; she was like a blessing to them all. She had brightened all of their lives.

Aissa picked up her pace as she reached the pasture. She loved this land. It was so different than the desert that lay to the north, east, and south. Here, by their pond and their spring-fed trees, it was hard to imagine that the brittle mesquite and sun-scalded sands were less than a day's ride away. She looked up the valley. Oak, cottonwood, and ash trees grew in abundance along the trail of the underground spring and in stands around the pond. Sprigs of wildflowers grew everywhere; white and purple sage, soapweed, and the deep blue larkspurs. She loved it here. Could Shadow Hawk ever feel the same love for this ranch?

He would never feel at home in Agua Prieta, she knew that. Nearly every time he went with them into town, some drifter would start in, insulting her, trying to start a fight. Indian women who were married to white men were bad enough in most people's opinions. A white woman with an Indian man was unthinkable. Most of the townspeople cared enough about her and Ben to keep their mouths shut, but the disapproval was in their eyes. Aissa felt it and she knew that Shadow Hawk did, too. She pushed the thoughts from her mind. There was nothing that she could do about people's attitudes.

Aissa walked up the dusty road to the house. She still couldn't believe that she, Shadow Hawk, and her father had built it themselves. It was everything she had ever dreamed of: two stories, with polished wood floors, bedrooms upstairs, and a large living area. Most of all, there was a real kitchen.

As Aissa got closer to the house, she smiled. Something smelled impossibly good. Christina had already started dinner. Aissa shook her head. No matter how many times she told Christina to relax, she would not.

Aissa stepped up onto the porch, stamped her boots free of the dirt and dust, and opened the front door. Her father was napping on the sofa, but Shadow Hawk and Christina were nowhere around. Aissa went into the kitchen. There was a large pot of stew bubbling on the stove and a basket of freshly baked bread was already on the table, wrapped in a towel. The table had been set and there was a small vase of fresh flowers in the center. Christina had forgotten nothing.

Silently, Aissa climbed the stairs to her room and went inside. She poured water into the bowl on her washstand and quickly cleaned up. She took off her dress and slip and put on a work shirt and a pair of men's pants. She put on her socks and sat on the bed to pull on her boots. Only then did she reach up to take the pins from her chignon and quickly braid her hair into one thick plait, tying it with a small ribbon. Then she allowed herself to examine the idea that was forming in her mind. Shadow Hawk was probably out mending the fence above the high pasture that had collapsed in last winter's snows. Christina was most likely out gathering her herbs or roots or just walking around the way she loved to do.

Making her decision and refusing to examine it further, Aissa went downstairs into the kitchen and put some sugar lumps into her pocket. Everything she needed was in the tackroom: blanket, bridle, and riding pad. She had been wanting to do this for a long time. Shadow Hawk's paint was in the corral. She'd never ridden him—Shadow Hawk said he wouldn't allow anyone else to ride him. But Aissa didn't believe that. The paint always let her pat him and he loved the sugar she always brought him. Shadow Hawk was like a selfish boy when it came to this horse.

Aissa opened the corral gate and hung the riding pad over the top rail. Slowly, carrying only the bridle, she walked toward the paint, holding out a lump of sugar in her palm. She had been feeding the stallion sugar for so long that she knew he wouldn't shy away from her. The paint snorted a few times as she approached, lifted his head, then took a few tentative steps.

"Come on, boy," Aissa urged, moving slowly forward until her hand was just inches from the stallion's head. She held still, quieting even her breathing as the stallion flared its nostrils, taking in her scent. A moment later, she felt the tickling warmth as he licked the sugar from her hand. She pulled another lump from her pocket and fed it to him.

"Good boy." She reached up and rubbed her hand along the animal's soft nose, marveling at the coloring of the stallion. It was as if someone had taken a bucket of black paint and splashed it over him.

Carefully, she patted his neck as she slipped the bridle over his ears. She led him to the fence and tied the reins around a rail. She took the blanket and riding pad from the corral fence and put them over the stallion's broad back. When she drew the cinch tight, the paint's skin rippled. He knows what saddles are, Aissa thought, but he would rather be bareback. She climbed up on the railing, carefully slipping onto the stallion's back. Purposefully calm, Aissa leaned forward and walked the stallion out of the corral. He pranced nervously in the yard. Aissa took a deep breath and loosened the reins, shifting her weight forward. The paint instantly leapt into a gallop.

Aissa held the reins tightly, trying to keep her fear from overcoming her as the stallion galloped across the open pasture. His strides seemed enormous and Aissa knew she could never control him. This horse was different from any horse she had ever ridden. He had been trained for war and for flight . . . and for an instant response from his rider.

Aissa knew that by gripping his sides with her legs and leaning forward to tangle her hands in his mane, she was urging him to run even faster. But she couldn't relax. She could only hope that he would soon tire, but when she tried to pull back on the reins, the horse fought her and jerked them from her hands. Aissa managed to get hold of the reins, but she was afraid to try to stop the paint again. He might jerk the reins so hard that they broke or fell free to drag on the ground.

Aissa suppressed a scream and forced herself to think. The stallion's thunderous strides had carried them across the meadow in seconds and now they were headed down a gentle slope. At the bottom, the oaks grew thicker, their twisting branches often low to the ground. Uncontrolled, the paint might kill them both trying to race through the trees and fallen logs.

Desperate, Aissa pulled back on the reins; again, the stallion jerked the slack he wanted from her hands. In moments, the paint would race blindly into the oak trees. Every muscle in Aissa's body ached and she felt helpless. There was a sudden shout, and Aissa saw Shadow Hawk riding toward her on one of the ranch horses. The animal wasn't as fast as the paint, but Shadow Hawk was coming at an angle and whipping him hard. Shadow Hawk yelled again, something Aissa couldn't understand, and the stallion slowed slightly at the sound of the familiar voice. His ears flicked back, then forward again. Shadow Hawk yelled once more. He was speaking Apache. This time the stallion reacted, turning, sliding to a heaving stop, then suddenly rearing, pawing at the air in front of him. Aissa hadn't been prepared for anything like this. She fell from the stallion's back and at Shadow Hawk's angry-voiced urging, rolled to the side. Heart racing, Aissa covered her head with her hands, certain the paint would trample her. But moments passed and the pounding of the stallion's hooves slowed then stilled. Aissa turned over and slowly sat up. Shadow Hawk had the reins of the paint and was patting the animal's sweaty neck to calm him. The ranch gelding, blowing hard, stood off to one side. As Aissa watched, Shadow Hawk left the stallion long enough to unbridle the gelding and slap its rump, sending it back toward the corrals. Shadow Hawk mounted the paint. Aissa rubbed her back and hip, looking up at him.

"What were you doing? I told you never to ride that animal!" There was no mistaking the rage in his voice.

"I thought I could—"

"Why? Why did you think you could ride him? When did you become a warrior?"

Aissa attempted to stand. He held his arm out for her but she ignored him. "I'm sorry. I shouldn't have ridden him." Slowly, she started back toward the house.

"Where are you going?"

"Home."

"I'll take you with me. Come."

Aissa bristled at Shadow Hawk's command. She stopped and glared at him. "I admit I was wrong to ride your horse, but this is my land, not yours. Don't tell me what to do." She started toward the house, her leg and hip stiffening with every step. She was more bruised than she thought, but she refused to give Shadow Hawk the satisfaction of knowing she was hurt.

"So, you are going to limp all the way back just to defy me?"

Aissa glared up at Shadow Hawk. "Why do you think everything I do is in defiance of you? Sometimes I do things just because I want to do them."

"Like riding the stallion?"

"Yes, like riding the stallion." Aissa kept walking, trying to make her sore leg carry her weight equally.

"This stallion means very much to me," Shadow Hawk said as he rode beside her.

"Yes, I know that," Aissa said, refusing to look up at him.

"He was my father's. The stallion is all I have left of him."

Aissa nodded, all her anger fading as he spoke. She felt

like a fool. "I know that, Shadow Hawk," she said slowly. She stopped. "If you hadn't seen us, he would've hurt himself badly. I'm sorry. I just wasn't thinking."

"No, you weren't." Shadow Hawk leaned forward, looking at her intensely. "The stallion is very valuable to me but if something had happened to him, my life would go on. If something had happened to you. . . ." Shadow Hawk shook his head. Slowly, deliberately, he swung his right leg over the stallion's neck, and without losing eye contact with her, he slid to the ground. "I could never replace you, Aissa. My love for you is much too strong."

"I'm sorry," she whispered, leaning against him.

"Promise me you won't do such a foolish thing again."

"I won't take the stallion again. I promise. I was scared to death anyway," she admitted, risking a small smile. But he did not smile back at her.

"Promise me you won't do something that foolish again. It's in your nature to act without thinking and that scares me."

"What does that mean?" Aissa asked defensively.

"You've done it before."

"When?"

Shadow Hawk touched her arm. "You almost died in that storm on the desert."

Aissa laughed harshly. "You can't even compare that to this. I was running for my life."

"But it was dangerous."

"Yes, it was dangerous. But I would do it again," she said defiantly. "We don't seem to be able to agree on much these days, do we?" Aissa started walking.

"No, we do not," Shadow Hawk said from behind her. He took the stallion's reins and followed her.

Aissa glanced at him. "You don't have to walk with me. I'll be fine."

"I could argue that with you all day long," Shadow Hawk replied, his voice sharp. "Perhaps it's time for me to visit my people."

Aissa kept her eyes straight ahead. "I know that you miss them very much."

"You want me to go?" Shadow Hawk stopped.

"You do miss them, don't you?" Aissa said without stopping. "You need to be with them."

"If I didn't want to be here, I would have left a long time ago."

"But I know your sense of honor," Aissa said. "You feel that you owe me and my father."

"You are enough to make a man question his sanity." Shadow Hawk breathed slowly, obviously trying to control his anger. "Don't tell me what I feel. You don't know what I think."

"I'm sorry, I—"

He pressed his fingers against her lips to silence her. "My love for you is so strong it frightens me. I seem to have no control over it. How many times do I have to tell you how important you are to me?"

Shadow Hawk was standing so close to Aissa that she could see the subtle changes in his eyes as they darkened from blue to gray. She was aware of his height, the scent of his skin, the way he set his mouth when he was angry. Why couldn't she just love him? Why was it so hard for both of them?

"Are you listening to me?" Shadow Hawk demanded.

"Yes," she responded, still staring up at him.

"What is wrong with you, Aissa?"

"I don't know," she stammered, stunned by her realization of how much she loved Shadow Hawk. If she lost him again, she wasn't sure she could survive it. Why did marriage matter so much to her? Impulsively, she stepped forward, pressing her body against his. She lifted her mouth, kissing him deeply.

Shadow Hawk pulled away, holding Aissa's hands. "What is the matter with you? I think that fall knocked what little sense you had out of your head."

"Maybe it did." Aissa kissed Shadow Hawk again, knowing that she wanted him more than she wanted anything else in this world. Suddenly marriage didn't matter at all. She was tired of being ashamed of her desire. The only thing that mattered was being with him. She took his hand and led him under one of the oak trees. He seemed hesitant at first, and Aissa decided to change his mind. She stood next to the trunk of the tree and slowly undressed until she was standing only in her shirt.

Shadow Hawk shook his head. "This isn't like you, Aissa."

"I know," she whispered, pulling him to her. She felt his arms go around her, and she leaned into him, her mouth searching his, her tongue probing. She brought his hands beneath her shirt and he made a low sound deep in his throat as his hands caressed her breasts and belly. His fingers stroked her, and for the first time, she touched him, moving her hand tentatively at first, then with determination as she saw his look of desire deepen. It excited her when he said her name, and she continued to explore his body as he explored hers. She put her head back against the tree trunk, reveling in the pleasure they were giving each other. Aissa closed her eyes as Shadow Hawk leaned against her, pressing his body close to hers. He lifted her leg and held it around his waist, gently guiding himself into her. She gasped when she felt him but she didn't shy away; she met his every thrust. This time there was no slow, sensuous lovemaking. This time they were both in a hurry. As Shadow Hawk thrust faster and deeper, Aissa felt him lift her from the ground, and her hips met his in an impossible fury until they both cried out, wrapped in each other's arms. Slowly, Shadow Hawk lowered Aissa so that she was standing, her head resting against his chest. She closed her eyes, her body still alive from the feel of him. They stood, until their breathing slowed, kissing each other softly for a long time.

"You're full of surprises," Shadow Hawk said, his fingers running through Aissa's hair.

She smiled, her heart still filled with the passion of their lovemaking. "Look what's happened to me. I'll take my clothes off in the afternoon and make love to you in a pasture." Shadow Hawk put his hands on her cheeks, and she closed her eyes. She felt his lips against hers, a gentle, sweet kiss.

"Sometimes I feel I'll go mad from my desire for you." His voice was deep, still full of passion.

"I've already gone mad," Aissa said, brushing his lips with hers.

"I've decided something," Shadow Hawk said, his voice suddenly serious.

"What?"

"I'll go to my people. I'll visit with them for a time and then I'll come back."

Aissa nodded, trying to contain her fear. He had left her twice before to go back to his people and he hadn't returned.

"I will come back, Aissa," Shadow Hawk said, kissing her. "And when I do, we will be married. I want you to plan it with your father."

"But—"

Shadow Hawk shook his head, a slight smile touching his mouth. "Do not argue with me on this. I want you for my wife. I want to go to bed with you lying next to me, and I want to wake up with you by my side." He looked at her, his expression one of love. "It is time, Aissa."

Aissa closed her eyes, unable to believe what she was hearing. "You're sure?"

"I'm very sure. I love you. I want to marry you. I want you to have my children."

Children! Her heart began to beat frantically. Was it really going to happen? "I haven't even thought of children," she stammered.

"I have often thought of children. I want many and I want them to have your hair and eyes. But," he said, his eyes narrowing, "I want them to have my ability to ride a horse."

Aissa smiled but her eyes filled with tears. She couldn't believe that after everything they'd been through they were finally going to be together. She laid her head against Shadow Hawk's chest and let him hold her. She had never felt so happy in her life.

Ataza stood on one of the high lookout points of his mountain stronghold. This had been a good camp for many, many summers. They had been lucky; no white man had ever followed them across the desert to these mountains. He knew that some would try eventually. But for now, this was still the safest place for them. If only his family had stayed here.

He thought of his sister, Broken Moon, and his daughter, Singing Bird. They had gone to visit relatives in the spring and now terrible news had come. They had been taken by slave traders. For nearly a generation, these slavers had tormented the Apache. How many of his people had died in the airless, disease-filled mines of Mexico? Others had been taken as well. Among them, his daughter's husband, Brave Heart.

Ataza turned and squinted southward, out over the desert. He knew he would have to find a way to get word to Shadow Hawk. Even though his nephew had chosen to live with his white woman, Ataza knew Shadow Hawk would be enraged when he found out that his mother, Broken Moon, and his younger brother, Brave Heart, had been captured. He would want to ride with them.

Ataza breathed deeply. He forced himself to remain strong. He had heard much of these mines. The slaves had to work long days with little food. He had heard other stories, uglier ones, of women being raped, of people choking to death from little air, of others being branded or beaten to death. Ataza thought of Singing Bird, his only daughter, and his eyes misted over. She was a kind and gentle soul. She would never last in such a place. They would break her.

Ataza closed his eyes, summoning his strength. As long as there was the slightest chance his family was alive, he would have to go after them. He would take his sons, Gitano and Miho. Together, they would find Shadow Hawk. Ataza hesitated. For a moment, he considered not telling his nephew, not taking the time to find him before heading south. But he knew if anyone could find their family, Shadow Hawk could. He had spent much time out of the Apache world, had learned to speak the white tongue and Mexican tongue. Ataza knew he needed Shadow Hawk's help.

Ataza nodded, feeling his decision becoming real. In the morning, they would ride. He took another deep breath and looked out at the distant mountains. It was on one of those mountains that he had found his medicine so many summers ago. Again, he closed his eyes and wrapped his fingers around the small bag that hung around his neck. His voice was low and even when he spoke. "Guide me, Great Spirit, on the right path to find my people. Give me the strength to see what others may not." He opened his eyes again and turned, walking back toward camp. It would soon be time to go.

Chapter Three

The heat of the day still rose from the hard ground, and Broken Moon knew that in a few hours she would be grateful for it. She was already grateful that the slavers had decided to let them rest for at least part of the night. Some of the people were near collapse, and the slavers probably had decided that to push them further would mean losing some of their profit.

Broken Moon wrapped her arms around Singing Bird, trying her best to still her daughter-in-law's fear. She understood it and that was why she did her best to comfort the girl. The women were kept in a separate group from the men and boys so they had only seen Brave Heart a few brief times.

Broken Moon sighed, resting her chin on Singing Bird's head. So, she was a captive again. Only this time, she knew it would be far worse than when she had been taken captive by a Comanche warrior when she was a young woman. As frightened as she had been at the time, she had quickly adapted to the Comanche ways, and to her surprise, she had found that she had fallen in love with her captor, Black Hawk. She had always missed her people, had always wanted to visit them, but after she had given birth to Shadow Hawk, she knew that Black Hawk would never permit her to take his son from the Comanche camp. Not until her husband had been killed on a raid and Shadow Hawk was fourteen summers old, had they gone to her people. Now, after years of living in freedom, surrounded by love, she knew again the old fear of captivity, of being treated like a slave, of knowing her value was like that of a horse or a mule. When she could not work, she would not be kept alive.

Then there was Brave Heart. He was not her blood son but she loved him as if he were, and she knew that Shadow Hawk loved him as if they were real brothers. She was worried about him now. She was afraid he would do something foolish trying to protect Singing Bird.

The Mexicans were talking quietly in the darkness. Broken Moon's Spanish wasn't perfect but she understood most of what they were saying, and it only confirmed what she had feared. They were excited about the fine price they would get for these Indians when they sold them to the mines. Ugly laughter and suggestive sounds followed one man's claim that he could get much more for some of the younger women if he sold them to flesh traders of another kind.

Broken Moon sat up when she heard Singing Bird's even breathing and was sure the young woman had fallen asleep. She stretched, careful not to make a noise that might attract the attention of the slavers. Mines—she had heard of them before. Broken Moon shivered at the thought of laboring down deep in the earth. It frightened her beyond all else. What of the dead who rested there? Would they not disturb them? Would they not be angry at such an intrusion? Broken Moon closed her eyes and forced the fear away. She had to be strong. She could not let her fear overcome her. She had to be strong for Singing Bird and Brave Heart.

She knew Ataza would come looking for them, but she hoped that he would not bring Shadow Hawk. It was futile to hope that her son would not come. He would stop at nothing to find her and his brother. But she didn't know if she could survive the loss of both of her sons if things went badly.

The ground was hard and she tried to rest but she couldn't get comfortable. She opened her eyes and looked up at the night sky. Stars were everywhere, twinkling and shining brightly. She wondered if Black Hawk could see her. Silently, she prayed, asking him to help guide and keep her strong. This would be a true test of her strength.

Aissa sat on the porch beside her father. Shadow Hawk had set up a target on an oak tree. He had already shot ten or fifteen arrows and then pulled them free. As he started back, Christina picked up his bow. Aissa watched Shadow Hawk approach her quickly. Although she could not hear his words, she knew Shadow Hawk was lecturing the girl, telling her that she should not handle his weapon. Christina only laughed. After a moment, Shadow Hawk reluctantly handed her the arrows. Christina notched the first one with a practiced ease and drew back the bow. When she let go, the arrow hit the target, almost dead center.

"She's full of surprises, isn't she?" Ben said, rocking back and forth in his chair.

Aissa nodded. "I think she could do anything if she put her mind to it."

"Reminds me of somebody else I know." Ben raised an eyebrow at his daughter.

"We're not at all alike, Father." Aissa shook her head. "There's something about Christina."

"What exactly?"

"I don't know, something wild. I get the feeling she could live off the land and do just fine."

"You live off the land. Hell, we all do out here."

"Not in the same way, Father. I live in a big house and I raise animals I think Christina could fend for herself if

you stuck her in the desert with just that bow and arrow."
Aissa watched as Shadow Hawk handed Christina the bow again. The girl hit the bull's-eye and whooped loudly. Aissa couldn't keep from smiling. Christina had grown in many ways in the few short months she'd been here. When Aissa had found out that Christina had never owned anything new in her life, she had bought her clothing and small presents of ribbons for the pure pleasure of seeing Christina's happiness.

In many ways, Christina was the younger sister she'd never had. They had even spent hours fixing each other's hair, giggling at the outlandish styles they created. But when Aissa gave Christina her reading lesson, she seemed less like a girl and more like a young woman. She was already reading some of Aissa's simpler novels and she pored over the newspaper everyday, trying to learn new words. She practiced her handwriting constantly and had begun to keep a diary. She was bright, and she was capable, and she was full of life.

"I think she's going to beat your boy," Ben said, leaning forward in his chair.

"If she can beat an Apache at this. . . . Or maybe, Father, he's letting her win."

"He wouldn't do that."

"Yes, he would." Aissa watched as Shadow Hawk held his left arm straight, deliberately pulling back on the bowstring with his right hand. He hesitated for a moment, squinted his eyes, then let the arrow fly. It landed to the left of the bull's-eye, not far off but apparently far enough. Christina started jumping up and down and threw her arms around Shadow Hawk's neck, kissing him on the cheek. Shadow Hawk shook his head in dismay but Aissa smiled. She knew he had done it on purpose. He had let Christina win.

"You were right," Ben said softly. "You know him pretty well, don't you?"

Aissa looked at her father, caught by an odd tone in his voice. Did he know of all the times she and Shadow Hawk had been together? Probably—he wasn't a fool. "Yes, I know him well, Father."

"You still love him, I mean, enough to spend the rest of your life with him?"

"Yes," she responded without hesitation.

"You've considered the problems you'll have? Your children will be half-breeds."

Aissa shook her head adamantly. "No one will ever call them that, not if I have anything to say about it."

"He doesn't even have a last name, Aissa." Ben shrugged. "I don't know why it should be so important, but you know that to most people it is."

"All that matters is that I love him and he loves me. He's a good man, you know that better than anyone. How can you question our love for each other?"

Ben reached out and took Aissa's hand. "I'm not questioning that, Aissa. Any fool could see how much you two love each other."

"So why does it bother you so much?"

"It bothers me because I know people, Aissa. I've been around. You forget I'm from the South. I know how much skin color can matter to some people. It could be hard on you and Shadow Hawk, and it will be hard on your children."

Aissa squeezed her father's hand. "I know you're only thinking of me, Father. But I'll be all right, I promise you." Aissa turned when Christina pounded up the porch steps.

"Aissa, did you see? I beat Shadow Hawk."

Aissa smiled broadly, nodding her head. "Yes, I saw. You're quite good with that bow and arrow." She looked at Shadow Hawk as he walked onto the porch after Christina. "Beaten by a woman."

Shadow Hawk shrugged his shoulders. "She was too

good. I should have listened to her." He reached into his pocket and started to hand her two coins.

Christina took a step backward. "No, I was only kidding about the bet. I couldn't take your money."

"But I would've taken yours," Shadow Hawk said seriously.

"No, you wouldn't have. Besides, I know you let me beat you anyway." She smiled. "I'll go on inside and bring us out something to drink."

Ben winked. "Fine shooting there, Shadow."

"Thank you, Gerard."

"But you did let her win, didn't you?" Aissa asked, watching Shadow Hawk as he leaned back against the porch railing, facing them.

"My last arrow was not so true as the others."

"A real gentleman," Ben said. "Since I have you two alone, when do you plan to make an honest woman out of my daughter, Shadow? And what kind of a name are you going to give her?"

"Father!" Aissa exclaimed, staring angrily at Ben.

"I'm your father. I can ask these questions."

"Father, not now. Please."

"It's all right, Aissa." Shadow Hawk looked at Ben. "I have decided to go once again to see my people. When I come back, I will take Aissa for my wife. We have talked about this."

Aissa looked at her father and could tell by his expression that he was upset and she knew why. She started to speak but Shadow Hawk held up his hand.

"I can see that you are troubled, Gerard."

"Damn right, I'm troubled. You left Aissa before, and you didn't come back until it was almost too late."

"I know," Shadow Hawk agreed.

"Father, please," Aissa pleaded but Ben didn't even look at her.

Aissa watched Shadow Hawk as he straightened up and

looked at her father. "I understand why you would have doubts, Gerard, but I also think that you have reason to trust me. I would do anything to protect Aissa and I have. My only regret is that Grimes escaped alive."

"But what about the future? How are you going to take care of my daughter? I won't have you making a squaw out of her."

"Father, don't do this."

Shadow Hawk faced Ben squarely. "Gerard, listen to me. I will do whatever it takes to provide for Aissa. Even now I am learning how to work this ranch."

"But you just said you were going back to your own people."

"I am going back for a visit, Gerard. If you were to live with Flora on her ranch, would you not want to visit Aissa sometimes?"

Aissa smiled slightly, knowing that Shadow Hawk had finally found a way to reach her father.

"I suppose, but it's not the same."

"It is the same. I want to see my family then I will return here. I swear this on my father's name."

Aissa looked at Shadow Hawk and then at her father. Ben knew what it meant for Shadow Hawk to make such on oath.

Ben stood up, rubbing his leg. He held out his hand to Shadow Hawk. "I don't expect you to swear on your father's name but I'll hold you to your word."

Shadow Hawk grasped Ben's hand firmly. "It will be my honor to marry your daughter, Gerard. And I do have a name to give her. I will take my grandfather's name. It is Bradley."

"Shadow Hawk Bradley," Ben said, shrugging. "Sounds all right. I guess."

Shadow Hawk grinned. "My grandfather gave me a white man's name, Gerard. I can use it if you prefer."

Ben shook his head. "Doesn't seem right somehow.

Your name is Shadow Hawk, and you shouldn't change it."

"If it is necessary I will use the name."

"Whatever you decide is fine with me, Shadow."

"Thank you, Gerard."

Aissa stood up and hugged her father. She kissed him on the cheek. "Thank you."

"Be happy, Aissa. That's all I want for you."

Aissa started to respond when she heard Christina's bubbly voice.

"Are you all as hungry and thirsty as I am?" Christina came out carrying a tray with a pitcher of lemonade and a basket of muffins. She held the tray out to Shadow Hawk. "I think you deserve the first drink since you're such a gentleman."

"Thank you, Christina," Shadow Hawk replied, pouring himself a drink and grabbing a muffin.

Aissa filled the rest of the glasses and handed one to her father and Christina, then took the tray and put it on the porch steps. Aissa watched in amazement as Christina downed the glass of lemonade in three gulps. She wanted to tell her that ladies didn't drink that way but she was so amused by it that she decided not to. There were some things that shouldn't be changed about Christina. In fact, Aissa could think of three or four proper ladies in town who would benefit from trying to emulate her.

"That was some contest, girl," Ben said between bites of his muffin. "Where'd you learn to shoot like that?"

Christina plopped herself on the railing next to Shadow Hawk and began eating. "My father and I used to go hunting for rabbit and squirrel. Had to be a good shot or you'd starve."

"You have a steady hand," Shadow Hawk said.

"You were very impressive, Christina," Aissa said, hesitating as she looked past Shadow Hawk and Christina. She could see a cloud of dust not far away. Riders.

Maybe it was Joe or Flora. She glanced back to hear what Shadow Hawk was saying and when she looked up again, the riders were cantering into the yard. They were Apache. "Shadow Hawk," Aissa said, her voice low as she interrupted him. She squeezed his arm and turned him around.

Shadow Hawk stood on the top step of the porch, looked for a moment, then descended the steps to the Apache who had pulled up and were walking their horses toward the house.

"My God, Indians," Christina whispered. "Should I get a gun or something?"

"No, they're not enemies," Aissa said confidently. She recognized them: Teroz, Ataza, and finally, Gitano. She followed Shadow Hawk until she stood next to him. She smiled up at Gitano. He had been her only friend in the Apache camp besides Ocha, Shadow Hawk's grandmother.

"You look well, white woman. It is good to see you."

"It's good to see you, too, Gitano." She looked over at Ataza. "Welcome, Ataza. Can we help you in any way?"

"I have need to speak to my nephew," Ataza said, his voice gentle.

Aissa nodded. Her eyes traveled over the man she didn't know, to the man she knew only too well: Teroz. Her eyes narrowed as she studied him. He had kidnapped her from her ranch, taken her to the Apache camp, and threatened to kill her if she disrespected him in any way. But in spite of his dire warnings he had never hurt her. He had turned out to be her ally and her protector. She nodded to him. "Hello, Teroz."

"It is good to see you, Aissa."

"Shadow Hawk, why don't you take your family up to the porch? I can bring some food and drink."

"That is not necessary," Ataza replied brusquely. "We do not have the time." He looked at his nephew. "We are in need of your help, Shadow."

"What is it, Uncle?"

"Your mother, Singing Bird, and Brave Heart. They have been taken."

"What do you mean?" Shadow Hawk's voice grew deeper.

Aissa watched as Ataza and then the others dismounted. The man she didn't know stepped forward and extended his hand to Shadow Hawk.

"It is good to see you again, Cousin."

Shadow Hawk grasped the man's hand. "It is good to see you, Miho." Shadow Hawk looked from Miho to Ataza. "Now tell me what you mean, Uncle."

"Miho can tell you."

Miho nodded slightly. "My wife's family went to visit the band where your mother was staying. But when they got there the camp had been destroyed and many of the people were scattered, hiding among the rocks. They said they had been attacked by slave traders."

"Slave traders?" Shadow Hawk looked at Aissa, dismay written on his face. "Do you know anything of these people?"

Aissa stopped forward. "I've heard some things. They raid many of the Apache camps and Mexican villages. They take the young men and women, anyone who is strong enough to work."

"Work where?" Shadow Hawk asked.

"They will be forced to work in the mines," Ataza said, his voice unable to hide his fear and anger.

"The mines," Shadow Hawk repeated, looking at Aissa. "We read about the shafts they dig in one of those books."

"Yes," Aissa replied.

"Is escape possible?" Shadow Hawk asked.

Aissa shook her head. "We should talk to my father. He would know more. He might even know where some of the mines are." Aissa listened as Shadow Hawk spoke in rapid Apache to the men, and they followed him to the porch steps, refusing to climb them. Ben and Christina were standing tensely at the top. Aissa glanced at Ataza's troubled face. "They need your help, Father," Aissa said gently, climbing the steps to stand next to Ben.

"What is it, Shadow?" Ben asked.

"My mother, my brother, and my cousin have been taken by slave traders to Mexico. My uncle says that they will be put to work in the mines. Do you know anything about these mines, Gerard?"

Ben descended the steps without hesitation. He looked at the men and immediately held out his hand to Ataza. "Tell your uncle I am pleased to meet him. Tell him he has a fine nephew."

Aissa watched as Shadow Hawk quickly translated. Ataza hesitated for only a moment then grasped Ben's hand and replied in Apache.

"My uncle says to tell you that your daughter has much heart and that her courage has served her well. He asks if you can help him find his daughter because she does not have the strength of Aissa."

Ben nodded, motioning for Ataza to sit on the bottom step next to him. "Translate for me, Shadow," he said. "This slaving business has been going on for years, at least as long as I can remember. Mostly they take Indians and Mexicans, but they've been known to steal white people, too." Ben waited for Shadow Hawk to translate and he continued, "I do know of two big mines down there. I went to one myself, trying to find a friend's daughter who'd been stolen."

"You know how to get there, Gerard?" Shadow Hawk asked anxiously.

"I can't go with you, Shadow. I'm not willing to leave Aissa alone. But I can draw you a map."

"I would not expect you to come with us, Gerard. A map would be very useful to us." Shadow Hawk translated for the men. "Are these mines far from here?"

Ben shrugged his shoulders. "Three, four days' ride, maybe. For your people, two days' ride."

Shadow Hawk translated, and Aissa thought she detected a hint of a smile on Ataza's face as he nodded. Ataza asked Shadow Hawk a question and Shadow Hawk translated.

"My uncle wants to know what kind of work is done in these mines."

Ben looked over at Ataza and then at Shadow Hawk. "They're sent down into the mines where it's dark. The only light comes from lanterns that're hung on beams. The air is stale, and it's hard to breathe. It's backbreaking work, killing work."

"Are they allowed to come out of these mines?" It was Gitano, his voice filled with fear. Aissa had forgotten how well he spoke English.

"They usually bring them out at the end of the day. They're fed and probably shackled so they can't run away."

Shadow Hawk translated for the men and nodded as he listened to Ataza's words. "My uncle wants to know how long a person could survive in such a place, Gerard."

Aissa watched her father. He shook his head. "I don't know, Shadow. They're ugly places. I went down in one once. I don't know if I could last a month in one." He took a deep breath. "But your people are strong. They know you'll be searching for them. If they can do the work, they'll probably survive until you get there." Ben waited until Shadow Hawk was finished translating. "There's something else, Shadow. Two of the biggest mines are controlled by the government."

"What does that mean?"

"That means there will be soldiers guarding them, lots of soldiers with lots of guns. You and your people just can't go in there like you're raiding a ranch. They'll shoot you dead before you can even get close. You'll have to think of a way to get inside."

"How is it possible, Gerard?"

Ben thought for a moment, looking at Shadow Hawk. "I don't know. Maybe you could pass yourself off as a Spaniard. You're too tall to pass as Mexican. There are still a lot of Spaniards in Mexico." Ben ran his fingers through his hair. "If you could somehow steal an officer's uniform, you might be able to get inside the camp. You speak Spanish well enough. I don't know how else you'd do it."

Shadow Hawk shook his head. "I don't know what an officer's uniform looks like."

"I can draw a picture of one for you, more or less. But you'll be able to tell. Watch and see which man is the leader. If you have to, kidnap him."

"You're suggesting I break the law, Gerard?"

"I'm not suggesting any such thing," Ben said, stretching his legs out in front of him. "I was a sheriff for too long. I don't take kindly to people breaking the law." Ben shrugged nonchalantly. "But who knows what the laws are like down in Mexico? They're probably completely different from ours."

"So, you don't think it would be an offense to kidnap a Mexican soldier?" Shadow Hawk shook his head. "You worry me, Gerard."

"I like your father, white woman," Gitano spoke up suddenly. "He thinks like an Apache."

Ben grinned. "Thank you, son. I take that as a compliment." Ben looked at Ataza. "Tell your uncle to water the horses, and we'll get him and the others something to eat."

Shadow Hawk translated. "My uncle says they are fine, but he gives you his thanks anyway."

Ben stood up. "Tell your uncle not to argue with me. It's a long ride and they could use some food. We must have something here they'll eat."

Shadow Hawk smiled. "I will tell him, Gerard." Shadow

Hawk translated again and looked at Ben. "My uncle says that he will not argue with one so stubborn as you, Gerard. He accepts your offer." Shadow Hawk spoke to the men in Apache and they led their horses to the water trough.

"Christina and I will get something together," Ben said, glancing from Aissa to Shadow Hawk. "We'll let you two talk."

When they were alone, Aissa turned to look up at Shadow Hawk. "You're going with them, aren't you?"

"I must, Aissa. It's my mother and my brother. And you have seen Singing Bird. If these places are as bad as your father says, none of them will survive."

"I know. I understand. I would go if it was my father."

"I must pack."

Aissa followed Shadow Hawk up the stairs to his room, watching him as he threw a few things together in a saddlebag. He put his bedroll next to the saddlebag.

"What about your medicine? You should have it when you find them."

Shadow Hawk nodded and took a rawhide bag from a drawer. He shook his head. "I am so used to playing at being a white man that I forget that which I need most."

Shadow Hawk walked to the window and looked out. "I will miss this place."

"I'm afraid," Aissa said softly, and Shadow Hawk turned to put his arms around her.

"I will be back, Aissa. You must believe me."

"Yes, I believe you."

Shadow Hawk took one of Aissa's hands and put it over his heart. "I will carry you in here with me until I return."

Aissa put her arms around Shadow Hawk's waist and rested her head on his chest. "Be careful. I don't know what I'd do if something happened to you."

"Nothing will happen to me. I will get my family and

take them home. Then I will come back here and marry you."

She smiled slightly, her mouth trembling, tears filling her eyes. She was more afraid than she was willing to admit.

"Do not cry, Aissa. I will be all right." Shadow Hawk kissed Aissa's face where the tears began to fall.

"I know," she said softly, trying to convince herself.

"I want you to promise me you will take care of yourself. Do not do foolish things."

Aissa nodded. She heard voices outside the window. "You should go now. I think they're waiting."

"I love you, Aissa, do not ever forget that."

Aissa closed her eyes as Shadow Hawk kissed her gently. She wished she could make love to him once more, but she knew it was impossible. Reluctantly, she pushed him away. "I'll walk down with you." She led the way down the stairs to the kitchen. Christina handed him a pack.

"There's enough food to last you for a day or two."

"Thank you, Christina," Shadow Hawk said. He walked to her, taking her firmly by the shoulders. "You look out for Aissa and Ben for me."

"I will," Christina replied seriously. "I'd give my life for them."

"You won't have to do that, just look after them and yourself. I will be back soon." He kissed her on the cheek and taking Aissa's hand, headed out the door.

Aissa noticed the paint standing next to the other men's horses. Ben stood holding the stallion's reins, conversing animatedly with Gitano.

"This cousin of yours claims to be the best Apache warrior in these parts, Shadow," Ben said as Shadow Hawk and Aissa came down the steps.

Shadow Hawk cocked an eyebrow at Gitano as he went to the paint and tied on his bedroll and saddlebags. "My cousin only says that because the others do not understand English. He would never say such a thing in Apache."

Ataza faced Ben and spoke.

"My uncle says to thank you for your kindness, Gerard. He will not forget what you have done for him."

Ben nodded. "It's all right. Tell him I wish him luck."

"Be safe, Gitano," Aissa said quickly, knowing that in moments he would be gone.

"I am always safe, white woman. The Great Spirit surrounds me wherever I walk." Gitano smiled broadly and mounted his horse.

Aissa started toward Shadow Hawk but hesitated when Teroz called her name.

"You are well, Aissa?"

Aissa nodded. "I'm very well, thank you."

"You are happy?"

Aissa searched Teroz's eyes, knowing what he was really asking. He wanted to know if she forgave him. "Yes, Teroz, I am happy. I love Shadow Hawk very much. When he comes back, we are going to get married.' "

Teroz nodded his head. "That is good."

Aissa couldn't resist a smile. Teroz had undergone an incredible change, or maybe there had been a gentle side to him all along, just as Singing Bird had said there was. "I hope you and Shadow Hawk will get along."

"I have no intention of fighting with my cousin. I am more concerned with finding my people."

Aissa was pleased that Teroz had called Shadow Hawk's mother and brother "his people." "I am glad you're going with them, Teroz."

"Thank you, Aissa." Teroz swung up on his horse.

Aissa glanced around to find Shadow Hawk. He was standing a little apart from the others. She forced herself to remain composed as she went to him. She took her locket from around her neck and put it into his hand.

"Take this for luck. Know that I am always with you."

Shadow Hawk dropped the locket into his pocket and pulled Aissa to him. "I will miss you."

"It is time, Cousin," Gitano called out.

Aissa looked up at Shadow Hawk. "We will be together soon. Then I will never let you go."

Shadow Hawk smiled. "I will look forward to that time." He kissed her then swung up onto the paint.

Aissa watched as the men turned their horses out of the yard and rode away. Shadow Hawk looked back once, raised his hand slightly, and rode on with the others. Aissa waved back. She tried to keep her fear under control, but it suddenly seemed overpowering. She couldn't shake the feeling that something bad was going to happen.

Ray had been watching the Gerard ranch for days. He had seen the Apache ride in and had seen Shadow Hawk leave with them. He smiled to himself. This was perfect. The Apache were probably on their way south to search for their people. What a surprise Shadow Hawk would have in store when he came back and found that Aissa was also gone. He relished the thought.

But he had learned a hard lesson—he wouldn't let Aissa's Apache lover see him again and he wouldn't let Ben Gerard know he was alive. He would let them all think he was dead but he would still have his revenge. The slavers would take Aissa south and she would be put to work in one of the mines. She would be forced to labor from dawn until dusk every day in the mines until gradually she would be broken. Her health would deteriorate, as well as her beauty. She wouldn't last a year down there. As far as Ray was concerned, if she wanted to live like a squaw she could die like one.

He grinned. Once she was out of the way for good, the

old man would fall apart. Then it would be just a matter of time before Ray could go back in and reclaim his land.

Aissa walked slowly, swinging the bag that contained her books. She sucked on a cinnamon stick she had bought at the General Store. She had bought several of them for Christina but they looked so good, she had decided to have one herself. It had only been three days since Shadow Hawk had left but it seemed like weeks. Aissa forced herself to smile. Soon she would be twenty-one years old and Shadow Hawk would be back. They would be married.

She bit off a piece of the candy stick and chewed it vigorously. She'd had a particular craving for sweets lately, maybe because she missed Shadow Hawk so much. She was trying anything to keep her mind from him.

As the dirt road wound its way toward her land, Aissa stopped. She looked behind her. Strange, she felt as if she were being watched. She started walking again, trying to shake the uneasy feeling that had come over her. Like a child walking in the dark, she began to hum to herself, walking so quickly that she was almost running. As she rounded a bend in the road, Aissa impulsively looked back over her shoulder. There were two riders behind her, not close enough to see their faces but closer than they should've been. If they had been behind her on the road all the way from town, she would've seen them long before this. Whoever they were, they had turned onto the road in the last few minutes, having come across open country.

Aissa felt her own thudding pulse as she fought the urge to break into a run. Glancing back, time after time, she saw that the riders were gaining on her. In her nervousness, she stumbled and fell, and when she regained her feet again, she saw two riders in the road ahead of her as well. The instant she realized that they were after her, she broke into an involuntary run. Over the pounding of her own heart, she heard hoofbeats behind her. Trying to keep her wits, Aissa flung away her book pack and lifted her skirt. She ran as she had never run before in her life, leaping over fallen logs, her eyes fixed desperately on a rock outcropping a few hundred yards away. Her breathing was so hard and fast that it hurt. But still she ran on. Just as she began to believe she might make it, the hoofbeats behind her got louder and closer, and she could hear the men behind her laughing. An instant later, she felt rough hands around her waist as she was lifted from the ground and flung face down across the horse's withers. Immediately, the rider pulled his horse back down from a gallop into a canter, then into a trot that bruised her ribs. Aissa squeezed her eyes shut, trying to block out the pain in her chest and sides, the fear in her heart, and the ugly boasting of the man who had caught her. He was speaking Spanish and although Aissa tried to lift her head to look at him, she knew that seeing his face wouldn't matter. These were slavers. The same kind of men who had taken Shadow Hawk's family. It would be a long time before anyone came looking for her, but Shadow Hawk would eventually. Until then all she could do was try to survive.

Chapter Four

Aissa was exhausted. After the men had taken her, they had ridden the rest of that day and the entire night before they stopped. When they finally rested, Aissa was up and given only a sip of water. It seemed like they had rested barely an hour before they forced her back onto a horse. This time at least, she was allowed to sit up and some of the pain in her stomach and chest began to ease. But it was almost worse to have the slaver's arms around her, holding her tightly as they rode. After a few hours, they stopped again, this time just long enough for the slavers to drink and for the man Aissa was riding with to shove her to the ground. One of the others caught her long braid and forced her to stumble alongside his horse for a little way before he bent down and swung her up in front of him.

By the second day, Aissa couldn't keep her eyes open. Very often she fell asleep, only to be jolted awake by the shout of one of the men or the uneven stride of whichever horse she was on. The men were careful not to say where they were taking her. The only thing she knew for sure was that they were in Mexico. She had been there before with her father and she recognized the little pueblos where the people lived in thick-walled adobe houses. The women who sold beans and rice to the slavers were dressed in colorful cotton skirts and blouses. They stared at her, as they carried baskets full of clothes or food, children clinging to their skirts. Carts led by flop-eared mules stirred dust wherever they went, and sleepy men dressed in their white pants and shirts sat underneath their sombreros in the shade taking naps in the hot afternoon sun. Aissa had even heard the bells of the church chime in one little town. It had been two o'clock in the afternoon.

The next time they stopped it was night and the moon was high in the sky. Again, Aissa was bound and given only a little water. When they left her alone, she lay on her side and immediately fell asleep, not even trying to listen to what the men were saying. Too soon, she was awakened and the group began riding. They rode until mid-morning and then slowed. Aissa could see how dreary and barren the land had become and soon, she could see the place where they were taking her.

As they headed downslope toward the mine Aissa tried to still her fear. She had never seen land this barren, this scarred. There was a dark opening in the face of the hill that had to be the entrance to the mine. Aissa could see people moving in and out, stoop-shouldered and with heavy steps. Parallel rails came from the entrance to the mine and ran down to the floor of the desolate valley. Aissa saw two people pushing a wheeled cart from the mine. As it began to roll downhill on its own, they stopped, straightened up, then turned and shuffled back into the entrance. Were they Indians? Aissa strained to see but couldn't tell. As they got closer, Aissa could see up the valley. There were low, rough barracks and corral-like enclosures that held no horses or cattle. The slavers rode straight toward the largest building, shouting.

Aissa was pushed to the ground. She stood apprehensively looking around her as some of the workers and all of the soldiers stared at her. One of the guards came up to her, lifting her heavy braid from her shoulder.

"Una rubia," he said, his voice harsh. *"Ella es para mi,"* he said, touching her shoulder.

Aissa flinched. He had said, "This one is for me."

The man whom Aissa had ridden with shook his head adamantly. *"No, mas tarde. Tiene que trabaja ella. Por eso paga el gringo. Me entiendes?"*

The man's words stunned Aissa. In spite of her fear, she felt a cold anger. *El gringo.* The white man. The white man had given orders that she be worked. The only white man who could've planned and arranged something this cruel was Ray Grimes. If Ray was behind this, it would be even harder for her to escape, and even harder for Shadow Hawk to rescue her. Could this be the same mine where his family had been taken? Had Ray arranged that, too? She knew that he would lay trap after trap and enjoy the scheming. As the guards shoved Aissa forward, a short, stocky woman wearing drab gray clothing came out of one of the barracks. *"Va a ensenarla el trabajo. Andale!"* The guard shouted.

Without hesitation, Aissa followed the woman. The woman was silent as they walked. Aissa noticed the carts that were filled with rock and ore, and workers were loading it onto burros that looked too small to bear the heavy weight. Soldiers with rifles constantly walked around the yard, intimidating workers, shouting for no apparent reason. Aissa stopped to watch as one man passively accepted two blows to the back of his head from the butt of a rifle without a fight. The soldier laughed when the man fell to the ground.

Aissa felt a tug on her arm and realized the woman was urging her forward. She strained to see. There had to be a way to escape this place. Before she could do more than glance around, the woman pulled her forward to the entrance of the mine shaft. Aissa hesitated, jerking her arm from the woman's grasp. The top beam of the opening came to her chest. She wouldn't be able to stand up inside. She looked around, suddenly feeling panicked. Where could she go? Maybe if she pretended to be sick she wouldn't have to work. But even as her thoughts swirled, she saw a guard approach them. Instantly, the woman dragged Aissa after her. The woman fit easily through the mine entrance but Aissa had to duck, keeping her shoulders rounded and her head lowered. She followed the woman into the shaft that was lit only by lanterns that hung from the wooden braces that reinforced the tunnel. The air was musty and dank, and the deeper into the shaft that they walked, the cooler it felt.

The tunnel was narrow and impossible for her to stand up in. Even the much shorter woman who walked in front of her had to duck under some of the reinforcing beams. Aissa stepped carefully over crudely hewn railroad ties. After ten or twelve steps, the Mexican woman pushed her roughly to one side and Aissa watched as sweating workers pushed an ore cart past them toward the entrance. Wooden timbers were all that held up the earthen walls. Aissa thought about the weight of hundreds of feet of earth above her head and fought the urge to run. Another ore cart rumbled past and Aissa stared at the dull gray chunks of rock. She didn't even know what was mined here.

The woman jabbed Aissa in the shoulder and gestured impatiently. Aissa followed the woman, numb and frightened but determined not to show her fear. As they walked, they passed people who chipped at the rock walls with steady, measured strokes, depositing the chunks into bags around their shoulders. When they reached a turn, the woman grabbed Aissa by the arm and led her down another tunnel. She took a small pick out of a cart and pressed it into Aissa's hands, showing her how to grip it. Taking a second pick, she began to cut into the rock walls with small taps, taking the chunks of ore and putting them into the cart. As soon as she was satisfied that Aissa was working, the woman left her alone. Aissa looked around, her stomach empty, her body already weary. How was it possible? Just a short while ago she and Shadow Hawk were talking about getting married. Now, she was a prisoner, forced to labor down in the cold, dark earth.

She watched the men and women around her, and she learned quickly. She choked up on the pick, getting a better grip. She hit the wall firmly, waiting until pieces of the ore broke off in her hand. She wasn't even sure what she was looking for but she put the pieces into the cart. The air was stale and thick with the odor of human sweat. There were times when she felt as if she might collapse, but she forced herself to continue. She had to stoop over in order to work, and her back and shoulders ached unbearably. Ray had thought this through very carefully.

The steady chinking sound of her pick against the stone seemed to mark out each second as it passed. At first Aissa tried to work efficiently but soon she was working as the others were—mindlessly—careful only to keep her pick moving. Already her hands had blisters and there were times she felt she would suffocate from the still, dank air. But whenever she felt like giving up, she thought of Shadow Hawk. She knew that however long it took, he would find her. All she had to do was stay alive.

Clayton Montrose handed out the food to the workers. They liked him as much as they were still capable of liking anyone. He was fair and he treated everyone well. He tried to make them all his allies. He knew there were a few of them who were not as beaten as they pretended to be. If he was ever going to get out of this hellhole, they would be the ones to help him.

Clayton had been here at the Xavier Silver Mine for over two long, grueling years. He shouldn't have been here, but he'd made the unfortunate mistake of killing a Mexican officer in a poker game. Rather than send him to prison, he was sent to the mine to work. But he was soon out of the mine.

It hadn't taken him long to ingratiate himself to the *Comandante* and soon he was serving food to the workers. Clay also was able to secure certain things for the workers. In return, they gave him what little they had: their loyalty. When they saw him walking where even he was not permitted to go, they did not betray him. If some of them knew about the money he had buried inside the mine, he felt sure they would never steal it from him. Whatever hope they had for extra food when they were sick or help when they were injured, they placed in him.

Getting the money had been ridiculously easy. The guards were almost as affected by the grinding boredom of the mine as the prisoners were. Petty cruelty was common, and although fighting among themselves was forbidden, it still went on. But the major outlet for the guards was gambling. Gambling had become their obsession. Every night, the soldiers gathered around two splay-legged tables in the barracks, eager to learn the dozens of variations of poker that Clay knew, as well as rummy, craps, virtually anything they could place a wager on. Clay used his quick wit and intuitive charm to control the men. When one seemed on the verge of remembering who was really in charge, Clay would see to it that that man had a winning streak. As the others became jealous or even suspicious, the guard would forget his anger at the gringo. By making sure that the guards were always preoccupied with their own rivalries, Clay preserved his dangerous role as the puppetmaster, pulling invisible strings.

Clay knew it couldn't last forever, and he didn't want it to. As soon as there was a diversion or an opportunity that allowed him to escape, he would be gone. Until then, he remained the happy-go-lucky gringo who helped the workers and who was friendly with the guards.

When Clay heard that the white woman had been brought in, he was eager to see her. The money he'd taken from Grimes was the easiest money he would ever make. He wouldn't have to do a thing. The white woman wouldn't last long anyway. No white woman would last in the heat and dust.

The only reason he'd made it as long as he had was because he'd gotten himself out of the mine as quickly as he could. For the short time he'd worked alongside the Indians and the Mexicans, he had been amazed at their strength and endurance. Even more than that, he had been astounded by their kindness toward each other.

Today, as always, Clay smiled at one of the pretty Mexican girls as he handed her an extra roll. He'd see her later. He spoke in fluent Spanish to the workers as they lined up for their sparse, midday meal. He had even picked up a few words of Apache, but he rarely talked to them. The Apache scared him; they scared everyone. Some of them wore shackles, earned by repeated attempts at escape. If most of the others had a kind patience deep in their eyes, the Apache had just the opposite. Anyone could see the smoldering hatred that they kept alive day after day under conditions that would have broken anyone else. The guards beat them, but they were careful to walk in threes and fours to the parts of the mine where the Apache worked. Because they were so hard to control, the government preferred to buy more docile slaves from southern Mexico, people who would work until they died and were easily replaced.

Clay was carrying on an animated conversation with Vincente, his helper, when he looked up and saw the white woman. She was a good head taller than the men around her, and her hair was so blond it was startling among the dark-haired workers. Even in her dusty clothes, with dirt smeared on her face, he could see she was a real beauty. Grimes hadn't told him that. He watched her as the line moved forward. He wasn't sure what he'd expected. The way Grimes had talked the woman was despicable, spiteful, someone who deserved this kind of punishment. But as he watched, the blond woman bumped into one of the workers and immediately apologized. The startled worker nodded and almost smiled. She didn't seem like the kind of woman who would've given a second glance to a man like Ray Grimes. Even in that first card game, Clay had known within five minutes that the only thing that separated Grimes from the lowest kind of drifter was his money. How would he know they were married? When she got to the front of the line, he lowered his voice as he filled her plate with beans and an extra roll.

"What's your name?"

She didn't answer.

"You must speak English."

She nodded without answering.

"Then tell me your name."

She looked at him. "My name is Aissa." Her eyes narrowed.

He smiled, knowing what she was thinking. He was as obvious to her as she was to him. He was tall, his hair was sandy blond, and his eyes were a light brown. Although she was covered with rock dust, he could tell she was fair-skinned, while his own face and arms were burnt brown by the sun. He knew she was wondering who the hell he was and what he was doing here. He couldn't tell her the truth, or at least not all of it, not if he ever wanted her to talk to him. And suddenly, that was what Clay wanted more than anything else. Not only was she pretty, he found himself intrigued.

The woman looked confused. The workers behind her were becoming impatient. Clay nodded his head toward a narrow strip of shade along one side of a storage shed. "Go sit over there. At least it'll give you a little protection from the sun."

She looked at him a second longer, mumbled a thank

you, and went to sit down.

Clay filled a few more plates and then asked Vincente to take over for him. He grabbed some extra rolls and walked over and sat down next to Aissa. He dropped the rolls on her plate. "Here, you might want these for later." When she looked up at him, he was astounded by the lightness of her eyes. Her gaze was steady, but there was no doubting the fear that was there.

Aissa put the rolls in her skirt pocket. She sat up straight, rubbing her back. "I can't repay you for these."

Clay ignored her remark. "You'll never make it in the mine. You're too tall. We'll have to figure a way to get you out of there." Even as Clay spoke, he was chiding himself. He wasn't supposed to help this woman, he was supposed to make her life miserable.

Aissa's eyes became guarded. "I'll manage."

"No, you won't. The pain will start in your back and creep up to your shoulders and neck. Pretty soon it'll become impossible for you to stand up straight. Your arms will start to turn numb on you. Your eyes will go next."

"My eyes?" she echoed, her voice fearful.

He nodded. "They'll become so accustomed to the dark that when you come out into the sunlight, you'll be blinded. Haven't you noticed the way the workers all squint?" Clay leaned closer to Aissa. "We have to think of something to get you out of there."

"Why would you want to help me? What do you get out of it?"

For a moment Clay could only smile. It was the same question he was asking himself. He covered his hesitation with a joke. "I don't suppose you have any money stashed on you?"

"Do I look like I have money stashed on me?" Aissa replied angrily.

Clay shrugged his shoulders, suppressing a smile. If she had that much spunk left after a day in the mines, she just might have a chance. "Thought I'd ask."

"I have some land. If you can help me get out of here and back to my home, I can give you enough to start your own ranch."

"I'm not interested in land, lady. Do I look like a farmer to you?" Clay watched as she lowered her head. She was a pretty thing. "How'd you end up here?" Clay asked. It'd be interesting to see if she had any idea who was behind all this.

"It doesn't matter."

"It does matter if you want me to help you. I need to know what I'm up against. People end up here for lots of reasons: they owe money to the wrong person, they end up on the wrong side of the law, sometimes they just plain run out of luck."

"My story's a little different than that."

Clay waited, hoping she would go on. This was going to be interesting.

"I was kidnapped," she said simply.

"Who would want to kidnap you?"

"A man I used to be married to."

"Your husband did this to you?" Clay tried to hide his surprise. Grimes had never said anything about them being married.

"He was never my husband," Aissa responded angrily. "I was forced into the marriage. I hated every day I was with him."

"Still, why would he do something like this?"

"Because I never loved him, and I took back the land that belonged to my family."

Clay shook his head. "Sorry, lady, I've seen lots of men who wanted to get back at a woman, but I've never seen one who would do something like this." He watched as she dropped her plate on the ground and faced him, eyes blazing.

"It's a long story, one I don't tell to strangers. But I'll

tell you this much, if it hadn't been for Shadow Hawk, I would've killed Ray Grimes." Clay watched as she picked up her plate, her movements suddenly precise and controlled. When she looked at him again, her expression was careful. "Don't ask me any more questions."

Clay held her eyes. "Just one more. Who's Shadow Hawk?"

She wiped the sweat from her brow, looking defeated. "He's the man I should've married."

Clay nodded, careful to conceal his surprise. "Indian?"

"Apache."

Clay stared at her in disbelief. "I don't know which is harder to believe, that an Apache talked you out of killing someone, or that you're actually crazy enough to marry one." He watched her mouth curve upward in a slight smile. But as quickly as it appeared, the smile was gone.

"Did you mean it about helping me?"

In spite of what he had promised Grimes, Clay nodded. "It's going to take some time, but I'll figure something out."

"I doubt if there's anything you can do anyway. I heard the slavers talking. He doesn't want me to leave here. I think he's arranged for me to work. . . ."

Clay watched Aissa's face as she hesitated. "Until you die?" He finished for her.

Aissa nodded.

Clay could only shake his head again. He barely knew this woman but he was willing to bet that she had never done anything in her life to deserve even one day here. He found it especially difficult to believe that she could've done something bad enough to hurt someone like Grimes. "I'm pretty friendly with the guards and maybe I can get them to leave you alone. Then we can think about how to get you out of here."

"And what will I have to do in return?"

Clay looked at Aissa, and he couldn't contain a smile. "We can talk about that later."

"No, we'll talk about it now."

"All right. I don't need your land." Clay shrugged. "I don't need much of anything."

"Then why are you here?"

"Had a little run-in with a Mexican soldier. Killed him in a poker game."

"And you expect me to trust you?"

"I don't see that you have much choice." Clay looked around him. "Look, you're pretty and you're white. You'll attract a lot of attention around here because you stand out. Won't be long before the guards are fighting over you." He could see the fear in her eyes. She couldn't hide it this time.

"You never answered my question. What do *you* want from me?"

"I don't want anything right now. If we get out of here, maybe then—"

"Never mind. I don't want your help."

"Look, lady," Clay lowered his head next to hers, "if you're worried that I might take advantage of you, don't be. I have plenty of women here. Fact is, I don't need your money or your land. My family has plenty of both. I just thought you looked like you could use a friend. Guess I was wrong." He started to get up but felt her hand on his arm.

"I'm sorry. I don't know who to trust anymore."

"I know what you're feeling. I'll try to help you if I can, but if I can't, I won't risk my neck. I've been planning my escape from here for almost two years and I won't let anything or anyone stop me from getting out."

Aissa pushed the loose strands of hair back from her face. "I understand. What should I do?"

"Just keep working. Don't cause any trouble. I'll do what I can."

"I don't even know your name."

"It's Clay. Clay Montrose." He smiled one of his most charming smiles.

"Thank you."

"Don't thank me yet, lady." Clay got up and walked back to the food line. He liked this woman. She reminded him of his sister. Clay thought about his family for a moment. He wondered if his father was worried about him. If he was, he'd never admit it. But his mother and Rayna would be worried. He glanced around at the dusty work yard and the cruel-faced guards. He had sworn that he'd never go back to his father's ranch, but now he knew he would. He didn't give a damn about his old man, but as long as his mother and sister lived there, it was still home. He hoped to be back there real soon.

At the end of each day, the workers were herded into a large area surrounded by a high wire fence. It served as a corral. The large circle was divided in the middle by another fence and men were kept on one side, women on the other. Pregnancy was a complication the government tried to avoid. Any guard that impregnated a woman was expected to solve the situation himself.

After Clay had dished up the evening meal, he waited until all the workers were inside the fence and darkness had fallen. Then he slipped across the mine camp and followed the narrow gauge tracks to the mine entrance. He knew there was a guard in the tower, but they were all used to seeing him walk around the camp. He had let it slip one night at the card table that he hoped to find some silver nuggets. They had all laughed, and one guard had suggested that Clay might prefer his old work assignment. Clay had turned his face so they couldn't see the sheen of sweat on his forehead in the lantern light. He was walking a dangerously thin line and he knew it. But they would remember his remark and when they saw him enter the mine at night, they would assume that he was poking around the fallen ore from that day's work. The guards all knew he had money hidden somewhere, but the mine was not the obvious choice because it was filled with workers everyday. What the guards did not understand and would never understand was the loyalty the workers had toward Clay and the basic honesty that they possessed.

Within a few moments, Clay had pushed the loosened planks aside and was standing in an unused tunnel. He pushed aside a large rock and dug into the loose dirt. He smiled, pulling out the crispest, newest bills. This was not what Grimes would've wanted his money spent for and that would make it even better. This was a long shot, but Clay thought it would work.

As he started back out of the mine, he rehearsed in his mind the conversation he was about to have with the *Comandante*. He would have to be very careful; the man was unpredictable.

Clay ducked under the timbers that reinforced the mine entrance and stood for a moment, breathing the fresh air, working his shoulders to ease the discomfort. "Unpredictable," he whispered the word in the darkness. The word seemed to suit him as well as the *Comandante*. He had played it close to his chest for almost two years. So, why was he willing to risk everything for a woman he barely knew, a woman he had promised to kill?

He jammed the money in his pocket and started back toward the camp, adjusting his stride to fit the distance between the rough-hewn ties. If there was a reason why he was going to help Aissa, he sure as hell didn't know what it was. But he was going to help her.

He passed the soldiers' barracks, hearing their loud and raucous voices as they bet their meager earnings in the nightly poker game. The *Comandante* lived in the largest building, away from the others, and it was a fairly clean place by these standards.

Clay had learned early on that if he pleased the *Comandante,* he could get just about anything he needed. If the *Comandante* wanted women, Clay got them for him, especially women who were willing to better their lives here in this miserable place. If the *Comandante* wanted a poker game, Clay arranged it. If the *Comandante* wanted a certain meal, Clay managed to find the right ingredients.

On one memorable occasion, Clay had traded firewood to a guard whose aunt lived in a nearby village. That aunt had chickens and paid for the firewood with two dozen eggs. With half the eggs, Clay had traded for flour and butter. Getting sugar had involved a goat, a pair of boots, and four of the remaining eggs. But when Clay was through trading, the *Comandante* got the cake he had wanted. In return for these small luxuries, the *Comandante* had given Clay an enormous amount of freedom. As long as he kept out of trouble, things would go well for him. The *Comandante* had even given Clay a storage shed for him to clean out and live in. It was barely large enough for him to stretch out in, but it afforded him privacy.

Clay took a deep breath and walked to the front of the *Comandante*'s office. Even though it was after dark, he knew the man would still be up. He was stern and hardworking but fair in his own way. Clay knocked twice on the door and entered when he heard the *Comandante's* voice.

"Sí, what do you want?" the *Comandante* asked without looking up.

"I'm sorry to bother you, *Comandante,* but I would like to speak to you about an urgent matter." Clay watched as the man continued writing methodically for a few minutes then put down his pen and carefully folded his hands in front of him on the desk.

"What is it?"

"It is the white woman who was brought into camp today."

"What of her?"

"I would like to have her for my woman."

The *Comandante* nodded patiently. "Yes, I'm sure you would, *gringo,* and so would every other man in this camp."

"She will cause trouble, *Comandante.*"

"In what way?"

Clay shrugged, trying to sound nonchalant. "It is like you said. The guards will fight over her, the workers will fight over her, she will be more trouble than she is worth."

"And what do you propose to do with her?"

"I propose to make her my woman. She will cook for me, help me feed the others, do whatever I tell her to do." Clay paused before continuing. "And she will warm my bed at night."

"It is said you have many women, *gringo.* Why do you want this one?"

"She is like me, a stranger here. I think she will listen to me and not cause any trouble."

"If she causes trouble, I will have her removed from this place. I do not need your assistance in this matter, *gringo.*"

Clay knew now was not the time to press. "Whatever you say, *Comandante.* It was just a thought. *Buenas noches.*" He closed the door and walked out into the cool night air. He looked up at the star-filled sky and took a deep breath, then he looked up at the guard tower. He couldn't wait to be free of this place. God, how he hated it here. He hated the way the workers were treated. He hated the way the guards took advantage of the women. And most of all, he hated what he had become in order to survive.

He smiled to himself, shaking his head. How could the son of a wealthy rancher wind up working in a mine in Mexico? But Clay knew that answer all too well. He had answered it dozens of times. Everything always came back to his father and the death of his brother. After his brother had died, he had started running and he hadn't stopped since.

He'd managed to get himself into plenty of trouble, and he'd seen his share of dirty jails. But he'd also learned the fine art of gambling, and it had supported him well at times. At other times, like this, he regretted ever having learned how to shuffle a deck. But the most important thing he'd learned was that he was strong and smart enough to depend on himself. He also figured out early on that he had the kind of personality people were drawn to, especially women. He'd taken full advantage of the fact.

He walked past the enclosure and heard the sighing and shuffling of the workers as they slept or tried to get comfortable. He thought about Aissa and wondered if she was all right. He hadn't lied to her when he told her she'd never make it here—she probably wouldn't if he didn't help her. If the mine didn't break her, the guards would . . . and Grimes had counted on both of those things. He had to come up with a better idea, one that would convince the *Comandante* that he should look after her.

He started toward the barracks, money in hand, but turned and walked to his small shack. He wasn't in the mood for poker tonight. He went inside, lying down on the blankets that served as his bed. He took off his boots and shirt and stretched out on his back. He couldn't stop thinking about Aissa. She was pretty and she was strong, but there was something else that he recognized. She wore an expression that mimicked fear but was really something beyond that; it was one of desperation. He'd seen that look before on people. People with that look had tried to escape, had ignored the shouts of the guards, and had been shot. He didn't want to see the same thing happen to her.

* * *

Aissa hit at the rock wall in front of her, taking the pieces and dropping them into the cart. It was amazing. She could barely see but somehow her eyes had adjusted to the dim light. Her hands were calloused and blistered, her arms and shoulders ached unbearably. Whenever there was no guard around, she got down on her knees and sat back on her heels, reaching out in front of her to stretch her back.

She ran her fingers over the rough plank, counting the notches she'd made there: twenty-six. She'd been here almost four weeks, yet it seemed like a lifetime. Her lungs ached for the want of fresh air, her eyes stung from the ore and dust particles that filled the dark tunnel. She was beginning to wonder if Shadow Hawk would ever find her.

Her days were all the same. She woke at sunrise with the others, was given some water and bread, and she toiled in the mine until midday when they were allowed out for one hour. After the hour, they were sent back into the mine to work until shortly before sunset. They were given beans, bread and occasionally a small piece of meat, and then herded into the enclosure like animals to sleep out in the open. She had tried to talk to Clay again but he had only ignored her. Somehow she'd offended him that first day they had talked, and in so doing, she had lost her only hope of escape.

As she chipped away at the rock, Aissa heard the bell sounding the lunch hour. She stopped, thankful that for once it seemed to come early. She dropped the pick into the cart and started out after the others. She hated this part—waiting while the others slowly filed out of the tunnel. It took every bit of courage she had to keep from shoving past them and running outside. She'd imagined all kinds of horrible things, but mostly she wondered what it would be like to be buried alive.

"What is your hurry, *rubia?*"

Aissa heard the guard's voice behind her and she cringed. It was the guard called Cinzo. He frightened her. He always followed her, stared at her, and made life generally miserable for her. If something extra needed to be done, he assigned the task to her. If someone had to work through the lunch hour, he made sure Aissa was the one to do it. He also made sure she knew he could make things easier for her if she became his woman. But Aissa had always refused his advances and, in so doing, had to suffer the consequences.

"You will take your lunch inside today with me," he said, taking her by the arm and leading her back into the tunnel.

"No, please, I'm so hungry."

"I have food for you. Just come with me."

"No, I feel sick. Please, I need some air."

"No, that is not what you need, *rubia*. I know what it is that you need."

"No!" Aissa responded adamantly, jerking her arm away. She saw him raise his hand and she ducked, running past him back the way she had come. She retrieved her pick from the cart and waited around the corner, the ax held firmly in her hand.

"What game is this, *rubia?* You know I will find you."

Aissa was shaking. She leaned against a heavy timber, her back pressed against it, bracing herself. She heard Cinzo as he approached and she raised the pick over her head.

"Hey, Cinzo, the *Comandante* wants to speak to you." The deep voice echoed in the mine shaft.

Aissa exhaled. It was Clay. How had he known she was in trouble, and why had he decided to help her?

"What is it now, *gringo?*" Cinzo's voice was filled with irritation.

Aissa could hear Clay's voice more clearly now. "The

Comandante wants to see you now."

"Ah!" Cinzo said, cursing under his breath.

Aissa stepped around the corner and almost ran into Clay. She was so relieved to see him she felt as if she could cry. "Thank you. Again."

"Are you all right? Did he hurt you?"

"No. How did you know I was in here?"

"I didn't see you in the line and I asked some of the women. I decided I better get you out of here."

"The *Comandante* doesn't really want to see him, does he?"

"It doesn't matter. The *Comandante* is resting now. The *Comandante* doesn't like to be disturbed when he's resting. When Cinzo wakes him up, he'll be sorry."

"What about you?"

"Cinzo won't say anything." Clay took Aissa's hand and led her deeper into the tunnel.

Aissa hesitated, pulling against Clay's hand. "Where are we going?"

"I want to show you something. Come on."

Uneasily, Aissa allowed Clay to lead her along. Within minutes, they had passed the tunnel that Aissa usually worked in. A few moments after that, Clay turned abruptly to his left and stopped. He pulled Aissa forward and placed her hands on a wooden ladder. "Go up," he urged her. Aissa hesitated, putting her hand to her chest, feeling as if she couldn't breathe.

"I can't. I've got to get out."

"You're fine, Aissa. This is important."

Aissa wanted to turn and run, but instinct told her to trust Clay. He'd done nothing to hurt her. She climbed the ladder and waited for him.

"There are four other levels, too," Clay said. "But they're only working on the bottom one now, trying to relocate the main vein." He took her hand and they walked straight until they reached a dead end. Clay took a candle out of his pocket and lit it. Aissa saw another ladder in front of them. Clay climbed it and she followed him reluctantly, grateful for the candle—there were no lanterns on this level. As they walked the tunnel became even smaller until Aissa's already strained back muscles were screaming with pain. After a few minutes, Clay squatted down, pulling her with him. He put his arm around her shoulders.

"Rest a minute, catch your breath."

Aissa stiffened and started to pull away but Clay held onto her. "Let me go."

"I'm not going to hurt you." Clay edged forward, holding the candle out in front of him. "You see this?"

"What? I don't see anything."

Clay moved a rotting old timber out of the way. "Give me your hand." He pressed it against the wall. The dirt was soft, moist, and it collapsed under the pressure.

Aissa tried to read Clay's face in the flickering candlelight. "What is it?"

"It's freedom."

"What do you mean?"

"You know the hill behind the barracks? This tunnel runs under it. It goes back nearly a hundred yards. I'm the one who built this false wall to conceal the entrance. The way I figure it, if I can lengthen it another twenty-five to thirty feet, I'll come out on the far side of the hill where the guard in the tower can't see me."

"What if someone finds it?"

"No one will find it. None of the guards ever come back this far."

"Why are you showing it to me?"

"In case something happens to me and I can't get you out of here, I want you to have a chance. You could probably talk some of the others into helping you dig."

Aissa covered her face with her hands, dropping to her knees. She was exhausted. Every muscle in her body ached. All she wanted to do was cry. "I don't understand why you're doing this."

"I just want to help you, Aissa. It's that simple. I don't want anything from you."

"But you'll be punished for helping me." Aissa started to turn around and go toward the ladder, but Clay took her arm.

"Listen to me, Aissa. I'm not a real honest man. I've lived life the way I've wanted to, I've done things I've regretted, but I never had to worry about anyone but myself. Now suddenly, I find myself thinking about you. I don't know why. Maybe because you remind me of my little sister. I can't explain it."

Aissa smiled weakly. "I don't know how to thank you."

"You're going to have to play along with me for awhile."

Aissa nodded in resignation. "Whatever you say. What do you want me to do?"

"Well, when we walk out of here, you have to look like . . ." Clay hesitated. "You know, like we've been together."

"Why?"

"If I can make the *Comandante* believe you're my woman, maybe you can stay with me."

"I'm scared, Clay." Aissa took a deep breath. "If he doesn't believe that I'm your woman and he gives me to one of his men, I swear I'll—"

Clay put his arm around Aissa and pulled her to him. "I'll make him believe it. You'll be all right."

Aissa nodded. "Okay."

"Let's go then. Careful on the ladder."

Aissa followed Clay down the ladder in the dim candlelight. She held his hand as he led her through the tunnel and back down to the next level. She tried to memorize the turns, repeating the sequence in her mind as they walked. When they neared the entrance to the mine, Clay stopped. He quickly unbuttoned his shirt. Gently, he undid Aissa's hair and ran his fingers through it, then grabbed the arm of her dress and jerked the cloth downward, tearing the shoulder seam. Then he took her hand and led her into the light.

As always, Aissa closed her eyes and turned her face away from the bright sunlight. She tried to stop, to orient herself, but Clay pulled her along behind him. The workers stared at her as they sat quietly eating their food, some shaking their heads in sympathy. She noticed that some of the guards were laughing. She lowered her eyes. Clay took her to the lean-to where greasy shelves were stacked with pots and tin plates.

"Help Vincente serve the food," he ordered and walked away.

Aissa watched him for a moment but quickly grabbed a plate and began serving up the food. She heard Clay laugh loudly and looked over to see him standing with the guards. They were staring at her and Aissa looked away, feeling sick. She knew what Clay was telling them.

After Aissa and Vincente had served all of the workers, Vincente dished out a plate for her. "Thank you," she said gratefully. "What about you?"

"I eat whenever I want. I do not have to work in that hole," he nodded toward the mine. "Eat now. You will need your strength."

Aissa didn't argue. She took her plate and sat down in the shade of one of the shacks. When she was finished, she laid her head back and closed her eyes. She didn't think she could make it. She thought being a captive in the Apache camp was hard, but it didn't compare to this. She rubbed her hands together, wincing at the stinging pain of the blisters. She felt her body begin to relax and in spite of the sounds—the laughter of the guards, the quiet murmurings of the workers, the carts going in and out of the mine shaft—she felt as if she could sleep forever.

"Get up, Aissa."

Aissa opened her eyes and stared up at Clay. His voice sounded strange. "What is it? What's wrong?"

"I had to make a bet. If I don't win it, you and I will both lose." Clay reached down and took Aissa's arm, dragging her to her feet.

She tried to pull free; this charade had gone far enough. "What are you doing, Clay?" But instead of answering, Clay lifted Aissa up and over his shoulder. She struggled against him but he held her tightly. She heard the laughter of the guards, and she wondered if she could really trust this man. If he was just keeping up an act, why was he hurting her? "Put me down," she said it so that only he could hear her. Again, he didn't answer. He kept walking toward his shack, his grip still painfully tight around her waist. His silence terrified her and she beat at his back, convinced that he hadn't meant anything that he'd said in the mine. He kicked open the slatted door, gripped her around the waist, and set her down in front of him. With his hands on her shoulders, he pushed her inside, dragging the door closed behind him. Aissa felt trapped. The shack was small, windowless, and stiflingly hot. She watched as Clay came toward her.

"Don't do this, Clay. Please." But he didn't stop. Instead, he knelt on the ground next to her and shoved her back, pinning her with his weight. "No!" Aissa screamed as loudly as she could. Not this. She could bear anything but this violation. She screamed again as she felt Clay on top of her, his hands pressing her into the hard, dirt floor. She tried to wrench free of him, to move away, but she was so tired, and he was so much stronger. She could feel his breath, hot and quick against her throat, and she felt as if he were taking the air she needed, as if he were suffocating her. Then she felt his mouth on hers, searching, forcing his tongue probing. She jerked her head to the side but he tangled his hand in her hair, holding her still. He kissed her harshly, bruising her mouth with his. Aissa tried desperately to push him off, but he held her fast, his kisses covering her throat and the tops of her breasts. Aissa thought she would die. She wanted to die. Too much had happened. And now the only man she thought she could trust was raping her. "Please, don't do this. Please," she begged, her voice ragged with pain. But even as she pleaded with Clay, she felt his hands moving over her body. She struggled, crying out as he pulled up the skirt of her dress. The sudden laughter from outside the door stunned and humiliated her. The guards were out there, listening, enjoying every moment of her ordeal.

"Come on, Aissa. I know you want it." He said it too loudly, and he spoke Spanish. Again raucous laughter erupted outside the door.

Aissa gasped as she felt Clay's hand touch her inner thigh. "Scream." Clay began to move as though he were raping her but he didn't enter her. Aissa steeled herself, but he didn't even push her legs apart. "Scream," he whispered again, pulling her hair. She screamed loudly, confused and terrified. After a moment, Clay cried out and then lay still on top of her. Outside the door, laughter rang out. Then she heard footsteps and the laughter died as the guards walked away.

"Aissa."

She heard Clay's voice, but she didn't respond. He sat up. But she lay motionless, silent. Sweat dripped down her temples and the air felt impossibly moist and heavy.

Clay touched her shoulder. "It's all right, Aissa. They're gone now."

She opened her eyes and looked at him. His shirt was torn and his hair was tangled, but his face had lost the ugly lust that had been there. He spoke her name again, reaching for something in the corner. "Here. Sit up."

Aissa struggled into a sitting position, pulling her dress down over her legs. She took the tin cup that Clay had pressed into her shaking hands and quickly drank the tepid water that was inside. She wiped the sweat from her face and took a deep breath. "What do you want with me, Clay?" Her voice was trembling.

"Calm down, Aissa."

"If you ever try that again, I'll find a way to kill you."

"I had to do it. The guards didn't believe me when we came out of the mine. Two of them were talking about taking you for themselves. There might've been some other way to stop them, but I sure as hell couldn't think of it."

"You should've told me."

"If I had told you, you wouldn't have been as convincing."

Aissa lowered her head. "I just want to go home."

He gently pushed her hair back from her face. "You can't go home yet, and while you're here, the only way I can help you is to make the guards and *Comandante* believe that you're my woman."

"You're just a prisoner. If they think I'm your woman, it's not going to stop them."

"The *Comandante* likes me. I think I can convince him to make sure the guards leave you alone."

She looked him in the eyes. "I will never let you do that to me again. I can't pretend something like that."

"You don't have a choice."

"There's always a choice." She lay back down on the cool, dirt floor, turning on her side. "I'm not sure I want to live badly enough to give up every scrap of pride I've ever had. Maybe you don't understand. Maybe no man could ever understand." She closed her eyes. It would be easy to die. It would be easy to lie here and never get up. She felt Clay's hand on her arm.

"I thought you were a fighter, Aissa."

"I'm tired of fighting. I'm beginning to believe I'll never get out of here."

Clay pulled her into a sitting position. She let him do

it, but then she moved away from him, leaning against the back wall of the shack. "Leave me alone."

"What about that Apache of yours? If he loves you as much as you say he does, he'll come after you."

"How can he find me here? It's impossible."

"An Apache can track a person anywhere he wants. He'll find you, unless I get you out first."

Aissa permitted herself to feel a glimmer of hope. "Do you think it really is possible to escape?"

"Of course it is."

"Then why haven't you done it before?"

"I got into a little trouble when I first got here and I was in shackles for awhile." Clay grinned. "After that, I played it smart. It took me a long time to earn the *Comandante's* trust and it's taken a long time to dig that tunnel out—I can't work everyday at it or they'd notice. But one way or another, I will get out."

Aissa wiped her face with the hem of her skirt. "Why are you really helping me, Clay?"

"I already told you—"

"You told me what you thought I wanted to hear. Now I want to hear the truth." Her voice sounded strong.

Clay cleared his throat. "You're a pretty woman, there's no denying that. When I first saw you in line, I thought I could finally have a woman for myself in this place to pass the time."

"That's what I thought," Aissa said quietly.

Clay held up a hand. "I'm not finished."

"I don't need to hear any more." Aissa started to stand up, but Clay pulled her back down.

"I know Ray Grimes, Aissa. I know all about you."

Aissa felt all the strength go out of her. If Clay was a friend of Grimes's, she could never trust him, and she had no chance. "You bastard," she whispered.

Clay held up his hand again. "Grimes was one of the players in the card game when I killed the soldier. He came to see me in jail before they brought me here. He didn't offer to help me then, guess he didn't need me for anything. Then he showed up here a couple of months ago and offered to pay me if I made sure you never made it out of here alive."

Aissa shook her head unable to believe that Clay had deceived her so easily.

"Grimes said if I did the job, he would come back in six months and pay me the rest of the money he owed me and help me to escape."

"That's easy money, Clay. Why don't you just get it over with now?" Aissa's voice was shrill. "And how were you planning to kill me? Push me down one of the mine shafts? Or were you just going to be patient and wait until someone did it for you?"

"I was never going to kill you, Aissa. I was just going to take his money and escape when I could. Then once I got to know you, I decided to do whatever I could to help you escape."

"You expect me to believe that?"

"I have no reason to lie to you, Aissa. I've done a lot of things, but I'm not a murderer. It wouldn't have been that hard to hide you away when Ray came and make him believe that you were dead. As soon as Ray left, I planned to take the rest of the money and buy my way out. The only change I've made in that plan is that I'm going to take you with me."

"Ray Grimes," Aissa shivered. "Even if I escape from here, I'll never be free of him."

Clay made an impatient sound. "Look, when you get out of here, go home, sell your land, and move on. Buy a ranch someplace else. He'll never look for you. He'll think you're dead."

Aissa shook her head. "I'll never sell my land. It belonged to my grandfather. Besides, that's what Ray really wants, the land. I'd rather die than give it to him."

"It's only dirt, Aissa. It's not worth dying over."

"You're wrong, Clay, it's much more than dirt. It's a part of my family. I've grown up on that land. It's a part of me. I want my children to grow up there someday." Aissa's eyes filled with tears. Would she ever have children? Would she ever see Shadow Hawk again?

"You can do whatever you want when you get out of here but just steer clear of Grimes."

Aissa shook her head. "If I do get out of here, I'll go looking for him. And this time, not even Shadow Hawk will be able to talk me out of killing him." Aissa felt stronger than she had in a long time. She was beginning to believe it. She would get out of this place, and she would somehow make sure that Ray Grimes never hurt her or her father again.

Chapter Five

Shadow Hawk had only been away from Aissa for three days and already he missed her. According to what Ben had said, there were two big silver mines: the Xavier Mine and the Crucero Mine. The Xavier Mine was closer so Ataza had decided to go there first in the hopes that the slavers had wanted to be rid of their Apache captives as soon as possible. The country around the mine was so bleak that it had taken them days to find a place where they could watch without being seen. The guards were all Mexican soldiers, armed and wary. There was one white man and a few Indians, but most of the mine workers were dull-eyed *campesinos* enslaved by their own hopelessness. They thought they had seen Apache, but just to be sure, Gitano and Shadow Hawk waited for the cover of darkness then made their way close to the laborers' enclosure. Imitating an owl's cry, they waited for a response. When none came, they knew that none of their people were there. Furious at the wasted time and worried about his people, Shadow Hawk led his uncle and cousins farther south.

The Crucero Silver Mine was set in the foothills of the Crucero Mountains. As they watched from their hiding place in the rocks above the mine, Gitano thought he spotted Singing Bird but he wasn't sure. The next day as the laborers were taken to the mine, Shadow Hawk was certain that he saw Broken Moon. Unbeaten and unbowed, her eyes were raised, scanning the rocky hillsides. The guards were not nearly so alert. Shadow Hawk cupped his hands to his mouth and made a cawing sound, the cry of a mother crow protecting her young. Broken Moon raised her right hand, palm up, for an instant, then quickly looked away. He knew she had heard his signal. When the sun set, he climbed the rocky hillside back to his camp.

"I have seen my mother and she knows we are here," Shadow Hawk told the others.

Ataza gripped Shadow Hawk's shoulder. "Did you see Singing Bird or Brave Heart?"

"No, Uncle, but they must be here. Gitano would not have mistaken anyone else for his sister."

Miho stepped forward. "We have time before the sun rises, let us ride."

Teroz shook his head. "You are not thinking clearly, Miho."

Shadow Hawk stepped between them. The enmity between his two cousins had begun in their childhood and had only grown stronger. The last thing any of them needed now was a fight between Miho and Teroz. "We will do nothing to endanger their lives, Miho."

"Shadow Hawk is right," Ataza said, the authority in his voice unmistakable.

"What is your plan, Brother?" Gitano asked, standing next to Miho.

"We have guns and we have the cover of darkness. What else do Apache need?"

"You may be ready to die, but I am not. I am going to become a father," Teroz said, his voice unable to mask his dislike for Miho. "I do not want Paloma to be left alone."

Shadow Hawk winced. Miho had once loved Paloma. Shadow Hawk could see Miho tensing himself for a fight. He spoke quickly. "We are here to help our people. You two can fight later if you must."

"I will not risk my sister's life," Miho said. "If my father advises caution, I will listen."

"Good," Ataza said. "Let us sit."

Shadow Hawk waited until everyone was seated and silent. "Aissa's father said we must look for the uniform of an officer."

"What is an 'officer'?" Ataza asked.

"A chief," Shadow Hawk said, explaining the differences in the uniforms as Ben had explained them to him.

"And how do we get this uniform?" Teroz asked.

"You have seen the soldiers ride in and out. We will have to ambush some of them."

Miho shook his head. "I do not like it. Too much can go wrong." He clenched a fist. "The Mexicans are not known for their fighting skills. We can go in there at night while there are only a few guards on watch. Before too many of the others wake, we will be gone with our people."

"Both plans have merit," Ataza said, quieting the group. "What do you think, Shadow?"

Shadow Hawk looked at Miho. "I agree with Miho. They will not be expecting us to come for our people. If we do it quickly, we can get away unnoticed."

"Yes, it is a good plan," Ataza nodded.

"I agree," Gitano added.

"And what do you think, Teroz?" Shadow Hawk asked, looking at his old enemy.

"I think we must wait. We must study these Mexicans and see what they do, especially at night. We must see where our people are kept. It will be much easier if there is a pattern to everything they do."

"You agree then?" Miho asked curtly.

"I agree only if we are patient. I will not agree to run in there and endanger the lives of our people just so you can play the hero, Miho."

"I cannot possibly be looking at Teroz," Miho spat. "In the old days, you would do anything for glory. You cared nothing for others. Am I to believe you have changed so much, Cousin?" Miho shook his head. "I do not think so."

"I do not care what you believe, Miho. But know this, I will stop you if I think your rashness is going to hurt our people."

"It is settled then," Ataza interrupted diplomatically. "I agree with Miho's plan, but I also agree with Teroz. We must wait and watch. We must pick the right time."

"We will be patient as long as we must," Shadow Hawk said. "I will take first watch." He stood up and walked to the rocks, positioning himself so that he could see without being seen. Even in the darkness he would take no chances. He wondered about his mother, brother, and Singing Bird and hoped that they were all well. He knew that Ataza feared for Singing Bird. It was true that the girl was gentle and kind, but he thought she was stronger than either her father or her brothers suspected. He heard grinding in the dirt, and he knew that Gitano had come to speak to him. He knew it was Gitano without even looking up. He could always smell his cousin. Gitano had always chewed on dried mint leaves and had never broken the habit.

"Are you well, Cousin?" Gitano asked, lying flat on his belly next to Shadow Hawk.

"I am well."

"But you worry."

"Of course I worry, Gitano. My mother, brother, and your sister are down there."

"There is something else that troubles you, Cousin."

"No, why do you needle at me so?"

"I know you, Shadow Hawk. Is it Aissa? Is there something wrong?"

Shadow Hawk turned to Gitano in the darkness. "There is no trouble between us. I plan to marry her as soon as we take our people back."

"Good. That is good."

"You don't sound convinced. I thought you liked Aissa."

"I like Aissa very much. She is a sensible woman, she

even thinks like an Apache sometimes," he said, spitting the mint leaves out of his mouth. "She is even rather pretty for a white woman."

Shadow Hawk smiled to himself in the darkness. That was quite a compliment coming from Gitano. "Yes, I could not ask for more in a woman."

"So, what is it?"

Shadow Hawk shrugged in the darkness, looking down on the amber lights in the mining camp. "It is a feeling, nothing more."

"What feeling, Cousin?" Gitano shifted his position. "By all the spirits, I can talk easier with my horse than I can with you."

Shadow Hawk smiled again. Gitano never lost his humor. "Every time I have been away from her, something has happened."

"Perhaps you should go back, Shadow. We know where our people are. We can get them out."

"No."

"Do as you wish. You will not do otherwise."

Shadow Hawk rolled over and lay on his back looking at the night sky. "What do you think of Miho and Teroz? It does not go well between them."

"You, more than anyone, know how I hate Teroz," Gitano said. "But I must admit he has been a good husband to Paloma. She is very happy."

Shadow Hawk didn't answer immediately. It was hard for him to remember his own treatment of Paloma without feeling ashamed. And he had not been the first man to wrong her. "Did Miho ever know of the child?"

"No, and it is probably well that the child died. It would have been yet another source of bitterness between Miho and Teroz. One might have wound up killing the other."

"That might yet happen, Cousin."

Gitano fell silent, and Shadow Hawk turned over and again looked at the lights below. He desperately wanted to free his family and get back to Aissa.

Broken Moon sat in the darkness, exhausted but unable to sleep. Singing Bird lay beside her. Broken Moon heard low voices coming from outside the enclosure. She shifted, trying to see without waking Singing Bird. Through the rough mesquite branches that had been bound together to form a fence, she could see the silhouettes of two of the guards. So far, none of the women had been raped. For that much, at least, Broken Moon was grateful. She had instructed Singing Bird to smear dirt on her cheeks and to keep her eyes lowered, but it would not work forever.

The guards had no women here as far as Broken Moon had been able to tell, and she was always wary of them. They lived in rough adobe shacks that stank of garbage and sweat. She watched for awhile longer until the voices faded and she relaxed, leaning back against the fence and looking up at the stars.

She thanked the Great Spirit for helping Shadow Hawk to find them and she prayed for his safety and their own. The people who had worked in the mines for a long time were as hopeless and sullen as beaten dogs, and that frightened her more than the thought of dying. Broken Moon looked down at Singing Bird and smoothed the young woman's hair back from her face. Even if they were killed escaping, at least they would die an honorable death.

Aissa lay on her side in the small shack that she now shared with Clay. She could hear his heavy breathing, and she listened as he mumbled in his sleep. She still felt uncomfortable lying next to him every night, but she had to admit to herself that she did feel safer. She had seen the way the guards had looked at her lately. If Clay hadn't done what he'd done, who knows what might have happened to her? She wondered how much longer she would have to stay here. It was hard to keep her hopes up even though she knew Clay was working on the tunnel.

She had practically given up all hope that Shadow Hawk would find her. The more she thought about it, the more she realized how impossible it would be for him to track her. There was no trail to follow, no witnesses who had seen her kidnapped. She knew her only chance for freedom rested with Clay.

She couldn't figure him out. What had made him decide to help her? He could easily have taken the money that Grimes had offered him and killed her without saying a word, but for some unknown reason he'd decided to help her instead.

Clay mumbled something again, rolled onto his side, and threw his arm across Aissa. She tried to lift it off but he stubbornly held it there. She sighed deeply. Maybe she needed to take matters into her own hands. Instead of waiting for Clay to help her, maybe she could escape on her own. She waited until Clay's breathing was steady, and she lifted his arm from her waist, moving away from him. She sat up in the darkness. She could do it. She already knew where Clay had hidden a rifle. And now that she helped serve the meals, she had access to extra food. She didn't need to rely on Clay. If she managed to escape, she could hide out in the hills for a few days until the soldiers gave up looking for her, then she would head north. It would be frightening and it would be difficult, but it would be no more frightening or difficult than it was in this place.

Shadow Hawk waited silently in the foothills above the mining camp. They had observed the camp for days and decided that they would free their people this night. They had spent hours hammering out the plan. They would wait until the moon was high and the guard in the tower had grown bored and sleepy. Then Gitano would climb the tower and kill the guard, while Miho took the horses and rode north, waiting for the others to reach him. Shadow Hawk, Ataza, and Teroz would go into the area where the prisoners were kept and get Broken Moon, Singing Bird, and Brave Heart out.

As Shadow Hawk waited, he could feel his heart beating. He had seen the way the soldiers treated the Mexicans and the Indians, and he was grateful that they would soon get their people out. He was also grateful that Aissa was far away and safe.

"It is difficult to be patient at a time like this," Gitano whispered in the darkness as he came up next to Shadow Hawk.

"I have never been patient," Shadow Hawk replied, careful to keep his voice barely above a whisper. "My father told me many times that I would never make a good warrior if I was not more patient."

"My father still tells me the same thing."

"Ataza is a wise man. We would all do well to listen more closely to him."

"Yes, you are right, Cousin, but sometimes it is too painful to listen to my father. Sometimes it is easier to make my own mistakes."

"Spoken like a true son, Gitano," Shadow Hawk replied, a smile on his face. He looked down at the mine camp. There was very little movement now. Soon everyone would be asleep except for the guard in the tower.

They waited in silence for a long while until no sounds came from the camp except an occasional rasping cough. Shadow Hawk glanced up at the sky; the moon was high, the hour was late. Soon they would go. Shadow Hawk tried to spot the others, knowing they were not far from him. He could see nothing and, even better, he could not hear them. He was glad he was with them and not their enemy.

Shadow Hawk was certain that Ataza would give the

word but he did not. They waited still longer, and Shadow Hawk knew Ataza was hoping the tower guard would doze off. Finally, Shadow Hawk heard the almost inaudible sounds of his family moving closer in the darkness. Ataza spoke in a whisper.

"It is time. You go first, Gitano. We will soon follow."

"Yes, Father," Gitano replied. One instant he was there, the next he was not.

"You go to the horses, Miho. We will meet you."

"Yes, Father."

Shadow Hawk listened for the telltale snapping of a stick or the sound of pebbles rolling beneath their feet, but there was nothing. Both Gitano and Miho went in the silence that so frightened any enemy of the Apache.

Ataza began to whisper again. "When we are inside, Shadow Hawk, you look for your brother. Teroz and I will find the women." Ataza was silent a moment and then he spoke again, his voice solemn. "Let the Great Spirit guide us."

They moved down the hill, spreading out. When Shadow Hawk was close to the perimeter of the camp, he found a hiding place and watched. He could barely make out a shadow seemingly gliding across the sand. The shadow paused near the barracks, then again, at the base of the tower. Shadow Hawk breathed a prayer for his cousin's safety.

Gitano was the natural choice to climb the tower. Even as a boy, he had made a game of leaping from boulder to boulder, climbing higher than anyone else wanted to go. Even as a man Gitano loved heights and he loved to climb. As Shadow Hawk watched, Gitano started up the tower. Moments later, he was just below the platform where the guard sat. He hesitated, then Shadow Hawk saw him pull himself up and over the railing. Shadow Hawk tensed. He had great confidence in Gitano, but it was always possible the guard would see him before Gitano was close enough to attack him with his knife. The silence continued unbroken and Shadow Hawk began to relax. A moment later, he saw Gitano again at the bottom of the tower, holding the guard's rifle high above his head.

"Let us go," Ataza said.

The four of them moved across the sand as swiftly and as quietly as Gitano had. When they reached the tower, Gitano was waiting for them.

"I will keep watch," Gitano said quietly, holding the rifle. Shadow Hawk watched for a moment as Ataza and Teroz headed toward the women's enclosure, and then he headed to the other side of the mesquite fence to the men's enclosure. He unlatched the gate and pulled it open, stepping inside. He could smell the fear; many of the men were aware of his presence but were too afraid to move. He looked around at the silhouettes of the sleeping men. The moon cast its pale light over them, but it barely illuminated their faces. It would be difficult to find Brave Heart.

Shadow Hawk slowly made his way around the enclosure, moving from man to man, trying desperately to see his brother's face. He had gotten more than halfway around the enclosure when he heard his name.

"Shadow Hawk. Here."

Shadow Hawk immediately went to his brother and squatted down in front of him, placing his hands on his shoulders. "Are you all right? Can you walk?"

"I can walk but not well. I have these chains around my ankles."

Shadow Hawk reached down and felt the thick, heavy chain. He had seen shackles before in the white man's jail. "They will make noise when you walk. I will carry you."

"Do not be foolish, Shadow. Take Singing Bird and mother and leave. Quickly. I will only slow you down."

Shadow Hawk looked down at his brother. "We must hurry, Brave Heart."

Shadow Hawk deftly picked up his brother and hefted

him over one shoulder. He would not wait for the others. He would be useless in a fight since he had to carry Brave Heart. So it made sense for him to leave now, carry Brave Heart to safety, then come back if the others needed his help.

Shadow Hawk waited until he was out of the camp before he risked running. The guards would probably never have heard his too-heavy footsteps or the muted clinking of the chain, but he would take no risk while his people were still inside the mining camp. Where he could, Shadow Hawk hurried, making his way directly to their camp. Breathing hard, he lowered Brave Heart to the ground and sat beside him. Together, they looked down the hillside.

After a moment, Shadow Hawk stood and moved to one side, trying to see if the others were coming. "I will go back down and see if they need my help," he said impatiently. But just as he spoke he heard pebbles sliding beneath moccasined feet. He stood quickly and followed the sound. Soon he could see the silhouettes of his people as they came over the rise. He walked to his mother, embracing her.

"It is good to see you, Mother," he said, his voice filled with emotion.

"It is good to see you also, my son."

Shadow Hawk walked to Singing Bird, waiting until she hugged her brothers and husband. Gently, he pulled her to him, kissing her on the cheek. "It is very good to see you, little Cousin."

"Thank you, Shadow. I knew you would come. I knew it. Broken Moon and I never gave up hope."

"We do not have time for this," Ataza said. "We must get to the horses. It will not be long until they discover the guard."

They fell into a silent ground-covering run. Teroz led the way, setting his pace so that Shadow Hawk, who was carrying Brave Heart, and the women could keep up.

Shadow Hawk ran just behind his mother, watching her carefully in case she stumbled. Broken Moon and Singing Bird ran light-footed and sure, and Shadow Hawk was proud of them. Freedom had given their spirits strength and they used it now to guide them. With every step away from the mine, Shadow Hawk felt his own spirits strengthen, and by the time they reached the horses he felt as though he could run until sunrise without tiring.

Now that they were a safe distance from the mine and the sound would not betray them, Shadow Hawk broke the shackles from Brave Heart's ankles. Brave Heart sat, feet as wide apart as the chain would allow, while Shadow Hawk and Teroz took turns pounding the heavy metal with rocks until it broke. Once they were mounted, Teroz set a killing pace, knowing that the horses were rested and surefooted.

Dawn found them in the foothills. As the sun rose, Teroz reined in his horse. As he had all night, Shadow Hawk watched his mother. She pulled her horse back to a canter, then slowed it to a walk. All the horses were heaving and flecked with sweat. Broken Moon still sat her horse proudly, but Shadow Hawk could see the exhaustion in the rigid set of her shoulders. Teroz led them uphill and Shadow Hawk knew what he was looking for. What they needed was a safe place to rest.

Shadow Hawk glanced back out over the desert. Ataza, riding behind him, caught his eye.

"Do not worry, Nephew. They will not follow us. They cannot know how many of us there are. They are afraid of the Apache."

Shadow Hawk nodded but still he scanned the desert below them. There was no flash of sunlight off metal, there was no dust from horses' hooves.

Before the sun had risen more than a hand's breadth above the horizon, Teroz had found what he was looking for. Leading the horses across an expanse of broken rock, they descended into a steep-sided valley. At the bottom they watered the horses. Brave Heart sat with his back against a rock, Singing Bird beside him. Broken Moon waded into the water to wash, holding up her tattered skirt in one hand. Miho and Ataza drank then went to the horses and pulled them back from the stream. Teroz untied a bundle of food and handed it to the others.

"I will go back up and watch," Shadow Hawk said as he walked away.

"I will go with you, Cousin," Teroz said, following Shadow Hawk up the hill.

Shadow Hawk ignored the aching in his muscles and set a fast pace. It amazed him how Teroz's presence still set him on edge, made him unwilling to show any weakness. Near the top of the ridge, Teroz caught up with him, and Shadow Hawk wondered if he felt it, too—the old rivalry between them.

The sun was well up now, and Shadow Hawk paused at the edge of the scree to look down the mountainside, then out over the desert. He squinted, trying to see anything out of the ordinary.

"Do you see anything?" Teroz asked, standing next to him.

Shadow Hawk shook his head. "I see nothing. Ataza was right. He said they would not follow us."

"They are cowards. They will kidnap innocent women and make them into slaves, but they will not fight men."

Shadow Hawk studied Teroz for a moment. He was built like most Apache—short of stature and powerful of build. But Teroz was the extreme. He was the strongest man Shadow Hawk had ever fought, and he always used his strength to his advantage. It was hard for Shadow Hawk to forget the days when he first came to the Apache camp, the days when Teroz's taunts and threats were a constant reminder that he was an outsider, a Comanche, not an Apache.

"What is it, Cousin? Why do you stare at me so?"

"Is it not strange to you, Teroz, that the two of us are

standing side-by-side on this ridge, and we are not ready to kill each other?"

Teroz considered the question for a moment and nodded his head. "It is strange, I must admit."

"Why did you come with the others, Teroz? You have never cared for my mother or brother."

"I have always respected your mother, and I never hurt your brother. And you know that Singing Bird is the only person who was ever my friend."

"Is it possible that you have changed that much, Teroz?" Shadow Hawk shook his head in wonder. "I remember the first time I saw you. You were bringing fresh meat into camp. Paloma was following you and she dropped some of the meat on the ground. You slapped her."

"Yes, and you were ready to fight me."

"She was just a girl, Teroz."

"And you were ready to defend her. I admired that."

Shadow Hawk raised an eyebrow. "What do you mean?"

"You and I never liked each other, but I always admired your honesty, Shadow Hawk, and your ability to give of yourself."

"That is hard for me to believe," Shadow Hawk replied, looking back down at the desert and shifting uncomfortably.

"It is true. That is why I was so surprised when I brought Aissa into camp and you did nothing to help her."

"What did you expect me to do?" Shadow Hawk asked angrily, his face close to Teroz's.

"I expected you to do anything to help her," Teroz said, sitting down on the rocky ridge.

"I could do nothing. I was married to Paloma," Shadow Hawk replied, sitting next to Teroz, his arms resting across his knees.

"But think of my surprise when suddenly you brought Paloma to my lodge and told me you had divorced her and you were giving her to me. And you said you wanted Aissa, but I could see by the look in your eyes that you did not want her in the way that a man loves a woman. You wanted to punish her."

"I grow weary of this talk," Shadow Hawk said shortly, starting to get up, but Teroz's large hand on his arm stopped him.

"Wait, Shadow Hawk. Please."

Shadow Hawk looked down at the hand on his arm until Teroz removed it, and then he looked up at Teroz. "You have more to say, Teroz?"

"I thought you were perfect, Shadow Hawk, and that is why I hated you so much. Everyone in the camp loved you and respected you. You could do no wrong. So when I saw you treat Aissa so badly, I realized that you were human, just like the rest of us."

Shadow Hawk's anger rose steadily but when he looked at Teroz's eyes, he could see no satisfaction there, only truth. Shadow Hawk looked back out at the desert. "I cannot deny it. I will never forgive myself for leaving Aissa alone to marry Paloma. I thought I would never leave her alone again, but now I have."

"Soon you will be home and with Aissa, Cousin. Do not worry."

"This is strange, is it not, you and I talking like this?"

"There is no longer any reason for us to hate each other. I am married to Paloma, and we are going to have a child together. You are living with Aissa in the white world. Our hatred for each other no longer serves any purpose."

"You are right," Shadow Hawk nodded, picking up a pebble from the ground and rolling it around in his hand. "My father once told me that hatred is like disease, that it eats away at a person until nothing is left."

"I think your father was a wise man, Cousin."

Shadow Hawk looked at Teroz and couldn't keep from laughing. How many times had Teroz made fun of his Comanche blood? "Even though he was a Comanche dog?" Shadow Hawk couldn't resist saying.

Teroz nodded and smiled. "I admit that sometimes I am slow to learn things. I did not hate you because you were Comanche, Shadow Hawk, I hated you because you were all that I was not. Your father could have been Apache; it would have made no difference."

"I thank you for your honesty, Teroz. In truth, my father was a good man. You would have liked him."

"Yes, I know I would have."

"So, what is this, Shadow Hawk?" Miho's voice rang from behind them. "You sit with this one and talk as if you are old friends." The contempt in Miho's voice was obvious.

Shadow Hawk didn't glance back at his cousin. He stared out in front of him. He had finally made peace with one cousin, only to cause anger in another. "Come sit with us, Miho."

"I will sit with you but not with him," Miho said coldly, standing next to Shadow Hawk.

"I will go then." Teroz started to rise, but Shadow Hawk grabbed his arm, forcing him to stay.

"No, there is no reason for you to leave, Teroz. You have done nothing wrong."

"Nothing wrong? Have you forgotten so soon, Cousin?" Miho's voice had grown loud and sharp. "What of all the times he beat Paloma? What of all the times he tried to hurt you and Brave Heart?"

"That was a long time ago, Miho. That is in the past."

"I have not forgotten the past."

"Leave it, Miho," Shadow Hawk said, his voice sharp. He knew what was going to happen if Miho didn't contain his anger.

"Why, Shadow, why are you defending him?"

"I am not defending him, Miho. I have no reason to hate Teroz now."

"But all of the things he did—"

"They are in the past, Miho!" Shadow Hawk declared angrily, standing up. "They are in the past."

Miho faced Teroz, looking down at him. "I will never forget the many times Paloma came running to me because you had mistreated her. How many times, Teroz?"

Shadow Hawk looked at Teroz, watching as his stout, muscular body tensed. But he didn't stand up. "I mistreated Paloma many times, Miho. I tried many times to hurt Gitano and Brave Heart even. I probably would have if you had not been there."

"See, did you not hear it for yourself, Shadow? He admits it."

"I heard, Miho. Now ask him about Singing Bird."

"What about Singing Bird? Did you hurt my sister as well?" Miho's rage was barely contained.

"No, Singing Bird was my only friend."

"That is not possible. My sister would not have a friend such as you."

"Do you not remember the times when you and Gitano chased Singing Bird out of the camp, Miho? The many times you left her up a tree alone crying, or down in the canyon at dusk?" Teroz's voice was controlled, betraying no sign of emotion. "I can remember finding her alone, sobbing. And each time I helped her back to camp. I could not believe that you and Gitano would treat someone as gentle as Singing Bird in such a manner."

"It was only child's play," Miho responded defensively. "We never actually hurt her."

"But she could have been hurt. She was only a child."

"Do you not see what he is doing, Shadow? He tries to compare us." Miho glared at Teroz. "What you did to Paloma and what we did to Singing Bird was different. We were her brothers. We loved her."

"As I loved Paloma," Teroz said gently. "Only I never knew how to show love."

"This bores me, Teroz. You try to build yourself up in my eyes, but it does not work. I know what you are really like. I grew up seeing the hatred in your eyes. Perhaps you can fool Shadow Hawk, but you will never fool me."

Shadow Hawk watched as Teroz stood slowly, his height barely that of Miho's, but his strength infinitely more obvious. "I am not trying to fool you, Miho. I only speak the truth."

"You do not understand what the truth is, Teroz. You never did."

"And you do?" Teroz's body tensed as he stood facing Miho.

Shadow Hawk shook his head. "We do not have time for this now. Let us go back to the others."

"No." Miho put up his hand, waving Shadow Hawk away. "I want to hear what Teroz has to say about the truth."

"I admit to everything that you have said about me, Miho. I was not a person of great courage or great heart. I was not like Shadow Hawk." He hesitated, his black eyes boring into Miho's. "Nor were you. But I have changed."

"That is not possible."

"It is possible, Miho. I have learned that a heart full of hatred is a cold thing, a lifeless thing."

"You sound like our grandmother Ocha. I did not expect this of you."

"That is my point, Miho. You no longer know me."

"Do you know what surprises me most of all, Teroz? I cannot believe that someone as gentle and as kind as Paloma would consent to marry you. Did you threaten her? Did you force her in some way?"

"That is enough, Miho," Shadow Hawk said, stepping between the two.

"Tell me, Teroz. I want to know."

Shadow Hawk looked at Teroz, amazed at his control. Shadow Hawk knew he could no longer prevent the truth from coming out. He stepped back as Teroz began to speak.

"Since we are speaking of truth, Miho, why do you not tell us why you left us so quickly to marry a girl from another band? Everyone thought that you and Paloma would one day marry. What happened?" Teroz's voice was controlled, but there was a hard edge to it.

Miho's dark eyes narrowed. "That is no concern of yours."

"But it is. It is especially a concern of Shadow Hawk's."

"Why would it be a concern of Shadow Hawk's?" Miho looked from Teroz to Shadow Hawk. "What is he talking about?"

Shadow Hawk shook his head in resignation. He would not have told Miho this, but Teroz had left him no choice. "When I came back to the camp, I was only going to visit with my family. I was planning to return to Aissa. But I could not."

"Why? Why could you not return to the white woman?"

"Because I found Paloma. She had tried to kill herself. She was bleeding badly. If I had not found her, she would be dead. If I had not married her, she would have tried again."

Miho's face was closed and his eyes were wary, disbelieving.

"Come, Miho, you freely accuse Teroz of being dishonest, but do you not truly know why Paloma would have done this to herself?" Shadow Hawk stepped forward, surprised at the anger he now felt. "Paloma was trying to kill herself because she was carrying a child, your child, and you left her alone."

Miho stared at Shadow Hawk. "I do not believe you."

"It is the truth, Miho. I would not lie to you."

Miho was silent again, his dark eyes penetrating as they looked from Teroz to Shadow Hawk. "How do I know I can believe anything you say now that you are friends with this one?"

"Do you not want to know what became of your child, Miho?" Teroz interrupted.

Miho stared at Teroz, his rage barely contained. "I had no child."

"You had a son, Miho," Teroz said evenly, his voice low.

"No—"

"You had a son. I buried him on the hill overlooking the valley." Teroz took another step closer to Miho. "Paloma almost bled to death having your child, Miho."

Miho stood without speaking, stunned. He looked up at Shadow Hawk. "Is this true? Is this true that I had a son?"

Shadow Hawk finally saw the pain in Miho's eyes, and he regretted what he had to say. "Yes, Miho, it is true."

"And Paloma?"

"She almost died. It was as Teroz said." Shadow Hawk gentled his tone. "But what he did not tell you was that he saved her life. If he had not gotten her to Ocha in time, she surely would have died." Shadow Hawk watched as Miho avoided Teroz's eyes. After a moment, Miho walked away from them, scrambling up the broken rock to stand alone, dangerously close to the edge. Miho stared off into the distance, silent and unmoving. Shadow Hawk wanted to go to him but he knew that Miho needed to be alone, to absorb what he had just heard. He knew that Miho was not a bad person. On the contrary, his cousin was one of the most courageous, honorable people he had ever met. He had probably loved Paloma in his own way. Shadow Hawk knew that he, of all people, was not one to pass judgment on Miho. He had put Aissa through enough pain himself. He looked up as Teroz walked over to him and spoke, his voice low.

"I will leave now."

Shadow Hawk nodded. He hesitated then climbed the broken rocks to stand next to Miho. Miho did not turn to look at him or speak. Shadow Hawk sat down, not knowing what to say or do. He reached down and picked up some of the pieces of loose rock. One by one he let them fall down the rocky hill, listening to the sound as they gathered momentum. Miho's shadow fell across him, and he looked up at his cousin, waiting for him to say something, but Miho only stood still, staring.

"Are you all right, Miho?" Shadow Hawk asked. "Do you want me to leave you?"

"It makes no difference," Miho shouted, his voice echoing down the hillside. He kicked at the rocks, his face suddenly almost pale. Shadow Hawk watched helplessly as Miho sent one rock, then another spinning out over the steep drop. Miho moved like a man in a dream, coming closer and closer to the very edge of the outcropping.

"Miho, get back."

Miho looked at him, his eyes glazed. "Why, Shadow? What does it matter if I fall to the bottom? I have shamed Paloma. I have shamed my family. I have shamed myself."

Shadow Hawk tensed, ready to try to restrain Miho if he had to. "We will talk about it, Miho."

"What will talk accomplish, Cousin? I will tell you, it will accomplish nothing. It will change nothing. I used Paloma in a way that someone so gentle and kind should never have been used. I left her knowing that my seed was inside her."

"It is over now, Miho. Paloma has forgiven you. She is happy now."

"Yes, she has forgiven me. She is now carrying the child of my enemy. Do you know what that feels like, Shadow?" Miho's voice rose to a fevered pitch as he stood on the edge of the outcropping.

Slowly, Shadow Hawk stood up next to Miho, his eyes never leaving Miho's face. "Yes, I know what it is like. You are not the only one to dishonor a woman, Miho."

"Do not tell me that you have done such a thing, Cousin? You, who is so pure of heart."

Shadow Hawk ignored the barb and continued. "When I married Paloma, Teroz was so angry that he kidnapped Aissa from her father and brought her to the camp."

Miho laughed but there was no humor in the sound. "You see? He has not changed. He is still the same."

"That was the beginning of his change, Miho, that is why I am telling you this. When I saw Teroz bring Aissa into camp, I wanted to kill him, but there was nothing I could do. I had made my choice. I had married Paloma. But the more I watched Aissa with Teroz, I realized that he was not treating her as a captive. He gave her the freedom to go where she chose."

"I hear hesitation in your voice, Cousin."

Shadow Hawk lowered his head, ashamed by what he was about to say but determined to say it. "I could not stay away from Aissa. I promised her that I would find a way to take her away from the camp."

Miho smiled knowingly. "She was afraid of Teroz then?"

"No, she was more afraid for me if Teroz found out that we had been together." Shadow Hawk looked at Miho. "I could think of nothing but her, Miho. She consumed my every thought. Then I saw Teroz and Aissa sitting together by the stream. They kissed." He shook his head, remembering. "I went crazy. I wanted to kill them both, but mostly I wanted to punish her. So the next morning I divorced Paloma and took her to Teroz, demanding Aissa in return. I took Aissa to my lodge and I punished her, I hurt her in a way that only a man can hurt a woman." Shadow Hawk stared off into the distance, wincing at the memory, remembering Aissa's cries as he forced himself on her. "I am not so pure of heart, Miho. I understand what you are feeling."

"But it is different with you, Cousin. You and she are now together."

Shadow Hawk looked up. Miho had moved away from the edge. "Still, Miho, what I did was wrong. She had kissed Teroz because he had just given her her freedom. Teroz was the honorable one, not I."

"I feel such shame, Shadow," Miho said, his voice barely above a whisper. "What should I do?"

Shadow Hawk shook his head. "You know what is in your heart, Miho. You did not mean to hurt Paloma. Perhaps you should go back and talk to her."

"If Teroz will permit it."

"Teroz will not stop you."

"You think highly of him now," Miho said, with no trace of rancor in his voice.

"He is a man of honor. He proved that."

Miho bent down and picked up a small rock, sailing it through the air. "It was much easier when we were boys, was it not, Cousin?"

"It was much easier, Miho," Shadow Hawk agreed, listening as the stone hit rocks below and fell away. Suddenly, he couldn't wait to get home, to get back to Aissa.

Chapter Six

Christina cleared the dishes from the table and took them to the sideboard. Ben hadn't touched his dinner again. It had been weeks since Aissa had been kidnapped, and Ben had tried everything he could to find her. He had formed several search parties, and they had ridden until exhaustion had forced them to quit. There had been no trace of Aissa anywhere. Ben had even tried to seek out different Apache bands, but they would not speak to a white man. Ben's only hope lay with Shadow Hawk, and every day that passed dimmed that hope.

Christina quickly washed and dried the dishes. She poured Ben a cup of coffee and handed him a slice of cake. "Here, Ben, I made you a chocolate cake. Your favorite."

"I'm not much in the mood," Ben said, wrapping his fingers around the coffee cup.

"I won't take no for an answer. You wouldn't touch my dinner, and I'll take it as a personal insult if you don't eat my cake." Christina pushed the plate in front of Ben.

"All right," Ben said absently, taking a bite.

"You have to admit it's good, isn't it?" Christina smiled broadly and was rewarded with a slight smile from Ben.

"Yes, Christina, it's good."

"Next time I expect you to eat your dinner, too. When Aissa comes back here and finds you all skin and bones, she'll blame me." Christina crammed a large bite of cake in her own mouth.

"She wouldn't blame you."

"Sure she would. She expects me to look after you. You're like a father to me, Ben." Christina put down her fork and covered Ben's hand with hers. "I know this is hard on you, Ben, but you must be strong. Just like you told me when I came here. I thought my heart would break for want of my ma and pa, but you and Aissa helped me to be strong. Now, that's what you have to do. Shadow Hawk will find Aissa. You'll see."

Ben nodded, finishing the cake on his plate. "You're right, that's mighty good cake."

"Told you."

"I can't help but worry about her, Christina."

"I know, Ben. But after all those stories you told me about her, she'll be fine. Aissa's real strong. She can survive anything."

"Anything but Ray Grimes."

Christina made a face. "Don't go thinkin' that way, now. You start thinking good thoughts."

Ben took Christina's hand and kissed it gently. "You are a light in the darkness, darlin'."

Christina shrugged her shoulders, feeling the color flood her cheeks. "I'm only trying to repay you and Aissa for what you both did for me, that's all." Christina stood up and cleared the dishes.

"Will you join me on the porch?" Ben asked, standing up and walking to the cupboard, where he poured himself a small glass of whiskey.

"Yes, I'll pour myself another cup of coffee and be right out." Christina watched Ben as he walked out. She smiled to herself. She couldn't believe it. It was the first sign she'd seen of his old self. She quickly poured herself another cup of coffee, spooned a generous helping of sugar into it, and followed Ben onto the porch. She sat in the chair next to him.

"You going to the dance on Saturday?" Ben asked,

holding his glass of amber-colored liquid to his mouth.

"The dance? Lord, no. 'Sides, no one has asked me yet."

"I happen to know that Joe is real interested in spending some time with you."

Christina almost spilled her coffee. "Joe?" She stared at Ben in disbelief.

"That's right. He told me just the other day how pretty he thinks you are."

Christina looked over the rim of her cup at Ben. "I think you're lying, Ben Gerard."

"Why would I lie?" Ben sipped at the whiskey.

"Cause you want me to go to that dance, that's why."

"No skin off my nose if you go or don't go. Just thought it might be nice for you to have a night out." Ben's gaze was fixed on the sunset.

Christina squirmed in her chair. "He hasn't even asked me."

"What if he does?"

"He won't," Christina said stubbornly.

"But what if he does?"

"I can't go."

"Why not?" Ben turned to face her.

"I just can't, that's all." Christina sipped at her coffee, avoiding Ben's eyes.

"What's wrong, Christina?"

Christina was quiet for a moment then she spoke. "I don't know how to dance."

Ben laughed, slapping his hand on his thigh. "Hell, most of the people there don't know how to dance. They just think they do."

"I wouldn't even know what to do, Ben."

"It's simple. Stand up."

"Here?"

"Yep." Ben got to his feet and moved to the center of the porch. "Come over here."

Reluctantly, Christina set down her coffee and went to stand in front of Ben.

He smiled at her. "Now, give me your right hand. That's good. Now put your left hand on my shoulder. Good. Now, you don't want any man to get any closer than this," Ben said, standing a good six inches away. "If they do, don't dance with them."

"That's it?" Christina asked in wonder. "That's all I need to know?"

"Not quite. We'll pretend there's some music playing. Why don't you hum one of those slow songs you're always singing?"

Christina knit her brows together but complied, humming a beautiful ballad her mother used to sing to her.

"Now, I'm going to step back and to the right, and you step forward and to your left. We go in a little box, just like that. See? You're doing it, you're dancing."

Christina grinned. "Am I really dancing, Ben?"

"You're dancing, Christina."

"I like this." She hugged Ben, holding onto him a moment, remembering the feel of her own father when he hugged her. She looked up at him, tears misting her eyes. "Thank you, Ben. You've been so good to me."

"Nonsense, I don't know what I would've done without you these last few weeks." Ben stumbled slightly. "Damned whiskey. I'm not used to drinking."

"Come on, you should be getting inside. Doctor says you should rest. All that riding didn't do you any good." Christina picked up their dishes and followed him inside the house.

Ben kissed Christina on the cheek. "I think I'll turn in now. I promise I'll eat dinner tomorrow."

Christina smiled. "Good night, Ben." She watched him as he carefully negotiated the flight of stairs. She put the bolt on the front door and turned down the lamps, slowly walking up the staircase to her room. She shut the door when she was inside and undressed. She put on her nightgown and crawled into bed, turning out the lamp.

She rubbed her eyes. She was tired, more tired than usual. She felt as if she were carrying a hundred pound weight on her shoulders. She would never admit it to Ben but she had a bad feeling about Aissa; she was beginning to wonder if she was ever coming back. Tears filled her eyes as she thought of Aissa's pretty face, sparkling blue eyes, and her ready laugh. Christina clenched her fists, trying to fight back the tears. Aissa had been like a sister to her, and now she'd been taken away. Was everyone she loved going to be taken away from her?

Christina turned her face into the pillow and for the first time in months, she cried as she hadn't cried since her parents had been murdered.

Shadow Hawk was weary. It had been a long hard journey back to his people. Miho had said almost nothing as they rode and even Gitano had been uncharacteristically quiet. The tension between Miho and Teroz had not eased. If anything, it had gotten worse, making the journey more difficult than it should've been.

But when they had reached their camp, the people had erupted into happiness and celebration at the return of the captives. For the first day, Shadow Hawk had drunk *tizwin* and talked with family and friends he had not seen for far too long. But soon he found that he couldn't celebrate with a free heart. It was hard for him to be with his family, knowing that he would soon leave them. There was no assurance that he would ever see them again. He was almost a day's ride from the Apache camp before the weight on his heart began to lighten. Soon he would see Aissa.

He took a deep breath and sat up straight. It was a clear night and the moon was waning. But he could see well enough. He knew he was close to the Gerard ranch. He could smell the tall grass that grew in the pastures, and he could smell the water in the ponds. He was almost back home, almost back to Aissa.

He had missed her so much. He ached for her. He smiled slightly. He wanted nothing more than to take Aissa outside under one of the oaks and make love to her, to feel her arms around him and her body next to his. He wanted to feel her warmth and the softness of her skin.

He could hear the nervous sound of the cows milling about in the pasture as he rode through. His stallion whinnied as they neared the pond, tossing its head up and down. Shadow Hawk let the paint drink then he slid off and washed his face and hands. On impulse, Shadow Hawk stripped and dove into the water naked. He swam the length of the pond, letting the cool water wash the dust and sweat from his body. He grinned as he waded out and pulled his clothes back on. He was turning into a white man. He had bathed on his way to see his woman.

Shadow Hawk mounted again and rode up to the corrals. He took his gear from his horse, threw it over the top rail of the fence, and slapped his stallion on the rump, sending it into the corral. Then he picked up his belongings and headed toward the house. The glowing windows reminded him of Aissa's hair.

Shadow Hawk walked up the porch steps and then stood in front of the door for a moment, trying to compose himself. As much as he wanted to make love to Aissa the moment he saw her, he would have to wait. First Ben and Christina would want to hear about how he had rescued his family. Christina would have a thousand questions. Shadow Hawk smiled as he thought of the secret glances he and Aissa would exchange. In this he was lucky. Aissa would want him as much as he wanted her. He would marry her soon and he knew how much that would mean to her. He took a deep breath and knocked on the door, respectful of Ben's custom.

"Yep, just a minute."

Shadow Hawk heard Ben's voice and the older man's heavy steps as he walked across the wooden floor. When Ben opened the door, Shadow Hawk smiled. "Hello, Gerard. I'm home."

"Shadow Hawk, you're back. Thank God."

Shadow Hawk was startled when Ben threw his arms around him and hugged him fiercely. "It is all right, Gerard," he said, feeling uncomfortable.

"I just can't believe you're finally here," Ben said, releasing him. "Come in, come in." Ben shut the door. "You hungry? Christina left a good pot of stew on the stove."

"Where is Aissa?" Shadow Hawk asked, looking around. But even as he asked the question, he knew that something was wrong. He looked at Ben's face, recognizing a bleak expression he had seen before. "Where is she, Gerard?"

"Come sit down, Shadow Hawk. Did you find your family?" Ben walked over to the leather sofa and sat down, stretching his legs out in front of him.

Shadow Hawk nodded, waiting, watching Ben's face.

"Aissa's gone," Ben said into the silence. "She's not here."

"Where is she?" Shadow Hawk stood still, unmoving.

Ben shook his head. "I'd give anything to know, but I don't. She just disappeared one day."

Shadow Hawk felt his heart constrict. "What do you mean she disappeared?"

"She was on her way home from school one day and she never made it. I saw hoofprints on the road, and I saw her footprints leading off the road into the pasture. I found her books scattered in the grass. And that's all I ever found. Whoever they were, the sonsabitches knew how to hide their trail."

Shadow Hawk dropped down onto the sofa next to Ben, his mind whirling. "When did this happen?"

Ben shook his head. "A few days after you left. I looked everywhere for her, Shadow. I organized three search parties. We rode every direction we could ride, asked people in every town near here if they'd seen her but . . ." Ben shook his head wearily. "But I didn't have any luck. No one's seen her."

Shadow Hawk leaned forward, resting his elbows on his knees, his hands covering his face. "How is this possible?"

"I think you and I both know how it's possible."

Slowly, Shadow Hawk sat up, looking at Ben. "Grimes. You think Grimes did it."

"I'm sure of it. Who else hates Aissa? She should've killed the bastard when she had the chance."

"And Christina? Is she all right?"

Ben nodded. "Christina's fine. She's taken good care of me. I forced her to go to a dance with Joe tonight. She hasn't left my side since Aissa. . . ."

Shadow Hawk stood up and paced the room. Everything in this room reminded him of Aissa. He picked up a small glass figurine of a bird and held it in his hand. Aissa had said it was not particularly valuable, but she liked it because it reminded her of an orphan sparrow she had found when she was little. He wrapped his fingers around the cold glass and walked away from the fireplace. "How can this be happening, Gerard?" he shouted, turning and throwing the figurine against the rock hearth, watching as the glass shattered and splintered into hundreds of tiny pieces.

"Sit down, Shadow." Ben's voice was soft but commanding.

Shadow Hawk nodded silently and again sat next to Ben, feeling the reassuring pressure of the older man's hand on his shoulder. "It's not right. Aissa and I were going to be married." He looked at Ben and saw the pain in the older man's face. Ben was trying to be strong, but he was just as scared as Shadow Hawk.

"She loves you, Shadow. You're her only hope."

"Hope? What hope can I be to her when I don't even know where to begin?"

"We'll talk tomorrow. You're tired. You need to rest."

"I don't need to rest, Gerard. I need to find Aissa."

"You aren't even thinking clearly, Shadow. You're so tired you don't know what you're doing. When you're rested, then you can search for Aissa. You won't do her any good this way."

Shadow Hawk nodded and stood up slowly. He faced Ben. "I am so sorry, Gerard."

"It isn't your fault, Shadow."

"Much of it is my fault, Gerard. That is the problem." Shadow Hawk walked upstairs, stopping in front of Aissa's door. He felt a great sadness. He walked into his room and closed the door. He didn't turn up the lamp. He walked to the window and stared out into the night. He wondered where Aissa was and if she was all right. Ben had been right—he should have let Aissa kill Grimes when she had the chance. He shook his head. He should have killed Grimes himself.

Beyond the tall oaks that grew in the yard, he could see the silhouettes of the distant mountains. But this time he was not thinking of his people; he was thinking of Aissa and of how much he loved her. "I will find you, Aissa," he whispered, "somehow I will find you."

Ben sat on the sofa, staring at the fire. He had never seen such a look of despair on Shadow Hawk's face. If he had ever doubted the man's love for his daughter, he didn't now. He heard the creaking of the buckboard as Joe and Christina came into the yard. He sat up straighter. No use in upsetting the girl. He listened to

Christina's girlish laughter, and he couldn't keep from smiling. Then he heard their footsteps on the porch. It was quiet for a few moments then he heard Christina say good night to Joe. She opened the door and walked inside, her cheeks flushed. She looked lovely.

Ben smiled. "Have a good time?"

Christina walked over to the fire, warming her hands in front of it. "It was wonderful. I danced and danced and danced. I even danced with some other men."

"You did? What did Joe think of that?"

Christina shrugged her shoulders. "Not much, he was too busy talking to some of the ranchers about some rustled cattle."

Ben nodded. "Sounds like Joe. Always working."

Christina loosened her shawl and sat down next to Ben. "I'm glad you talked me into going, Ben. I had a really good time. I even visited with some of the ladies. They were real nice to me."

"I'm glad." Ben patted her hand. "Shadow Hawk came back tonight."

"Shadow Hawk's back? Is he here?"

"He's upstairs."

Christina hopped to her feet. "I need to see him."

"Not now, Christina."

"But I want to talk to him."

"He's sleeping. Let him rest, Christina," Ben implored.

Christina nodded. "I'm just so anxious to see him. Is he all right?"

"He seems fine, but you know how he feels about Aissa." She stood up. "I think I'll go on up to bed now."

"Christina."

"Yes?"

"I'm glad you had fun tonight."

Christina leaned down and kissed Ben on the cheek. "Thank you, Ben. Good night."

"Good night." Ben watched Christina as she left the

room. She was a pretty thing, full of life and enthusiasm. He'd already begun to think of her as one of the family. But she wasn't Aissa. No one could ever take Aissa's place. He felt the tears form, and he quickly brushed them away. No time for crying. He had to do his best to help Shadow Hawk figure out a way to find his daughter.

Shadow Hawk couldn't sleep. He heard Christina when she came upstairs and went to bed, and later, Ben's heavier steps as he went to his room. Shadow Hawk couldn't still his thoughts. He tried to think of every place Grimes could have taken Aissa, but the list was endless. Grimes was the kind of man who would want Aissa to suffer, and there were many ways he could do that.

Shadow Hawk stood up, unable to deal with his bleak thoughts anymore. He pulled on his pants and left the room, feeling the cold, hardwood floors underneath his bare feet as he walked. The fire was a glowing bed of coals when he got downstairs, and he threw in more logs, watching as the flames flickered and danced. If he had been in the Apache camp, he would've gone walking in the mountains until dawn to clear his thoughts. Here, he was afraid that Ben or Christina would hear him leave and worry. He poured himself a whiskey and stood in front of the fireplace. Quickly, he drank it, coughing as the liquid burned his throat. He poured another, remembering how his white grandfather had used whiskey to chase sadness away and bring sleep.

He sipped from the second glass and placed it on the mantel. He looked down at the floor and realized that all of the broken glass had been picked up. Shadow Hawk shook his head. That had been a stupid thing to do. He had broken something that meant a great deal to Aissa. Ben was right. He really wasn't thinking very clearly.

"Shadow Hawk?"

Shadow Hawk heard the soft, girlish voice and turned to see Christina. She was dressed only in a thin, white nightgown. Shadows from the fire played on her nightgown and he found himself transfixed for a moment. "Hello, Christina. How are you?"

"Shadow Hawk," she breathed his name then grinned. "I'm so glad you're back." She took a few tentative steps forward and stretched her hands out toward the warmth of the fire.

Shadow Hawk stepped back to let her get closer to the fire, then realized that the firelight shone through her nightgown, silhouetting her graceful and womanly body. Then he turned away, drinking some more of the whiskey.

"Are you sure you're all right?" Christina asked him.

"I would be better if I knew where Aissa was."

"You'll find her, I know you will."

Shadow Hawk looked at Christina. Her brown hair tumbled in thick waves over her shoulders, and her green eyes reflected the fire's flames. She was becoming a beautiful woman.

"Did you find your family?" Christina turned her back to the fire, crossing her hands behind her.

"Yes. They are all well."

"I knew you'd find them. Did Ben tell you that I went to a dance tonight?"

Shadow Hawk nodded.

"It was fun. I danced for the first time in my life. I wasn't going to go, but Ben forced me. He taught me how to dance and gave me one of Aissa's dresses to wear."

Shadow Hawk nodded again, turning away from Christina. He took another drink of the whiskey, wishing she would go upstairs to bed.

"I'm sorry. I didn't mean to upset you."

"You didn't upset me."

"Yes, I did. I won't wear any of Aissa's clothes if you don't want me to."

"I don't care if you wear her clothes," Shadow Hawk said angrily, drinking the rest of the whiskey. He could feel it coursing through his veins, and he was sorry he'd drunk it. He closed his eyes.

"Are you sure you're all right?" Christina asked.

Shadow Hawk didn't move, didn't open his eyes. "I'm fine."

"I worry about you, Shadow Hawk," she said.

He could feel her body close to his, and he tensed when he felt her hand on his bare back. Her touch was amazingly soft and gentle. He moved away from her. "I think you should go back upstairs, Christina. I'll be fine."

Christina moved closer to him, and he could smell Aissa's perfume in her hair. "I missed you so much, Shadow Hawk. I worried about you. I thought you might be dead." She placed her hand on his chest.

Shadow Hawk took her hand in his. "Don't," he said gently. "I love Aissa."

"I know that, I just want to help you."

"You can't help me, Christina. Not this way."

"Why not?"

Shadow Hawk closed his eyes for a moment. He could imagine her firm body pressed against his, and it awakened a need in him that had gone unfulfilled for a long time. He opened his eyes and looked at her. "Go back upstairs, Christina."

"No," she whispered, putting her arms around his waist and standing on her toes so that her mouth was close to his. "I just want you to hold me."

Shadow Hawk felt her lips brush his. He wanted to pull away, knew that he should, but he didn't. He put his arms around her and pulled her even closer, covering her mouth with his, feeling the sweet softness of her lips. But as he felt her body against his, he knew it wasn't Christina that he wanted. He wanted Aissa, and it was wrong to use Christina in this way. Gently, he took her hands and stepped back. "Go upstairs, Christina. Now," he said firmly.

"Why is it wrong for me to want you?"

Shadow Hawk looked at her, pressing his fingers into the soft skin of her shoulders. "I want you, too, Christina, but for all the wrong reasons."

"I don't understand."

He pushed her hair back over her shoulders. "You're a pretty young woman. A man would be crazy not to want you. But I love Aissa. It would dishonor both of you if we made love."

Christina shook her head. "I never meant. . ." Tears ran down her cheeks.

Shadow Hawk reached out and gently wiped the tears from Christina's face. "I know that. In many ways you're still a child, Christina."

Christina lowered her head. "I'm not as much of a child as you think I am. I'm a grown woman."

Shadow Hawk started to stroke her hair, then let his hand fall. "It's late, why don't you go back upstairs?" Shadow Hawk turned away from her and looked into the fire. A moment later he heard her soft footsteps as she left the room. Shadow Hawk smiled, nodding his head. The man Christina chose to love would be very lucky.

Shadow Hawk waited until he heard Christina's door close, then went silently to his own room. His restlessness was gone, leaving only determination. He would find Aissa.

Clay held the lantern as he walked in the tunnel. He looked behind him, making sure no one had followed him. The guards had not noticed him going in. As he walked through the workers, he saw several of them glance at him, then avert their eyes. He had been in the mine so often lately, that some of them had to have figured out what he was doing. Clay walked faster, wishing he could take them all with him. Maybe some of them would find the tunnel after he and Aissa were gone and manage to get away. As he passed one of the workers, the man bent double, coughing the dry, wracking cough that so many of them had. Aissa's cough had cleared up. He was glad he had managed to keep her out of this dust.

He climbed the first ladder, then waited, listening again to make sure he hadn't been followed. He walked quickly down the passage and climbed the second ladder. He had been digging more and more often on the tunnel and he was close. Or at least he thought he was. By his reckoning, he only had ten or fifteen feet more to dig. He removed the plank and went into his tunnel. It had gotten narrower and narrower as he had piled the dirt from his digging along the sides. He carried as much of the dirt out of the mine as he could. But since he'd been trying to work faster, he had resorted to simply spreading it out.

He dug until his arms began to ache and he stopped, tilting his head backward and moving it around. He hated it here in this cramped little place, but he knew it was the only way out. He closed his eyes for a minute and thought of Aissa then he picked up the spade and began to dig, trying to push thoughts of the beautiful, blond-haired woman from his mind. But the harder he worked, the more he thought of her.

He put down the spade, gathering the loose dirt in a pile and pushing it to the side. He thought of the night before, when he'd turned over and accidentally thrown his arm across Aissa's breasts. He hadn't meant to touch her but the feel of her had excited him. He had wanted to take her right then, but he couldn't do it. She was scared and she still didn't completely trust him. But it would be different when he got her out of here and took her to his ranch. It would be real different.

He picked up the spade again and poked it at the top of the hole, his mind reeling with thoughts of Aissa and escape. He wasn't paying attention when the dirt fell on him and seemed to keep coming. He quickly moved away and brushed the dirt from his face. Then he looked up. There was a small blue patch . . . he could see the sky. He had finally broken through.

Carefully, he stuck the spade up to the top of the hole and created a bigger circle, lowering his head as the dirt showered down on him. He looked up again, grinning at the circle of blue above him. He couldn't wait to tell Aissa. Using the spade like a pike, he climbed toward the light. Managing to get high enough to see, he almost shouted. He had come out even better than he had imagined. He was well down the slope. There was no way anyone from the mine would see them escaping.

He slid back down into the tunnel. Before he replaced the false bracing, he dug up his cache of money, sticking the roll of bills into his pocket. If he and Aissa were seen entering the mine later that night, the money would probably be enough to convince one of the guards to let them go.

They would escape tonight. He almost ran down the tunnel, imagining Aissa's face when he told her that the wait was over. There would be no moon tonight. They would wait until the guards and the workers were asleep. It wouldn't be that hard to get from the shack to the mine entrance. After that, they would only have to be careful not to let the lantern light show. Clay was weighing the advantages of stealing a burro against the dangers, when the ground beneath his feet began to rumble. Immediately, he began to run.

When he came to the first ladder, he crouched and jumped, barely able to hold onto the lantern as he stumbled back into a run. The second ladder was longer, and he climbed down it frantically, hoping that the few seconds he had lost by not jumping would not mean the difference between life and death. He broke the lantern glass as he stepped off the last rung. He threw the lantern down and ran toward the murky glow at the end of that tunnel.

The ground shook a second time, and he pounded around the corner and back into the main tunnel. The air was thick with dust, and it was almost impossible to see. He could hear women shrieking and men shouting as he stumbled forward. Clay screamed at the workers to calm down and stop clawing at each other. The urgency in his voice carried enough authority to break the hysteria. Once they stopped shoving each other, the workers were able to pour out the entrance. Clay pushed those ahead of him, and he pulled a woman who had fallen back onto her feet so that she wouldn't be trampled. The human tide carried Clay out of the mine entrance just as an eerie groan in the earth rose to a deafening roar. When he turned to look, the mine entrance had collapsed and dirt and rock spewed out in all directions. The workers lay on the ground gasping for air, some crying for those that were left inside the tunnel. The guards were yelling at each other, but no one seemed to know what to do.

Clay made his way back to the entrance of the mine, elbowing his way through the guards who stood gawking. Quickly, he began clearing debris with his bare hands. There were still people trapped inside. "Help me!" he yelled to tbe people around him. Someone handed him a spade and he dug furiously. One by one, the workers who were able to bent their backs to the task, organizing a line of people who passed rocks from hand to hand and dumped them thirty or forty feet back from the entrance. The work seemed to go unbearably slowly, but before long Clay and the workers had reopened the entrance. Dust poured like smoke out of the tunnel. Clay could see three people lying on the ground. He crawled in and dragged one of them into the yard, while the workers got the others.

"It is no use, *gringo,*" one of the soldiers behind him said. "If there is anyone in there, they will be dead already."

Clay shook his head. "There are different tunnels. There could he people trapped in some of them with no way out. We have to dig our way to them."

"Listen, *gringo—*"

"No, you listen," Clay said angrily, holding the shovel up to the man's throat. "Either you and your men help, or I'll take your goddamned head off right now."

"All right, all right."

Clay started digging as the guard shouted out orders. He tried to imagine what it would be like to be trapped inside the tunnel.

"Señor."

Clay stopped, looking up when he heard Vincente's voice. "What is it?"

Vincente hesitated, his eyes avoiding Clay's. "The woman, she is inside."

"What?" Clay felt a surge of almost uncontrollable panic seize him. He dropped the shovel, grabbing Vincente by the shirt. "What do you mean she's inside? She was supposed to be helping you cook."

"She was worried about one of the women who is with child. The woman didn't come out for lunch so the *gringa* took her some water and extra food. I could not stop her, *señor.*"

Clay nodded numbly, turning back to look at the collapsed mine entrance. "Do you know which tunnel the pregnant woman was working in, Vincente?"

"I do not know, *señor.* I am very sorry."

Clay picked up the shovel and went back to digging alongside the grim-faced workers. Without anyone to give them orders, they worked like demons. When people tired, they passed their shovels to others who relieved them for a time, until they grew tired and passed the shovels back. Twice Clay had to give up his shovel and step back, fighting for air. Both times he began digging again as soon as he could breathe without coughing.

"Look," one of the women shouted. "The tunnel is clear." She started to run inside.

"Wait," Clay said, grabbing her arm. "It's too dangerous."

"But how will we get the people out?" one of the men asked, his voice frantic with worry. "My brother is in there."

"Only a few of us can go," Clay said, trying to keep his voice calm. "Those of us who do go in must go very slowly. Any loud noise or quick movement and the tunnel could cave in again."

"I will go with you, *gringo*," one of the men offered.

"And I," said another.

Clay nodded as man after man offered to go inside the mine with him. He stared at the soldiers who stood silent and dumbfounded, not offering to do anything. He looked directly at the one he had threatened earlier. "Get us some lanterns and rope." The man hesitated and Clay took a step toward him. One of the workers came to stand beside Clay, his spade raised to shoulder level. A moment later, there were twenty men standing with their spades held like weapons.

The guard nodded. "*Sí, señor.* Lanterns and rope."

Clay turned back to the men who had volunteered to go with him. "I'll tie a rope around my waist. Amado, you do the same. Ricardo, you too. Someone can hold onto the ends from out here." Clay pitched his voice so that the rest of the volunteers could hear him. "If something happens, the rest of you can follow the rope and dig your way in to us." The soldiers appeared with the rope and lanterns. Clay quickly tied a rope around his waist, picked up a lantern and spade, and moved toward the entrance to the mine. He turned to the others one more time. "Remember, we must move very slowly. If you have to talk, whisper."

Clay led the way into the dark tunnel, bending over as he carefully wound his way through the main artery, stepping over fallen rock and timbers. He felt the others close behind him and when the tunnel forked, he stopped. "I will go straight," he whispered. "Amado, go to the left, Ricardo go to the right. *Vaya con Dios.*"

Clay continued to move slowly forward, holding the lantern out in front of him. He continued to advance until he saw the pile of dirt and rocks that blocked the tunnel. He set the lantern down and began digging, carefully moving pieces of rock and trying to move the partially broken timber. He worked until he had made a hole large enough for him to crawl through. He picked up the lantern and crawled forward carefully, holding it in front of him. As he emerged from the hole, he saw a hellish scene. There were people lying on the ground, some of them twisted into impossible positions. One man had died standing up. His body remained upright, propped up by fallen rock. He stared unblinking, his skin ghostly white. Clay could hear women crying the groans of the injured.

"Señor!" one of the women cried out, reaching forward.

"Easy," Clay said reassuringly. "Real easy. I want all of you who can walk to come out of there real slow. If you move too quickly or make too much noise you might cause another cave-in. Understand?" Silently they nodded their heads. "When you get out here, just grab the rope that's around my waist and that'll lead you to the outside." One by one, Clay helped the men and women through the hole. The last one to get up was the woman who was pregnant. She was sobbing and holding her stomach. Clay reached in and took hold of her hands, gently guiding her through.

"Thank you, *señor,*" she said gratefully.

"Where is the white woman? Is she with you?"

"She is back there. She was hit on the head and fell down. I tried to help her, but I could not, *señor.*"

"It's all right." He put the rope in her hand. "Hold onto this and it will lead you out."

"You will look for the *gringa?*"

"Yes, I'll look for her. Go now." Clay helped her climb through the narrow opening he had dug. Once she had started her way out, he climbed back through, hanging the lantern on a piece of broken timber. He didn't have to walk far. Aissa was only about thirty feet from the hole. Her face and hair were so coated with rock dust that he almost walked past her, assuming she was one of the workers who had been killed. He bent down, trying to rouse her. She didn't move, but her skin was warm. He knew she was alive.

Clay picked her up and began walking slowly. There was a distant rumble in the earth and Clay froze, sweat beading his forehead. The rumbling faded, then stopped. One of the upper levels had probably collapsed. Clay carried Aissa back to the pile of rubble that blocked the tunnel. He laid her down gently and put his hands underneath her shoulders. Crawling backward, he pulled her with him until they reached the other side. Barely able to see from the dust that was swirling around in the tunnel, Clay picked Aissa up and staggered toward the mine entrance, following the rope. He wasn't able to stand up straight and his arms shook from holding Aissa, but still he quickened his step, wanting desperately to get out of the tunnel before there was another cave-in.

When Clay stepped into the blinding sunlight, someone took Aissa from his arms and laid her on the ground, well away from the entrance. Clay drank some water from a tin cup and then knelt next to Aissa, touching the cup to her lips. She still didn't move. Blood covered her forehead.

"Here, *señor.*"

Clay looked up. It was the pregnant woman. She handed him a wet piece of cloth. "Thanks." He gently wiped Aissa's forehead, cleaning the blood away from a large gash.

Slowly, the woman knelt down next to Clay, her hands in a protective gesture over her round belly. "She was in there because of me. She brought me food and water. It was not the first time she was kind to one of us." The woman reached out and stroked Aissa's hair. "One of the big timbers fell. It knocked her backwards. Will she be all right?"

Clay wanted to reassure the woman, "I hope so. God, I hope so."

The woman began to cry.

Clay reached out and touched her arm. "It's all right. You're safe now."

"We will never be safe here, *señor,* not as long as we have to go back in there."

Clay nodded silently, lifting Aissa into his arms. He carried her down the hill and across the camp to his shack. Gently, he laid her down. "I'll get you some help or die trying, Aissa," he promised her. Then he spun and went back outside. He headed toward the *Comandante*'s office, determined to talk to the one man who might be able to help Aissa. He kicked the door open. The *Comandante* looked up, pen in hand.

"What is it, *gringo?* I am busy."

"You're busy?" Clay repeated, his voice hard. "Did you know there was a cave-in out there? You have people trapped in that mine, *Comandante.*"

"Yes, I have been informed." He lowered his head and began writing again.

Clay kicked the *Comandante*'s desk. "The white woman is

badly hurt, and I want a room for her, not the shack I'm living in."

"You know I cannot do that. You are a prisoner here."

"I want a room and I want a doctor brought in to look at her and anyone else who was hurt."

The *Comandante* looked up, his eyes unreadable. "And if I do not do these things, what do you propose to do, *gringo?*" The *Comandante* opened his top drawer and took out a pistol.

Clay stepped forward, staring at the older man, willing to die if he had to. He kept walking until the barrel of the pistol was almost against his chest. The *Comandante* stood up and backed away from him, glancing around to find the door. The instant the *Comandante* averted his eyes, Clay sprang forward and knocked the gun from his hand. It fell to the floor with a loud clatter and Clay scooped it up. As he straightened, Clay leveled the gun at the *Comandante*'s head, narrowing his eyes as if he meant to shoot. Clay could see the beads of sweat rolling down the man's face. He let the sweat trickle down the *Comandante's* temples as he counted slowly to ten. Then he lowered the gun. "If I wanted to kill you, I could have done it long ago. I haven't asked you for much, *Comandante.* You treat these people like animals. It's wrong and you know it."

"I did not start this. I was sent here by my superiors."

Clay shook his head. "But you could make things better for these people.

"Why should I do that?"

"Because I'll kill you if you don't."

"I don't believe you. You are a coward, *gringo,* and you know that if you shoot me, you will die for it."

Again Clay lifted the pistol, pointing it at the *Comandante*'s head. "I had no reason to kill you before now. But now things have changed. You either help her or you die."

"There are twenty guards close enough to hear the shot."

Clay smiled, squinting as though he were sizing up a target. "Do you seriously think that your men will arrest me? Think about it, *Comandante*. I have played cards with these men for two years. I have fed some of them, tended to the wounds of others. I have even loaned some of them money I think they would rather have me alive than you." Clay could see the fear in the *Comandante*'s face. He could no longer hide it. "It is not uncommon for you to grant me special favors. No one will question this." Clay waited patiently, watching as the man fought to control his fear.

"All right, I will give you my cabin."

"Your cabin?"

"Yes, these papers," the *Comandante* held them up. "I am being sent elsewhere. I leave tomorrow. There will be a new *Comandante* arriving in a few weeks. Until then, use my cabin. I will sleep in here tonight."

Clay nodded. "Thank you."

"Do not think of escaping, *gringo*. Captain Morales will be in charge. He is much tougher than I."

"I only want to help my woman," Clay said. "And the doctor, will you get one?"

The *Comandante* nodded. "I will see that one is sent here as soon as I reach Ciudad Guadalupe."

Clay stepped forward. "You are a decent man."

"I hope your woman survives." The *Comandante* looked at the pistol a moment longer then went back to his paperwork

Clay stood uncertainly. He thought of giving the pistol back, but he knew he might need it. He shoved the barrel of the pistol into his waistband. He walked back to the shack and picked up Aissa, walking to the *Comandante*'s cabin. Freeing one hand, he opened the door to the cabin and went inside. It was small but it was clean. There was a cot against one wall, a small desk and chair against another wall. A rock fireplace was built into the wall opposite the door and on the hearth there was a kettle, some pans, and a large pot.

Clay put Aissa on the cot and walked to the hearth. There was some water in the kettle and he poured it onto one of the towels that hung from the chair. He went back to Aissa and cleaned her face. The gash in her head was still oozing blood. He pressed the cloth against the wound, trying to stop the flow. He heard her moan and he touched her cheek. "Aissa." She moved her head slightly, crying out.

"It's dark," she said in a soft, puzzled voice.

Clay gently lifted her up, holding her in his arms. "Aissa, wake up. You're not in the darkness anymore. Open your eyes."

Aissa opened her eyes and looked at Clay, tears streaming down her cheeks. "I can't see you, Clay. I can't see you."

Clay looked at her sparkling blue eyes, eyes that were bluer than the sky itself, and saw that she was looking right at him but she could not see him. His body tensed and he felt a tightening in his stomach. He held his hand directly in front of Aissa's eyes. "Can you see my hand?"

Aissa's eyes did not move and slowly she shook her head. "I can't see anything, Clay. I'm blind."

Chapter Seven

Shadow Hawk stared at the man who sat across the table from him. He was about thirty years old but looked about fifty. He was fat, sweaty, and he was missing most of his bottom teeth. He dragged his dirty hand across his mouth and slammed the glass down on the table, filling it again. "So, what you wanna know, half-breed?"

Shadow Hawk concealed his disgust, refilling the man's glass. "Tell me about the slave traders." Shadow Hawk watched as the man drank yet another glass and sat back in his chair, belching loudly. Shadow Hawk poured another, hoping to get the man to talk more.

"Slave traders, can't say as I know much about 'em." The man reached for the glass, but Shadow Hawk put his hand over the man's, preventing him from lifting it.

"I've heard you know all about them, Cady." Shadow Hawk didn't release his grip, staring coldly into the man's eyes.

Slowly, Cady pulled his hand away. His eyes darted around the saloon, watching as one of the women walked by. He smiled at her with his toothless grin. When she ignored him, he looked back at Shadow Hawk. "What do you want to know?"

"Where are they?"

"Who? There are lots of them."

"Tell me about the men who kidnapped a woman from Agua Prieta." Shadow Hawk studied Cady, and he knew that the man was going to lie.

"Don't know nothing about it."

"You're lying, Cady."

Cady lowered the chair onto the floor and sat forward, his husky forearms on the table. "I don't take kindly to strangers callin' me a liar. Especially half-breeds."

"Do you know what half Indian I am, Cady?"

"No, why should I care? You're all the same, far as I'm concerned."

"I'm half Apache. Do you know about us, Cady?" Shadow Hawk watched Cady's eyes as he struggled to remain calm. "You can insult me all you want, but I am a very patient man."

"What the hell's that supposed to mean?"

Shadow Hawk shrugged his shoulders. "It means if you don't tell me what I want to know now, I'll make sure that you tell me later."

Cady held up his hands. "Hey, look, I don't want no trouble. I ain't done nothing wrong."

"Then tell me about the slave traders and there won't be any trouble." Cady reached for the glass and this time Shadow Hawk let him drink it. "Now talk, Cady."

"There's a group of five or six of them. Heard they attacked a wagon a while back. Killed the man and woman and stole their valuables."

Shadow Hawk remembered the bodies of Christina's parents but did not let the memory show on his face. "Go on."

Cady drank the shot of whiskey and refilled it again. "The same group kidnapped the white woman, I hear."

"How do you know?"

"I talked to one of them before it happened. Right here in this saloon."

"What did he say?"

"Said he had a job, an easy job this time. Said he was getting paid real good for it."

"Did he say who was paying him?"

Cady shook his head, his long greasy hair barely moving. "Nope, didn't say. Just said they were to kidnap the white woman and take her south."

"To Mexico?" Shadow Hawk forced himself to remain calm. He didn't want to betray anything to Cady. But after two weeks of searching for clues, this was the closest he'd gotten.

"Yep."

"Do you know where exactly?"

"Hell, I don't know." Cady drank another glass and lifted the now empty bottle. "Jesus, I could sure use another drink."

"I'll buy you a whole bottle if you tell me where they took the white woman."

Cady smiled slightly, revealing his few remaining decaying teeth. "A whole bottle?"

"If you give me the right information." Shadow Hawk leaned closer his eyes narrowed. "But if I find out that you lied, I'll find you, and I'll personally skin you alive, Cady. Among white men that is merely a saying. Among Apache, it is a promise."

Cady nodded slowly, setting the empty bottle down on the table. "They were taking her to a silver mine in Mexico. I can't exactly remember the name of it, but he said it's a place where they keep prisoners."

Shadow Hawk sat up. How had it been possible? He had just returned from Mexico. Had he been to the mine where Aissa was probably taken? "One more thing, tell me what the woman looked like."

"I don't know what she looked like. I didn't kidnap her."

"The man must've told you something about her. Anything."

Cady nodded. "There's one thing but if anyone ever asks me, I'll deny I ever talked to you."

"What is it?"

"He said it was the sheriff's daughter. Doesn't make

sense to me, considering the sheriff's so young. Anyway, that's what he said."

Shadow Hawk stood up, taking some coins out of his pocket and dropping them on the table. "This should pay for your bottle. And remember what I said, Cady. This better be the truth."

Shadow Hawk walked out of the saloon, ignoring the stares of the men who still were uncomfortable with seeing him around town. He mounted his paint and rode toward the Gerard ranch. It wouldn't take him long to get his gear together. He could leave in the morning, as soon as it was light. He knew Ben would want to come along but he wouldn't allow it. Ben wasn't up to the ride and Shadow Hawk knew he could move faster alone.

As he rode back to the ranch, he didn't think of Aissa or Ben or Christina. He thought of only one thing: what he would do to Ray Grimes when he found him. And this time, he wouldn't make the mistake of letting him live.

Aissa's head pounded. The pain had worn her down. She wanted to be brave but in the blackness that surrounded her she could no longer find her courage. The pinpricks of light that sometimes whirled across her vision had given her hope at first, but it had been a false hope. She wanted to cry, but she didn't. She didn't even want to be alive.

Aissa turned her head to the side, reaching up to touch the bandage that covered the gash on her head. She wasn't sure how long it had been since the accident in the mine, three or four days maybe. Long enough for her to realize that her life would never be the same. Not only was she a prisoner in this awful place, she was a prisoner confined by her own sightless eyes. Ray couldn't have thought of a better punishment for her.

She heard the voices in the yard and knew that Clay

was coming. She didn't know how he had managed to get a cabin for them but she was thankful. She had the luxury of her own cot and the peace of knowing that no one would bother her. Clay had been a good friend to her. She was afraid to think what might happen when he left. She jerked her head toward the door when she recognized Clay's footsteps. He dragged a chair across the floor and sat down.

"Hello," he said, touching her hand briefly.

"Hello." She felt calmer suddenly. She trusted Clay, and she felt safer when he was with her.

"I've brought you dinner. Vincente made it just for you. You'll hurt his feelings if you don't eat it."

She smiled slightly. "That was nice of him."

"Do you want to sit up?"

"I don't know." Aissa dreaded the throbbing pain that always came when she lifted her head. The only time she got up was when one of the women helped her wash.

"I'll prop the pillow and blankets behind you. You need to eat, Aissa."

"I'm not very hungry." She turned her face away from Clay, trying to still the tears that welled up in her eyes. But she felt his fingers on her chin.

"Please try."

Aissa couldn't resist Clay's gentle tone, and she reached out for his arm and let him help her to a sitting position. Immediately, her head began to throb harder and she pressed her fingers to her temples. "I wish it would go away."

"The doctor said it will take some time. Are you seeing any more light?"

Aissa shook her head. "No, only the same sparkles of light sometimes. That's all."

"That's a good sign, Aissa. The doctor said your sight may come back someday. But you need time to heal."

"I'll never see again, Clay. You know that." She pressed

her fingers harder, trying to make the pain go away.

Clay held a cup to her mouth. "Drink this."

"What is it?"

"Drink it. Vincente says it will help your headaches."

"Do you know what it is?"

"No, but he's part Indian and he's helped a lot of people around here. I'd drink it if I were you."

Aissa took the cup and drank the bitter-tasting liquid. She handed the cup back to Clay. "Tell him thank you."

"I'll tell him when you eat the dinner he made for you."

Touched by Clay's gentle urging, Aissa nodded. Clay placed a fork in one hand and put the plate of food in her other hand. She tentatively jabbed at the food but hit only the bare metal of the tin plate. She tried it again but couldn't manage to get any food to stay on the fork. She shook her head and pushed the plate back at Clay. "I can't."

"Yes, you can." Clay put some meat on the fork and held it to Aissa's mouth. "Open."

"No," she said, embarrassed and humiliated. "I don't need you to feed me."

"Yes, you do. Either I feed you or you'll starve to death. Now open."

Aissa opened her mouth and felt the stringy texture of the meat. She chewed slowly, enjoying its spicy flavor. When she swallowed, Clay held another bite to her mouth. This time, she didn't resist. She let Clay feed her until she was full.

Impulsively, Aissa reached out, touching Clay's bare arm. She remembered his smooth, dark skin and his long, blond hair. "Why are you doing this, Clay?"

"Doing what?"

"Why are you going to so much trouble to help me?" She felt Clay's hand on her own.

"Because I want to, it's that simple."

"But you can't stay here with me."

"Who said I was planning to stay?"

Aissa was stunned. She knew that Clay was still planning to escape, but she hadn't expected him to be so blunt about it. What would she do without him? She tried to take her hand away from his arm but he held onto it. "Please, don't."

"Listen to me, Aissa. I'm not staying here and neither are you. You're coming with me."

Aissa heard the words but they didn't bring her comfort. "No, I can't," she stammered, frightened at the thought of leaving this room which had become her sanctuary.

"You don't have a choice. If you stay here, you'll die."

"But there's nothing for me out there."

"There's plenty for you out there if you'd stop feeling sorry for yourself."

Aissa jerked her hand away. "What do you know about it?"

"I don't know, Aissa," Clay said gently. "Why don't you tell me?"

Aissa felt Clay's weight on the cot as he sat down. She didn't struggle as he pulled her into his arms. She closed her eyes and let the tears fall. "I'm so scared. I keep thinking it's only a dream and I'll wake up. But I open my eyes and I still can't see. It's as if the world as I knew it is gone. I feel completely alone."

"You're not alone, Aissa."

Aissa could hear the sincerity in Clay's voice, and she began to cry. She felt his arms around her and she held onto him, clinging to him as if he were her last hope. "I'm so scared."

"Don't be scared. I won't leave you."

"You can't take me with you, Clay. I'll only slow you down."

"Don't worry, all you have to do is stay on a horse. Can you do that?"

Aissa nodded slightly, sitting up and wiping her face. "I think so." She sat back against the pillow. "Where will we go?"

"I have a place in mind."

"Where?"

"It doesn't matter now. Our only concern is getting out of this place. And we have to do it before the new *Comandante* arrives.

"When will that be?"

"A week, two at the most."

Aissa shook her head. "No, I can't. I'm not ready."

"You don't have a choice, Aissa. Listen to me." Clay grabbed Aissa's shoulders. "What do you think the new *Comandante* is going to do with a blind woman? He can't put you to work in the mine. You can't help cook like you did before. He'll think there's only one thing you're good for . . . and you know what that is, Aissa."

Aissa turned away, resting her cheek against the rough wooden wall. She knew exactly what Clay was talking about. But still, she couldn't imagine trying to cross the desert without being able to see. What would she do if something happened to Clay? "I'm not ready to go. I can't."

Clay let go of Aissa. "All right then, stay here. I can't make you go. But don't expect any of these men to be nice to you when I'm gone. As soon as you don't have my protection, you're going to be somebody's woman, Aissa. You won't have any choice in the matter."

"Stop it!" Aissa cried out, trying to hide her face. She couldn't stop crying and her whole body began to shake. She felt Clay take her hands from her face and hold them tightly.

"Look at me," Clay said softly.

"I can't look at you, don't you understand?"

"But you know where I am. All you have to do is reach out to me, Aissa. I'm right here."

Aissa lowered her head, unable to make sense of anything. She wanted to live but she didn't want to live in complete darkness the rest of her life. And if she stayed here? Clay was right. It was just a matter of time before someone, some man, took her for his woman. She would rather be dead than have that happen.

But what if she and Clay did manage to escape, what then? Would she go with him, or would she ask him to take her back home? She knew instinctively that the world wouldn't seem so dark if she were with him, but it wouldn't be the same as before. And what about Shadow Hawk? How would he feel about her now? She knew his sense of honor. He would stay with her, but it would be out of pity. She couldn't bear that. She loved him so much, but she was thankful he couldn't see her like this. At least she knew what Clay felt for her wasn't love, and thank God, it wasn't pity either.

Tentatively, she reached out her hand and touched Clay's arm. "I've never been this scared in my life. What if I'm a burden to you, Clay? I'll just slow you down."

"You won't be a burden, Aissa. Besides, these soldiers aren't going to waste their time chasing us."

"How do you know?"

"Because we aren't that important to them. Without someone really in charge, they aren't going to take the chance of injuring men or horses just to chase after us."

"You never did tell me where we were going."

"I guess that means you're coming with me."

Aissa nodded, shoving her hair back from her face. "I have to ask you something, Clay."

"Anything."

"What if I want to go back to my father? Will you take me?"

"If that's where you want to go, I'll take you. I'm not kidnapping you, Aissa. I'm just helping you escape from this place and Ray Grimes. Hopefully, Ray will think you're dead. No one is going to want to tell the new *Comandante* that we escaped. If Ray comes nosing around asking questions, they'll just say you and I died in the cave-in."

Aissa sighed, trying to sound as confident as she could. "All right. I'll do it."

Shadow Hawk looked over at Ben, who was seated on the sofa. They'd both been quiet over dinner. This was Shadow Hawk's last night here. Shadow Hawk knew they were both thinking the same thing: Aissa had been taken to a mine but they didn't know if she was still there or if she was even alive. He pulled one of the chairs close to Ben, so he could see Ben's face.

"This is not an easy night to smile, eh, Gerard?" Shadow Hawk said.

Ben nodded, staring into the fire. "I want you to promise me something, Shadow."

"What is it, Gerard?"

Ben looked up, his eyes glassy. "As soon as you find Aissa, if you find Aissa, I want you to marry her. I want you to marry her and take her away from here. This land is going to wind up killing her."

"Gerard, listen to me," Shadow Hawk said patiently, patting Ben's arm. "It is not the land that is doing anything to Aissa, it is Ray Grimes."

"Yes, but if she lived someplace else, she'd be safer."

"There are men like Grimes everywhere, Gerard. You know that."

"I want her away from here, Shadow. Can't you just do that for me?"

"I would do anything for you, Gerard. You know that. But it's up to Aissa. I know her. She will want to come back here and be with you."

"Then I'll move. I'll sell this damned land. It's caused us nothing but trouble anyway."

"Gerard, listen to me." Shadow Hawk grasped Ben's arm. "It is up to Aissa. If she wants to leave here, I will take her. But if she wants to stay, I will stay here with her."

"And what about Grimes, Shadow? When he finds out she's still alive, he'll come after her again."

"I will deal with Grimes," Shadow Hawk said, his voice cold and hard.

Ben looked at Shadow Hawk, nodding slightly. "All right. Just find her and bring her back, Shadow. She deserves to be happy."

"She will be happy, Gerard, do not worry."

"You have everything you need? Are you sure I can't send some men with you?"

"No, I can move faster on my own."

"What about your cousins? They could help you."

Shadow Hawk shook his head. "No, I will find Aissa. And I will find Grimes. You must trust me, Gerard."

Shadow Hawk rode out of the yard before sunrise. Ben and Christina said goodbye to him and then Christina talked Ben into going back upstairs to rest for awhile. When she was sure Ben was in his room, she went to the barn, quickly saddled her horse, and led it into the yard. She left her letter to Ben on the table and grabbed her saddlebag and bundle of food from behind the sideboard. Quietly, she opened and shut the door and led her horse out of the yard, mounting him only when she was well away from the house. She kicked the horse into a canter and followed Shadow Hawk's tracks. She knew the direction he was riding so she stayed well behind him. If he discovered that she was following him, he would make her go back.

Christina took a deep breath and looked around as the early morning light cast its glow over the countryside. She reached back and rummaged through the food in her saddlebag until she found a blueberry muffin. She took a bite and savored its sweetness. She probably wouldn't be eating well for a long time so she would enjoy the food she'd brought along.

She had decided days ago that she would follow Shadow Hawk. If he found Aissa, she could be there to help; if he didn't find Aissa, she could be there to comfort him. In any case, she needed to be near him. She loved him. She would never do anything intentionally to come between him and Aissa. But if Shadow Hawk needed her, she would be there. If it weren't for him, she wouldn't be alive.

Christina spent most of the first day riding at an easy lope, becoming slightly panicked when she actually saw Shadow Hawk at one point. She pulled up instantly and waited until he was much farther ahead of her.

She looked around her as she rode, still unaccustomed to the arid countryside. She didn't like the desert. She would always be reminded that her parents had died here, far away from anything or anyone. She would never get used to the rattlesnakes, the scuttling lizards, and the coyotes who howled like demons in the night. Even the things that grew here weren't pretty: cactus, agave, yucca, tumbleweed. Everything in the desert reminded her of death.

Christina lifted her water bag and took a drink, letting her horse walk at its own pace. The sun blazed overhead, and she pulled her hat down further over her eyes. She kicked her horse into a canter, making sure that she didn't lose Shadow Hawk's tracks. She thought about Aissa. Was she alive? Was she thinking about Shadow Hawk and wondering if he was coming to get her? Christina shook her head, suddenly feeling guilty about her feelings for Shadow Hawk. But how could it be wrong to love someone?

As the sun sank in the sky, Christina began to grow nervous, and she rode with one hand on the stock of Ben's old rifle. She knew she had to spend several nights alone but now, with the sun so close to setting, it seemed foolish. She took a deep breath and braced herself.

In the distance Christina saw an outcropping of spiny red rock. She veered toward it, knowing that she could find Shadow Hawk's tracks in the morning. He wouldn't stop riding this early, she was certain, but she wanted time to set up a comfortable camp before darkness. She found a place where the jutting rock formed a three-sided shelter. She spread out her bedding and dug a small firepit. As the sky darkened, she gathered enough mesquite to build a fire. She ate a meal of cheese, bread and apples, then hunkered down between the safety of the rocks to sleep. She awoke at gray dawn, packed her horse, and started riding south again, knowing the sun would soon rise.

On the third morning Christina spotted Shadow Hawk again and reined in, watching him as he crossed the river at the bottom of the valley. After he was out of sight, Christina started down the slope. As she rode, she decided that the next day she would let him see her. Late in the day, following Shadow Hawk's tracks across rocky ground, Christina's trepidation came back. By the time she camped under the oak trees in a dry wash, she couldn't shake the feeling that she was being followed. After she ate, she sat with her back to a large oak tree, her rifle in her lap. She was in the middle of a stand of ancient oaks and the ground was covered with dry leaves. It would be impossible for someone to walk through them without her hearing them.

Christina watched the sky turn pink, then darken. The sounds of an owl announced the coming of nightfall. Christina fought to stay awake and for a long time she did. But by moonrise, her head had fallen forward and she was sound asleep. The sharp crackling of the oak leaves snapped her awake.

Her first instinct was to raise her rifle, but it was no longer across her lap. She patted the ground in a frantic search for the weapon but it wasn't there.

"Are you looking for this?"

Christina instantly recognized Shadow Hawk's voice. He stepped out from behind a tree. "How long have you been here?"

"Long enough to slit your throat without you even noticing it," Shadow Hawk replied, his voice cold.

Christina sat up straight, pressing her back against the tree. "I can explain—"

"I don't want to hear any explanations from you. Nothing you can say will make any sense." He dropped the rifle on the ground next to Christina. "When the sun comes up tomorrow, I want you to turn around and ride back home."

"I can't do that. I won't."

"This is not a game, Christina. You could get hurt out here. Why would you take such a chance?"

"I wanted to help you."

"I don't need your help."

"But Aissa might."

"I can help Aissa."

"But what if she's badly hurt? I can help take care of her."

Shadow Hawk sank into a cross-legged position, his arms resting on his knees. "Why are you really here, Christina?"

Christina couldn't see Shadow Hawk's features in the darkness, but she could imagine his blue eyes deepening in color as he asked the question. "I told you before, I want to help you. You've done so much for me."

"And I told you you don't owe me anything."

"But you saved my life."

"Anyone would have done the same thing."

"No, that's not true. Not everyone is like you, Shadow Hawk. You care about people."

"Stop it, Christina. We've had this talk before. I want you to go back home tomorrow."

"I won't go back."

"Then I'll leave you. Aissa is my main concern, not you. You'll only slow me down."

"I won't slow you down, I promise. I was able to keep up with you for three days and I wasn't even riding that hard. You didn't even know I was following you."

Shadow Hawk paused. "I knew you were behind me that first day. I heard your horse leave the yard. I thought you would turn back on your own."

Christina reached forward in the darkness and touched Shadow Hawk's leg. "I won't go back, so you might as well take me with you."

Shadow Hawk stood up. "I will not take you with me and I will not take you back. You are on your own, Christina."

Christina stood up to run after Shadow Hawk then stumbled to a stop. She couldn't even tell which way he'd gone. She was afraid that it would be different now; he wouldn't be so easy to follow. From now on he would make it more difficult for her.

She walked back to her place by the tree and sat down, grabbing her rifle and again putting it in her lap. She put her head back and closed her eyes, forcing down the fear that threatened to rise to the surface. She knew Shadow Hawk—he wouldn't leave her out here all alone, almost a hundred miles away from home. Would he?

Shadow Hawk shook his head, taking a bite of the rabbit he had just roasted. It had been five days since he had left the ranch and Christina was still following him. He had been sure that she would've turned back but her tenacity had surprised and infuriated him. He had ridden much more slowly than he had wanted to. Now he cursed himself for not taking her back the first day. He would have to keep riding slowly; he couldn't leave her and she knew it. Whether they rode together or separately, he was taking her with him. If something happened to Christina as well as Aissa, he would never forgive himself.

He was afraid of the look he saw in Christina's eyes. He wanted to make her understand that he wasn't in love with her. The only way to make her understand that was to show her how much he loved Aissa. Riding alone with Christina day after day and sleeping beside her at night was only going to make things worse—but he couldn't avoid it.

He finished his rabbit and licked his fingers, then took a drink of water. He repositioned the roasting stick that held the second rabbit. He didn't want it to burn before he got back. He stood up and mounted the paint, riding back in the direction of Christina's camp. Although she was trying to be careful, she was still easy to find. For one thing, her horse always gave her away. The nervous animal continually nickered at everything that moved. And Christina was no better than the mare. She continually hummed, which could be heard for miles around. He was surprised she hadn't run into trouble already.

When Shadow Hawk got close to Christina's camp, he guided the paint through a willow thicket, then continued along the stream bottom, letting the slender branches snap back into place. He wanted Christina to hear him—even over her humming. As he rode into Christina's camp, she stood tall, her rifle held in front of her. He spoke without dismounting. "Get your things. You're coming with me." He didn't have to say it again. Within minutes, Christina had packed her horse and mounted, following him to his camp. Shadow Hawk slid off the paint and squatted next to the fire, pulling the second rabbit off the coals. He handed the still sizzling rabbit to Christina.

"Are you sure?"

"I'm sure. Eat."

Christina didn't say another word but took the stick from Shadow Hawk, carefully taking off strips of meat and blowing on them before she put them into her mouth. Shadow Hawk handed her a water bag. She drank deeply, then ate some more. Shadow Hawk watched her. Christina was different from Aissa, there was no doubt about it. There was something untamed about her. He thought back to the night she had expressed her love for him. He would have to be careful.

"Why are you staring at me?" she asked, wiping her mouth with her hand.

"I don't understand you. You puzzle me."

"Why?" She looked at him across the fire with her large green eyes, eyes that hid nothing.

"Why would you risk your life to follow me? I do not understand that."

"Why would you risk your life to follow Aissa?"

"That is very different, Christina."

"No, it's not," Christina replied evenly, putting the stick down on a rock next to her.

"Yes, it is. I love Aissa. I would do anything for her."

Christina shrugged her shoulders. "I love you and I would do anything for you. It's the same thing."

"It is not the same thing," Shadow Hawk said patiently. "I do not love you, Christina."

"That's all right, I don't expect you to."

"Then why are you here?" He couldn't hide his exasperation.

"I told you before. I want to help you and I want to help Aissa. I owe you both."

Shadow Hawk shook his head, unable to understand Christina. "You shouldn't have come. It's too dangerous."

"Well, I won't go back." Christina stood up, taking her bedgear from her horse and laying it down on the ground near the fire. She sat down, staring at Shadow Hawk. "There's nothing you can do to make me change my mind. There's nothing you can say." She lay on her side, facing the fire.

"What do you think will happen when I find Aissa?" Shadow Hawk asked, his voice calm.

"I'll go back to the ranch with you two."

"But what if we leave? What if I decide to take Aissa away? What will you do then, Christina? You can't follow us everywhere we go." Shadow Hawk didn't want to hurt her but better to hurt her than to mislead her.

"I'm not going to worry about that now," Christina said, her voice barely audible.

Shadow Hawk stared at Christina, wondering what would become of her. She was still so young in so many ways, and she needed to be loved. But he was not the man to love her.

Clay chewed on the end of the handrolled cigarette, squinting his eyes through the smoke as he looked at his cards. He'd gotten a lousy hand: King, nine, eight, a three, and a two. He'd kept the King and discarded the rest. He hated to do it; it let everyone know just how bad his hand was. Now as he looked at his new cards, he struggled to maintain his composure. He'd gotten two Kings and two Queens, a full house. It hadn't happened to him in a long time. Maybe it was a good sign. He studied the others' faces as they looked at their cards and bet. He knew he had them. He shook his head, only slightly, so that someone might assume he was disappointed. He didn't want to be too obvious. He was known as a great bluffer. He had only meant to keep up appearances by playing tonight, but this was an opportunity he couldn't let slide by. Everything seemed to be going his way.

Three days earlier, two of the soldiers returned from visiting their families with a dozen saddle horses. He'd taken two of them the night before and led them away from the mine, leaving them tethered in a thicket of buckbrush. Then he had scattered the others. The next morning the soldiers had rounded them up, furious that two of them had managed to wander away. Clay had packed food and blankets and had his bankroll hidden in the *Comandante's* cabin. He even managed to steal some ammunition for the rifle. Now, if he could only win this cash. . . .

"Are you playing, *gringo*, or are you feeling sad?" one of the soldiers asked, laughing.

"I think the *gringo* is trying to be brave, Juan, but he is not doing a very good job of it. What do you think?" The men started to laugh loudly.

"What's the bet?" Clay asked, as if he hadn't been paying attention.

"Forty dollars. I do not think you can afford it, *gringo*."

Clay put his fingers on a stack of coins, moving them back and forth in front of him as if he didn't know what he was going to do. Finally, with a sigh, he pushed the stack forward. "I'm in."

"He's in, Juan," Enrique said. They all burst into drunken laughter.

"I'll see the forty and raise twenty more dollars," Ricardo said. He was sitting to Clay's left. Ricardo never drank as much as the others and hated to lose.

"I think you are bluffing, Ricardo," Juan said, seeing the twenty dollars. "I'm in." He turned to his left. "What about you, Luis?"

Luis shrugged his shoulders, acting as if he didn't know what he wanted to do. He lifted a bottle of tequila, poured some into a shot glass, and downed the contents. "Sixty dollars is a lot of money to lose. That is more than I make in one month."

"Either you're in or you're not," Clay said evenly, staring across the table.

"The *gringo* is right," Juan said impatiently. "You do this every time, Luis. Either play or drink. You are not good at both."

Luis took another drink and pushed his money into the middle of the table. "I'm in," he said nervously.

They went around the table until everyone had matched the bet but Clay. He glanced at the money in the center of the table. He knew he had a good hand but he also knew that Ricardo didn't usually go this high unless he was sure of himself. Clay glanced at his cards again and swallowed. He decided to take the chance.

Clay pushed the twenty dollars forward. "I see you and I call." He looked at Ricardo and watched as the man laid down his cards in a single stack. A Jack showed. Ricardo fanned the rest of the cards out: Jack, Jack, Queen, Queen. A full house, Jacks high. Clay didn't change his expression. He looked at Luis.

Luis was shaking his head, his face pale. "I told you I cannot afford to lose this kind of money," he muttered, throwing his cards face down on the table.

Ricardo smiled broadly. "What about you, Juan? Let's see your cards."

Juan turned over his cards: two pair, Aces and nines. "Not good enough to beat you, Ricardo. Too bad." He turned his cards over and shoved them forward. He turned to the man next to him. "Your turn. You can beat Ricardo, eh?"

Enrique shook his head and shrugged. "I have never beaten Ricardo," he said, a huge grin on his face. "But I still like to play the game." He pushed his cards away.

Now all eyes were on Clay.

"So, *gringo*, it is up to you," Luis said, taking another drink. "Let us see if your luck is with you tonight."

"Yes, let us see," Ricardo agreed.

Clay took the cigarette stub from his mouth and threw it on the floor. He set his cards down, face up, his hand covering them. "I have to beat a full house?" he asked, his eyes meeting Ricardo's.

"Come, *gringo*, you aren't afraid, are you?" Ricardo asked.

Clay shook his head, amused that the normally quiet Ricardo was suddenly so cocky. Clay turned over his cards, fanning them out slowly. He watched as Ricardo's eyes darkened. "Full house, Kings high. Sorry, Ricardo, you lose." Clay leaned forward and slid the pile of coins toward himself. Clay looked up at Ricardo. "You wouldn't be interested in a little side bet, would you, Ricardo?"

Ricardo glanced down at the money on the table. "What did you have in mind, *gringo*?"

"How about one card, high man wins?"

"You have all my money, *gringo*. I have nothing left to bet."

"I'm not that stupid, Ricardo. I know you have some silver." Clay hesitated a moment. "Don't look so surprised. I know you all steal it."

"And what do you have in return, *gringo?*"

"I'm not finished. I want something else, Ricardo." Clay's eyes were steady as he looked at the other man.

"You, a *gringo* prisoner, are now demanding things from me." Ricardo laughed. "What is it? I cannot wait to hear."

"I want you and the others to let my woman and me walk out of here." The silence in the room was immediate and complete. Clay knew he was taking a chance, but he was betting on the fact that these men hated their superiors and much like the prisoners, money could mean freedom for them, too.

Clay looked at the faces around the table: Luis, with

the frightened animal eyes; Ricardo, wearing his confidence like a badge; Juan, a face that was open, yet unreadable; and Enrique, his habitually jovial expression not in any way masking his shrewdness. They could have easily taken Clay and shackled him and stolen his money; they could have done it anytime over the last two years. But they hadn't. It was as if there was an unwritten code of honor between them all. Clay was counting on that honor now.

"So, what is the bet, *gringo?*" Ricardo broke the silence, pouring himself some tequila.

"Five hundred American dollars," Clay said, rolling himself another cigarette. He lit it, inhaled deeply, and looked around the table at the others. "And one hundred more for each of you who doesn't say a word."

"You have that much money?" Ricardo asked.

"You know I have more than that, Ricardo," Clay said, setting the cigarette on the edge of the table. "Think of all the money I've won from you thieves over the last two years." Clay smiled.

Ricardo seemed to consider for a moment and nodded his head. He stood up and brought a small bag out of his pocket. He dropped it on the table. "It is a bet. I do not care if you and the woman leave. In fact, it will be easier for me to win if you are gone."

Clay started to shuffle the cards, but Ricardo held up his hand.

"Let Juan shuffle."

Clay watched as Juan deftly shuffled the cards and pushed the stack toward the men. "Let him cut," Ricardo said, nodding toward Clay. His hand steady, Clay reached out and turned over the top card. Eight of spades. He kept his face carefully impassive as the men around him laughed.

"Not so good, *gringo,*" Ricardo said, shaking his head in mock sympathy. He reached out and drew the next card.

Without looking at it, he put it face down on the table. "You and your woman may not be going anywhere, *gringo,*" Ricardo said, a grin on his face.

Clay smiled ruefully. He'd never been able to quit while he was ahead. He fixed his eyes on Ricardo's hand as he slowly turned over his card. Luis doubled over in suppressed laughter and Clay had to clench his teeth to keep from whooping aloud. Ricardo had drawn the five of hearts. Clay had won.

"I cannot believe it," Ricardo said, shaking his head.

"Do not feel bad, Ricardo," Enrique said, laughing loudly. "We have always said the *gringo* is lucky."

Clay counted out some money and passed it to Ricardo. "Here's three hundred dollars."

Ricardo looked at him in astonishment. "But you won the bet, *gringo.*"

Clay reached out and touched the stripes on the arm of Ricardo's uniform. "You could've had me killed anytime during the last two years. This is my way of thanking you." He looked at the others.

"I will be sleeping when you leave," Luis said anxiously. Clay counted one hundred dollars and passed it to him.

"Me, too," Juan said, gratefully accepting the money.

"I will be with my woman," Enrique said, pulling the money toward him. "I let nothing disturb me when I am with my woman."

"When will you be leaving, *gringo?*" Ricardo asked.

Clay pocketed the remaining money and the bag of silver. "As much as I am going to miss you gentlemen, we will be leaving tonight."

Chapter Eight

Aissa looked exhausted and Clay was worried about her. The ride had been harder on her than he thought it would be. He'd considered going home before they'd escaped, but now Aissa's condition had left him no choice. As much as he dreaded seeing his father, Aissa was too weak to keep traveling. She needed to be cared for.

He looked back at Aissa, as he held onto the reins of her horse. It had been a rough journey, but she had never once complained. As soon as she had made the decision to go with him, she had allowed herself few moments of self-pity. Although he had seen her wince involuntarily many times, pressing her hands to her head, she had stoically refused to complain about her headaches. He was amazed at her strength. He was also amazed at her beauty.

Clay shook his head, angry at himself. He couldn't afford to have feelings for a woman, especially not this one. He would help her recover, he would do that much, then get her back to her father if that's what she wanted. Then it would be over. She didn't love him, and he wouldn't let himself fall in love with her.

He pulled up. "Thirsty?"

Aissa nodded and reached out. Clay handed her the bag. She drank then held it out to him. "Thank you," she said.

Clay put the bag to his mouth and drank generously,

pouring some of the water into his hand and rubbing it on the back of his neck. "Are you hungry?"

"Not really."

"You should eat something." Clay took some bread from the food Vincente had packed for them. "At least eat this. It will fill you up." He watched Aissa as she took the bread and bit into it. She had a beautiful full mouth, and he wondered what it would be like to kiss it. He turned away, staring out at the trail ahead of them.

"How much longer until we get to your ranch?" Aissa asked.

Clay looked at her and realized how tired she sounded. "We could rest here."

"Can we make it to your ranch tonight?"

"If we ride straight on, we can probably make it in a few more hours. Are you up to it?"

"Yes, I think so."

"Okay. Let's ride. I'm going to pick up the pace a little." Aissa nodded and Clay kicked his horse into a canter. He glanced back once to make sure Aissa was all right. She sat her horse well and he faced forward again.

He dreaded going back home. It had been a long time. His mother would hover over him, and his father would tell him what a failure he'd been. He smiled. He really couldn't argue with that. He had been a failure. He hadn't done much with his life up to this point except gamble, fight, and get thrown into jail. Maybe that's why Aissa had come into his life. To make him think about somebody besides himself.

As he rode, Clay thought about Rayna, his sister. She had always defended him, even when it had put her in an awkward position with their father. She was small and pretty and about the sweetest thing he'd ever known in his life. He couldn't wait to see her again. And she'd be good for Aissa.

By the time the sun was low on the horizon, Clay had

recognized familiar landmarks. He saw the first split-rail fence he'd ever built in his life. He'd been just twelve years old when he helped his father build the mile-long fence. Clay could still remember the ache in his arms and shoulders from setting the rails. At the time, Clay thought be wouldn't survive it. But as he looked at the fence now, he felt a certain kind of pride that he'd never felt then.

"Clay?" Aissa's voice came out of the twilight. "Yes."

"Is the sun down? It's getting cool."

Clay looked behind Aissa, the sky had turned orange and pink. He shook his head, feeling sad suddenly. He'd taken the sunset for granted and Aissa couldn't even see it. "Yes," he told her. "It's almost down."

Aissa nodded.

"Are you cold?" Clay pulled up suddenly, untying a rolled blanket from the back of his saddle.

"No, I'm fine."

"Just the same," Clay said, leaning over and draping the blanket over Aissa's shoulders, "you should wrap this around you. It won't be long now. We're only a few miles from the ranch."

Aissa held the edges of the blanket. "I don't want to be a problem for your family, Clay."

"You won't be a problem, Aissa," he said, reaching out and taking her hand. He held it for a moment, comforted by the fact that she didn't try to pull away.

As the sky darkened, Clay saw the lights of the ranch in the distance, and he shifted in the saddle. It would be strange seeing his family again after all this time. He knew his mother and Rayna would be kind to Aissa, but what about his father? He didn't know. All he knew for sure was he wouldn't let his father hurt or embarrass her in any way.

"We're almost home, Aissa. There are lights up ahead."

"I feel uneasy about this, Clay."

Clay pulled up, his voice low. "If it's your blindness you're worried about, don't be. I'll be your eyes, Aissa."

"But they're your family. They haven't seen you in a long time. They don't need to be fussing over me."

"They won't be fussing over you, I'll be fussing over you. I don't want to hear anymore."

Clay guided the horses up the familiar tree-lined road that led to the house. He could hear the rustling leaves of the tall aspen trees as the wind blew through them. Where the road split, Clay bore left toward the stables. The instant he dismounted in the stable yard, he was greeted by a man holding a rifle. Nothing had changed; his father was still wary of strangers.

"Who goes there?"

Again Clay smiled. "I go there, Jeb."

"Who's that?" The man stepped forward, the rifle slightly lowered.

"You'd better be careful, Jeb. Pa sees that rifle lowered, you'll lose yourself a job."

"Damnation, is that you, Clayton?" Jeb lowered the rifle to his side and walked forward.

"It's me, Jeb." Clay shook Jeb's hand. "How you been?"

"Been as well as can be expected for an old coot. What about you? Last I heard, you was in some Mexican jail."

"Not quite. Is my father here?"

Jeb shook his head, looking past Clay to Aissa. "No, he's away on business. Should be back in a week or so. Got yourself a gal?"

Clay walked back and helped Aissa down from her horse. "Aissa, this is Jeb. He practically helped raise me."

Jeb took his hat off with a flourish and shook Aissa's hand. "Very pleased to meet you, ma'am. Hope this fella's been taking good care of you."

"He's been taking very good care of me, Jeb. Thank you."

"Is there something I should know about you two, Clayton?" Jeb asked, looking from Clay to Aissa.

"No, Jeb, Aissa and I are just friends. She's going to be staying with us for awhile. She's injured her eyes and can't see. We'll all be looking out for her while she's here."

"I'm sorry to hear that, miss. Real sorry."

"It's all right, Jeb."

"Well, you must be tired. Clayton, take the young woman into the house and I'll bring in your things. Your mother and Rayna will be real happy to see you."

"Thanks, Jeb." Clay led Aissa along a stone pathway. It curved along the side of the hill then under the old oak that shaded the west side of the house. Clay stopped at the bottom of the broad, stone staircase that led up to the courtyard. "These steps are pretty steep, Aissa, and the rocks are uneven. Hold onto my arm." Clay guided Aissa up, pausing when she faltered.

"Where are we, Clay?" Aissa asked, stopping suddenly. She turned her head, as though she were straining to see.

"Sorry," Clay replied. He had to constantly remind himself that Aissa couldn't see. "It's a courtyard. There's a fountain with a stone bench built around it. A statue of an angel's in the middle of the fountain spitting out water. I always thought that was kind of strange but my mother likes it."

"It sounds lovely. What else?"

"There's a high adobe wall that surrounds the courtyard and the house. My father built it after Indians attacked and tried to burn down the house. There's broken glass set into the mortar at the top."

"Broken glass? Why?"

"He built the wall because we were having a lot of Indian trouble. The very next time they raided us they came right over the wall. They never did much really, never hurt anyone, just stole livestock mostly. But my father hated them. So he put broken glass on top the wall to keep them from coming in."

Aissa winced. Clay knew she was imagining what it would be like to climb the wall and discover the glass with her hands. He and Rayna had had the same reaction at first.

Clay led Aissa farther into the courtyard. "There's also a bench next to the wall and there are flowers everywhere. My mother loves flowers.

"Where is the house from here?"

"We're facing the house. The whole place is built around this courtyard. Most of the rooms open onto it." He squeezed her hand. "Are you ready?"

Aissa turned her incredible ice-blue eyes toward him and slowly nodded.

He led her to the heavy, carved door, put his hand up to knock, and decided against it. He opened the door, pulling Aissa inside, then closed the door silently behind them. They walked into a small entryway, turned to the right, toward an arched doorway that opened onto a large dining room. Clay stopped and touched Aissa's lips, whispering for her to be silent. His mother and Rayna were seated at the table eating dinner. They were both dressed in velvet and lace, and the table was set with fine china and silver. The scene seemed unreal after his time in the silver mine. Nothing has changed, he thought. He squeezed Aissa's hand and led her into the dining room. His mother's back was to him, but Rayna saw them instantly. She had the same sandy blond hair that Clay did, but her eyes were a light brown, almost caramel in color. Rayna's face lit up when she saw him, and she leapt to her feet, her chair crashing to the floor behind her.

"Rayna!" her mother exclaimed. "What in heaven is the matter with you?"

Rayna ignored her mother and hurried around the table to her brother, hugging him fiercely as he lifted her off her feet. "I can't believe you're here," she said, laughing.

"I'm here, Sis." Clay set Rayna down and moved slowly forward to greet his mother. It seemed she had grown thinner, more fragile in the last two years. She was still a beautiful woman, elegantly dressed, but the years with his father had taken their toll on her. Clay smiled broadly, leaning down to kiss her on the cheek. "Hello, Mother."

Dorothea Montrose looked up at her son, gently touching his face. "But I thought you were in jail. The last letter we received—"

Clay took his mother's hands in his. "I'm here now, Mother."

"Are you going to stay for awhile? You're not going to run off again, are you?" She looked past Clay to Aissa, who was standing very still, her eyes seemingly focused on Clay and his family.

"I'm going to be here for awhile." Clay stepped back and took Aissa's arm, urging her forward. "Mother, Rayna, this is Aissa. She is a very good friend of mine and she needs our help right now. She was in an accident and she lost her sight."

Rayna took Aissa's hand and spoke warmly. "Hello, Aissa, I'm Rayna. You should feel honored, or maybe cursed. You're the first woman my brother has ever brought to meet us."

Aissa smiled. "It's nice to meet you, Rayna."

Dorothea stood up, her full skirt rustling. She put her arm through Aissa's, leading her to the table. "You sit down right here, dear. I'm Clayton's mother. We'll take good care of you."

"Thank you, ma'am." Aissa felt around for the back of the chair, then slid into it and folded her hands in her lap.

Dorothea was watching her, smiling. "You just call me Dorothea."

"I hope I won't put you to any trouble, Dorothea. As soon as I'm able, I plan to go home."

Velvet rustled against lace. "You'll be no trouble at all, dear. It'll be good to have someone new to talk with." Dorothea glanced at her son. "Sit down, Clayton. You look like you haven't had a good meal in months."

"I haven't, Mother."

Dorothea rang a crystal bell and within seconds a maid appeared. "Please bring two more place settings, Elaina. Clayton is home and he has brought a friend."

A small, middle-aged woman with dark skin and a long dark braid smiled at Clay and he grinned back at her. "So, you are finally home, *Señor* Clayton. I knew you would come back eventually."

"I couldn't stand being away from your cooking, Elaina. I could smell that pork from miles away."

Elaina waved away his praise. "You have not changed at all." She bustled out, returning almost immediately with plates and silver.

Clay sat down and filled Aissa's plate with generous portions of pork, potatoes and corn. He took her fork, put some food on it, and put it in her hand. "There you go."

Aissa hesitated and shook her head. "No, you go ahead and eat first. I'll wait until you're done." Her cheeks flushed pink, and it was obvious to everyone that she was embarrassed.

"I'm not really that hungry."

"I'm done with my dinner," Rayna said, getting up and going to the other side of the table. She sat in the empty chair next to Aissa. "Do you mind if I help you, Aissa?"

"It's not necessary, really," Aissa said, nervously knotting the napkin that Clay had handed her.

"Nonsense," Rayna replied, taking the fork and putting it in Aissa's hand. Patiently, she guided Aissa's hand so that she was able to get the food on the fork. "I don't think you'll need my help for long. Looks to me like you aren't having much trouble at all." Rayna continued to help Aissa as she looked at her brother. "So, Clay, are the *federales* after you? Do we need to put more guards out at night?"

Clay laughed and leaned over, kissing his sister on the cheek. She hadn't changed one bit. "No *federales*, Sis. Just Aissa and I."

Dorothea leaned forward, scrutinizing him. "You look terrible, Clayton. Lord knows when you had your last bath."

"They weren't too keen on letting us bathe where we were, Mother."

"We?" Dorothea said, raising an eyebrow and looking at Aissa.

"Yes, Aissa was in the same place I was," Clay said nonchalantly, taking a hefty bite of pork and corn wrapped in a tortilla.

"Just where were you exactly?" Dorothea asked, dabbing at her lips with an ironed linen napkin.

"We were prisoners in a mine in Mexico. Not a real pleasant place." Clay poured himself a glass of wine and took a drink. "How's your headache?"

"It's not too bad," Aissa answered quietly. Clay could tell she was concentrating on eating her food without dropping it on the table or herself.

Again there was a rustling as Dorothea turned to face him. "Why were you a prisoner there, Clayton? You never said what happened."

Clay sighed. What point was there in lying? "I was in a card game and a man accused me of cheating. He pulled a gun on me, and I had to shoot him. Unfortunately, I killed him."

"Cards! I told you when you were just fifteen years old and your father caught you gambling with the hands that cards were going to get you in trouble."

"And you were right, Mother," Clay said playfully, winking at Rayna as he took another drink of wine.

"I don't think that's very funny, Clayton. I've been worried sick about you."

"I'm sorry, Mother," Clay said quickly. He had forgotten how easily his mother got hurt.

"Why did they send you to a mine? Why not a jail?" Rayna asked.

"It's hard labor working in a mine. I suppose they figure it's a worse punishment than sitting in a jail cell." Clay glanced over at Aissa, who was wiping her mouth with a napkin. Her eyes looked so bright, so normal, it was hard to believe she couldn't see.

His mother looked over at Aissa. "However did you wind up in a place like that, dear?"

"Mother, that's not really any of your business," Clay said as gently as he could.

"No, it's all right," Aissa said. "I don't mind." She looked in the direction of Dorothea's voice, her head held high. "I was kidnapped."

"Good heavens," Dorothea murmured. "Who would do such a thing to you?"

Aissa hesitated and Clay reached to touch her hand. "You don't have to say anything, Aissa."

She shook her head. "It's all right. The man who did it hated my family. He wanted our land, and my father wouldn't sell it to him. I guess he thought he could get it by kidnapping me."

"So he took you to Mexico? What a horrible thing." Dorothea took a sip of wine.

Clay watched his mother. She had gone pale.

"Does he know you've escaped?" Rayna asked.

"Who said we escaped?" Clay asked, looking at his sister. Her impish expression made him smile.

"I know you, Clay. So, Aissa, does this man know you've escaped?"

"I pray he doesn't find out." Aissa shook her head closing her eyes.

"That's why I want Aissa to stay with us for awhile," Clay put in. "It'll be safer for her here. She's still suffering bad headaches from the accident. She really needs time to recover, to rest."

"You can stay here as long as you like, dear."

"How did you get hurt, Aissa?" Rayna asked, her voice direct but gentle.

"I was inside the mine when there was a cave-in." She turned her head toward Clay. "Clay saved my life. He went back into the mine to get me out."

"So, you're a hero," Rayna mused. "Never would've thought it."

"Me either," Clay agreed, grinning at his sister.

"I don't understand how you two can joke about something that's so serious," Dorothea said in an agitated voice.

"You worry too much, Mother. Clay is well and with us now."

"Yes, but who knows what tomorrow will bring?"

Clay looked at Rayna and contained his smile. As much as he wanted to laugh, he couldn't. He knew the hell his father had put his mother through. He supposed she had nothing much to laugh about. "Rayna is right, Mother. I'm just fine, and I'm going to be around for awhile."

"I can't help but worry when it comes to you, Clayton. You know that."

Clay nodded, drinking the rest of his glass of wine. "So, Sis, why aren't you married? Or did you chase all of the eligible men away?"

Rayna playfully slapped Clay on the arm, "I have a few who are still interested in me, I'm just not interested in them, that's all."

"You're going to be an old maid before too long, Sis. You better hurry up."

"Look who's talking. You're three years older than me. If you don't give our mother and father a grandchild soon, they'll never forgive you."

"Would you two stop it?" Dorothea pleaded. "I'm sure Aissa would like a nice hot bath, wouldn't you, dear?"

Aissa's face lit up. "Yes, that would be wonderful. If it's not too much trouble."

"No trouble at all," Rayna said. "Clay will be glad to bring in the tub for you."

Aissa smiled. "Have you two always been so hard on each other?"

"Can't remember a time when we weren't," Rayna said, glancing at her brother. "Except when there was trouble. We always stuck together when there was trouble."

Clay reached behind Aissa and squeezed Rayna's shoulder. "My sister is tough and stubborn. That's probably why no man will marry her."

"That's enough, Clayton," Dorothea said. "Bring that tub into the kitchen so we can start filling it up for Aissa."

Clay winked at Rayna. "Yes, Mother." He stood up and left the room.

Dorothea stood also. "I'd better follow him to make sure he doesn't get sidetracked. Rayna will help you, Aissa."

"Thank you, ma'am," Aissa said softly, tilting her head to one side.

"What is it? Does your head hurt?" Rayna asked as she looked at Aissa.

"It's nothing."

"Come on, Aissa. If you're going to be staying here for awhile, you'd better be honest."

"It just seems that your mother treats Clay like a small boy."

"You're right, she does. She always has. But that's because of my father."

"Why? Clay didn't say much about your father."

Rayna nodded, tapping a spoon on the table. "Clay could never do anything right in my father's eyes. So after awhile he tried to do things deliberately to upset him."

"Why? Clay's smart. He could do anything."

"I know," Rayna said, pushing the spoon away. "It really has nothing to do with Clay. It has to do with Russell."

"Who's Russell?"

"Russell was our older brother. He was a year older than Clay, four years older than me. Russell was thirteen, Clay twelve, when the accident happened." Rayna took a deep breath and continued. "They were out hunting one day. They went up into the foothills. They were looking for a mountain lion my father had wounded. But unfortunately the lion found them first."

Aissa remained silent and Rayna nervously tapped the edge of her wine glass with her finger.

"They were riding up a trail and the lion was on some rocks above them. They never saw it. Russell was in the lead. The lion knocked him from his horse and attacked him. Clay's horse threw him and he dropped his rifle. By the time he got to it, it was too late. The lion had already killed Russell. Torn his throat open."

Aissa reached out, groping until she found Rayna's hand.

Rayna hesitated, her voice shaking and barely audible. "Clay didn't talk for months. He blamed himself for not saving Russell. But there was nothing he could do, he was only twelve years old." Rayna's voice rose sharply. "But my father blamed him and kept on blaming him. He never let him forget that Russell might be alive if it weren't for him."

"I'm so sorry, Rayna," Aissa said.

"Clay could never do anything right in my father's eyes after that. So he started getting in trouble. First it was school, then it was chasing one of the rancher's cattle into another pasture, then it was getting caught drinking in the saloon with one of the saloon girls. He didn't much care what he did as long as he embarrassed my father."

"What did your father do when he found out Clay was a prisoner?"

"He said he probably got what he deserved." Rayna reached for her glass and sipped from it.

"Your father probably won't be too happy to find me here, will he, Rayna?"

Rayna hesitated, tapping her glass again. "Probably not, Aissa, but then he's not too happy to see anyone these days."

"What about Clay? What will he do when he sees Clay?"

"I don't know," Rayna shrugged her shoulders "My father is not a pleasant person. In fact, I dread that he's coming home so soon."

Aissa thought about her own father, and she couldn't still the tears that filled her eyes. She couldn't imagine feeling about her father the way Rayna and Clay felt about theirs. Aissa felt Rayna squeeze her hand.

"Are you all right, Aissa? Did I say something to upset you?"

Aissa wiped the tears from her face. "No, I was just thinking about my father."

"Tell me about him."

"He was sheriff in our town for as long as I can remember. He's a good man. That's why he made such a good sheriff."

Rayna squeezed her hand again, encouraging her to go on.

"When my mother died, I thought he'd go crazy from grief. I thought I'd lose him, too, but it only brought us closer. He's stubborn as can be sometimes, but then so am I."

"You miss him a lot, don't you? Why didn't Clay take you back home, Aissa? It would be much better for you there."

Aissa shrugged her shoulders. "I'm not sure I could've made it that far yet. Clay thought it would be safer for me here."

"All depends on what you consider safe," Rayna said, unable to hide the sadness in her voice. "My father is not at all like yours, Aissa."

Aissa reached out until she touched Rayna's arm. "Don't worry about me, Rayna. I might look helpless, but my mind and my mouth still work just fine. I'm not afraid of your father."

"Good," Rayna said, hugging her. "I like you, Aissa. I think we're going to be good friends."

Shadow Hawk lay on the ridge overlooking the mine. He and Christina had been here for two days and he'd seen nothing. There was only one way to find out about Aissa and that was to get inside. If she had been here, someone would know what had happened to her.

He pushed himself back from the ridge and made his way to their camp. As she always did, Christina jumped up as soon as she saw him, her eyes full of concern and questions.

"Did you see anything?"

Shadow Hawk shook his head. "I'm going to have to go in and find out what I can. If I don't come back, you go home," he told her. She stared at him, and he couldn't stand the look in her eyes. It was obvious how much she cared for him.

He waited until well after dark then made his way into the mine camp. The prisoners were kept in much the same way as the other mine, but Shadow Hawk was almost certain that Aissa was not among them. If she were, he would've seen her in the lines of workers that went into the mine every morning. He had waited until only a few lights shone in the cabins that were scattered behind the barracks. He moved silently and swiftly toward one of the lighted cabins. He heard voices and looked in the solitary window. Four men were seated around a table playing cards. Two bottles were on the table. Shadow Hawk pulled away from the window and hid on the side of the cabin away from the door. They were drinking. It wouldn't be long before one of them came out. Shadow Hawk squatted in the darkness, his arms wrapped around his knees.

A half hour later, laughter came from the inside of the cabin, and he could hear a chair as it edged across the wooden floor. There were footsteps and soon he heard the front door open. A man walked over to the other side of the cabin. Shadow Hawk waited until the man was rebuttoning his trousers, then he moved silently toward him. The man was drunk, leaning against the side of the cabin. After a moment, he pushed himself upright and started for the cabin door. Shadow Hawk moved quickly, coming up behind the man. He wrapped his forearm around his throat, drew his knife, and held it next to the man's face. He dragged him to the back of the cabin.

"Tell me about the white woman." Shadow Hawk spoke in Spanish.

"What white woman?" the man asked, frightened.

Shadow Hawk pressed the point of the knife into his cheek. "I do not have much time. Tell me about the white woman with the light hair or I will slit your throat and find another who will talk."

"All right," the man said desperately, his fingers digging into Shadow Hawk's arm. "She is gone."

"Gone?"

"She was here but she is gone now."

"Make sense or I slit your throat. What happened?"

"She went away with the *gringo*. She was his woman."

Shadow Hawk tightened his grip until the man began gasping for air and clawing at his arm. Shadow Hawk loosened his hold slightly. "What *gringo?* Tell me his name."

The soldier sucked in a huge breath of air. "His name is Clayton Montrose."

"What does he look like? Quickly!" Shadow Hawk pressed the knife into the man's skin.

"He has light hair like the woman but dark skin. And he was a prisoner like her."

Shadow Hawk was surprised. He loosened his hold on the man, allowing him to breathe more easily for a moment. "Why was the *gringo* here?"

"He shot a soldier in a card game, that's all I know."

"Do you know where he came from?"

"I don't know."

"Think!" Shadow Hawk touched the blade of the knife to the man's throat.

"All right, all right. I remember he said his family had a ranch in New Mexico territory."

"Anything else?"

"No, no!"

"The woman's name, can you remember it?"

"I do not remember her last name but the first name was Aissa. That's all I know." The soldier sounded almost sober. His fear had overcome the whiskey.

"When did they leave here?"

"Almost three weeks ago."

Shadow Hawk released his hold on the man and with the butt of his knife hit him sharply on the back of the head. The soldier crumpled then dropped to the ground. Shadow Hawk quickly made his way out of the camp and back to where Christina was waiting. She wanted to ask him questions, but he refused to answer her. "Pack everything, we are leaving."

Christina's eyes flooded at his coldness, and Shadow Hawk wished that he could be kinder to her now, but he could not. All he wanted was to find Aissa and having Christina along meant that he would have to travel more slowly. As they broke camp, Christina kept glancing at him, her hurt evident on her face. Shadow Hawk knew she was upset but he had no comfort to give her. The soldier's words kept echoing in his mind. "She went away with the *gringo*. She was his woman."

A cool breeze blew against Aissa's cheeks and she leaned her head back, enjoying the feel of the air against her skin. Her hair hung loose around her shoulders and she liked the way the wind picked it up and tossed it lightly around. She heard footsteps on the stone path and nodded slightly. She was proud of herself. Just two weeks ago she would never have paid attention to the sound. She would've depended on her eyes to tell her who was coming.

"Aissa."

Aissa raised her head, smiling. She liked the sound of Clay's voice. It was calm and reassuring. "Hello."

"Are you all right?"

"Yes, I was just enjoying the peace and quiet." She felt him lift a strand of her hair from her shoulder and run his fingers through it.

"You have beautiful hair, do you know that?"

Aissa shrugged, embarrassed. "It's just hair, Clay."

"No, you're wrong."

She felt his hand on her shoulder, rubbing it gently, then moving to the curve of her neck. His fingers brushed the place under her right ear. She moved her head slightly. "Clay, what are you doing?"

"I'm just admiring your beauty. Do you mind?"

Aissa was caught off guard. She felt his roughened fingers as they traced a path from her cheek to her mouth. She closed her eyes, allowing herself to remember how she had felt when Shadow Hawk had done the same thing.

"Clay, please. . . ." But her words were smothered by his kiss. It was a gentle, but demanding, kiss. Aissa was surprised by the passion in it and she pulled away. "Please don't," she said softly.

"I'm sorry. I didn't mean to force myself on you."

Clay's voice was kind and gentle, and Aissa found herself responding to it. "You didn't force yourself on me, Clay. I'm just not ready for anything like that." Aissa turned away, wishing she could see his face. She hated the darkness at times like this. "I'm still in love with someone else," she said, her voice sounding unconvincing and weak. She felt his hand on her chin, turning her back to face him.

"I know," he said, brushing his lips against hers.

Aissa closed her eyes again, enjoying the feel of Clay's lips on hers. She liked him. He had risked his life to save hers, and she was grateful to him. But did she love him? She didn't think so, not like she loved Shadow Hawk. She could never love anyone like she loved him. She thought of the last few times Shadow Hawk had made love to her, how urgent and passionate he had been, and she felt her cheeks burn. She stood up suddenly, not wanting Clay to see her face, as if he could read her thoughts. She walked toward the sound of the fountain but caught her boot on one of the chipped stones and fell forward. She put her hands out in front of her to break her fall, but she felt Clay's strong hands catch her before she hit the hard stone.

"You have to be careful. I told you," he said, leading her back to the bench.

Aissa shook her head, feeling clumsy and stupid. "I'm sorry. I feel so helpless sometimes."

"You're not helpless, Aissa. It will get easier."

"I don't think so," she said, her voice shaking with emotion. She couldn't imagine herself going for a ride alone, or going for a walk, or baking bread, or doing anything. . . . She felt Clay's arm go around her shoulders, and she couldn't resist the strength she felt there. She rested her head on his shoulder and cried, letting him hold her as he had so many times before. He stroked her hair and kissed her cheek, telling her everything would be all right. And it suddenly occurred to her that this man was prepared to accept her the way she was. She thought of Shadow Hawk. He was too fiercely independent; he couldn't build his life around a blind woman. Tears filled her eyes again, and she wrapped her arms around Clay's neck; crying because she had lost her sight, but crying also because she knew she had lost Shadow Hawk.

Shadow Hawk sat up on the rocks and watched as Christina bathed in the stream. She was muscular and strong, and she had made sure that Shadow Hawk had seen her before she stepped into the water. She was not as long and slender as Aissa, but she was the kind of woman a man could. . . .

Shadow Hawk shook his head. It had been too long

since he'd been with Aissa. And it didn't help that he was with Christina every day. She didn't hide the fact that she cared for him. Just the night before, a pack of coyotes had come too close to camp and Christina had snuggled close, holding on to him. He had wanted to push her away but hadn't; even through the thick blankets she'd felt too good. Now he watched her as she bathed, occasionally standing up to show off her firm, young body.

Shadow Hawk lay back on the rock and emitted a deep sigh. He stared up at the white patches of clouds as they raced by. He wondered if Aissa was looking at the sky, and he wondered if she was alone. He closed his eyes and remembered every detail of Aissa's face: eyes so blue it seemed as if you could look through them, a small, delicate nose, and full lips that trembled slightly when she was upset or crying. He could imagine running his fingers over her lips and pressing his mouth to them.

He put his arm over his eyes, blocking out the sun. The soldier said Aissa had been the *gringo*'s woman. What had he meant by that? Maybe the *gringo* had taken Aissa by force, made her go with him.

"Are you resting?"

Shadow Hawk heard Christina's voice, but he didn't want to open his eyes. He was afraid she was standing in front of him without any clothes on. "Just waiting for you to finish your bath, " he said, his eyes still closed.

Christina sat down next to him. "Well, I'm finished. You can open your eyes now. I'm dressed."

Shadow Hawk waited a moment then slowly lowered his arm and sat up. Christina was next to him on the rock, dressed only in a slip. The thin white material stuck to her body and Shadow Hawk forced himself to look away from her wet breasts as they pressed against the slip. "You shouldn't run around like that, Christina.

You never know who could be around here."

"You act like you've never seen a naked woman before," Christina said, pulling on her stockings.

He looked at her. The slip slid up her thighs as she pulled on her boots. She didn't seem to be the least bit embarrassed. In fact, she seemed quite proud of her body. He'd never seen anything like it. All of the Apache women were so shy they'd never be seen without their clothes. And Aissa was still shy even though she had begun to overcome it with him. "Get dressed, Christina," Shadow Hawk said brusquely, picking up his rifle and climbing down from the rock. He went to the stream and splashed water on his face then took a long drink. He heard her come up behind him but he didn't turn. He sat back on his haunches and looked across the stream at the cottonwoods that grew along the bank.

"Why don't you like me?"

Shadow Hawk turned finally, staring up at Christina. Her hair hung in dark, wet strands down her shoulders, and the wet slip still clung tightly to her breasts, but she had slipped on her skirt. "I do like you."

"You don't act like it, " Christina said, sitting next to him. "In fact, you act like you hate me."

"How old are you?" Shadow Hawk asked suddenly.

"I'm eighteen years old. Why are you asking me that? You know how old I am."

"Have you ever had a beau, Christina?"

Christina thought about it for a moment then shook her head. "Not really. Why?" She looked at him quizzically.

"I don't think you quite understand some things," Shadow Hawk said, easing into a cross-legged position, wondering what he was going to say.

"Understand what?"

Shadow Hawk looked into her clear, green eyes. "I don't think you understand the effect you have on men,

Christina. You shouldn't let a man see you in your slip."

"Why not?"

"You know why not. There are some men in the world who would take advantage of you if they saw you like this."

"You wouldn't."

Shadow Hawk shook his head, his eyes darkening. "You're not as grown up as you pretend to be, Christina." Without another word, he pulled her close, pressing his mouth against hers. He kissed her deeply, pushing her backward roughly. For a moment she kissed him back, then, as he shifted his weight to straddle her, he felt her hesitation. Pinning her with his weight, he began to push her legs apart. She began to struggle, twisting under him, finally freeing her mouth from his. Before she could cry out, he was on his feet, looking down at her. "If I were another man, I would not have stopped. I could ride away right now and leave you carrying my child."

Shadow Hawk shook his head impatiently, walking toward their horses. He took some dried meat from the saddlebag and began chewing on it. He couldn't stand it much longer. He had to find Aissa.

Chapter Nine

Clay had found his father's will by accident. He had been looking through the old oak desk for some papers and had come across the metal box. He had opened it, realized what the document was, and had read it. When he had finished, he sat down slowly in his father's worn leather chair.

"I, Bradford Montrose, being of sound mind, bequeath all my earthly goods to my daughter's husband, if, in fact, she is married at the time of my death. If she is unmarried at the time of my death, I bequeath all that I own to my wife and daughter, to be administered by an executor of my choice, Nate Summerfield. My wife and daughter shall handle no money nor any of the business dealings of this ranch. They will live on a monthly trust to be determined by said Nate Summerfield."

Clay scanned the next few paragraphs. His father had made provisions in case Nate Summerfield died and had then gone on to detail the assets of his businesses and his ranch. The last line of the will leapt out at Clay, stunning and wounding him.

"I bequeath nothing to my son, Clayton, which is what he deserves."

"You bastard," Clay said, folding the paper up and putting it back in the box. He sat at the desk, remembering the times when he and Russell used to watch his father conduct business. Occasionally, his father would wink at them and they would laugh, knowing that they had been included. But those were the days when his father still considered him a son, in the days before Russell had died.

Clay shook his head. He couldn't believe his father was so cold. It hadn't surprised him that he, himself, had been left out of the will; he'd expected that. But he was surprised that his father had left no control to Rayna. Rayna was as smart and as capable as any man he knew and she could probably run the ranch better than their father. But then Bradford Montrose didn't think much of women. He'd always treated their mother like a child and he'd made it perfectly clear early on that she was to keep the house and produce children, nothing more.

But then came Rayna, the youngest and the smartest. Clay smiled as he thought of her throwing off her dresses to wear his and Russell's clothes so that she could follow them. Their father had berated her, but Rayna never flinched, never apologized. She had never feared their father and that confused him.

Clay wondered why Rayna had never married. She was a pretty woman, and he knew that men were attracted to her. Why did she continue to stay at a place that held no fond memories and could only make her life miserable? He knew why as soon as he asked himself the question. Rayna would never leave their mother alone with their father. If she did, Rayna knew that their mother would be destroyed. She put her own life aside and continued to protect their mother and battle their father.

Clay looked down at the desk. There was a blotter, an inkwell, a pen, a neat stack of paper, and a pair of bronzed baby shoes. Russell's shoes. Clay picked them up, feeling the coldness of the metal, amazed at how small the shoes were. He had always thought Russell was so big. The door opened, and Clay looked up. Quickly, he put down the bronzed shoes. Rayna was standing at the door, dressed in a light blue skirt and blouse, her hair pulled back loosely in a ribbon. She smiled at him and he smiled back. She was so pretty.

"So, I found you," she said, closing the door behind her as she entered the room and sat down across the desk from him. "What're you doing in here? I thought you hated this room."

"I didn't always hate it. Russell and I used to come in here sometimes. Pa used to let us sit here while he talked business. Made us feel real important."

"Men talk," Rayna said sarcastically, "something my little pea brain wouldn't understand."

"Does it ever bother you that he loved Russell more than us?"

Rayna reached out and picked up the shoes, studying them for a brief second then putting them back. "It used to, but it doesn't anymore. If Russell had lived, Pa would've wound up hating him, too."

"No, I don't think so. Russell was always his favorite."

"You're wrong, Clay. Russell became his favorite when he died. He couldn't disappoint Pa then. He became the perfect child."

Clay studied Rayna for a moment. Her voice was calm, not betraying any sign of bitterness, but her tone was cold, almost unfeeling. "Are you all right, Sis?"

He saw her face soften slightly. "You could always tell, couldn't you?"

"Talk to me," Clay urged.

Rayna looked at him. "I hate him, Clay. I swear, I hate him more than I thought it was possible to hate anyone."

"Then leave. Why do you stay here?"

"What about Mother? I couldn't live with myself if something happened to her."

"Rayna," Clay said gently, leaning forward and taking her hand. "You're a grown woman. Mother is no longer your concern. You're entitled to your own life."

"If I left, he'd put her through even more hell than he already does. It wouldn't be fair, Clay."

"Fair?" Clay laughed bitterly. He let go of Rayna's hand and stared past her at the painting of Russell that hung on the wall. "Sometimes I hate her, too, you know."

"Who? Mother?"

"Yes."

"Why? She tried her best."

"Why the hell didn't she ever stand up to him like you always did?"

Rayna stood up and paced the room. "I was never married to him, Clay. It's different for her."

"No, it's not. I can't imagine you ever taking that from any man."

Rayna stopped behind Clay, her hands on his shoulders. "It's easy for us to sit in judgment of her. But I don't think we have the right."

"Why are you defending her, Rayna? She never defended us."

Rayna shrugged her shoulders. "She's our mother, Clay. That's reason enough to defend her."

Clay took one of Rayna's hands and kissed it lightly. "I'm sorry. I'm glad she has you. God knows, she never had me to look after her."

"I don't blame you for being angry, Clay. Mother never defended you against Pa, but she was frightened. You know how he used to beat her."

"Yes, I know," Clay said in disgust, recalling the many times he had heard his mother cry out. He shook his head. "What do you think of Aissa?" Clay turned so that he could see his sister's face.

"I think she's one of the most beautiful women I've ever seen."

"That's not what I meant."

Rayna nodded. "I think she's very nice and she's very scared."

"Can you blame her?" Clay asked defensively.

"No, I don't blame her, Clay. I was just wondering about something."

"What? I hate it when you start wondering," he grinned.

"Are you and she just friends? Is that all there is between you?"

"That's all there is between us, Rayna, believe it or not."

"When are you taking her back to her home, Clay?"

"When I think it's safe."

"When will that be?"

"I don't know. I want to make sure the man who put her in that mine isn't waiting around for her."

"You're in love with her," Rayna stated, her eyes fixed firmly on her brother's.

"I'm not in love with her, damnit!" Clay stood up.

"I've never seen you treat any woman like you treat her, Clay. She's touched you in some way."

"Is that so bad?" Clay demanded.

"You have to think of her, Clay. You just can't keep her a prisoner here and make her fall in love with you."

"I'm not doing that," Clay said angrily. "She's free to leave anytime she wants."

"And how does she do that, feel her way home?"

Clay held up his hand. "All right, all right, I care for her, I admit it. That doesn't mean I'm in love with her."

"I think you should get her out of here before Pa comes back. . . ." Rayna hesitated, narrowing her eyes. "That's part of the reason you're keeping her here, isn't it? You know it'll infuriate Pa if he thinks you've fallen in love with a blind woman."

"You're crazy."

"No, I'm not. We all know how he feels about anyone who is less than perfect." Rayna shook her head. "You can't do this, Clay. You can't do this to Aissa."

"I'm not doing anything to Aissa. Don't be so melodramatic, Rayna. As soon as Aissa is able, I'm going to take her home."

"I worry about you, big brother."

"Some things never change, do they?" Clay drummed his fingers on the desk. He looked challengingly up at her. "Have you ever read Pa's will?"

"His will?" Rayna shook her head. "No. Why?"

"I read it."

"When?" Rayna lowered her eyes to the drawers in front of Clay. "You didn't. How could you go through his private papers?"

"Why shouldn't I?" Clay leaned forward. "Don't you want to know who gets the ranch?"

"You get the ranch, of course. We all know how Pa feels about a woman's ability to do anything."

"You're wrong, little sister. Since you're not married, the ranch doesn't go to anyone in this family."

"What?" Rayna couldn't hide her surprise. "What do you mean?"

"I mean I don't get anything, and you and Mother get a monthly allowance. You know Nate Summerfield?"

"What does he have to do with our ranch?"

"He's the man Pa has picked to run things if he dies. You won't have a say in how anything is done around here."

"Summerfield? Summerfield's a banker. Pa wouldn't—"

Clay opened the drawer and pulled out the box. He handed the will to Rayna. "Read it." When Rayna hesitated, Clay shoved the papers toward her. "Read it, Rayna."

She took the will reluctantly and began to read. When she was finished, she folded it neatly and handed it back to Clay. "Once a bastard, always a bastard," she said softly, putting her hands in her lap.

"I'm sorry, Sis. I didn't think he'd do it."

"Neither did I," she said mournfully.

"How are you fixed for money?" Clay asked suddenly.

Rayna looked at him. "What kind of question is that? You know I don't have any money of my own."

"But he must give you some to buy clothes and supplies for the house. And what about the bills? You used to pay those."

"I still do."

"Good," Clay nodded approvingly.

"I don't trust you when you get that look, Clay. What're you planning to do?"

"I'm going to make sure you get what's rightfully yours."

"What does that mean?"

"I'm going to start getting into some card games. I'm a damned good gambler, you know."

"Sure, that's why you've wound up working in a mine in Mexico. Don't be crazy, Clay. I'll be fine."

"No, you won't be fine. Don't you understand? Pa will try to run your life even after he's dead. I won't let him do that to you."

Rayna reached out and squeezed her brother's hand, smiling at him. "I appreciate what you're trying to do but I'll be fine. It says he's leaving us a monthly allowance."

"You deserve more than that. Do you want some stranger coming to live here on the ranch and telling you how to run it? If Summerfield comes here, it'll be like you're married to that sour-faced old geezer." Clay shook his head. "Is that what you want?"

"Clay—"

"Don't argue with me, we're going to be partners. You're going to start funneling money away from the ranch, and I'm going to get into some friendly card games. Once we have a substantial amount of money, I'll invest it for you."

Rayna looked at Clay for a moment and then burst into laughter.

"What's so damned funny?"

"Did you learn something about money while you were working in the mines?"

"I know all I need to know, Rayna. I knew how to run this ranch when I was sixteen years old, and I bet I could still run it better than Pa does now." He leaned back in the chair and propped his boots up on the desk. "Anyway, I have some money of my own."

"How's that possible? You've been working in a mine for the last two years."

"I got on friendly terms with the guards, and we played a lot of cards. I was lucky. I won a lot of money."

"And they let you keep it?"

"I hid it in the mine just in case."

Rayna shook her head. "You'll never change. I can see why you drove Pa crazy."

"Don't you dare start feeling sorry for him, Rayna. He doesn't deserve your pity. Any man who would leave his entire estate to a goddamned stranger. . . ." Clay stood up and walked around the desk to his sister. He leaned down and kissed her on the head. "I love you, Sis. I won't let the bastard drive me away this time. I'm going to make sure that you and mother are set for life."

Bradford Montrose sat his horse with a straight back, his head held high. As tired as he felt, he would never think of letting it show in his posture. That was a sign of weakness and he despised weakness.

He'd been to Chicago, negotiating the sale of cattle and then he'd stopped in Santa Fe to see his mistress. Lila was young, redheaded, and full of fire. He'd known her for three years and she'd made life worth living again. God knows, Dorothea didn't provide him with much pleasure these days. Truth was, he could barely tolerate his wife anymore.

Then there was Rayna. Bradford shook his head. His daughter was the most headstrong human being he'd ever met or run across. She wasn't afraid to stand up to him on any occasion. He smiled slightly, as he thought of her face. How was it possible for such a pretty little thing to be so strong? How was it possible that Dorothea had produced such a daughter? But he knew that Rayna had gotten her strength and will from him, not from Dorothea.

He wanted more for Rayna. He wanted her to be married and have children of her own. She'd be a good mother; he knew she would. But she'd never leave the ranch as long as Dorothea was alive. She was too loyal.

Bradford had never meant for it to be this way. When he had married Dorothea, he had genuinely loved her. She was pretty and bright; she gave him two sons and a daughter, all of whom were healthy and strong. No man could've asked for more from a wife. But then that dark day came, the day that Russell got killed, and all of their lives changed. He pulled a silver flask from his saddlebag and took a drink of whiskey.

Tears stung his eyes as he thought of his oldest son. He had loved him so much; they had all loved him so much. But when Russell died, a part of Bradford had died.

And he would never forgive Clay.

He wondered if Clay was ever coming home. He shook his head, holding tightly onto the reins. Clay was a lot like Rayna, strong, outspoken, and totally unafraid of him. But after Russell died, that independence had turned into rebellion.

Bradford topped a rise and reined in his horse. He looked out over the green pasture that was dotted with cattle and horses. He'd done well for himself. He'd started out with a quarter section and a small herd of cattle, and now he owned thousands of acres and his herd was bigger than he had ever imagined it could be.

He kicked his horse into a canter and rode across the

pasture. Bradford drank in the beauty of the land. He had missed it all right, he always did. But as much as he was glad to be home, back to his land, he dreaded going back to his family.

He rode for miles across the pasture land, recalling the times he used to ride with Russell and Clay. He could remember how they had laughed and joked together. He remembered how much they had loved each other. The memories were still painful to him after all this time. He slowed his horse when he saw the even rows of quaking aspen that he had planted to line the road up to the house. It was a beautiful sight.

Bradford rode up the long tree-lined road to the barn. Jeb greeted him when he pulled up.

"How you doin', Mr. Montrose?"

Bradford dismounted. "I'm just fine, Jeb. I think we'll be getting a good price for the cattle this year. As long as we can keep them fat and healthy." He removed his saddlebags and threw them over his shoulder.

"Shouldn't have no problem doin' that, sir."

"Everything all right while I was gone?"

"Yessir, nothing amiss." Jeb hesitated, holding onto the reins of Bradford's horse. "There is one thing though."

"What is it?"

"Clayton is back. Been back for a couple weeks now."

Bradford concealed his reaction. "Clay's home?" He nodded. "Good." He walked away toward the house, trying to stay calm. So Clay had come home. He was surprised, but only mildly. He knew he'd come home eventually, especially when he ran out of money.

He climbed up the stone steps and walked the pathway that led into the courtyard. He stood for a moment. Every time he walked into it, it was as if he'd gone into another world. He had to give Dorothea credit. She had kept this courtyard as beautiful and as pristine as she had kept the house.

He stopped at the fountain, putting his saddlebags down on the small circular bench that surrounded it. He dipped his hands into the water, splashing it onto his face. He picked up the saddlebags and as he walked toward the house, he kicked each boot against the other, making sure there was no excess dust. He opened the door and walked inside. It was quiet. If Clay was home, he sure as hell wasn't in the house. He smelled food immediately and almost went into the kitchen but decided against it. Instead, he walked upstairs. There were three rooms on the left side of the staircase and three rooms on the right. His room was at the end of the east side, overlooking the courtyard. Dorothea's was on the opposite side of the staircase. It had been that way for years.

Bradford opened the door and went inside, closing it behind him. He put his saddlebags on the floor and walked across to the window, pushing back the curtain. He could see past the courtyard to the corrals and beyond to the pastures and foothills. He walked back and sat down heavily on the bed, then leaned back with his hands tucked under his head. He closed his eyes. It felt peaceful here. But he knew that wouldn't last long now that Clay was home.

He rested in the stillness of his room for an hour and then got up and went downstairs to the kitchen. He stood at the arched doorway and looked in. Dorothea was kneading bread on the table. She was still an attractive woman but they'd had nothing in common for years. He walked into the kitchen.

"Hello, Dorothea."

Dorothea looked up, her dark eyes startled when she saw her husband. "Bradford, you're home." She reached for a towel and started to wipe her hands but Bradford shook his head.

"You don't have to stop. I'm going to check on things."

"No, it's all right." Dorothea cleaned off her hands. "Are

you hungry? Let me get you something to eat."

"No, I'll eat later." He looked around. "Where's Clay?"

"You heard," she said, her voice low.

"Yes, I heard. When did he get here?"

"A couple of weeks ago. Bradford, there's something you should know. He has a woman with him."

Bradford laughed harshly. "A woman, he brought a woman here? I should've known he'd do something like that."

"No, it's not what you think," Dorothea said, gently taking his arm and guiding him out of the kitchen and through the dining room. Without speaking, they walked through the double doors to the courtyard.

Bradford shook free of Dorothea's grasp. "I don't want him here, Dorothea."

"But he's your son," she said somewhat defiantly.

Bradford paced around the courtyard and then came back to stand next to Dorothea.

"He causes nothing but trouble whenever he's here. He gets you and Rayna upset."

"He doesn't upset us, Bradford. He upsets you."

"Don't start it, Dorothea," he said, clenching and unclenching his right fist.

"This is my home, too, and as long as I'm here, Clay is welcome." Her voice shook but her eyes were challenging.

Bradford leaned down, his mouth close to Dorothea's face. "This is not your home. You don't own any part of this place, do you understand? You're only here because I let you live here."

Dorothea lowered her head, her eyes filling with tears. "You know I don't have anyplace to go, Bradford."

"Yes, I know," he said coldly. "So if I were you, I'd keep my mouth shut about Clay. Do you understand?" When she didn't respond, Bradford grabbed her upper arm, pressing his fingers into the soft flesh. "Do you understand, Dorothea?"

Dorothea nodded without raising her head. "Yes," she mumbled.

"Mother?" Rayna was standing just inside the wide doors.

Dorothea quickly walked toward her daughter. "Your father is back, Rayna." Dorothea dabbed at her eyes with a hanky, smiling.

"Are you all right, Mother?" Rayna gently took her mother's hand.

"I'm fine. I just have some things to finish up in the kitchen."

Bradford watched as his wife ran away, her head lowered in defeat, as usual. And then he saw his daughter. Rayna walked toward him, her head held high, her face set in a grim expression. She was ready for a fight. "How are you, Rayna?"

Rayna walked up to him, meeting his eyes. "What did you do to her?"

"I didn't do anything to her.. You know your mother; she cries over every little thing."

Rayna shook her head. "How long have you been home, a few minutes? And already you have her in tears."

"Your mother is emotional, Rayna. Always has been. There's nothing I can do about it. So, how's the ranch? Anything I should know?"

"The hell with the ranch!" Rayna shouted. "Do you think I actually care about this place?" She took a step closer to her father. "Why should I work so hard for a place that will never belong to me anyway?"

"What're you talking about?"

Rayna narrowed her eyes. "You don't have to hide it anymore, Pa. I saw your will." She shook her head. "I know you're not leaving anything to me or Clay, but how could you do that to Mother?"

Bradford was so stunned he couldn't speak for a moment. "My will? How the hell did you see my will?"

"It doesn't really matter, does it, Pa? What matters is we are nothing to you. We never have been." She laughed bitterly. "I wish Russell had lived."

"So do I," Bradford said, his voice catching slightly.

Rayna walked forward. "But I wish he would've lived for a different reason than you. If Russell had lived, he would've grown up and disappointed you, just like Clay and I have."

Bradford shook his head. "No, he wouldn't have. Russell was too good."

"Russell was a boy when he died, Pa. He didn't have a chance to disappoint you."

Bradford sank down onto the stone bench of the fountain. "No, Russell was different. He was so eager to please. He would've done anything for me."

"That's because he was scared to death of you," Rayna said angrily.

"No, he wasn't. He loved me."

"He loved you because he would've suffered if he hadn't." Rayna looked down at her father. "Did you know that he often told Clay and me that he was going to run away when he was old enough?"

Bradford looked at Rayna, shaking his head slowly. "No, he wouldn't have said that."

"He did, Pa. He said that and plenty of other things."

"You're just trying to hurt me," Bradford said, suddenly feeling weary. It had been a long ride and as usual his welcome home was more exhausting than the trip.

"You're right, I am trying to hurt you. I'm trying to hurt you like you've hurt all of us. You've made all of us suffer for something none of us was responsible for, Pa."

"Clay was responsible. He killed Russell." Bradford's voice was suddenly hard.

"Would you stop it, Pa? Clay was younger than Russell. How could he have saved him?"

"He was stronger than Russell. He was a better shot. He could've done something."

"He did try, Pa, but he was only a boy. When are you going to forgive him?" Rayna's voice softened slightly.

"Forgive?" Bradford looked up. "I'll never forgive him. It should've been Clay who died, not Russell."

"You bastard," Rayna said, backing up. "You're dead inside."

Bradford reached out to his daughter, wanting to say something, but nothing came out. He watched her as she ran out of the courtyard. He closed his eyes, shaking his head. Rayna was right about one thing: he felt dead inside. He had been that way for a long time.

Clay dismounted and walked to Aissa's horse, helping her down. He took her hand, leading her across the yard and up the stairs to the path. They had had a good ride and Aissa had actually laughed a few times. She was beginning to learn her way around, and he could see her confidence building. He stopped.

"What's wrong?" Aissa asked.

"Nothing is wrong. I just want to look at you." Clay brushed some strands of hair from Aissa's face.

"It makes me uncomfortable when you stare at me and I know you are."

"Why?"

"Because I can't stare back."

Clay smiled and lowered his mouth to Aissa's, gently pressing his lips to hers then quickly pulling away. "I love your mouth," he said, his voice deep.

"Clay—"

Clay put a finger on Aissa's lips, "It's rude to interrupt a man when he's trying to be romantic."

"Clay, please don't. I keep telling you, I'm not ready for this."

Clay nodded, rubbing Aissa's cheek. "All right, I'm

sorry."

"Don't be sorry. I wouldn't be here without you."

"I don't want your gratitude, Aissa. I want more than that."

"I can't give you more than that. You know that, Clay."

"Yes, I know," he said, trying to hide his disappointment.

"I'm sorry."

"Don't be sorry. You've been honest with me. Come on. Let's get something to eat." Clay took Aissa's hand and led her along the path, telling her where to step and warning her where the stones were loose. He had to be patient, he reminded himself. He couldn't push Aissa.

Clay was looking at Aissa when they entered the courtyard, making sure she didn't trip on the uneven rocks of the path. He had his arm around her waist and had said something to make her laugh when he looked up and saw his father sitting by the fountain. He stopped abruptly, holding onto Aissa so she wouldn't stumble.

"Clay, are you all right?" Aissa asked.

"It's my father. He's here."

"Here? In the courtyard?"

"Yes." Clay walked toward his father, holding tightly onto Aissa's hand. His father was leaning back against the fountain, his legs stretched out in front of him. Clay was surprised that a man of Bradford's age could still look so robust, so fit. He was still lean and muscular, and his light brown hair had only tinges of gray in it. It was as if nothing touched the man, not even time. "Hello, Pa," he said. When his father opened his eyes and looked at him, the hatred burning there was even stronger than he had remembered. Only then, did Clay realize, that he had hoped that his father might have learned to forgive him after all these years.

"So, you're back," Bradford said, looking from Clay to Aissa. He looked her up and down. "And you brought a woman."

"This is Aissa, Pa. Aissa, this is Bradford Montrose."

"I'm pleased to meet you, sir," Aissa said politely.

"What is this, Clay? Is this another attempt to get back at me?"

"What're you talking about?"

"Her? Why did you bring this woman here? You know how I feel about women like that."

Clay let go of Aissa's hand and stepped forward. "Women like what?"

Bradford looked at Aissa and shrugged. "Well, she's cleaned up but it's easy to see she's a whore. You've never had a woman without paying for her, have you, Clay?"

Clay fought an urge to throw himself at his father, but he heard Aissa say his name. He stepped back and took her hand. "Have you noticed anything about Aissa, Pa? I mean, besides the fact that she's beautiful." He waited a moment and then continued before his father could speak. "Have you noticed her eyes? Pretty, aren't they?"

"Clay, what is—"

"Aissa is blind, Pa. She can't see. That's why I brought her here."

Bradford looked at Aissa, studying her face. "That's true?"

"Yeah, Pa, it's true. And for your information, she's a schoolteacher."

"I can speak for myself, Clay," Aissa said firmly, letting go of his hand. "Mr. Montrose, I'm sorry I intruded on your hospitality. I will be leaving at the soonest possible moment. I can only pity a man who has earned the hatred of his children."

Bradford stood up. He was visibly shaking. "I don't need to take that kind of talk in my own house."

"No, you don't," Aissa agreed. "That's why I will be leaving."

"Then why don't you go and take him with you."

"That's enough, Pa," Clay ordered. "Aissa is my guest. She can stay here as long as she likes."

"And what gives you the right to invite people to stay here. This isn't your home."

Clay shook his head, a slight grin on his face. "You're wrong, Pa, it is my home. It's as much my home as it is yours."

"You little—" Bradford stepped forward, his hand raised.

"You want to hit me? Go ahead. I've been waiting for this for a long time."

Aissa touched Clay's arm.

"I'll take you inside, Aissa."

"No, I'll be all right." Clay watched Aissa as she carefully walked over the rough paving stones toward the dining room doors.

Clay turned back to his father. "How could you call her a whore? You don't even know her."

Bradford shrugged his shoulders and sat down. "So I made a mistake. It's not like you ever brought home a decent woman, Clay."

"It's nice to see some things don't change," Clay said, walking over to the fountain and reaching his hands into the cool water.

"I was just thinking the same thing about you, Son."

Clay splashed his hands against his face and looked at his father. "I meant what I said about the ranch. I'm not leaving."

"I could make you leave."

Clay considered what his father said and nodded in agreement. "I suppose you could, but I'll always come back."

"You showed Rayna the will, didn't you?"

"Why not? I thought she deserved to know that she wasn't going to get anything for all her years of loyal service to you." Clay stared at his father. "So, feel like hitting me? Come on, Pa. You used to do it all the time."

Bradford's face flushed in anger. "I want you gone from here."

"I told you before, I'm not leaving." Clay leaned close to his father, his voice low. "I'm different now, Pa. You can't make me run away anymore. I'm here to stay."

Bradford calmed himself. "So, why the newfound interest in the ranch? You think you'll mend your ways, and I'll just hand over this land to you?"

"I don't expect you to hand anything to me, but I do expect you to do right by Mother and Rayna. They both deserve it for putting up with you for all these years."

"They've had a good life, had everything they ever wanted."

"Everything?" Clay asked, laughing bitterly. "Do you consider all the beatings you gave Mother and me everything we deserved?" Clay saw his father's hand clench. Bradford had slowed down some. Clay saw the blow coming and blocked it. He held his father's wrist in an iron grip. "I don't think so, Pa. Not this time." He forced his father's hand back down. "And you'll never lay a hand on Mother again as long as I'm around."

Bradford stood up, almost as tall as his son. He looked at Clay, wearing an ugly smile. "Why are you suddenly so protective of your mother? You never cared how she felt all those times you were caught stealing cattle or you were thrown in jail."

"I've changed," Clay said calmly, "and I'm staying."

"We'll see about that," Bradford said angrily, striding across the courtyard and into the house.

Clay watched his father walk away. He didn't like fighting with him; he never had. But as far as Clay was concerned, his father was in for the fight of his life. It was time to stop running away.

Chapter Ten

Christina brushed off her skirt and pushed back her hair, making sure she looked as neat as possible. She stepped onto the plank sidewalk and passed some stores until she reached the General Store. She smiled as she looked up at the sign; she'd never been able to read a store sign before. She went inside, tentatively touching the colorful dresses that were hung in neat rows on a rack. Then she went to the counter, glancing at the fancy bottles of perfume that stood on the shelf behind it.

"May I help you, miss?" The man behind the counter stepped toward her. He was dressed neatly in black pants and a white shirt. He had gray hair and a slight belly and he had a friendly face.

Christina smiled broadly. "Yes, I just got in from out of town. I'm visiting the Montrose ranch, but I don't know how to get there," she said innocently. "And I'm kind of scared. I've never met them before. My parents are sending me here for a visit."

"Oh, they're nice enough folks, at least the mother and daughter are. The father, now he's pretty hard to figure."

"They might not be too happy to see me," Christina said uneasily.

"Don't you fret now, it'll be just fine. Let me tell you how to get to the ranch. It's easy to find. You just go about ten miles due west out of town and you'll run right into it. You can rent a buggy at the stable."

"Thank you so much," Christina said politely. She looked at the candy sticks in the jars and reached inside, picking out two of them. She handed the man two cents.

"No, no. I couldn't take your money. You just enjoy these. Come by and say hello if you come back into town."

"Thank you so much," Christina said and left the store, walking hurriedly to the stable. Shadow Hawk was watering the horses. He looked up when he saw her.

"Did you find out?"

"Yes. He said it's about ten miles due west of town. He said we'd run right into it." Christina offered him a candy stick.

"No," Shadow Hawk said, shaking his head. "Did you find out anything about these people?"

"Not much," Christina shook her head. "Said they were nice people." Christina sucked on the candy stick like she was a five-year-old child.

"What about the son? Did he say anything about him?"

"No, not a thing."

Shadow Hawk nodded, stepping to the side of the stable and looking out into the street. He didn't like towns. There was always too much going on. It was too hard to keep track of people. "We should get going. You ready?" He couldn't help but smile when he looked at Christina. She was eating the candy stick with a fury.

"Guess so," she muttered and walked to her horse.

Shadow Hawk and Christina mounted up and rode slowly out of town. He ignored the hostile stares and glanced over at Christina. If she were bothered by the disapproving looks, she didn't show it. Shadow Hawk knew that Aissa often concealed her uneasiness for his sake. It was more likely that Christina hadn't even noticed.

Shadow Hawk urged the paint into a lope and as they passed the last whitewashed house, he gave the stallion his head. He glanced back once to make sure that Christina was behind him, then rode hard.

In less than a mile the wild grass became sparser and the loam soil hardened into sunbaked red clay. The cottonwoods and oaks that had shaded the houses in town gave way to tough-barked pinon pines and twisted mesquite. Shadow Hawk let the stallion run until the animal was flecked with sweat and breathing hard. Only then did he rein in and turn to see Christina. She was riding hard and well, but was nearly a half mile behind. He slowed his stallion to a walk and waited until she caught up with him.

They rode in silence, following the contour of the dusty, rolling hills. Slowly the land became greener again. They crossed streams and rode through stands of ponderosa pine. The meadows were now thick with pasture grass, and twice Shadow Hawk heard the distant bawling of cattle.

When Shadow Hawk saw the Montrose ranch he reined in abruptly. Even at this distance, the house looked enormous. The path that led to it was lined with tall trees. The whole place looked so foreign, so unnatural. Without explaining to Christina, Shadow Hawk wheeled his stallion around and started uphill, toward the mountains. He would wait until darkness. He would not give this white man a chance to stop him. He would find Aissa, and if she were willing, take her with him before the sun rose. For an instant, he allowed himself to imagine that she might not want to come with him, that she was happier with the white man, but he pushed the thought from his mind. Before morning, Aissa would be in his arms, and they would be on their way home.

Shadow Hawk led his horse out of camp, mounting

only when he was far enough away. He had waited until he was sure Christina was asleep, not wanting to take the chance that she might follow him. He rode in the darkness, guiding the stallion along the rocky path and down into the valley. The moon wasn't up yet and could not offer him light, but he had ridden many times in the black of night. His eyes could adjust to the darkness, learning to discern certain shapes from others. He was momentarily distracted by a calf bawling for its mother and realized that he was in one of the pastures surrounding the ranch. He rode until he saw the silhouettes of the tall trees. Even though the stallion was unshod, its hooves made a loud clumping sound on the hard dirt path. He slipped off the animal and tied him to one of the low-hanging branches. He took a length of rope from his pack, patted the animal on the neck, and ran up the dark path that opened up to the ranch.

He stopped when he reached the end of the path, waiting in the safety of the trees until he was sure no one was in the yard. He started to step out but stopped, checking to see if there were dogs. He could see the house up to the right. The barn, corrals, and bunkhouse were to the left. He would have to cross the yard and go up some steps. The only way into the house was through the courtyard, and he knew he would have to go over a wall or high double doors. He had heard of these kinds of houses before, and Gitano had told him of the high walls topped with broken glass. He had also told him how to climb one. What he needed was a white man's saddle. He stood tensely for an instant longer, listening. If there were dogs, they were either sleeping or locked into the courtyard at night. Shadow Hawk started toward the barn.

The saddles were hanging neatly along one wall. As Shadow Hawk ran his fingers along the well-kept leather, the ink-like blackness lightened as the moon rose and he could see the silver ornaments worked into the leather of the saddles. He slung a heavy saddle with a high cantle over his shoulders and silently slipped out of the barn.

He ran across the yard and up the steps to the stone path. His moccasined feet made barely a sound as he passed the doors and went to a corner of the wall. The heavy timber that reinforced the corner was encased in adobe bricks. It extended above the wall, half a man's height. Its sides and top would be encrusted with glass, but that wouldn't matter.

Shadow Hawk took the rope, made a slipknot, and threw it up over the corner post. He pulled the rope carefully, knowing that the glass would only cut through it if he were careless enough to allow it to rub back and forth against the sharp edges. Settling the saddle on his left shoulder, he began to climb. Near the top of the wall, Shadow Hawk steadied himself. With a quick circular motion of his left foot, he wrapped the rope around his instep and tightened the grip with his right hand. In one fluid motion, using a pendulum-like swing of his left arm, he lifted the saddle to the top of the wall. An instant later, he swung himself up and across the saddle. Still holding onto the rope, he climbed down the inside wall, lowering himself silently until his feet touched the courtyard stones.

The courtyard was dark and the sound of a fountain was all that Shadow Hawk could hear. The house was quiet. He had no idea where Aissa would be, but he assumed the bedrooms were on the second story. A man who had built a wall like he had just climbed would not be likely to sleep where an intruder could easily get to him. He looked up at the second floor. It would be easy enough to climb, but what if he climbed onto the wrong balcony and the white man or his father was awake? He went to the glass doors and carefully turned the handle. They were bolted. He stepped back and looked up again at the balcony. The doors of the room on the left were open to catch the night breeze. That was the only way to get in.

Shadow Hawk found a thick vine that grew up the wall of the house. It supported his weight easily enough and he pulled himself up onto the balcony. He smiled inwardly at the white man's folly—top the wall with glass but leave a natural ladder for the enemy to climb. He moved slowly into the room, letting his eyes adjust to the shapes inside of it. There was someone lying in the bed, but he couldn't tell if it was a man or a woman. He silently drew back the curtain. The moonlight fell across the bed. Dark hair framed the face of an older woman. Shadow Hawk let the curtain fall and moved across the room toward the door.

Silently, he went out into the hallway. He tried the next room, hesitating as the door creaked slightly. When he heard no sound from inside, he opened it. A woman lay sleeping in the bed but it was not Aissa. He went to the room at the end of the hall. He touched the handle, hesitating. If Aissa was in this room and she refused to come away with him, what then? He pushed open the door and in the moonlight he could see Aissa's golden hair spread out over the pillow. His heart leapt when he saw her. He closed the door and went to her bedside. He sat down, reaching out to stroke her soft hair.

"Aissa," he said softly, continuing to stroke her hair.

She stirred in her sleep. "Shadow Hawk?"

Aissa's voice was like a pain in his heart. He lowered his mouth to hers and whispered, "Yes, Aissa, it's me." He kissed her gently, savoring the feel of her lips. For an eternal moment, the warmth of her mouth opened to him and she pulled him close. Then, suddenly, he felt her pull away.

"Shadow Hawk," she whispered, "I have to tell you something."

Shadow Hawk touched her lips with his fingers. "No." It didn't matter what had happened to her, or what her feelings were for this white man. Now that he was looking at her, touching her, he knew that nothing could come between them. He kissed her again and although she struggled against him for an instant, she could not hide her desire. He pulled the sheet down. She wore a white gown of thin cotton and he could see her firm breasts pressed against the cloth. He traced the line of her throat and then, without thinking, slipped his hand beneath her nightgown. The warmth of her skin inflamed him, and he fumbled with the pearl buttons on her bodice. Aissa reached up to slide the nightgown straps from her shoulders. Her head was thrown back and her lips were parted.

Shadow Hawk pulled at the buttons and the thin cloth began to tear. Unable to control himself, Shadow Hawk ripped the gown from her body. Intoxicated by her beauty he stood and undressed, trembling with passion.

"Shadow Hawk." Aissa whispered his name.

Her whisper excited him as though it had been a physical touch. He bent to kiss her again, silencing her protests with his passion. His hands moved over her smooth skin, exploring and remembering how beautiful she was. Her body arched against him and he felt her legs open. Oblivious to the danger all around him, Shadow Hawk touched her. The warm wetness between her legs shattered his last vestige of control. He entered her, wanting nothing more than to possess this woman. He had ached for her for so long. Aissa answered the rhythm of his thrusts, her lithe body molded to his own. The heat of her belly and thighs drove him beyond passion into ecstasy. He felt his body tremble as he lost himself in her, covering her soft cries with a deep, passionate kiss, until they were both spent. He rolled to the side and held her against him, kissing her forehead.

"Aissa." His voice was a soft caress. He closed his eyes, remembering. How was it possible to feel such passion with a woman? And then he heard her soft cry as she buried her face in his chest. He could feel her tears. "Don't cry, Aissa. It's all right."

"You don't understand."

"Not now," he said gently. "There is nothing you can say that will change the way I feel about you. Do you understand me?" He held her until she quieted, and he felt her body relax. He wanted to stay here, holding her in his arms, for as long as he could. But it was time to go.

"You should go now," she said quietly. "Come back again tomorrow. We'll talk then."

"What are you saying? You're coming with me now."

"No, I can't."

"Aissa—"

"Please, Shadow Hawk. Just come back tomorrow."

Shadow Hawk felt her pulling away from him. Even her voice had grown distant. "What is it, Aissa?" He propped himself up on an elbow, staring down into her beautiful face. Her eyes were closed. "Please look at me, Aissa."

"No." Aissa turned her head away from Shadow Hawk.

"Do you want me to leave?"

"Yes." Her voice trembled slightly.

He cupped her chin in his hand and turned her face toward him. He lowered his mouth, pressing his lips to hers. "All right, I will come back tomorrow if that's what you want."

"Yes," Aissa mumbled.

Shadow Hawk stood up and quickly dressed. He bent down and kissed Aissa once more. "I will see you tomorrow." He stepped out onto the balcony and climbed over the side, lowering himself until he was able to jump to the ground. He ran around the narrow side yard until he reached the courtyard. He ran to the wall, gripped the rope, and quickly scrambled to the top, throwing his leg over the saddle. He swung the rope to the other side and climbed off the saddle, pulling it off the wall and letting it fall to the ground as he climbed down. Once more he scaled the wall. If he was going to meet the people that owned this ranch it was better that he left no trace.

Shadow Hawk held onto the rope with his left hand while he cut against the loop with his right. He ran the sharp blade back and forth until the rope was almost severed, then he began his descent. Halfway down, the rope broke. He fell to the ground with the rope on top of him. He gathered the rope, put it over his shoulder, and picked up the saddle. He searched the yard for people or dogs and again made his way across, replacing the saddle where he had found it. Without a backward glance, he ran from the barn down the tree-lined lane to his horse. Quickly, he mounted, turning the stallion toward the mountains.

Shadow Hawk rode hard across the pasture and the sparsely covered foothills, all the while plagued by the thought that something was wrong with Aissa. Their lovemaking had been intensely passionate, as always, but there had been an underlying sadness. He was troubled that he couldn't help Aissa and that she didn't seem to trust him enough to tell him what was wrong.

He pressed his thighs against the paint's muscular shoulders as the animal started up the mountain path. He had not come this far to find Aissa only to lose her again. He would go back to the ranch tomorrow and he would find out what was bothering her and then he would take her home.

Aissa tensed as she heard the footsteps on the stone path. She was sitting on the bench by the fountain and she could tell from the heavy, deliberate footfall that it was Clay's father. She dreaded having to speak to him. When the sound of the steps stopped, she felt him standing in front of her, staring at her.

"Can I help you, Mr. Montrose?" She turned her head in his direction.

"How are you enjoying it here, missy?" His tone wasn't harsh but it wasn't friendly.

"Your family has been very hospitable."

"I'm sure they have, especially my son."

"Your son is a very good friend. He saved my life."

"My son has a weakness for a certain kind of woman, so don't think—"

Aissa held up her hand. "I have no intention of marrying your son, Mr. Montrose. I'm only here until I'm able to travel."

"Clay said you have a father."

"Yes."

"Why doesn't he come here and take you home?"

"Because he doesn't know I'm here."

"Why not?"

"I want to be able to get along on my own before I go back home. My father will be frightened enough as it is."

"So, you think that's Clay's job? To teach you how to do everything?"

Aissa shook her head. "I never said it was Clay's job. I'm the one who's blind, and I'm the one who has to learn how to deal with it."

"If you don't need Clay's help, why don't you leave? You said you wouldn't be here long."

"Does my being blind bother you, Mr. Montrose? Or is it that I'm a woman?"

"Didn't your father ever teach you any manners, missy?"

"My name isn't missy, it's Aissa. And my father is one

of the finest men you'd ever want to meet, sir." Aissa stood up. "By the way, I plan to pay you for the food I'm eating and any other inconvenience I've caused your family." Aissa began walking carefully across the courtyard.

"Wait." Bradford caught up with Aissa, taking her arm.

"I don't need your help." Aissa tried to shrug her arm away, but Bradford held on to it.

"You do if you don't want to trip over the pot that Dorothea left in the middle of the path." Bradford tugged at Aissa's arm. "To your right."

"Thank you," Aissa said, trying again to take her arm away. "I don't need your help, Mr. Montrose."

"You planning on going down the steps alone?"

"Yes."

"Have you ever done it before?"

"No, but Clay has told me where each one is. I count them. I even know the third one down is uneven and I have to step carefully and move to the left side."

"Well, if you've never done it before, you better let me help you. If you fall down and break your neck, I'll never hear the end of it from Clay."

Aissa smiled and didn't fight this time when Bradford took her arm. He led her slowly down each step, talking to her as she went. When they reached the bottom, Aissa let go of his arm "Thank you. That was very kind of you." She started walking across the yard.

"Where in the hell are you going now? Don't you know you could get knocked over by a horse?"

"I'll be fine. I may not be able to see but I can hear."

"Just the same," Bradford took Aissa's arm again as they began to walk across the yard. "I can hear too but hearing is no substitute for seeing."

"It is when you're blind," Aissa said firmly.

"I'm sorry, I didn't mean that the way it sounded. Sometimes I can be a little . . ."

"Unfeeling. Abrupt," Aissa said.

"Yes." Bradford hesitated. "So tell me, what can you hear? How could you find your way around here without getting hurt?"

"I didn't say I wouldn't get hurt. I'm sure I'll get hurt quite a few times until I learn my way around. But hearing everything makes me feel alive, like I'm not cut off from everyone and everything." Aissa stopped and took a deep breath. She closed her eyes. "I can hear the birds in the trees and there are some cows bawling in the pasture. The smithy is pounding out some new shoes, and I can hear some of the men yelling in the corral. I can also hear the horse that they're trying to break. He's scared. I can hear the hens in the barnyard and a couple of the roosters fighting. I can also hear you shuffling your feet. Are you nervous?"

"Me? No, I'm just amazed that you noticed so much. I guess I didn't really hear all that, or maybe I did. I don't know."

"You probably heard some of it but saw the rest. That's because you rely on your eyes to tell you everything."

"You're not afraid of me, are you?"

Aissa shook her head. "No, should I be?"

"Most people are."

"I'm not most people, Mr. Montrose."

"No, I reckon you're not. You remind me a lot of Rayna. She's spunky like you."

Aissa smiled. "I like Rayna very much. She's been very helpful to me."

"She's always been helpful to everyone, that's her problem."

"I don't understand.

"Doesn't matter. Where were you planning to go?"

"I was supposed to meet Clay by the barn. We're going to go riding."

"He shouldn't be riding this time of day. He has work to do."

"He's a grown man."

Bradford stopped. "He's never acted responsible."

"Maybe he's changed since you've seen him last. It's been over two years, hasn't it?"

"Closer to three. He was so seldom here before he went to Mexico, it was like he never lived here even then."

Aissa smoothed her skirt. "May I ask you a question, Mr. Montrose?"

"Suppose. Doesn't mean I'll answer it though."

"Aissa!"

Aissa turned her head at the sound of Clay's voice.

"What did you want to ask me?" Bradford cleared his throat.

"It doesn't matter," Aissa said.

"All right then. Looks like Clay's expecting you."

"Maybe someday you can answer my question. Thank you for your help." Aissa let go of Bradford's arm.

"Just walk straight ahead. Clay's coming to meet you."

Aissa put her hand up to wave goodbye and started forward. She had hardly begun to walk when she felt Clay's hand on her arm. "What're you doing?"

"I'm trying to get you across the yard away from my father."

"I'm fine. I thought I was supposed to find my own way to the barn."

"You can find your way back alone. Right now, I'd like to mount up and get out of here. Come on."

Aissa took Clay's hand as he led her to a horse and helped her mount up. He handed her the reins. She took a deep breath. She wasn't sure she'd ever be able to ride without being able to see.

"Are you still scared?"

"A little."

"Don't worry, Jilly's a good mare. She'll do what you want."

Aissa nodded, listening to the sound of Clay's horse as it walked out of the yard. She urged her mare into a walk, giving her her head so that she could follow Clay's horse. Aissa had a vision of her horse going off on its own way and winding up in the feed shed all alone. The thought made her smile.

"You all right?" Clay asked.

"Yes, I'm fine." Aissa patted Jilly's neck. Aissa tilted her head. The sound of the horses' hooves was suddenly muffled. As she had done a hundred times before, Aissa listened with her whole attention. A breeze was blowing and she could hear the papery rustling of the Aspen leaves. The ground was covered with them. Once they reached the pasture, Aissa felt the sun on her face and the breeze blow through her hair.

"Want to run a little?" Clay asked, reaching out to touch Aissa's arm reassuringly.

"Yes, I think so."

"Just let Jilly have her head. She's a smart mare. She won't take you anywhere dangerous. Besides, I'll be keeping an eye on you."

"All right."

"Let's go then," Clay said.

Aissa kicked Jilly into a gallop and grasped the saddle horn tightly. But soon she relaxed as the old familiar feeling of freedom came back to her. She loosened her hold on the reins and leaned forward, enjoying the wind in her face. She was both frightened and exhilarated. It took her a moment to realize that Clay was yelling at her to slow down and she pulled back on the reins, slowing Jilly to a canter, then a walk. She heard Clay's horse beside her.

"I was afraid you were going to take off and never come back," Clay said, his voice strained.

"It felt good," Aissa said defensively.

"I know, Aissa, but you have to be careful. If Jilly had stumbled, you would've gone down."

"It doesn't matter, Clay. Nothing happened." She felt the mare stop abruptly, and she realized that Clay had reached over and jerked the reins back.

"It does matter, Aissa. If you had been thrown and hit your head again, there's no telling what could've happened. You might never get your sight back then."

Aissa loosened the reins and let Jilly graze, feeling the mare shifting from hoof to hoof. Aissa had never realized that Clay had counted on her regaining her sight. "The doctor didn't say I would get my sight back, Clay."

"But he said you might. He said there's always that possibility. Are you still seeing light sometimes?"

Aissa shrugged, unconsciously running her fingers through the mare's mane. "Sometimes, but I don't think it means anything."

"What about the headaches?"

"I almost always have the headaches."

"Aissa, I've been thinking about something."

"What?" Aissa refused to turn her head toward Clay.

"I'd like to take you to see a doctor in St. Louis who is an expert on eye injuries. He might be able to tell us something different."

"Clay, I couldn't allow you to pay for a doctor."

"Why not?"

"Because I'm not your responsibility." Aissa swung her right leg over the horse and dismounted, putting her hands on the mare as she walked. She took some tentative steps, not knowing which way to go. Without warning, panic swept over her like it had the first time she discovered she was blind. She started running, not stopping when she heard Clay's voice. She felt as if the world was closing in on her, as if the darkness had let her out for only the briefest of moments. The ground felt uneven, as if it was moving. Suddenly she had no perspective, no way to tell if she was running uphill or down. She was breathing hard, gasping for air, when she stumbled and fell to her knees. She got up and started to run again but the toe of her boot caught on something. She sprawled face forward on the grass. She felt Clay's arms go around her as she struggled to stand up but she pushed him away. "Don't do that. Why do you always do that?" She turned her head, trying to hear, trying to let the sounds be her guide, but suddenly her senses failed her. She felt as if she were suffocating. She covered her face with her hands.

"Aissa, let me help you," Clay said gently, putting his arms around her.

Aissa wanted to pull away but didn't. She wanted to be on her own but knew it was impossible. She wanted to see again but knew she would not. So she sought comfort in Clay's arms, remembering how passionate she had been only the night before with Shadow Hawk. He had made love to her thinking she could see, but what would he do when he found out she was blind?

"Aissa, listen to me." Clay tilted her face upward. "I want to take you to see that doctor. Let me do that for you."

"Clay, I—" Her words were cut short by Clay's lips touching hers. His mouth sought hers, asking only that she give him some sign. She leaned her body against his, unable to fight anymore. She needed his strength. She needed him to help her. She kissed him back. As she felt his arms go around her and his kiss become more passionate, she stilled the tears that stung her eyes. She couldn't think of Shadow Hawk. As much as she loved him, this was best.

* * *

Shadow Hawk sat in the hills above the Montrose ranch, watching and waiting. He had gone back to camp after leaving Aissa and tried to sleep, but he could not. He could only think of the way their bodies had met yet again and the sadness he had sensed in her. He had wanted to ride into the ranch as soon as the sun had risen but had decided against it. For whatever reason, Aissa didn't want him there. Instead he went to the hills that overlooked the pasture and the ranch beyond, and sat there most of the morning. He didn't know what he was looking for.

And then he had seen the riders. As soon as they came out of the tree-lined path, he could see that one of them was Aissa. He watched her as she rode, leaning forward over her mare, a smile on her face. And then he had seen her stop. She and the white man talked for a time and then she dismounted and started running. Shadow Hawk had ducked down in the tall grass, not wanting to be seen.

Something was wrong with Aissa. Was she hurt? There was something about the way she ran. She stumbled and fell to her knees, got up, and began to run again, only to fall once more. Shadow Hawk had wanted to go to her, but the white man was there, helping Aissa to her feet. She was upset, had covered her face with her hands, and the white man had put his arms around her. More words were spoken, calmer words, and suddenly the white man kissed her, gently at first, and then more passionately. Shadow Hawk felt a pain. This was not like the time he had seen Aissa kiss Teroz because he had been kind to her; this was different. Just the night before he and Aissa had made love, and he had known something was wrong with her. Now, as he watched the white man kiss her and hold her, he knew what was wrong. She had fallen in love with someone else.

Shadow Hawk turned away in defeat. He closed his eyes, trying to blot out the pain. This was something he had not allowed himself to imagine. Slowly, he raised his head and looked at Aissa and the white man as they walked toward their horses. He helped her mount up and then they turned their horses toward the ranch. When they were out of sight, Shadow Hawk stood, feeling as if the only thing he had ever wanted had just been taken away.

Bradford and Jeb rode across the stream and up into the foothills. They had lost some mares, mares that Bradford was sure hadn't just wandered off. Stories of a wild stallion and his herd had been around for years, but no one had actually seen this phantom horse. Clay claimed to have seen him once, but Bradford hadn't believed him.

"Look there, boss," Jeb said, pointing to an area of grass that was trampled down. "They've been grazing here."

"Yep," Bradford said, lifting his hat back and scratching his head. "What're they coming up so high for, Jeb?"

"Who knows, boss. Might smell the stallion."

"Oh, hell, Jeb, no one's ever seen that damned stallion." The saddle creaked slightly as Bradford twisted around in it, looking for signs of the mares. He pointed down toward the far pasture. "Why don't you ride over across the lake? They might be in that little canyon over there."

"Okay, boss."

Bradford kicked his horse and he rode upward, again noticing that the grass had been trampled. He dismounted and ran his fingers over the ground. The hoofprint was still clear but wasn't one of his mares. It was an unshod horse. It was probably one of the wild herd.

Bradford started to mount his horse but the gelding

snorted loudly, tossing its head. The horse backed up a few steps, moving from side to side.

"Whoa, boy, settle down." Bradford held onto the reins and attempted to mount the horse again but it shied away, pulling the reins from Bradford's hands. Bradford started toward the gelding but it pawed the ground nervously. It tossed its head again and a frantic whinny escaped the animal as it bolted down the hill.

"Where in hell are you going, you stupid animal!" Bradford shouted after the gelding. Bradford kicked the ground angrily. "Damnit!" He started down the hill but stopped and turned around. Something had frightened the gelding. What was it? Bradford scanned the hills but could see nothing. He thought of Aissa and closed his eyes; perhaps he was relying too much on his sight. His eyes had been closed only moments when he heard the angry snort of a horse. He opened his eyes and looked above him. Still nothing. Then slowly, out of the rocks, a large black stallion appeared, tossing its magnificent head up and down, its nostrils flared. Bradford couldn't take his eyes from the animal. So, Clay had been telling the truth; there was a stallion.

Bradford didn't move. Wild stalllions could be as dangerous as any animal when cornered, but in the open like this, Bradford was sure the animal would turn and run. He waited, hoping the stallion would quickly sense that he was of no danger to him. But incredibly, the stallion stood staring at him, pawing the ground. Bradford started to move cautiously toward the trees, keeping his eyes on the powerful animal. He had made it halfway across the clearing when the stallion charged. Bradford tried to run but within an instant, the thunderous hoofbeats were right behind him and he dove to one side, rolling as he hit the ground. When he looked up, the stallion was rearing above him. Bradford froze, unable to move. He had seen stallions pound the life out of rattlesnakes with their hooves. He knew he should try to get away. Before he could move, the stallion dropped his forelegs and a crashing pain shot through his shoulder, knocking him to one side.

Bradford stood, trying to climb upwards toward the rocks, but the stallion came at him again, knocking him to the ground with such force that he pitched forward, face first. He tasted blood in his mouth and he lifted his head slightly. His shoulder ached, and he thought it might be broken. Slowly, he stood and broke into a stumbling run, knowing it was his only chance. He expected the stallion to come at him again, but he heard the sound of a man's voice.

Bradford stopped and turned. He shook his head. It was like something out of an adventure novel. Above him was an Indian on a paint, cutting off the stallion so that the animal couldn't charge Bradford. The Indian yelled something but Bradford couldn't understand it. It looked like he was calming the stallion while the paint stood, head held high, whinnying a challenge to the other horse. The wild stallion stood for a few moments, eyeing the Indian and the paint. Then he whinnied loudly and turned, his tail flared out behind him as he headed up the rocky path and disappeared. It was the most incredible thing Bradford had ever seen.

Slowly, Bradford stood up, holding his arm. His left ankle ached and so did his back. He looked down at his shirt. It was spotted with blood. He watched as the man rode toward him and then dismounted. He was Indian, but he was tall, taller even than Clay. His hair was barely shoulder length, held back by a headband. As he got closer, Bradford could see that the Indian's eyes were a dark blue, almost gray color. The Indian had white blood in him. Bradford was slightly apprehensive but not really afraid. He didn't believe the man meant to kill him.

"Is your arm broken?"

Bradford was astonished that the Indian's English was so good. He nodded absently. "Yes, I think it is."

"What about your leg?"

Bradford shook his head. "It'll be all right. Where in hell did you come from anyway?"

"It doesn't matter."

"It matters to me. You saved my life." Bradford attempted to extend his right hand but winced, instead he extended his left. "I'm Bradford Montrose. I want to thank you."

"My name is Shadow Hawk." Shadow Hawk shook Bradford's hand.

"You're not Apache."

"My mother is Apache, my father was Comanche."

"Where did the white blood come from?"

"From my grandfather. You will need help getting down the hillside. You can ride my horse."

"No, that's all right." Bradford started to walk and stopped, the pain shooting up his leg. "Maybe I will borrow your horse if you don't mind."

"You may ride him, you may not borrow him," Shadow Hawk said in a firm voice.

Bradford smiled slightly as he watched the man. When he came back with the paint, Bradford looked at the blanket on the animal's back. "Bareback?"

"You cannot ride bareback?"

"I haven't for a long time but I'll do it if I have to. You might have to give me a little help." Bradford waited as Shadow Hawk gave him a boost onto the paint's back, and then Shadow Hawk took the reins and began leading the animal down the hill. "Aren't you going to ride?"

"I will walk," Shadow Hawk said simply.

Bradford wiped at the dried blood on his face and

looked down at his arm. It looked like it might be broken and was beginning to throb. "Where did you come from anyway? Trying to steal a cow?"

Shadow Hawk stopped without turning his back. The paint shifted uneasily. "There is no need for me to steal white man's animals. I hunt all that I need to eat."

"I'm sorry, I meant no disrespect," Bradford said, realizing that he might've offended the man. "I thought I was going to die back up there."

"You probably would have," Shadow Hawk said matter-of-factly.

Bradford shrugged. Making conversation with this man wasn't easy. "Have you ever seen a horse come at a man like that? Never saw anything like that in my life."

Again, Shadow Hawk stopped but this time he turned, looking up at Bradford. "I have seen horses kill men many times. Either men are too stupid or too arrogant to understand the animal. Which are you, white man?"

Bradford was stunned. "I didn't do anything to that horse. I was down on the ground checking tracks, that's all."

"For what reason?"

"I was looking for some lost mares. Does that make me stupid?"

"It makes you stupid if you know that the stallion is around."

Bradford looked around sheepishly. "I guess I never much believed in that stallion. My son told me a long time ago that he had seen him, but I didn't think there was an animal like that around here."

"Perhaps next time you will believe your son when he tells you something." Shadow Hawk continued to lead the paint down the hill.

"I've heard your people know more about horses than any other Indians. Is that true?"

"It is true," Shadow Hawk replied, carefully leading the paint through some mesquite.

"So, you never did tell me why you're on my land. This is my land, you know."

"Yes, I know."

"But you're not going to tell me anything."

"I was not going to steal anything, white man, and if I had wanted to kill you or any of your family, you would all be dead by now." Shadow Hawk stopped and looked over his shoulder, narrowing his eyes. "And your walls topped with glass would not have stopped me."

Bradford felt somewhat like a child who had just been caught cheating. So, he even knew about the glass on top of the walls. "Shadow Hawk," Bradford persisted, "please tell me why you're here. Is it Clay, my son? Has he done something to offend you or your people?" Bradford watched as he said Clay's name, and he swore he saw a reaction in Shadow Hawk's eyes. But his voice betrayed no emotion.

"I do not know your son, white man. I am traveling with a white woman. We camped in your hills last night. I was out looking for game when I saw the stallion attack you."

Bradford nodded. "This white woman you're traveling with, is she a captive?"

"No, she is not a captive."

"Is she your woman?"

"You are lucky, white man, that I do not have more Apache blood in me or I would have cut out your tongue by now. You ask far too many questions."

Bradford smiled and shrugged his shoulders. "It's my nature, I guess. Is she your woman?"

"No, she is a friend. Her parents were killed by slave traders and she escaped. I am helping her, that is all."

"You sure seem to be in the right place a lot."

"Lucky for some people, is it not?" Shadow Hawk answered dryly, leading the paint around a fallen log.

Bradford nodded and smiled. He liked Shadow Hawk. This was a man of integrity. "I don't suppose you could use a job?" He knew it was useless asking the question as soon as he uttered the words.

Shadow Hawk didn't stop. "What kind of a job?"

Bradford couldn't believe it. "Well, you're good with horses. Why not teach my hands how to really break a horse?"

Shadow Hawk stopped this time and looked up at Bradford. "You are serious?"

"I'm real serious. It's the least I can do for you. You saved my life."

Shadow Hawk seemed to consider the offer. "It would be good to rest for a time. Christina, the white woman, is weary."

"Good, then you both can stay in the house. Christina can stay in my daughter's room, and you can stay in the guest room in my wing. What do you say?"

"Your men will not be happy to have an Indian giving them orders or staying in your house."

"My men will do as I say. If they don't, they can turn in their goddamned saddles. Besides, they could use a few lessons in horse breaking."

"All right," Shadow Hawk said, "but only for awhile. When I think it is time, I will leave."

"That's fair."

"What about pay?"

Bradford laughed. "You're not like any Indian I ever met. Well, let's see. You won't be doing what the other hands do, you'll strictly be working with the horses. I'll give you five dollars for every horse you break." Bradford smiled inwardly, knowing there was no way Shadow Hawk could break more than a couple horses a week. No matter how good he was, it took days to get a horse used to a man, a halter, and a saddle. The most Bradford would be out was ten dollars a week for a couple weeks. And he'd have some well-trained horses. He was getting the good end of the deal. "That's a lot of money. My top hands make forty dollars a month doing a hell of a lot more than that. Is it a deal?"

Shadow Hawk was silent a moment then nodded his head. "I will do it for five dollars a horse."

"Good, now let's get down this mountain before that damned stallion decides to come back."

"He won't be back," Shadow Hawk said over his shoulder.

"How do you know for sure?"

"Because I told him to leave."

"That's the damndest thing I ever heard," Bradford laughed. "You told him to leave." Then Bradford remembered hearing Shadow Hawk speak to the stallion. Was it possible? It was said there was no better man with a horse than a Comanche.

Bradford looked at the tall man who walked in front of him. If that was true and Shadow Hawk was that good a horseman, Bradford would be out a lot more than forty dollars.

Chapter Eleven

"I still don't understand why I have to pretend I don't know Aissa. It doesn't make sense," Christina said, dragging a stick through the dirt in their camp.

Shadow Hawk grimaced. How was he going to convince Christina that he needed her silence for now. He didn't want to tell her that he'd been with Aissa, and he sure as hell didn't want her to know that he'd seen Aissa with another man. Christina didn't need on excuse to think that he might love her one day. "Can't you just do this for me, Christina? If you're going to cause trouble, I'll take you home."

"And I'll just follow you."

"No, you won't. If I have to get Joe to lock you up, I'll do it." Shadow Hawk's voice was stern, his expression set.

"Oh, all right, but you still haven't told me why. I don't understand."

"You don't have to understand. When you and Aissa are alone, you can speak with each other, but in front of the others, pretend you don't know her. Just for now. Do you understand?"

"Yes," Christina said tersely, digging her stick into the ground. "Why did you have to take a job anyway? Why don't we just get Aissa and go back home?"

"Listen to me, Christina," Shadow Hawk said angrily, waiting until she turned her eyes to his. "I didn't ask you to follow me. I didn't want you along. If you don't like it, then you can go back to Gerard's ranch."

Christina continued to jab her stick into the ground until it snapped. She looked up at Shadow Hawk. "All right, I'll do as you ask, but it seems real silly to me."

"Get your things. We're going there today." Shadow Hawk set about packing his gear and cleaning out the camp.

Christina knelt down, rolling her bedding into a tight bundle. "I'm only trying to help."

"You can help me by doing what I ask you to do." Shadow Hawk shook his head. Christina was an exasperating young woman and sometimes he wanted to shake her. He finished packing his equipment and tied it onto the paint. While Christina was finishing up, he kicked at the still-warm coals from the early morning fire, making sure they were spread out, then he covered them with dirt.

As they started down the grassy hillside, Shadow Hawk was struck by the differences in this land and his. The land of the Apache was desolate and forbidding—this land seemed more forgiving.

"I don't want to stay here," Christina complained.

"I told you what you can do, Christina," Shadow Hawk said sharply. "Either you stay here with me or you go back to Gerard's ranch. But do not interfere with my plans."

"What plans?" Christina demanded.

Shadow Hawk pulled up suddenly, stopping the paint. "I will say this only once more. Do as I ask or leave. If you interfere with my plans in any way, Christina, I will not forgive you. Do you understand me?" Shadow Hawk's blue eyes darkened as he glared at her.

Christina lowered her head, nodding. "All right. I'm sorry, Shadow Hawk. I promise I won't do anything to interfere."

"Thank you." Shadow Hawk continued toward the

ranch wondering why he had accepted the white man's offer of a job. He could not forget the disturbing sense of sadness he had felt from Aissa when they had made love. There was something wrong, something he couldn't yet name.

He slowed to wait for Christina as they neared the tree-lined road that led to the house. He felt less white now than he ever had before. He would be a true outsider here.

"I've never seen a place like this before," Christina said, as she looked up at the perfect row of aspens on either side of the road.

When they came out of the trees and into the stable yard, Shadow Hawk pulled up, looking at the house, trying to push memories of Aissa and their lovemaking from his mind.

Shadow Hawk turned his horse toward the corrals and barn, dismounting even as a group of men ambled over to take a look at him and Christina. He tied the horses to the corral rail.

"We ain't got no jobs, Injun," one of them said. "Unless of course, you'd like to clean out the stables." The man spit out some chew and laughed.

Shadow Hawk remained silent, motioning for Christina to stay behind him.

Another man stepped forward, a toothpick sticking out of the side of his mouth. "What is it you want here, Injun?" When Shadow Hawk didn't respond, the man jabbed his forefinger into his chest. "What's the matter, don't understand English?"

"That's a pretty little woman you got there," an older man elbowed his way forward. "You steal her, Injun?"

"Of course he stole her, Clyde. How else would a red-skin have a white woman?"

Shadow Hawk stepped around the men, taking Christina's hand and walking toward the house.

"Hey, Injun, where you going? Don't you walk away from me." The cowboy spit some tobacco juice on the ground and shoved Shadow Hawk to the side. This time Shadow Hawk reacted. He let go of Christina's hand, pushing her out of the way, and punched the man full in the gut. As soon as the cowboy straightened, Shadow Hawk hooked his foot behind the man's boot heel and jerked it forward, knocking him to the ground. Without speaking, Shadow Hawk took Christina's hand and continued on toward the house. He saw Bradford coming down the stone steps.

"Don't even think about it, Grady," Bradford yelled out.

Shadow Hawk turned; the man had stood up and was pointing his gun at Shadow Hawk's back.

"Come with me," Bradford said brusquely, brushing past Shadow Hawk and Christina. Bradford called all the hands together and waited until they quieted. "Grady, you pack your things and get the hell off my ranch. I want you gone within the hour."

"But boss, that Injun—"

"Get out of here, Grady. I won't have any man work for me who'll shoot another man in the back." Bradford waited until Grady picked up his hat and walked away, ignoring the man's angry curses. "Now, the rest of you. This here's Shadow Hawk. He's Comanche. He saved my life this morning. I gave him a job." Bradford waited for the words to sink in. "He'll be breaking horses, and I want the rest of you to try to learn something from him. You all know there's no better horseman than a Comanche." He hesitated, looking from man to man. "Now I know how you all feel about Indians. Feel the same way myself, or I did until this morning. But he saved my life, and I owe him."

"But boss—"

"I don't want to hear it, Bill. You been around here long enough. I wouldn't have hired him if I didn't think he could do the job. That's all I expect of any of you, is to do your job. Now get back to work." Bradford waited until the men left. "Sorry about that. Grady's hotheaded."

"It doesn't matter." Shadow Hawk released Christina's hand. "Montrose, this is Christina Marley."

Bradford shook Christina's hand. "Pleased to meet you, I'm Bradford Montrose. So, you're a friend of Shadow Hawk's?"

"He's more than a friend."

"So, you've known him for sometime?"

Christina started to answer but hesitated, glancing at Shadow Hawk. "We haven't known each other all that long but like you, Mr. Montrose, I feel I owe Shadow Hawk my life."

Bradford nodded. "I understand. Both of you come inside. I'll show you to your rooms and then we'll have some lunch."

Shadow Hawk and Christina followed Bradford up the steps, through the courtyard, and into the house. Shadow Hawk smiled as he watched Christina staring at everything in wide-eyed wonder. When they reached the top of the staircase, Bradford stopped.

"Your room is to the left, the second door down, Christina. You'll be sharing with my daughter, Rayna. I'm sure you'll find everything you need. Come down to the courtyard as soon as you're finished cleaning up."

"Thank you very much, sir," Christina said, flashing a grin at both Bradford and Shadow Hawk.

"A charming young woman," Bradford said, walking down the hallway to the right.

"Yes," Shadow Hawk agreed.

Bradford opened the door to the middle room. "There's everything you need except clothes. I'm not sure we have any that will fit you."

"I'm fine."

"We do dress for dinner."

"Christina and I will respect your custom but we will eat outside." Shadow Hawk walked to the window, pulled the curtain aside and looked out. There was a view of rolling pastures and hills. "You have said nothing of your family." Shadow Hawk turned and looked at Bradford.

"I have a wife, daughter, and a son."

Shadow Hawk walked to the washbasin, wondering why Bradford spoke of his family with so little affection. He poured some water in the basin and washed his face and hands. When he was finished, he dried himself with the towel that was next to the pitcher and basin.

"You ready for lunch?"

"Yes." Shadow Hawk followed Bradford back down to the courtyard. A table was already set and two Mexican women were bringing out bowls.

"Sit down. We don't want the food to get cold."

"Your family will not join us?" Shadow Hawk waited until Bradford seated himself.

"My wife and daughter are in town and my son and his . . ." Bradford hesitated, "and his woman friend are having a picnic by the lake."

"Your son is not married?" Shadow Hawk asked as he sat down.

"Clay?" Bradford laughed loudly. "I'd drop dead a hundred times over if Clay ever got married."

"Is he in love with his woman friend?"

"I doubt it," Bradford said, reaching into a bowl and grabbing a tortilla. He handed one to Shadow Hawk. "They're best hot."

"And your daughter, what is she like?"

"Ah, Rayna, she's a little spitfire. I've scared many a man in my day, but I've never scared Rayna."

For the first time Shadow Hawk heard warmth in Bradford's voice. "You speak of her with fondness."

"Yes, I'm real proud of the kind of woman Rayna's turned out to be." Bradford looked up and smiled. "Here comes Christina." He stood up and helped her into her chair.

"Thank you. This all looks wonderful. It's just like one of those fancy restaurants I saw in one of. . . ." Shadow Hawk caught Christina's eye and she hesitated. "That I saw in one of my teacher's books."

"I have two of the very best cooks around." Bradford pointed to the various bowls. "We have beef, corn, sweet potatoes, squash, tortillas and butter. And in this bowl is some of the hottest *salsa* you ever tasted."

Shadow Hawk ate in silence as the women filled and refilled their glasses with water. He felt uncomfortable; this was unlike anything he had ever experienced at Gerard's ranch. But he could see that Christina was enjoying herself and that Bradford Montrose was enjoying Christina. They talked animatedly throughout lunch. Shadow Hawk finished eating and studied Bradford. Here was a man of many contrasts: he was strong and obviously powerful, yet he had been so helpless that morning. He gave freely of himself to Shadow Hawk and Christina, yet he barely spoke of his family. And Shadow Hawk sensed by what Bradford had said of his son that he was not very proud of him.

"How about some *flan?* Elaina makes the best *flan* you ever ate."

Shadow Hawk held up his hand. "No." He looked around the courtyard, wondering when Aissa would return and how she would react when she saw him.

"What's *flan?*"

Bradford explained the traditional Mexican dessert to Christina as Shadow Hawk pushed back his chair and stood up.

"I think I'll go look at the horses."

"The men are still a mite put out with you." Bradford stood up. "If you don't mind, Christina, I think I'll go with Shadow Hawk."

"No, I don't mind at all. I could stay in this courtyard all day."

Shadow Hawk grinned at Christina and left the courtyard, taking the stone steps two at a time.

"What's your hurry?" Bradford asked, catching up to him.

Shadow Hawk stopped.

"What's got you all worked up? The big house and the fancy table?" Bradford asked.

Shadow Hawk nodded. "Do you enjoy seeing people feel out of place, white man?"

"I felt out of place most of my life. And since I'm going to be your boss, don't you suppose you can call me something besides 'white man'?"

Shadow Hawk wanted to smile but didn't. "What do you wish to be called?"

"How about Bradford? That's my name."

Shadow Hawk hesitated. He didn't like the sound of the name or the way it rolled off his tongue. "I will call you by your last name."

Bradford shook his head. "You're a strange one. All right, call me Montrose if you like."

As they got within sight of the corrals, Shadow Hawk saw that the cowhands were still standing around in small groups. As he and Bradford got closer, they looked up. A few of them walked away hurriedly before Bradford could notice that they weren't working. The others went back to mending tack or repairing equipment. Shadow Hawk ignored the hostile stares of the cowhands as he and Bradford reached the first corral.

Shadow Hawk leaned against the top railing and watched. Two cowboys were holding a horse, its eyes were covered with a bandana. They dug their boot heels into the dirt holding the horse still as another man quickly mounted. The instant they released the horse, it half-reared, bolting into a gallop. When it felt the man's weight on its back, it began fighting him. It reared, leaping almost straight up, then slammed itself sideways, twisting as it came down. It was a powerful animal, and Shadow Hawk could see the cowboy trying to withstand the vicious jolting, trying to keep his balance. But inch by inch he was losing it. The horse went up again and a moment later, the man was on the ground and the horse was running around the corral, his head high in triumph.

"That horse has been giving us trouble for days."

"No one is talking to him."

"You said that before. . . ." Bradford stopped as Shadow Hawk walked away, climbed the corral railing and jumped down on the other side.

Shadow Hawk watched the buckskin and he waited patiently, walking slowly toward the animal. At first the horse ran from him but Shadow Hawk persisted, speaking in a calm, low voice, letting the horse know that he wasn't going to hurt it. Shadow Hawk ignored the taunts from the ranch hands and slowly walked around the corral as the buckskin ran. When the horse quieted and stood still, Shadow Hawk took a few steps toward the animal, moving slowly, his hands and arms loose, relaxed. Then he waited, letting the animal get used to his scent. When the buckskin lowered its head and extended its muzzle. Shadow Hawk stepped closer. The taunts from the cowhands lessened, then died as the buckskin took a step toward Shadow Hawk. Shadow Hawk could've grabbed the bridle but still he waited. "Why do you fight me so, my friend?" Shadow Hawk asked softly. The horse tossed its head up and down but didn't move away. Slowly, Shadow Hawk reached up and stroked the horse's sweaty neck.

"You are a strong horse, a good horse. You will no longer roam the ranges freely, my friend. You must accept your destiny."

Shadow Hawk continued to stroke the horse's neck until the animal was breathing steadily, its head lowered, the tenseness gone out of its muscles. Then he reached out and stroked its silky, soft muzzle.

"Let me help you, my friend. I will teach you what it is like to carry a rider." Shadow Hawk stepped so close to the buckskin that its muzzle was pressed against his chest. "That is enough for today. I will let you think on what I have said."

Shadow Hawk reached up once more and ran his hands over the horse's face and neck. Moving quietly along the horse's body, Shadow Hawk lifted the stirrup and undid the cinch. The buckskin shuddered as he pulled the saddle from its back. Shadow Hawk dropped the saddle in the dirt, then slid the bridle over the buckskin's ears, careful to give the animal time to let go of the bit. Once the tack was removed, Shadow Hawk again touched the buckskin, walking around it, still speaking in a low voice. He crossed behind the animal, telling it that there would have to be trust between them. He ran his fingers through its tail, working out a few burrs, then smoothed the hair on the horse's belly where the cinch had rubbed.

He pulled gently on the buckskin's mane. "You will one day carry a rider better than most horses." Finally, Shadow Hawk blew his own breath into the buckskin's nostrils, then stepped back. The buckskin stood, looking at Shadow Hawk as he turned and walked toward the fence, quickly climbing it and jumping to the other side. He continued to ignore the stares of the cowboys.

"That was pretty impressive," Bradford said, coming up next to him.

"He is far from broken but he understands what he must do."

"I don't know what the hell you're talking about but if it works, I won't complain." Bradford nodded toward the other corrals. "What do you think of my horses?"

"It appears you have many fine ones."

"I could sure use another good stud. I'll pay you two

hundred dollars for that paint of yours."

Shadow Hawk's stern mask cracked and for the first time he laughed. "And to think you accused me of being a thief, Montrose."

"What do you mean? That's more than fair."

"That paint and its sires has been in my family for four generations. I do not wish to see its blood weakened."

"Then you'll see the last of that animal when he dies."

"The paint has already sired many colts."

"All right, three hundred dollars then."

"The paint is worth at least five hundred of your dollars, but he is not for sale." Shadow Hawk started toward the house.

"You make a hard bargain, I tell you that. All right, five hundred dollars for the paint."

Shadow Hawk stopped and glared at Bradford. "You are a man who is used to getting what he wants."

"Yes, and I usually do."

"Well," Shadow Hawk said, his eyes narrowing, "you will not get it this time."

"Why?" Bradford persisted.

"To my people, a horse is everything. It takes us on the hunt, it takes us into war, it takes us from camp to camp. When a warrior dies, it is custom for him to be buried with his horse. Do you understand?"

"I think so."

"My father's stallion was a great war-horse. It took him into many battles. When my father died, my mother would not kill the paint. My father wanted me to have it, so that it would carry me safely through this life. This horse has great meaning to me, Montrose. The paint still carries my father's spirit."

Bradford nodded. "I envy your father to have a son who loved him so much."

"You have a son, Montrose, and a daughter."

"But they will never speak of me the way you speak of your father."

"I respected my father greatly because he treated me with respect."

Bradford shook his head. "It has never been that way with me and my children, except my oldest." A pained expression touched Bradford's face and he bent over to pick up a stone from the ground. He rubbed his fingers over it. "Russell was everything to me. He was bright and strong and he loved me. He shouldn't have died."

"You still have two children, Montrose."

Bradford shook his head. "It's not the same."

"Why do you find it so difficult to love your children? Do you blame them for being alive?" Shadow Hawk reached out and took the stone from Bradford's hand and threw it far out into the field. "The stone is gone now, Montrose. You will probably never find it again. But if you look on the ground, you can find others to replace it."

Bradford looked at Shadow Hawk, unable to hide his pain. "I loved that boy. I can't get over losing him."

"I loved my father, but I cannot die because he died. He would not want it that way. It is not the right way."

"What do you mean?"

"It is your duty to love your children."

Bradford shook his head. "I don't know if I can."

Shadow Hawk looked at Bradford, saw his pain, and decided he had gone too far. "I will start with the horses tomorrow. You have some good men. I watched them with the horses."

"Yes, I do. They're not all as difficult as Grady."

"I will not interfere but I will teach the ones who are willing."

"Good," Bradford nodded absently. "Listen, take Christina and walk on up by the lake. You'll probably run into Clay and his friend. It's a pretty walk. Christina will like it."

Shadow Hawk hesitated. He didn't know if this was the best way for Aissa to find out that he would be staying on the ranch for awhile. He shook his head. "I think it is best if you introduce me to your family."

"All right."

They walked into the courtyard. Christina was still there, sitting on the stone bench that surrounded the fountain. Her boots and stockings were off, her bare feet stretched out in front of her. She had her hands folded behind her head and her eyes were closed. Shadow Hawk thought she looked like a little girl. Bradford's boots clicked on the stones of the courtyard, and Christina opened her eyes, quickly pushing her skirt down to cover her ankles.

"I was just enjoying the sun and the sound of the fountain."

"That's what it's here for," Bradford said. "I'll see you two later. Dinner is at six o'clock."

Shadow Hawk sat down next to Christina. "You like it here."

"I think it's the most beautiful place I've ever seen."

Shadow Hawk nodded, leaning forward, resting his elbows on his knees. He stared at a black bug that skittered across the stones and then disappeared underneath one of the flowerpots.

"Are you nervous about seeing Aissa?" Christina asked.

"It has been awhile since we've seen each other." He felt Christina's hand on his shoulder. It was a comforting gesture.

"What's wrong, Shadow Hawk? Why won't you tell me?"

Shadow Hawk sat up, sighing heavily. "I think it's possible that Aissa might be in love with Montrose's son. If that is so, I don't want to force her to return with me."

"But she'll want to go back with you. I know how much she loves you, Shadow Hawk."

Shadow Hawk thought of the previous night, when he and Aissa had made love. He thought that Aissa loved him, but now he wasn't sure. He didn't know what to believe anymore. "I don't want to push her, Christina. That's why I need you to keep quiet. If Aissa does come back with me, I want it to be her own decision."

"I understand."

Shadow Hawk got up and walked to one of the pots, breaking off a bright pink flower. He held it in his fingers a moment then walked back and handed it to Christina. "Here."

Christina blushed slightly and took the flower. "Thank you."

"You should find a man who will bring you flowers all of the time, Christina. A civilized man."

"What does that mean?"

"That means," Shadow Hawk said, sitting back down, "that I am not the man for you. I can never love you, Christina."

Christina twirled the delicate pink flower in her fingers and looked at Shadow Hawk, her eyes glistening slightly when she looked at him. "I know you don't want to hurt me and I thank you for your honesty." She kissed him on the cheek.

Shadow Hawk stood up. "I'm going for a walk. Will you be all right?"

"I'll be fine."

Shadow Hawk nodded, leaving the courtyard. He turned once to look at Christina and found her bent over, her face in her hands. He shook his head, angry with himself for making her cry. But he had no choice. Even if Aissa decided not to go home with him, he would never love Christina. He wasn't sure he could ever love any woman but Aissa.

Shadow Hawk stood in front of the mirror, surveying

his reflection. Montrose had gotten him clean pants and shirts, knowing that he would never get him to wear a suit. Shadow Hawk shook his head and smiled. He wasn't even sure how he'd agreed to this much, but he felt it was the least he could do for Montrose. And there was Aissa. He hadn't seen her since he and Christina had arrived. Even if Montrose's dinner table would be an awkward setting for their reunion, he couldn't put it off any longer.

Shadow Hawk left his room and started down the stairs but stopped, wondering if he should wait for Christina. He knew it would be hard for her to keep pretending that she didn't know Aissa. He crossed the landing and walked down the hall, knocking on the middle door. A moment later it opened and a slight, young woman with blond curly hair looked him up and down, then smiled.

"You must be Shadow Hawk."

"Yes. I just came for Christina."

"She's almost ready. Why don't we wait out on the landing?" She shut the door and took Shadow Hawk's arm, leading him to the area above the stairs. "I've been curious about you ever since I got home. My father has always hated Indians, you know. By the way, my name is Rayna."

"Hello, Rayna."

"How did you get him to hire you?"

Shadow Hawk shrugged. "I saved his life. I suppose he thought he owed it to me."

Rayna laughed. "You don't know my father very well, he doesn't think he owes anyone anything."

"Still, it is good of him to let us stay here. I hope that Christina—"

"She's a delight. We have more people in this house right now than we've had in a long time."

"Your father told me that your brother has a friend staying here, too.

"I think Aissa is more than a friend to Clay. I've seen

the way he looks at her. I think he's in love with her."

Shadow Hawk looked quickly away. "Are you close to your brother?"

"I love Clay more than anything in this world. He's always been my best friend. He's been gone for a long time, but I think he's thinking about settling down now." Rayna turned. "Here comes Christina."

Shadow Hawk looked as Christina walked down the hall. She wore a simple yellow dress and her hair was pulled back in a braid. She was scrubbed clean, and she looked lovely. She was wearing the flower he'd given her behind one ear. He smiled. "You look very pretty, Christina."

"Thank you, so do you," she said approvingly.

Shadow Hawk looked down at the clothes he was wearing and frowned.

Rayna laughed. "Don't be embarrassed, you do look quite handsome."

"I don't know if I'm dressed the way your father intended—"

Rayna held up her hand. "Don't be silly, you're dressed just fine. Let's go down now."

They followed her down the staircase into the dining room. Aissa and Clay were already seated. Their heads were close together, and they were laughing. Shadow Hawk squeezed Christina's hand and leaned close to whisper to her.

"Remember, don't say too much."

"But, Aissa knows—"

"Please, Christina." Shadow Hawk was relieved when she nodded.

Bradford entered the room and sat at the head of the long table, opposite Dorothea, who smiled graciously as everyone stood around the table waiting to be seated. Shadow Hawk found himself wondering how Bradford's wife could breathe with her waist laced in so tightly.

"Sit down everyone," Rayna said as she pulled out the chair and sat between her father and brother.

Clay looked up at his sister. "You look beautiful to-night, Rayna."

Shadow Hawk tried to catch Aissa's eye but her gaze was directed downward as she toyed with a linen napkin. Christina pulled out a chair and sat to Bradford's left. Shadow Hawk remembered too late that a white man would've helped her with her chair. He stood uncertainly, unable to stop glancing across the table at Aissa.

"Sit down," Bradford commanded.

Shadow Hawk realized that everyone but Aissa was looking at him. He sat down quickly, then looked up to find Bradford's son's eyes on him. For an instant their gazes locked then the white man looked away. Shadow Hawk couldn't tell what he had been thinking.

"Excuse me, everyone," Bradford said in a deep voice. "I want to introduce our guests. The one in the pretty yel-low dress is Christina Marley and this is Shadow Hawk. He will be handling the horses for a while."

Dorothea leaned forward. "I'm Dorothea Montrose. I'm very pleased to meet you."

Shadow Hawk smiled and bowed his head slightly. "It is my pleasure, Mrs. Montrose." Shadow Hawk stole a look at Aissa and saw her face suddenly lose its color. But she still didn't look up at him. Bradford began talking again but Shadow Hawk didn't pay attention, he watched Aissa. Bradford continued talking, describing the incident with the wild stallion, but Shadow Hawk didn't pay attention, he was watching Aissa. She was tilting her head, listening. Shadow Hawk felt a cold knot forming in his stomach. He recalled Aissa's awkward run across the pasture and how the white man had helped her up. Bradford's son was speaking to her now and she angled her head as she lis-tened. The knot in Shadow Hawk's stomach tightened. He knew another person who listened that intently, his grandmother, Ocha. She was blind.

"So, you saved my father's life," Clay was saying, holding up a glass of wine to Shadow Hawk, "You're to be commended."

"It was nothing," Shadow Hawk said, barely able to conceal his feelings. This man had taken his woman from him—was he also the one who had put Aissa into danger? Was he responsible for her losing her sight? Aissa had tried to tell him last night, why hadn't he listened? Clay was still looking at him, and Shadow Hawk realized that the white man was waiting for him to say something more. "Your father makes it sound like more than it was."

"I suppose to a brave warrior like you, it was nothing." Clay drank half of the glass of wine.

Shadow Hawk hesitated before he spoke. "I never said I was a brave warrior."

"That's enough, Clay," Bradford admonished. "I thought we could have a nice, friendly dinner for a change."

"When was that ever important to you, Pa?" Clay challenged, finishing the rest of his wine.

"Please, Clayton," Dorothea implored, "let's not argue tonight."

"Come on, Clay, we have guests. Let's try to act civilized, shall we?" Rayna said through clenched teeth. "Christina and Shadow Hawk, this is my brother's friend, Aissa Gerard. And in case you haven't guessed, this is my oafish brother, Clay." Rayna jabbed Clay in the arm with her elbow.

Clay's angry face relaxed, and he smiled at his sister. He looked across the table. "Pleased to meet you, miss. . . ."

"Christina, my name's Christina."

"Pleased to meet you."

"Pleased to meet you, too." Christina looked down the table at Dorothea. "You have a lovely home, Mrs. Montrose."

"Thank you, dear."

"So, Pa, you never did explain why you hired Shadow Hawk to help with the horses. Do you think he can do a better job than all our hands put together?" Clay poured himself another glass of wine.

"From what I saw today, I wouldn't be surprised," Bradford said, glaring at his son.

"I've never talked to an Indian before," Dorothea said shyly.

Shadow Hawk looked at her and smiled politely. She had a friendly face, a kind face, but he could see the unhappiness that was etched there. He knew she wasn't trying to insult him, unlike her son. "Thank you for having us here, Mrs. Montrose. You're very kind."

Dorothea touched her hair and smoothed the bodice of her dress. "You're more than welcome to stay as long as you like, Shadow Hawk."

Shadow Hawk nodded politely and glanced across the table at Aissa, hoping that she could feel his eyes on her.

Dorothea followed Shadow Hawk's gaze. "Oh, Aissa has lost her sight, Shadow Hawk."

"I'm sorry, miss," Shadow Hawk said gently, still looking at Aissa. "How did it happen?"

"It happened in a mining accident," Clay said. He put his arm around Aissa's chair. "Lucky I was there to save her."

"Yes, lucky," Shadow Hawk echoed, not knowing what else to say.

"Let's eat," Bradford said, reaching for the meat platter. "These steaks are better than anything you'd get from here to Kansas City."

Shadow Hawk ate very little, making polite talk with Rayna and Dorothea. Christina, for once, did not talk incessantly. She listened to Bradford and answered him quietly. Whatever she was saying, it made Bradford smile.

Shadow Hawk couldn't take his eyes from Aissa. He

couldn't believe she was blind. She would never again be able to see her primrose or her father's face. Shadow Hawk grimaced, thinking about how hard it would be for Ben to accept this.

"I saw that paint of yours, Shadow Hawk. He's magnificent," Rayna commented.

Shadow Hawk tore his eyes from Aissa. "Thank you. He belonged to my father."

Bradford leaned forward. "Shadow Hawk says that stallion and its sires have been in his tribe for generations. Can you imagine?"

"So you didn't break the stallion yourself?" Clay asked. "Your father did it for you."

"No," Shadow Hawk said slowly, "my father broke the horse for himself. The stallion was his war-horse. He valued it almost as much as his family."

"Sounds pretty much like our family," Clay said, slamming his glass down on the table and picking up the pitcher.

"That's enough, Clayton!" Dorothea admonished. "We have guests in our home and I expect you to behave with some civility. If you cannot, I will have to ask you to leave the table."

The room grew silent. Dorothea's family, especially, was shocked. It was unlike her to speak up in front of strangers.

Clay was obviously surprised. "I'm sorry, Mother."

"I'm not the one you should apologize to," Dorothea said shortly.

Clay stared across the table at Shadow Hawk. "I apologize. I guess I've had too much wine."

Shadow Hawk nodded, accepting the apology.

Shadow Hawk tried to be polite as the conversation went on around him. But all the while he kept looking at Aissa. She had yet to say a word to him, and she kept her head lowered, speaking only when Clay leaned close to say something in her ear.

Bradford pushed his plate away. "I'm going to have a cigar and a glass of brandy. And I'm going to have both in the courtyard. Anyone care to join me?" Bradford was looking at Shadow Hawk.

Shadow Hawk shook his head, declining.

"Why, I'd love to join you for a cigar, Pa," Clay said, standing up, scraping his chair back noisily.

"Will you be all right, Aissa?"

"She'll be fine," Rayna said quickly. "You go on. If she needs anything, I'll help her."

"Have you had enough to eat, Shadow Hawk?" Rayna asked.

"Yes, thank you."

"What about you, Aissa? You're awfully quiet tonight."

"I'm fine, Rayna."

"You must've eaten a lot on your picnic with Clay," Rayna laughed. "You've hardly touched your dinner."

"I'm not hungry."

"Would you like to go to the library? We have a piano. I could play us some music."

"Yes, I'd like that," Shadow Hawk said, standing and walking around the table to Aissa. "May I help you, miss?"

"No, it's all right. I can do it," Aissa stammered, pushing away from the table and standing up. She reached out to find the wall but stumbled on the chair leg next to her. Shadow Hawk steadied her, his arm around her waist.

"Why don't I help you? We'll follow you, Rayna."

Shadow Hawk kept his hand firmly on Aissa's waist as they followed Rayna. "Why didn't you tell me?" he whispered.

"I tried but you wouldn't listen."

Her voice sounded so anguished that Shadow Hawk wanted to take her into his arms and comfort her. "I want to talk to you alone."

Aissa squeezed his hand. "Not now. Please."

"Here we are," Rayna said, waiting for them in the library doorway. "Both of you sit down there," Rayna said, pointing to a small blue sofa.

Shadow Hawk led Aissa to the sofa. She shrugged free of his grasp and sat down. He sat next to her. As Rayna situated herself at the piano, Shadow Hawk looked around the room. There were two floor-to-ceiling bookcases on either side of the door, and they were filled with leather-bound volumes. It occurred to Shadow Hawk that Aissa would enjoy reading all of the books if only she could.

Centered in front of a bookcase was a dark wood pedestal that held a statue of a running horse that had been carved from white stone. Shadow Hawk had never seen anything like it. He wished that he could take it back to his people so that they could see the ice-smooth texture of the polished stone.

Shadow Hawk understood something for the first time—money could buy amazing things in the white world; things of beauty, and things that were wonderfully made. But it could not buy the kind of simplicity that was always part of true beauty.

Rayna's fingers gracefully glided over the keys of the piano and the soft, melodious music touched Shadow Hawk. He looked over at Aissa. Her face was perfectly set, her mouth in a tight line, but her eyes were closed. He moved his hand over and touched hers, lightly. She opened her eyes but didn't turn toward him. He lifted her fingers and wrapped his underneath. He had so much to say to her, but he didn't know where to start. He saw a tear course down her cheek, and he reached over and wiped it away. She turned her head, but she didn't move her hand. He leaned close to her. "Can we talk tonight?"

Aissa shook her head. "I don't know. Why didn't you tell me you were going to work here?" She turned toward him, her eyes staring past his.

Shadow Hawk studied her for a moment. Her eyes were so beautiful; it was impossible for him to believe that she couldn't see. "I didn't plan this. It was an accident."

"I can't leave here right now, Shadow Hawk. I owe Clay so much."

Shadow Hawk tensed at the sound of the other man's name. "You owe Clay?" He moved his mouth so that it was close to her ear. "What about us, Aissa? Don't you owe something to us?"

"Keep your voice down, please," she pleaded.

"Rayna can't hear us and the others aren't here yet. Are you prepared to stay with this man, Aissa? I want to know." But before Aissa could answer, Shadow Hawk heard the voices of the others coming toward the library. He stood up, quickly moving away from Aissa. He walked over to a portrait on the wall.

"That's Russell," Bradford said, coming up behind him.

Shadow Hawk nodded. "He looked like Clay." The similarity was uncanny, he thought.

"No, they were nothing alike."

"So, you've met the prince," Clay said, coming up behind Shadow Hawk and Bradford.

"That's enough, Clay," Bradford said angrily.

"Why, Pa? Haven't you told Shadow Hawk that Russell was the best and brightest child in this family? Why don't you tell him the whole story?"

Shadow Hawk looked at Clay. The pain in Clay's eyes was clearly evident. Surprisingly, Shadow Hawk found himself feeling sorry for him.

"Clay, darling, please don't," Dorothea implored her son. She touched his arm gently. "Come sit down with Aissa. Listen to the music."

Clay hesitated a moment, locking eyes with his father, then turned and followed his mother across the room.

"He's so damned mean and stubborn sometimes I'd like to whip some sense into him."

"He's not a horse, Montrose. He's a man."

"You heard him. He's mean and spiteful."

Shadow Hawk turned to look at the portrait of Russell again.

"Perhaps he says things because you do not let go of the past." Bradford said something, but Shadow Hawk ignored him. He walked to the other side of the room. Rayna was playing another song, and Christina was engaged in conversation with Dorothea. Clay was sitting next to Aissa on the couch, his arm protectively around her. His head was close to hers as it had been all through dinner. Shadow Hawk could barely stand the sight of them together.

When Rayna finished the song, she stood up, curtsied, and smiled. She walked over to Shadow Hawk. "What did you think?"

"I liked it."

"I looked at you while I was playing. You seemed sad."

"I'm just tired," he said, trying to tear his eyes away from Aissa. "Perhaps I was thinking of things gone by."

"Why is it you speak English so well?"

"My grandfather is white. I spent every summer with him when I was a boy. He taught me many things."

"My father likes you." Rayna looked across the room at Bradford. "It's the strangest thing."

"Why?"

"Because you won't take his bullying, just like Clay. And you're an Indian. He should hate you. I don't understand him at all sometimes."

"Do you want him to hate me?"

"No," Rayna said softly, touching Shadow Hawk's arm. "I didn't mean it like that. I just wish he liked Clay more."

"They don't give each other a chance, do they?"

"No," Rayna said, shaking her head. "And they need each other."

Shadow Hawk heard Aissa laugh and again looked over

at the sofa. Clay was playing with a strand of her hair as if it were something he always did. "Would you mind if I went for a walk? I'm not used to. . . ." Shadow Hawk didn't know what to say, and he could see Rayna following his glance.

"I'll come with you." Rayna put her arm through Shadow Hawk's.

"No, you don't have to do that."

"I want to." Rayna steered Shadow Hawk out of the house and into the courtyard. They walked down the steps to the yard. "I like it here at night. When Clay and Russell and I were little, we used to sneak out when our parents were asleep and lay down in the grass and look up at the stars. Once we all fell asleep and Pa found us out here the next morning." She laughed. "When he was through yelling at us, we each got a beating. None of us could sit down for days."

Shadow Hawk laughed. "Can I ask you something, Rayna?"

"Ask me anything."

"Why is it so hard for your father to forget about Russell?"

Rayna stopped, tilting her head back and looking up at the sky. "I've wondered about it for years and I think I finally have it figured out. Russell's like a dream for Pa, a son who never failed, never really disobeyed. He's as good as Pa's imagination can make him and he always will be."

"He could be proud of you and your brother if he wanted to be. You aren't failures."

"To him, we are." Rayna started walking again. "What about you? You spoke about your father at dinner. You were close to him?"

Shadow Hawk nodded. "My father was my greatest teacher. I was with him when he died." Shadow Hawk could still recall vividly that cold winter day when the Kiowas attacked him and his father. His father had saved his life but, in so doing, had died.

"I'm sorry."

"Do not be sorry. He died like a great warrior. He died an honorable death."

"And your mother?"

"My mother. . . ." Shadow Hawk thought about Broken Moon. He wished she were here now. She could certainly offer him some words of wisdom. "My mother is a very wise and strong woman."

"Don't you miss her?"

"I miss her, but her words are with me even when I travel far from her."

"And what about Aissa?"

Shadow Hawk stopped. Was his love for Aissa that obvious? "What do you mean?"

"I saw you looking at her. What is she to you, Shadow Hawk?"

"She is nothing to me." He continued walking, attempting to ignore the question.

"You're a terrible liar. Remind me to play poker with you sometime."

"And you're a very direct woman." Shadow Hawk took Rayna's arm from his.

"Yes, I've been told that before. So, are you going to tell me about Aissa?"

Shadow Hawk shook his head. "Is it so easy for you to see what is inside my heart?"

Rayna nodded. "You're in love with her, aren't you?"

"We were to be married," Shadow Hawk said simply.

"What happened?"

"I was with my people. When I returned, I found Aissa had been kidnapped. It took me a long time to find her and I suppose it was during that time that she met your brother."

"Oh my," Rayna said. "I'm sorry. I didn't realize."

"I tracked her here." Shadow Hawk glanced back at the

house. "I never knew she was blind."

"When you came here today, why did you pretend that you didn't know her?"

"I saw her with your brother. She seems to care for him. I don't want to force her to come back with me if she doesn't want to. We planned to be married, but everything seems to have changed."

"And you're just going to let Clay fall in love with her?"

"I cannot blame him for that. I know what it is like to love Aissa."

Rayna shook her head. "I love my brother very much, and I'd do just about anything for him. But you have to understand the way he thinks. He's a gambler, he'll play every card that's dealt him. If he wants Aissa, he'll do anything to keep her. Even use her blindness. He'll force her to rely on him just so she'll stay here."

"Perhaps that's what she wants." Shadow Hawk started walking toward the corrals, and Rayna fell in beside him. "Do you know what caused her blindness?"

"There was an accident in the mine, a cave-in. She suffered a head injury. Clay saved her life. Aissa says she was ready to give up, but Clay talked her into going on, into trying to escape and coming here."

"She is fortunate he was there." Shadow Hawk's voice held little resolve. He stood on the bottom rung of the corral and leaned on the top, looking at the horses.

Rayna climbed onto the top rail and sat down facing Shadow Hawk "Doesn't it make you mad to see them together?"

"No."

"I told you, you're a terrible liar. I saw your face."

Shadow Hawk smiled. This was a woman he could easily like. "Yes, it makes me angry," he admitted.

"Then what're you going to do?"

"I will be patient. She cannot see me, but she can hear my voice. We have shared many things together. I will have to remind her of those things."

"You are going to fight for her."

"I will not fight your brother, Rayna. He is already fighting a battle."

"With my father."

"Yes. He is in much pain, I can see that. But I love Aissa. I cannot leave here unless I know for sure that she no longer loves me." Shadow Hawk felt Rayna rest her head on his shoulder for a moment.

"I don't think the poor girl stands a chance."

Shadow Hawk grinned, unable to resist Rayna's charm. But he hoped she was right about Aissa. He couldn't bear the thought of leaving here without her.

Chapter Twelve

Shadow Hawk had spent most of the night walking. By gray dawn, he found himself near the corrals. The big buckskin stood wakeful and alert in his corral.

"That is good, my friend," Shadow Hawk greeted the animal. "You do not sleep through the approach of a stranger." Shadow Hawk kept talking in a low, soothing voice as he climbed the corral fence and dropped silently to the ground. The buckskin tossed his head but the tenseness and fear that had been in his eyes before was gone. He took a tentative step toward Shadow Hawk.

"Ah. You remember me." Shadow Hawk moved toward the stallion, careful not to startle him. He ran his hands lightly over the animal's smooth coat. "It is the time to accept new things, my friend." Shadow Hawk knew he was talking to himself as much as he was talking to the stallion. The night of walking had not resolved his feelings. He knew he would be patient. He also knew it would not be easy.

Without quite realizing that he was going to do it, Shadow Hawk put one arm over the buckskin's back. When the animal didn't flinch away from his weight, he swung up. The buckskin snorted and shifted nervously, but he didn't buck and didn't try to run. He kept his weight perfectly balanced, aware that any clumsiness on his part would destroy the fragile trust between them. After a time, the buckskin took a step forward. Then another. Shadow Hawk felt him experimenting with the new weight on his back, and with the new idea that he might allow it to stay there. After a moment, the buckskin lowered his head and broke into an easy canter, veering into a wide circle. Shadow Hawk made no attempt to stop, or even to guide the horse. He felt the buckskin's strength and hoped that one day he would be able to find out how fast he really was.

As the sun turned the eastern horizon pink and gold the buckskin slowed to a trot, then to a walk, then stopped in the center of the corral, his head high. Shadow Hawk slid from his back and stood beside him, facing the sunrise.

"If I hadn'ta seen that for myself, I woulda called anyone who told me about it a damned liar."

Shadow Hawk turned to see the old cowboy Bradford called Jeb, leaning against the corral. "Do not come into the corral," Shadow Hawk said as he walked toward the man.

"Look, boy, I ain't that stupid. I saw how hard you worked to gain that buckskin's trust."

Shadow Hawk grabbed the top rail and vaulted over. Jeb had iron gray hair and a three-day stubble of beard. There was something direct and honest in his eyes that Shadow Hawk liked immediately.

"You s'pose you could do what you just did with that horse again?"

Shadow Hawk nodded.

"You're sure?"

Shadow Hawk nodded again.

"Sure enough that if I placed a little wager I wouldn't be riskin' my money?"

"How much money are you going to wager?"

Jeb shrugged. "I got some stashed away. If you break another horse like you just broke that one, I'll bet what I have and split the winnings with you."

Shadow Hawk watched the buckskin as he walked around the corral. "Why would you do that?"

"I like you."

"You do not even know me."

"Any man who can break a horse without hurting him is a good man. I know you well enough."

Shadow Hawk looked at Jeb. "It doesn't matter to you that I am Comanche?"

Jeb shrugged. "Hell, why should I care whether or not you're Comanche? It don't make me no nevermind. I wouldn't give a damn if you were a dirty Apache."

Shadow Hawk grinned widely. "That's very good, Jeb, because only my father was Comanche. My mother is Apache."

Jeb shrugged. "Like I said, if you can break horses like that, I don't care where you came from."

Shadow Hawk extended his hand. "My name is Shadow Hawk."

"I'm Jeb. Good to meet you."

"You have been with Montrose a long time?"

"Seems like a lifetime," Jeb muttered. "Mr. Montrose is a hard man sometimes. Oh, don't get me wrong, he's good enough to the hands, it's his own family that he mistreats."

"Were you here when the oldest son died?"

"I was here." Jeb reached into his pocket and took out a knife. He pulled out the blade and dragged the point underneath a fingernail.

"What happened?"

Jeb examined his clean nail and moved the knife to the next. "Hunting accident. A mountain lion attacked the boys. Russell was thrown from his horse and was attacked by the cat. Clay didn't have time to get a shot off before the cat killed his brother."

"And Montrose blames Clay?"

"Yep, and it'll never change. He doted on that boy." Jeb

looked around. "You best get on up to the house and get yourself some breakfast. The hands are starting to stir, and they don't much like the sight of you. Come on back later, but don't show that trick of yours. I want to make sure I make some wagers first."

"Don't let anyone ride the buckskin yet. I don't want him picking up any bad habits."

"I'll make sure they stay away from him. Go on now."

Shadow Hawk went back up to the house and went inside. He didn't want to eat with the others; he didn't want to see Clay and Aissa together again. So he walked to the kitchen. Elaina and Lita were already busy making breakfast. The heavy smell of *chorizo* hung in the air, and he gratefully accepted a cup of coffee from Elaina. As he turned, he saw Aissa standing next to the large adobe oven, her hands held in front of it.

"Here you are, *señorita,*" Lita said, handing Aissa a warm biscuit. "You eat now. You are much too skinny."

"Thank you," Aissa said, taking a bite.

Shadow Hawk walked over to the oven, standing next to Aissa. "Would you like something to eat, *señor?*" Lita asked.

"I'll take one of those biscuits, please." Shadow Hawk took the biscuit and nodded his thanks. "You're up early," he said to Aissa.

"Yes, ever since the accident, I can't tell the difference between night and day. I don't sleep well anymore."

Shadow Hawk looked at her. Aissa did look tired. He didn't want to make things worse for her. "I just came in here to get something to eat. I'll leave you alone."

"No, wait," Aissa said, turning toward him and extending her hand. "Why don't we have breakfast together? We can eat in the courtyard."

"What about Clay?"

"He won't be up for awhile."

"All right." Shadow Hawk went to the table, took two

plates, and handed them to Elaina. "Could you please put some food on here? The *señorita* and I will be eating in the courtyard."

"Sí, senor."

Shadow Hawk waited impatiently until Elaina was done filling the plates, then he walked to Aissa. "Hold onto my arm." He led Aissa outside to the stone bench, waiting until she was seated. "Here is your plate," he said, making sure she had it securely in her hands before he let go. He sat down next to her. He watched as Aissa felt for the fork. It took her several tries before she was able to get a bite to her mouth.

"Please stop staring at me." She laid her fork down on the plate. "I am blind, and that's not going to change."

"I'm sorry," he said, his voice barely audible. "I just wish I could help you."

"Why? So I would look at you and remember."

"What's wrong with that? Is it so bad to remember, Aissa?"

Aissa slammed the plate down on the bench beside her, sighing deeply. "It's not bad to remember, it's just painful." She turned her head away from him.

Shadow Hawk reached over and took her chin. "Look at me."

"I can't look at you!" she shouted, her voice shrill. "I can never see you again."

Shadow Hawk forced Aissa to turn toward him. He moved his head close to hers. "You can see me, Aissa." He took her hands and put them on his face. Slowly, fingers trembling, Aissa felt his forehead and the line of his nose, his prominent cheekbones, and the curve of his mouth. Her palm rested on his chin, her fingers still touching his mouth. Shadow Hawk gently kissed her fingers, wanting desperately to take her into his arms. Tears formed in her incredible eyes, but she quickly wiped at them, pulling her hand away.

"Is your hair still short?"

"It's longer now, almost to my shoulders. Feel." He put her hand up to feel his hair.

"And I can tell by your silent steps that you still haven't gotten used to white man's boots." She smiled when she said it.

"No, I don't think I'll ever be able to wear boots."

"So," she said, sitting up straight, her hands folded in her lap, "how is Christina?"

"Christina is . . ." Shadow Hawk fumbled for the right word. "Christina."

Aissa smiled. "Is she still so enthusiastic about everything?"

"Everything, especially this house. I think she'd like to live here forever." Shadow Hawk felt like an awkward young boy. He couldn't think of anything to say.

"How is my father?" Aissa turned away slightly, and he knew she was struggling to maintain her composure.

Shadow Hawk knew how much Aissa loved her father. "He misses you. You know better than anyone how much he loves you, Aissa."

Aissa nodded. "I know," she mumbled, choking on her tears.

Shadow Hawk put his arm around her and drew her close. "Why won't you let me take you home to Gerard?"

"No," Aissa said, sitting up. "I don't want him to see me like this."

"Like what?"

"I'm helpless. I can't do anything for myself. If it hadn't been for Clay, I would've died down in Mexico."

Shadow Hawk tensed at the sound of Clay's name. He dropped his arm from Aissa's shoulders. "Then have Clay take you to see Gerard."

"Shadow Hawk, I—"

"You're not being fair to him, Aissa. You're wasting time feeling sorry for yourself. Your father loves you, he doesn't care if you're blind."

"He would care. I wouldn't be able to do all the things I normally do for him. Our lives would be so different."

"Gerard doesn't need you to wait on him, he needs to know that you are well."

Aissa shook her head. "I can't. I can't go back. Not now."

Shadow Hawk stood up. "You are a very selfish person, Aissa. How can you deny Gerard the one thing he cherishes most in this world?"

"Don't, please."

"But it is easy here, is it not? You have Clay to wait on you and make you feel safe. And if he grows weary of the task, there are servants who can do it for him. You never have to go out into the world again if you don't want to."

"Shadow Hawk—"

"You know it would be different with Gerard and me. We both love you too much to let you give up. We would force you to rely on your own strength."

"Stop it!" Aissa shouted, covering her face with her hands. She was silent for a moment and then took a deep breath. "You don't know what I've been through, neither does my father. You have no idea what it is like to live in constant darkness."

"And Clay does? Clay understands this?"

"Clay was there when it happened. He saved my life. He willed me to go on when I was ready to give up. I owe him my life, Shadow Hawk. Can't you understand that?"

Shadow Hawk squatted down in front of Aissa, resting his arms on her knees. "Can't you understand that when I found out you had been kidnapped, I went to Mexico to search for you. When I tracked you down at the mine and found out you had left with a man, I was scared. I could only hope that the man was kinder than Grimes." Shadow Hawk stopped, wanting to put his head in Aissa's lap, wanting to wrap his arms around her. He sighed. "Tell me why you have chosen this man over me, Aissa. I do not understand it." His voice broke slightly. "When I left to search for my people, we were planning to be married. Have you forgotten so soon the many times we were together? Can you feel such passion for another man?" He gave into his impulse and rested his head on her lap, knowing that she might push him away. But she did not. Instead, he felt her fingers stroke his hair, and he closed his eyes. "I love you, Aissa. I cannot leave this place and forget about you." He lifted his head and took her hand, placing it over his heart. "You are here. You will always be here."

Aissa began to cry and Shadow Hawk leaned forward, pulling her into his arms. He held her, stroking her hair, kissing away her tears. But she pulled away suddenly.

"I can't go back with you, Shadow Hawk."

"Aissa. . . ." He stopped as he looked at her face. Her eyes were filled with tears and her cheeks were red. She had almost come to him, and it had scared her. He would have to be patient. "All right," he said gently, standing up. "You must do what is best for you." He walked out of the courtyard, not looking back.

The pain in his heart was almost more than he could bear. He knew Aissa so well. She was a proud woman and she didn't want to burden either him or her father, but he would have to teach her again the meaning of love. It mattered nothing to him that she couldn't see, but she didn't understand that. He would make her love him all over again.

Shadow Hawk walked over to the corral, stepping onto the bottom rung and leaning on the top. He watched as the cowboy inside mounted and attempted to ride a chestnut mare. The chestnut was quick on her feet. When she bucked, she doubled back on herself, and the rider could not anticipate her moves quickly enough. In moments, he was sitting in the hard dirt, wiping blood off his chin and grinning ruefully.

"So, I thought you was gonna show us some Indian tricks on how to break horses," one of the cowboys said to Shadow Hawk.

"Sometimes it is best to watch."

"Oh, I get it, you watch and learn from us, and then you convince the boss that you taught us everything. That's pretty darned smart."

Shadow Hawk looked at the man, his gaze never wavering. "What is it you and your friends have to teach me?"

The man hesitated, looking at some of the other men and then back at Shadow Hawk. "I saw you talking to that horse yesterday. That don't mean nothin'. Only thing that matters is when you get on him and ride."

"And you can do this with a wild horse?"

"I can break any horse. Hasn't been one that's stopped me yet."

"And the buckskin?"

The man shrugged. "I ain't had a chance to work with him much. If I could, I could break him."

"You wouldn't want to make a wager on that, would you, Frank?" Jeb walked from around the other side of the corral to stand between Shadow Hawk and Frank.

"What kind of wager?"

"Well, I was thinking along the lines of five hundred dollars," Jeb said casually.

"Five hundred dollars! Hell, that's more than I make in a whole year working here."

"Yeah, but it's not more than you make playing poker, Frank. Course, if you don't have any confidence that you can break that buckskin, then we won't worry about it."

Shadow Hawk looked at Frank. He was worried, and he had every right to be. Five hundred dollars was a lot of money.

"What about him?" Frank said, pointing to Shadow Hawk.

"He never said he was wagering, I said I was wagering. The only thing he's gonna do is break that buckskin."

"That's not right, Jeb."

"What's not right?"

"Bettin' against your own kind."

"Now you tell me, Frank, what's my own kind? Just so's I know."

"Hell, Jeb, you're bettin' for a Comanche against me. It ain't right."

"Is it a bet or not?" Jeb asked.

"I'll take a part of that," one of the cowboys said.

"Me, too," another added.

"It's only a wager if Frank is willin' to participate." Jeb stared at the younger cowboy. "Well, come on, Frank. You're always tellin' everyone what a great cowboy you are. I think I even heard you say once you broke a hundred horses in one week." Jeb looked at the other men. "Did any of you other boys hear that story?"

"You tell that story every time we play poker, Frank," one of the cowboys said.

"Come on, Frank. He's just a Comanche. You can beat him."

Frank looked at the men then jammed his hands in his pockets. "All right, it's a wager. Who gets first crack at the buckskin?"

"I'll flip a coin," Jeb said.

"Is there a time limit?" Frank asked, eyeing Shadow Hawk nervously.

Jeb shrugged. "I'll give you each one hour."

Frank kicked at the dirt. "One hour! That's not enough time. What if he gets to work with him first and he breaks him, I'll never get a chance."

"He might get to work with him first and not break

him. That'll just wear him down for you, Frank."

"I have to ride him for how long?"

"Ten seconds oughta do it." Jeb looked at Shadow Hawk. "What do you think, Shadow Hawk? Are you up to it?"

Shadow Hawk nodded. "I will do it."

"Good. Tomorrow morning right here. Get lots of rest tonight, Frank. You'll need it."

Shadow Hawk shook his head as the cowboys walked away. "You do know that it is possible for me to lose."

Jeb's eyes widened. "What do you mean? You told me this morning that you could break that durned buckskin. Something happen between then and now to change that?"

"I said I could break him if no one else rode him. You should have made the wager on two different horses." Jeb slapped his forehead. "Five hundred dollars. That's my traveling money. I been saving up to go visit my daughter and her family in San Francisco."

Shadow Hawk lowered his head. "Then I will speak to the buckskin tonight. Perhaps if I explain the situation to him, he will not be angry with me. Perhaps he will let me ride him tomorrow."

Jeb spit and turned away. For a long moment, he stared out at the horizon. "That's not funny. You're makin' fun of me."

Shadow Hawk grinned. "I am sorry, Jeb. I do not want you to lose your money, but you should have waited."

Jeb shook his head. "Doesn't matter now. I can't back down."

Shadow Hawk slapped Jeb's shoulder. "Then I will do my best." He walked away, smiling as he heard Jeb mumbling to himself. Shadow Hawk went to the far corral and unlatched the gate. The paint walked up to him, pressing its head against Shadow Hawk's chest. Shadow Hawk ran his hands along the stallion's head and stroked the silky forelock. The stallion whickered softly. "What is it, old friend? Are you happy to see me?" Shadow Hawk walked to the stallion's side, running his hand along his neck and patting his shoulder. He laid his head against the stallion's withers for a short moment, remembering the times as a boy he had watched his father mount this fine animal and ride off to the hunt or to war. Sometimes those days seemed like yesterday, other times like a lifetime ago.

"He's a magnificent animal."

Shadow Hawk didn't turn. He recognized Clay's voice but he'd been so deep in thought, he hadn't heard his approach. "Yes, he is a fine stallion."

"May I ride him?"

Shadow Hawk patted the stallion once again and turned to look at Clay, slowly shaking his head. "No one rides this stallion but me."

Clay swung his leg up and over until he was sitting on the top rail, facing Shadow Hawk. "You think you're the only one who can handle him?"

"I did not say that." Shadow Hawk ran his hand down the stallion's left foreleg, gently bringing it up so that he could check the hoof for stones.

"I still don't understand why this horse is so important to you. It's just a horse."

Shadow Hawk turned around and bent to lift up the stallion's left rear leg. Again he checked for stones. He did the same thing on the right side and then stood, scratching the horse underneath its neck. "This stallion is more than just a horse to me."

"Why, because your father gave it to you?"

"Yes, because my father gave it to me." He patted the stallion once more on the neck and walked to the gate, opening it and walking out. He paused only to latch the gate and then started across the yard. He hadn't gone far when he heard Clay calling after him.

"Wait up, I'll walk with you."

Shadow Hawk didn't wait, and he didn't slow his pace.

He headed down the tree-lined road and absently grabbed at the low-hanging leaves as he walked by. He could hear Clay walking behind him. The white man kept pace with him, never saying a word. When they got to the end of the road, Shadow Hawk stopped. "What do you want to say to me?"

"I know about you and Aissa. Why're you trying to keep it such a secret?"

"She told you about us?"

"In the camp she did. She even said your name once but I had forgotten it. I pretty much guessed you were the one last night. Why don't you just come right out and say you are here to take her back home? I don't get it."

"It is Aissa's decision whether she stays here or goes back home." Shadow Hawk started walking again, heading out into one of the pastures.

"Shadow Hawk, wait a minute." Clay caught up to him and stood, facing him. "I know you love her, so do I. Where does that leave us?"

Shadow Hawk regarded the man in front of him. He didn't like Clay Montrose, but he didn't hate him either. He just didn't want Aissa to fall in love with him. "That is not up to me. That is up to Aissa." Shadow Hawk started walking again, trying to put distance between him and Clay. He stopped when he reached the top of a hill that overlooked the pasture and the ranch. It was beautiful here, peaceful and serene. But after a moment, he saw Clay at the base of the hill. Shadow Hawk turned, refusing to watch the white man as he walked toward him.

Clay didn't stop until he was beside Shadow Hawk. He stood silently for a time, then spoke. "It's something, isn't it? My brother and I used to come here all the time. We'd pretend we were soldiers fighting Indians."

Shadow Hawk looked at Clay sharply. He couldn't tell if he was trying to insult him or not. "And you won, I suppose. You killed all of the Indians."

"No, sometimes we lost." Clay walked a few steps, bending down to pick some wild grass. He ran his fingers along the fine shaft. "You have a brother?" Clay asked, sticking the grass in his mouth and chewing on the stem.

"Yes, I have a brother."

"Have you two always been close?"

"We were not always brothers. We adopted Brave Heart into our family when I was fourteen years old."

Clay looked surprised. "How did you feel about that? Were you jealous?"

Shadow Hawk reached down and freed a moth from a spider's web. "It was my idea to adopt him. He was a small boy and mistreated by his family. He was seldom given food. He was the weak one of the tribe." Shadow Hawk thought for a moment and looked at Clay. "Have you ever seen wolves attack a herd of buffalo? They do not attack the bulls or even the full-grown cows, they attack the sick and the weak. That is the way it was with my brother. Everyone singled him out."

"Except for you."

Shadow Hawk looked at Clay, expecting to see resentment or anger in his eyes but there was none. He seemed sincere. "Brave Heart was a friend, and he had great courage for one so small. Many a time he stood with me against the others who made fun of my white blood."

"Then he is your true brother," Clay said simply.

"Yes." Shadow Hawk found himself wondering if there were more to this white man than he had thought. The idea of liking this man made Shadow Hawk uneasy. He walked along the hill, staring down at the valley. "This is good land. It gives of itself." He glanced back to see Clay smile and nod.

"Yeah, I never really realized how much I missed it until I was a prisoner in that damned mine." Clay shook his head. "I couldn't wait to get back here."

Shadow Hawk couldn't help but understand what Clay

meant. Many times Shadow Hawk wished he could go back and see the land where he was raised as a Comanche. He sometimes still had dreams about the river where he and Brave Heart had swum as boys. "Rayna feels this way about the land also?"

Clay nodded. "Maybe she loves it more. Rayna's never allowed herself any other life but this one. Hell, it's not like she isn't pretty or anything. She's always had one beau or another, but she could never leave. It's the land and my father. He keeps her here."

"I don't understand."

"My father can be a very charming man when he wants to be. You've seen that side of him. But he can also be a bastard. He's treated my mother badly in many ways, and he's never much respected Rayna's ability, even though she already half-runs this place. And me," he shrugged his shoulders, "hell, you've seen how he feels about me."

"Montrose is a bitter man."

"You could say that."

Clay started back down the hill. Shadow Hawk hesitated then caught up with him. "I didn't plan to meet your father. It was something that just happened."

"Hell, I don't care. Bradford Montrose does what he pleases, and everybody else be damned." Clay stopped, pointing over into the pasture. "Do you see that? That's something over there."

Shadow Hawk looked. He did see something moving, something that didn't belong. He started forward but stopped when Clay held onto his arm.

"Wait. Could be a rustler. They'd just as soon shoot you as look at you."

"It is not a man," Shadow Hawk said with confidence born of years of experience.

"You're sure?"

"Yes. I think it's an animal." Shadow Hawk started walking and then began to run. The eerie, ugly sound of a vulture overhead made him run faster. Why hadn't he heard the vulture before? Where had his senses gone?

Clay kept pace with him, and Shadow Hawk could see before they reached the pasture that it was a horse lying on its side. He slowed down. He could hear the animal's labored breathing from where he was, and he could see its large, frantic eyes as the animal struggled to lift its head.

"Jesus," Clay muttered, coming to a stop next to Shadow Hawk. "What the hell happened?"

"Mountain lion," Shadow Hawk said without hesitation. Clay had gone silent, and Shadow Hawk looked at him. He realized how difficult this must be for the white man, what memories this must bring back. "Are you all right?"

"Me?" Clay responded nervously, rubbing his hands together. "I'm fine. Let's take care of the mare." Clay looked around. "She just had a foal. I bet the bastard went for the foal."

Shadow Hawk walked around the horse. Clay was right. Shadow Hawk could see the bloody trail where the cat had dragged off the foal. The mare had given a good fight. The grass was trampled where she had tried to kill the cat, but the cat had been too cunning. And it had had the advantage of the darkness and the surrounding trees and rocks. The cat had probably jumped onto the mare's back, clawing and chewing until the horse was too weak to fight any longer. There was a deep gash along the right side of the mare's neck, and there were deep cuts in the right side of her stomach. The mare nickered pathetically, and Shadow Hawk knelt next to her, slowly reaching out to calm her. She tried to raise her head again, but Shadow Hawk forced it down, talking in a soothing voice to the animal.

Then he glanced up at Clay. "Go back to the house. Bring me a large needle and thread. Ask your mother. She will know what I need. And bring me something to clean off the blood."

Clay was shaking his head. "You can't save her. She's half-dead already."

Shadow Hawk looked up at Clay. "I know this is your horse, but let me try to save her. If she suffers too greatly, I will put her out of her misery."

Clay looked at the mare and then at Shadow Hawk. He nodded. "All right."

"Wait. There is a leather pouch in my bedgear. Bring it. It has my medicine."

"Whatever you say."

After Clay had left, Shadow Hawk sat down on the ground next to the mare's head, stroking the area between her eyes and rubbing her nose. "I promise you, I will not let you suffer." He then began to sing a song in Comanche he had learned as a boy. It was a chant his father had taught him just before he had gone on his first hunt alone. He had spent the night by himself in the woods and he had been frightened. "I will not leave you. I am by your side. Take comfort in my presence." Shadow Hawk repeated the words over and over, perhaps for himself as well as for the horse.

He heard the riders before he saw them and glanced up in surprise. Clay had brought Jeb, Christina, and Aissa. Shadow Hawk frowned for a moment when he saw Aissa with them and then he pushed her from his mind.

Clay dismounted and handed Shadow Hawk a long, sturdy needle and a spool of thick thread. "Here, Mother said this is what you'd need. She's already threaded it."

Shadow Hawk nodded. "Hold her head, Clay. Jeb, you be ready to help him."

"You sure you want to do this, boy?" Jeb asked, kneeling next to Shadow Hawk.

"Yes. I must try."

"Can I do anything to help?" Aissa asked.

Shadow Hawk started to dismiss her but realized this would be the perfect time for her to realize just how capable she still was.

"I think you and Christina should stay out of the way, Aissa," Clay said.

"No, I want her help," Shadow Hawk said, taking Aissa's hand and pulling her down next to him. "I want you to hold the wound together while I sew. Can you do that?"

"Yes."

"Good. Clay, did you bring my leather pouch?"

"Right here." Clay tossed it to Shadow Hawk.

He turned and looked at Christina. "I want you to make a poultice out of this. There's a creek back that way where you can get some water." He tossed the pouch to Christina. She caught it and turned, walking fast in the direction of the creek.

Shadow Hawk looked around. Clay sat next to the mare's head. If he was shaken it didn't show. Jeb's seamed face was calm and determined. Aissa had her head tilted in the odd way that meant she was listening with her whole attention. Shadow Hawk reached up once more and patted the mare's nose, speaking to her in Comanche. Then he nodded to the others and took Aissa's hands and put them on the edges of the gash in the mare's neck. The mare tried to raise her head but Clay held her down, and Aissa held the skin together while Shadow Hawk sewed deftly and quickly.

The mare lay remarkably still, although her eyes were wide with fear. Once Shadow Hawk had closed the wound on the neck, he took Aissa's hand and they moved so that he could focus his attention on the gashes on the mare's stomach. With Aissa gently pressing the ragged edges of the cut together, Shadow Hawk sewed the wound closed. Everyone worked together, holding the mare still. When Shadow Hawk was finished, Christina applied some of the poultice mixture to each wound. Then everyone stood back, Clay taking Aissa's hand. Shadow Hawk stroked the mare under her neck: "You must get up now. If you stay here, you will die."

Shadow Hawk stood up, watching as the mare raised her head and struggled to get to her feet. Her anguished cries rang out in the still air, and Shadow Hawk felt Aissa's hand on his arm. He glanced down, her beautiful face was twisted in sympathy for the mare. Hoofbeats caught his attention and he looked up. Montrose was riding toward them at a gallop. He pulled up sharply, his horse dancing nervously at the smell of the blood and the cat.

"Dorothea told me." He looked at the mare as she tried again to stand up and failed. "We have to put her out of her misery, Shadow Hawk," Bradford said, shaking his head. "It's not fair to her."

"Give her a chance, Montrose. Please."

"She'll never make it, boy," Jeb said sympathetically.

"Give her a chance."

"Please, Mr. Montrose," Aissa pleaded, squeezing Shadow Hawk's arm as she spoke. "Let Shadow Hawk try."

Shadow Hawk walked to the mare, squatting down next to her head. He stroked it gently. "It is time. You must get up now. You are strong. You are not ready to die." The mare nickered lightly and attempted to get her feet beneath her. Shadow Hawk tried to steady her, hooking one arm around her neck. Without saying a word, Clay moved next to Shadow Hawk and set his shoulder against the mare's side. Soon everyone, even Aissa, was pushing, encouraging, willing the mare to get to her feet. She scrambled wildly to gain her balance, to fight the pain that could so easily overwhelm her and keep her down. The gallant mare managed to right herself and to avoid stepping on anyone. At last, with the help of Shadow Hawk and the others, she staggered to her feet and stood, her head high as she swayed, breathing hard.

Shadow Hawk walked around the mare, grinning,

stroking her, careful to avoid touching the wounds. "Yes, you are strong and courageous. You would make a good Comanche war-horse." He turned and saw Clay looking at him, a smile on his face. "What?"

"A Comanche war-horse?" Clay raised an eyebrow.

Shadow Hawk made an impatient gesture. "This mare would not flinch in battle. She showed great courage today."

"I think you should have her," Clay said, then looked at Bradford. "What do you think, Pa?"

"I think that's a good idea. If this mare makes it, she belongs to you, Shadow Hawk. She probably won't have anything to do with anyone else now."

"Thank you," Shadow Hawk said simply. He walked to Clay's horse and got a rope. He looped it around the mare's neck loosely. "I will walk her back to the ranch."

"That's going to take awhile. She's not in real good shape," Bradford said.

"I do not mind."

"Damn that cat," Bradford said, looking up toward the hills. "You're going to have to go after it, Clay."

Clay followed his father's gaze. "It's probably gone now, Pa. I won't be able to find it."

Bradford glanced sharply at his son. "It's had a taste of blood. It'll be back. Do you want us to lose more livestock? I want you to go after that cat, damn it!"

Shadow Hawk saw the tenseness in Clay's face. He also saw the way Montrose was pushing his son. "I will go with him, Montrose. I have tracked cats before."

"I don't need your help," Clay said defensively. "I can get the cat myself."

Shadow Hawk looked at him, his expression calm. "I want to help destroy the cat that did this to my mare. If you will let me, I would like to go with you."

Clay looked up at the hills again and prodded. "Okay. We'll set out in the morning."

"Well, we best be getting back," Bradford said.

Shadow Hawk looked at Bradford. There had been a cold satisfaction in the man's voice.

"I'll help you mount up, Aissa," Clay said, taking her hand.

She stopped. "No, I'd like to walk if you don't mind." She hesitated. "I'll walk back with Shadow Hawk."

Clay looked from Aissa to Shadow Hawk and slowly nodded his head. "All right, I'll see you back at the ranch. I'll take your horse."

"Thank you."

"Do you need any more help, Shadow Hawk?" Christina asked. She held out Shadow Hawk's medicine bundle.

"No, thank you," Shadow Hawk said and tied the pouch to his belt. He looked up and saw Christina looking side-long at Clay. "Would you mind if Christina rode back with you?"

Clay looked startled and then smiled. "No, I'd welcome the company."

Jeb hung back as the others rode away. He shook his head. "Damndest thing I ever saw. You're gonna make me a fortune when you break that buckskin."

Shadow Hawk smiled. "I won't be able to do it until we find the cat."

"Frank'll wait." Jeb grinned and nodded his horse, glancing back once to wave as he rode away.

Shadow Hawk stood with the mare, stroking her, gently pulling at the rope, trying to start her walking. As the mare began to move, Shadow Hawk wanted to take Aissa's hand but he didn't. Instead, he watched her. She stood still for a moment and then, listening, followed the sound of the mare's hooves on the soft dirt. He led the mare over the smoothest path he could find. Aissa followed a pace back, a hand on the mare's shoulder. The mare stopped and staggered slightly, and Shadow Hawk let her rest.

"Is she all right?" Aissa asked.

"I don't know if she'll make it. She's very weak."

"There's a stream not far from here. Maybe she'll drink."

Shadow Hawk nodded. "We can try. We'll walk this way." Shadow Hawk led the mare and again Aissa rested her hand on the mare's neck. "There's the stream." Shadow Hawk led the mare to the water. She extended her head, shifting from foreleg to foreleg in an effort to find a comfortable position. "She is thirsty." Shadow Hawk slipped the rope from her neck. "Stand back, Aissa. I think she'll do better on her own."

The mare inched forward, stepping cautiously in the mud. Once she was close enough, she spraddled her forelegs and lowered her head, sucking greedily at the cold water.

"Help me to the edge. I want to wash my hands."

Shadow Hawk took Aissa's elbow, leading her to the stream. She dropped down to her knees and put her hands into the swiftly running water, rubbing them together. She splashed water on her face and cupped her hands so she could drink. Shadow Hawk watched Aissa as she sat back. She was dressed in a blue skirt and a white blouse. Her hair was tied at the nape of her neck by a blue satin ribbon. On the hem of her skirt he noticed spatters of blood from the mare. She had missed one smudge of dirt on her face and he smiled. He had never seen a woman more beautiful than Aissa in his life.

Shadow Hawk knelt next to her, using a handful of sand from the creek bottom to scrub his hands and arms. He drank and splashed his face. He sat down, leaning back on his hands. The mare had finished drinking and was attempting to eat some grass. "The mare is eating."

Aissa nodded. "I can hear her." She crossed her legs underneath her skirt. "You were wonderful back there. I knew you would save the mare."

Shadow Hawk looked at her. "How could you know it? I didn't even know it."

"I have confidence in you."

"If that is so, why don't you come back home with me?" Shadow Hawk watched Aissa's face as he spoke, and he could see the sadness there.

"I've told you why I can't go back."

"Yes, you've said many things." Shadow Hawk reached up and barely brushed Aissa's cheek with the back of his hand.

Aissa turned her cheek away. "Don't do that."

"Why not? Why does it bother you so?"

"Because I can't see you."

"You couldn't see me the other night," Shadow Hawk said in a low voice, brushing his hand along her arm.

"Don't touch me, please."

Shadow Hawk jerked his hand away. "Why did you stay here? I don't need your help to walk the mare back."

"I wanted to be with you," Aissa stammered, her voice trembling slightly.

Shadow Hawk turned his head. "This won't work, Aissa. I can't be around you like this. You expect me to treat you like a friend. But unlike you, I cannot forget the times we were together." He gripped her arm. "Have you forgotten those times already?"

Aissa shook her head. "No, I haven't forgotten them. I will never forget them."

Shadow Hawk sighed in resignation, dropping his hands from her arms. "So, you have made your decision."

"I think it's best that I stay here. At least for awhile."

"Do you love this man? Just tell me that, Aissa."

"No, I don't love him. But we are the same, he and I."

"You are both white, you mean." Shadow Hawk laughed harshly "I really thought it didn't matter that I was an Indian. I can see that I was wrong."

"It's not that—"

"Stop. I don't need to hear any more." Shadow Hawk stood up and walked to the mare. He slipped the rope over her head and led her in the direction of the ranch.

"Shadow Hawk."

Shadow Hawk turned around. Aissa still hadn't moved. She looked helpless. "I will send the white man for you. He can help you get back."

"Don't leave me out here. Please." Aissa stood up, reaching toward him.

Shadow Hawk thought about the hundreds of ways she could get hurt and shook his head. He couldn't leave her. He sighed. "I am here." He let his voice guide her. When she got close, he took her hand and squeezed it then helped her find the mare's withers. They walked in silence. Shadow Hawk couldn't think of anything to say. He loved this woman, but he would not beg for her to love him back. He could take her by force, make her go back with him, but he had done that once before and had almost lost her. He wouldn't force her to do anything this time. Maybe it was just time for him to leave.

The mare walked slowly but she didn't stop again. Soon they reached the road leading to the ranch. Shadow Hawk looked up at the canopy of trees. Gerard had planted saplings all around the house. One day, they would be as beautiful as these.

Shadow Hawk glanced back at Aissa. She was crying. He wanted to take her in his arms, but he knew she would only push him away. When they reached the yard, Shadow Hawk stopped. "We're here. I'm going to take the mare to the barn. Can you find your way to the house?"

"Yes."

Shadow Hawk tugged gently at the rope, and the mare obediently began to walk. He led her to the barn. He called to Jeb, asking the older man to take care of the mare. He knew Aissa. She was stubborn. Even if she couldn't get to the house, she would've said she could do it on her own. He walked back toward the house, surprised to see a flash of blue cloth through the trees. Aissa had only walked a few steps.

When she heard his footsteps she looked up, startled. "Shadow Hawk." Her voice was filled with anguish.

Shadow Hawk stopped. "What is it?"

"Give me time. This is all so new to me. I'm frightened."

"Then, let your father and me help you. We are the ones who should be caring for you, not these people, these strangers."

"I'm just asking for some time."

Shadow Hawk shook his head. "I can't give you anymore time, Aissa. You want me to stay here and wait until you decide between me and another man. I won't do that. I think you've made your decision anyway. There's no reason for me to stay."

"You can't go."

"I can't stay, Aissa. Don't you see that? I cannot watch you with the white man any longer."

Aissa started to walk toward the house. Shadow Hawk watched until she had turned up the path that led to the stone steps. He was about to go back to the barn when Aissa began to run. "Aissa, wait," he called, rushing after her. But Aissa had already reached the steps. Her foot slipped on the rough stone and she tumbled forward. Shadow Hawk could hear the sickening thud as she hit. An instant later, he was kneeling next to her, gently pulling her into his arms. She had cut her scalp and was bleeding badly.

"Don't leave now. Promise me." Aissa grabbed his arm tightly.

"I won't leave you, Aissa," he said, picking her up and carrying her toward the house.

"It hurts," Aissa said, resting her head against Shadow Hawk's chest.

Shadow Hawk had barely entered the courtyard when he saw Dorothea. "Aissa has fallen. She's hurt."

Dorothea stood up, quickly wiping her dirty hands on her garden apron. "Let's get her to her room." Dorothea led the way, directing Shadow Hawk to put her on the bed. Dorothea poured some water into the washbowl and wet a soft cloth, wiping Aissa's head. "It's not too bad, dear. But there's going to be an awful bruise."

"Where is Shadow Hawk?" Aissa asked, moving restlessly on the bed.

"I am here, Aissa." He picked up her hand and held it, ignoring the look that Dorothea gave him. "Does your head still hurt?"

"Yes."

Shadow Hawk looked at Dorothea. "Is there a doctor in the town?"

"Yes."

"Don't go," Aissa pleaded with him.

Shadow Hawk squeezed her hand. "Aissa, I have no medicine for this. I cannot help you. I don't know what to do."

Dorothea glanced sharply at Shadow Hawk. She stood up. "Don't worry, dear. I'll send one of the hands into town. You just rest."

When Dorothea left the room, Shadow Hawk sat on the bed, still holding Aissa's hand. "How do you feel?"

"I feel clumsy and foolish." She held her hand on her forehead. "My head hurts again."

Shadow Hawk reached into the bowl that was still on the bed, rinsed out the cloth, and wiped the still bleeding cut on Aissa's head. He pressed the cloth there, holding it until the bleeding stopped. "Have you had these headaches before?"

"Yes, after the accident. For the first few days I thought I'd die from the pain."

Gently, Shadow Hawk took Aissa's hands away from her

face. He placed his fingers on her temples and rubbed her skin in slow circles, watching her visibly relax. He couldn't stand seeing her in pain. "Is that better?"

"I'm scared." Her voice broke and she began to cry. "I'm sorry."

Shadow Hawk put his arms around her and lifted her up to him, holding her next to his chest. "I won't leave until I'm sure you are all right. Don't worry."

"But I don't want you to leave at all." Aissa buried her face in his chest, still sobbing.

Shadow Hawk could feel Aissa's fear and he held her tightly. "I'll always be with you, Aissa," he whispered, kissing her cheek. As her crying subsided and she lay in his arms, Shadow Hawk knew that he couldn't love any woman more than he loved Aissa. He loved her too much to stay here and watch her be loved by another man.

Chapter Thirteen

Aissa lay in Shadow Hawk's arms, feeling his strength and love. Her headache was getting worse. She held onto his shirt, pressing her face against his chest. She could feel his heartbeat and it comforted her. But she knew something was wrong; she shouldn't be in this much pain.

"Aissa."

Aissa heard Clay's voice as he walked into the room, but she didn't respond.

"What happened?" Clay demanded.

"She fell on the steps," Shadow Hawk said, still holding Aissa.

"How the hell did that happen? You were supposed to be watching her."

"She doesn't need to be watched," Shadow Hawk said calmly.

"Well, it's obvious she does when she's with you." Clay sat on the other side of the bed next to Aissa. "Are you sure she's all right?"

Aissa lay back down as Shadow Hawk released her and stood up.

"There's blood. My God, you hit your head." Clay reached for Aissa's hand. "Does it hurt like the first time?"

"It's worse."

"I'll get you something for the pain. I think Mother has some laudanum."

"No!" Shadow Hawk protested. "She doesn't need that."

Clay glared up at him. "How the hell do you know what she needs? You weren't there when she was hurt. I was. I saw what kind of pain she was in."

"And I'm telling you she doesn't need laudanum."

"Listen—"

"Please, don't." Aissa's voice was barely audible.

Shadow Hawk motioned Clay outside the room. "You don't understand," he said as soon as they were in the hallway.

Clay shook his head adamantly. "No, I think you're the one who doesn't understand. She almost went crazy the first time this happened the pain was so bad. I didn't have anything to help her. At least the laudanum will make her sleep."

Shadow Hawk took Clay's arm and led him farther down the hall away from Aissa's room. "Did she tell you about Grimes?"

"I know about Grimes. Why?"

"He forced her to marry him and when she wanted to leave he beat her. Then he forced her to take laudanum until she couldn't live without it. When I found her, she would've killed me or her father just to get another bottle of it. Do you understand now?"

Clay shook his head. "I didn't know. I just wanted to help her."

"You can't help her that way."

"What other way is there?"

"My grandmother is a healer in our tribe. She uses many different kinds of medicines for pain. I have some of them with me."

"In that leather pouch?"

"Yes. I can make her a tea that will help with the pain and she won't crave it like she will the laudanum."

Clay nodded. "All right."

"A doctor is coming?"

"Yeah, but he'll probably prescribe laudanum first

thing. They always do." Clay held up his hands. "Don't worry, I won't let him."

"What about her eyes? Why does she have these headaches?"

"I don't know for sure. The doctor who looked at her at the mine said something was damaged."

"Will she ever see again?"

"Don't know that either. That's why I'd like to take her to see a special doctor in St. Louis."

Shadow Hawk nodded. "I'll make the tea. You stay with her."

Clay walked back to the room. "How's it feel?"

"It feels terrible." Aissa lay on her back, her head propped up by some pillows. "Where is Shadow Hawk?"

"He's making you some tea, some kind of medicine."

Aissa smiled in spite of her pain. "He was right about the laudanum."

Clay took her hand. "I know, he told me. I'm sorry. I had no idea." Aissa was laying back against the pillows, her hair wet around the dark line of the cut. He could tell that she was still in pain, but she looked better now. Some of the color had come back into her cheeks.

"Something is happening, Clay."

"What do you mean?"

"I'm seeing flashes of light. The pain isn't letting up."

Clay touched Aissa's cheek. "That's good. Maybe your sight is going to come back."

"Or maybe something bad is happening. I'm scared."

"Don't be scared." Clay brought Aissa's hand to his mouth and kissed it. "As soon as you're able to travel, I'm taking you to see that doctor in St. Louis. No arguments."

Aissa nodded. "Don't tell Shadow Hawk about the light. Please."

"Why not?"

"I don't want to get his hopes up. If I get my sight back completely, then I'll tell him."

"All right." Clay held Aissa's hand tightly. "What're you going to do if you don't get your sight back?"

Aissa turned her face away from him. When she spoke her voice was so low that he had to strain to see her. "I don't know. I guess I haven't thought about it."

"I want you to stay here, Aissa."

"Clay, I can't do that to you. I'll always be in love with Shadow Hawk."

"Yes, but you're still here. You haven't gone back with him."

"You know why I haven't. I can't make him change his life for me."

"But I want to make my life around you just the way you are. Are you listening to me, Aissa? I love you. I don't care if you can see or not."

"Why would you love a woman who doesn't love you back?"

"You will, Aissa, you just don't know it yet." Clay leaned down and touched his mouth to Aissa's.

Aissa heard something in the hallway and pulled away.

"Here is the tea." Aissa felt Shadow Hawk sit on the bed next to her. "You'll recognize this," he said. "It's one of Ocha's mixtures."

Aissa smiled weakly. "Yes, I recognize the smell." She took the cup in her trembling hands and sipped at the bitter-tasting liquid. "Thank you." At that moment, she would've given anything to see Shadow Hawk's face, to try to read his eyes. Had he seen Clay kissing her? And if he had, was he angry or relieved? She felt Clay shift his weight and Shadow Hawk stood up.

"It will help with the pain." His voice was controlled.

She couldn't tell anything. "Are you going?"

"Yes, I think it's best." He hesitated a moment, and Aissa heard him head for the door.

"Will you be back?" Aissa called out.

"I'll check on you later."

Aissa heard Shadow Hawk as he left the room. She couldn't stop the trembling in her hands. She put the cup to her mouth and sipped again, closing her eyes. She was so confused. She knew she would always love Shadow Hawk and that she would never love Clay. But she still didn't know what she should do. Here, in this big house, she felt sheltered. But if she stayed here, when would she see her father again?

"Are you all right?"

Clay's voice startled Aissa out of her thoughts. "Yes, I'm fine. The tea is helping." She took the last swallow of the warm liquid and held out the cup. Clay took it from her.

"Think about what I said, Aissa."

Aissa nodded as she heard Clay leave the room, but she wasn't thinking about him or what he had said. She was thinking about Shadow Hawk.

Christina tiptoed down the hall. She had waited until Clay and his father were down at the barn and Dorothea and Rayna were busy in the kitchen. She didn't want to make Shadow Hawk mad but she wanted to talk to Aissa. She missed her. Aissa was the closest thing to a sister she'd ever had in her life. Christina eased the door open, she didn't want to knock in case Aissa was sleeping and she was. Christina felt her eyes sting with disappointment. She slipped inside and closed the door behind her. Maybe she would just wait until Aissa woke up.

Christina sank into a chair by the bed. She could see the awful wound on Aissa's scalp. Christina knew that both Shadow Hawk and Clay were worried about Aissa. She could also tell that both men were in love with her. It was easy to see why. Even now, when she was hurt, Aissa was the most beautiful woman that Christina had ever seen. She was one of the kindest, too. Christina grimaced, remembering that she had thrown herself at Shadow Hawk. The truth was, she wasn't so much in love with him, as she was in love with the idea of having a man care about her the way Shadow Hawk cared about Aissa. In a strange way, Christina was in love with them both. They had what she wanted someday.

Aissa stirred on the bed, and Christina watched as her eyes fluttered and opened. Christina smiled then realized that Aissa couldn't see her, didn't know she was there. Afraid she would startle Aissa but not knowing what else to do, Christina cleared her throat.

Aissa turned toward her. "Who's there?"

"It's just me . . . Christina."

Aissa smiled and reached out her hand. "I was hoping we'd get a chance to talk soon."

Christina took Aissa's hand. "I've missed you so much and so does Ben. He's been so worried, Aissa."

"How is he, Christina? Is he taking care of himself?"

For a moment, Christina didn't answer. She squared her shoulders and looked up. "I took real good care of him while I was there, Aissa. I made cakes just like you did, and I made sure he ate his meals just like he was supposed to. And we went for walks all the time."

Aissa sat up slowly. "How's my father's heart?"

Christina looked up, studying Aissa's face. "He talks about it sometimes. I mean he. . . ."

"What you mean is," Aissa said deliberately, "that when he wants to get out of doing something, he suddenly has a pain in his chest."

Christina burst out laughing. Aissa laughed, too, but softer, touching her temple.

"Does your head hurt a lot?" Christina asked. "Clay said that right after the mine accident, you were in horrible pain."

"It's better now."

"When are you going to come home, Aissa? We miss

you. It's not right for you to leave Ben and Shadow Hawk alone for so long."

"I'm not ready to go home yet, Christina."

"Why?"

"I just—"

"You're not in love with Clay, are you? You couldn't possibly love him the way you love Shadow Hawk. I mean he's handsome and all, but. . . ."

"I'm not in love with Clay, Christina, although I'm grateful to him, and he's been very good to me."

Christina stood up and walked around the room. "I think you have too much time to sit in here alone and think. What you need is somebody to talk to, somebody to keep you company. I'm moving my things in here today." Christina waited for Aissa to tell her to mind her own business, but she didn't. Instead she smiled.

"You're really amazing, Christina. Has anybody ever told you that?"

Christina could feel herself blushing, and she was glad Aissa couldn't see her. She knew she needed to act more mature. Christina stood up straight and glanced at Aissa, a determined look on her face. Aissa had helped her through the most horrible time she'd ever been through; in a way, she owed Aissa her life. Now it was Christina's turn to help Aissa.

Shadow Hawk patted the mare, scratching her nose affectionately. "You're mine now. I'll take care of you." He tried to push the memory of Aissa and Clay from his mind, but it was still too fresh.

"Shadow Hawk."

Shadow Hawk turned when he heard Rayna's voice. She was standing by the stall door. He hadn't realized before how pretty she was. Her hair was darker than Aissa's but it was curly, and she had soft brown eyes. She was small but not delicate-looking like other small women he'd seen. She was dressed in pants, a shirt, and boots.

Rayna looked down at herself. "What're you gawking at? Haven't you ever seen a woman in a pair of pants before?"

"Yes," he replied, thinking of Aissa, "many times. But I didn't expect to see you dressed like that."

"Why?"

"You seem too proper." Shadow Hawk turned back to the mare, leaning over to check her wounds. They had bled some more but not too badly. So far, she was doing all right.

Rayna shrugged her shoulders. "I suppose I've always been too proper for my own good. That's why I'm twenty-two years old and still living with my parents."

Shadow Hawk grinned. "You aren't in the grave yet, Rayna."

"Sometimes I feel like I am." She pointed to the mare. "Pa told me all about her. You're quite the talk around here. Think she'll make it?"

"I don't know. She has great courage."

"Why did you do it? Why did you go to so much trouble? Most people would've put her down."

"Horses are very important to my people. I was taught that they are a gift from the Great Spirit to us."

"You are the most interesting man I've ever met."

"Why?" Shadow Hawk asked. "Because I am Indian?"

Rayna followed Shadow Hawk as he walked outside to the corrals. "No, that's not why."

Shadow Hawk walked to the first corral, watching as the buckskin lifted its head warily.

"I hear you're going to break the buckskin."

Shadow Hawk had been avoiding Rayna's eyes but now that was impossible. Standing on the fence rail, she was as tall as he. He glanced at the powerful animal in the corral. "It's possible. It's up to the buckskin." He walked along the fence line, studying the horse.

"Don't you ever answer anything directly?" Rayna got down from the corral and followed Shadow Hawk.

Shadow Hawk stopped. "Sometimes."

"What are you going to do about Aissa?"

Shadow Hawk leaned on the corral, sticking his hand out to the buckskin as the horse walked slowly toward him. "I am not going to do anything about Aissa."

"You know Clay wants to keep her here, don't you?"

"Aissa wants to stay here." Shadow Hawk reached his hand out as far as it would go. The buckskin took a tentative step forward, smelled Shadow Hawk's hand, and then snorted and trotted around the corral.

"She's a fool then."

"Why do you say that?"

"My brother has never stayed with one woman for very long. I think he thinks taking care of a blind woman will right all of his past wrongs."

Shadow Hawk glanced sharply at Rayna. "Why do you talk like that about your own brother?"

"Because it's true. If I were you, I'd take Aissa and go back home."

Shadow Hawk walked away from Rayna, uneasy at her directness. As he passed the corrals, he looked in, checking the horses carefully. Rayna followed alongside him, stubbornly hurrying to match his long strides. "What is it you want, Rayna?" Shadow Hawk stopped suddenly and Rayna bumped into him as he turned.

Rayna shoved her hands in her pockets and shrugged her shoulders. "I don't know. I guess I want things to be the way they used to be when my brothers and I were young." She kicked at the ground and looked up at Shadow Hawk. "I guess I want someone to love me the way you love Aissa."

"You don't give yourself a chance to be loved. You never leave this ranch."

"Well, why don't you take me for a ride? Get me out of here." She was grinning.

Shadow Hawk almost decided against it, but reconsidered. It would be good to be with Rayna and get away from Aissa and Clay for awhile. "All right."

"Can I ride your paint?"

"I thought you were going to ride your own horse."

"Please. I'd love to know what it's like to ride a horse like that."

"Do you always get your own way?"

"Almost always."

They walked to the corral that held the paint and Shadow Hawk went inside, quickly putting the hackamore and saddle blanket on the paint. He led the stallion out of the corral. "Will you settle for almost getting your way?" Before she could answer Shadow Hawk had his hands around Rayna's waist. He lifted her onto the paint's back, then swung up behind her.

They rode out of the stable yard and Shadow Hawk kept the paint reined in. At first the spirited animal obeyed him, but as they started down the long tree-lined road the stallion began to prance nervously. Shadow Hawk slipped his right arm around Rayna's waist to steady her. He chided himself as he fought to keep the stallion under control. If Rayna got hurt he would not forgive himself. He could feel the tension in her body and drew her closer. He knew she was frightened, and he admired her courage in keeping silent.

Down the road, Shadow Hawk could see dust. It was several riders, probably ranch hands riding in to eat the noonday meal. He let the paint canter, holding Rayna closer. He did not want to run into anyone. They reached the end of the tree-lined lane before the cowhands, and Shadow Hawk turned the paint west, away from them. For once he wished the paint were not so easy to recognize. He could only hope that the cowhands had not seen Rayna. He had enough things to worry about without offending Montrose.

Rayna leaned back against his chest, turning to grin up at him. "Let him run. Give him his head."

Shadow Hawk loosened the tension on the reins and tightened his arms around Rayna. The stallion stretched out, the cadence of his hoofbeats quickening. Shadow Hawk realized that Rayna was an excellent rider. She was leaning forward over the paint's withers, her weight balanced correctly. Shadow Hawk let the paint gallop for almost a mile, relishing the warm wind and Rayna's girlish excitement. When he finally pulled the stallion back into a canter, then to a walk, Rayna straightened and turned to grin at him again, her hair wind-tousled.

"Thank you," Rayna said, loosening her hold on the stallion's mane. "I know why your father wanted you to have him."

"You've ridden fast horses before. It was no different than that."

"You know it was," Rayna said, playfully slapping Shadow Hawk on the leg. "You can tell he's afraid of nothing by the way he runs. He never hesitates."

"You know horses."

"I know them well enough. I know more than I let on to my father."

Shadow Hawk did not answer immediately. He turned the paint and headed back toward the ranch. "Your brother says you can run this ranch alone. He has great respect for you."

"And you wonder why I speak about him the way I do?"

"I didn't say that."

"I could hear the disapproval in your voice."

"He loves you very much."

"I love him, too. I never said I didn't," Rayna snapped.

"I'm sorry. I didn't mean to make you feel uncomfortable."

"I don't understand you. You are much too honorable for me."

"I am not so honorable, Rayna. I have done things I am not proud of in my life."

"That's hard for me to believe." Rayna was quiet for a moment before she spoke. "I'm sorry. You must think I'm horrible, but I do love my brother."

"I know what it is to love someone who does dishonorable things." Shadow Hawk was thinking of Miho.

Rayna lapsed again into silence, and Shadow Hawk realized that was another thing he liked about this woman. She could be content with her own thoughts. Before Shadow Hawk could understand Rayna's sudden sidelong grin, she had pulled the reins out of his hand and was urging the paint back into a gallop. His first reaction was anger, then, when he saw that she was controlling the paint, his anger became admiration. As they thundered up the road to the stable yard, Shadow Hawk put both arms around Rayna's waist, pretending to be afraid. Rayna immediately understood the joke and sat taller and more confidently. As they flashed by the lower paddocks, Shadow Hawk leaned forward to take the reins from Rayna. She half-turned to kiss his cheek as the paint slowed to a controlled gallop. In that instant, Shadow Hawk saw Clay and his father standing side-by-side, fence-mending tools in their hands, and disbelief on their faces.

At the barn, Rayna was flushed and laughing, and Shadow Hawk cursed himself for not anticipating the trouble his friendship with her could cause. Without being too abrupt, he made sure that Rayna returned to the house while he remained at the barn currying and caring for the paint. He stretched out the work, then went to look at the buckskin again and to check on the injured mare. By the time Shadow Hawk went into the house, it was nearly dark. He could hear the others gathered in the dining room, but he stopped in the kitchen and asked Elaina to tell Montrose that he would not be eating dinner that evening. He took the food that Elaina had given him and quietly went upstairs to his room. Once inside, he closed the door. He was not in the mood to talk to anyone.

He set the plate of food down on the night table and turned up the lamp. He paced around the room. He was sure Aissa wasn't well enough to go down to dinner and he wanted to see her. But he didn't want to risk running into Clay again.

He kept pacing around the room, stopping only to grab a piece of bread from the plate. He went to the window, looked out at the courtyard, and sat down on the bed. He had promised Montrose he would hunt for the mountain lion with Clay in the morning. How would he do it? How could he continue to be around the man Aissa was beginning to love?

He lay back on the bed and covered his eyes with his arm, blotting out the light from the lamp. Why was he staying here? What was the point? Aissa had already made her decision to stay, and there was nothing he could say to change her mind. Even Christina seemed to like it here.

Shadow Hawk sighed deeply. As soon as he and Clay came back from the hunt, he would go. It was time.

Aissa rested her head against the pillows. The pain was minimal now; the tea had helped. She didn't want to stay in bed, but the doctor had warned her against moving. She had never felt so helpless in her life. She missed her father more than she realized. She longed to hear his voice and feel his husky arms hold her and tell her everything would be all right. She missed her home.

As soon as she heard the footsteps coming down the hall she knew it was Clay. He had a heavy footfall that was unmistakable.

She looked toward the door. "Clay?"

"How'd you know?" Clay came toward the bed. "Elaina sent some food up. I thought I'd eat with you."

Aissa shook her head. "I'm tired, Clay. If you don't mind, I'd rather be alone."

"You sure?"

"Yes, thank you."

"All right. The tray is on the table to your right. Be careful. Elaina made some very hot hot chocolate."

"Tell her thank you."

"How is your head?"

Aissa shrugged. "It's not so bad now. I think Shadow Hawk's medicine helped."

"Good," Clay answered, his tone cold.

"What is it? What's bothering you, Clay?"

"Nothing. Just thinking about going after that cat tomorrow, I guess."

Aissa held her head as she sat up straighter. "Do you have to go? Can't your father send some of his men instead?"

"It's a test, Aissa. He wants to see if I can go out there without getting myself or someone else killed."

"Shadow Hawk is going with you, isn't he?"

"Yes. What about it?"

Aissa shrugged. "He's a good tracker, that's all. You'll find the cat with his help."

"I don't need his help, Aissa. I've hunted mountain cats before." Clay's voice was hard.

"I'm sorry. I didn't mean to make you angry."

"Don't be sorry," Clay said, sitting on the bed next to her, "it's not your fault." Clay put the cup of hot chocolate between Aissa's hands: "Try this. Elaina makes the best hot chocolate."

Aissa held the cup but didn't drink. "What else is the matter, Clay?

"It's Shadow Hawk."

"What about him?" Aissa tried to contain her fear.

"He took Rayna for a ride today."

Aissa shrugged her shoulders, relieved.

"He took her on his paint. She sat in front of him and when they came back into the stable yard, they were both laughing and acting like kids. She even kissed him in front of all the hands."

"Rayna kissed Shadow Hawk?" Aissa tried to make her voice sound calm.

"Yes, and he didn't look like he minded too much either. I didn't like it."

"What, the fact that he kissed your sister, or the fact that he's an Indian?" Aissa asked angrily.

"Both. How would it make you feel?"

Aissa felt the anger rise in her. She wished that she could see Clay so she could slap him. "I know how he makes me feel," she said, leaning her head back against the pillows.

"I'm sorry, I didn't mean that the way it sounded."

"How did you mean it, Clay? Are you trying to hurt me on purpose? Did you think by telling me about Rayna and Shadow Hawk, I would stop loving him?"

"No, I—"

"I think your sister is a very smart woman. Shadow Hawk is a handsome man and he's very trustworthy."

"There's no use talking to you about this."

"You're right." Aissa turned her head away.

"Listen, Aissa, I can't control what you're going to do, but I can keep my sister from making a mistake. I'll be damned if I'm going to let her fall in love with an Indian."

"You might not have anything to say about it, Clay." Aissa stopped after she spoke. She couldn't believe she was defending Rayna's right to love Shadow Hawk.

"Like I said, there's no talking to you about it. I'll be back up later to check on you."

Aissa waited until Clay's footsteps faded then she sat up, putting her bare feet on the cold, wood floor. Slowly, she stood, trying to gain her balance. She measured her steps to the door. Once she touched it, she felt the door frame and then pressed her fingers along the wall until she reached the landing. Carefully, she felt for the table at the top of the stairs and walked along it until she got to the other side of the landing and the other hallway.

She put her hands on the wall again and slid them over the smooth surface until she reached the end of the hallway. Then she walked across, touching the curtains that hung on the window. She felt her way past the first doorway, until she reached the second. She put her head to the wood and listened. She didn't know if Shadow Hawk was in his room or not. She knocked lightly. When there was no response, she turned the doorknob and opened the door, stepping into the room.

"Shadow Hawk," she said softly, unable to hear any sound. Then she heard the bed as he moved on it, and she knew he was here.

"Aissa. What are you doing here?"

"I wanted to talk to you." She reached out, her hands in front of her, making her way across the room. She felt Shadow Hawk's hand on hers as he led her to the bed.

"You shouldn't be up. You should be resting."

"I want to talk."

"We can talk in your room. Let me take you back there."

"No, I want to talk here. It's more private. Shut the door, please."

Shadow Hawk closed the door and sat next to Aissa. "Is it your head? Is the pain worse?"

"No, it's not my head. I just wanted. . ." Aissa

couldn't find the words. "I just wanted to hear your voice."

"I'll make you some more tea. It will help you sleep."

"I don't want more tea. Just sit and talk with me. Please."

"This isn't a good idea, Aissa. If Clay finds out you're in my room, he'll be angry."

"When did you begin to worry about what Clay thinks?"

"I don't care what he thinks, but I know it upsets you to see us fight. It's easier for me not to be around him."

Aissa touched Shadow Hawk's arm. "What about tomorrow? You can't avoid each other on the hunt."

"We're hunting for a cat, we're not going to a dance. We won't need to talk."

"You sound like you hate him."

"Part of me does hate him for being there for you when I couldn't be."

Aissa looked toward Shadow Hawk and squinted. Vague patterns of light danced across her eyes and she covered them with her hands.

"Aissa," Shadow Hawk said softly. "Let me take you back to your room."

"No," she said, shaking her head. When she opened her eyes again, the light was gone. She was still in the darkness. "I don't think I can live like this."

"You're not alone, Aissa. Many people love you."

"It doesn't matter, I still can't see."

"Clay says he wants to take you to see a doctor in St. Louis. I think you should go."

"No one can help me."

"You don't know that."

"Do you want me to stay here?"

"Isn't that what you want? You're the one who keeps telling me you can't go back with me. I won't force you, Aissa."

Aissa was silent for a moment before she spoke. "Clay

told me you took Rayna for a ride today. On the paint." She felt like a jealous young girl.

"I figured he'd tell you."

"Is that why you did it?"

"I took Rayna for a ride because she asked me, and I like her. What's the matter with you? Ever since I got here, you've been telling me that you're going to stay here with Clay." Shadow Hawk touched Aissa's cheek. "But you keep giving me little signs, Aissa. You want to stay with Clay, but you don't want me to go either."

"I owe Clay so much, I—"

"I'm tired of hearing how much you owe Clay. You've made your decision, and I've made mine."

"You're leaving?" Aissa tried to control the panic she felt.

"As soon as Clay and I get back from hunting the cat. I've told you how I feel. You know how much I love you, and you know how much your father loves you. For your own reasons, you've decided to stay with Clay. I respect your decision, Aissa, but it doesn't mean I have to like it."

Aissa nodded, her head beginning to throb. "I've been selfish, I know. I'm sorry." She felt his arm go around her shoulders and pull her to him.

"Don't be sorry." Shadow Hawk's voice was gentle.

Aissa rested her head on Shadow Hawk's shoulder. "I don't want you to leave."

"Aissa—"

"Let me finish." She sat up straight, her fingers reaching to touch his face. "I love you more than I could ever love any man. I know that you love me, and I know that you will take care of me. But after awhile, I would become a burden to you. It would never be the same between us. I don't want you to remember me as a helpless, pathetic woman."

"Aissa," Shadow Hawk said, kissing her cheek. "You will never be a helpless woman. Why don't you trust my love for you?"

"Because we are so different. I saw it even before you left to look for your family. When you and Father were working on the house, I'd see you looking out at the mountains. I know you miss your people. Now you can go back to them."

"I don't want to go back to my people."

Aissa shook her head. "It's not fair to make you live in a world where you don't feel comfortable. I want you to be happy, Shadow Hawk." Aissa's eyes filled with tears, but she quickly wiped them away.

"And what about you, Aissa? Will you be happy?"

"It doesn't matter, don't you see?" Aissa stood up. "I will never be happy as long as I'm wandering around in the dark." She shook her head, angrily wiping the tears from her eyes. "That's why you have to go and I have to stay." She started for the door but felt Shadow Hawk's arms go around her from behind, pulling her back to him. She leaned her head against his chest, feeling his arms wrapped tightly around her waist. She put her hands on his arms. "I'm so sorry," she said, her voice full of sadness. "I know I've disappointed you. I—I should've been stronger."

"Aissa, you are the strongest woman I have ever known."

Aissa turned around in Shadow Hawk's arms and reached up to touch his face. "I do love you, please remember that." She moved her mouth tentatively toward his and was met by an urgent, passionate kiss. She wanted to let him make love to her, but she knew that would only make it harder for them both. Reluctantly, she pulled away and reached for the door.

"I will walk with you," he said, his hand on hers.

But Aissa shook her head. "No, I have to go alone." Slowly, she walked back to her room, unable to fight the tears any longer.

* * *

Clay hurried through dinner and excused himself, going out to the courtyard. He dreaded going hunting in the morning; he especially dreaded having to go with Shadow Hawk. But there was no getting out of it now. If he didn't go, his father would think he was a coward.

He paced around the courtyard, furious with Shadow Hawk for thinking he could take Rayna for a ride in front of all the hands. What did he think gave him the right to come into his family and act like he was a part of it? But he knew why. His father had made Shadow Hawk feel welcome, had even let him stay in the house. Clay knew there was a purpose in what his father was doing, and he hated him for it.

"Damn it" he said, walking around the courtyard. He couldn't get Aissa out of his mind. He wasn't sure if he loved her. Hell, he wasn't sure if he even knew what love was, but he certainly cared for her more than he had any other woman. There was a kindness and caring in Aissa that fascinated him. And she needed him. That made him feel good. He hadn't felt needed in a long time.

Footsteps sounded on the stone behind him, and he turned around. Christina was walking toward him. "Am I bothering you?" she asked, folding her hands in front of her.

"No, I was just thinking. Why aren't you in with the others?"

"I wanted some air. Besides, I like this courtyard. It's so pretty."

Clay watched her as she walked around, staring up at the stars. He had seen her in the house with his mother asking questions. She seemed endlessly interested in everything. There was something distinctly childlike about her, as though she hadn't been out in the world on her own for very long. "How'd you end up with Shadow

Hawk?"

Christina continued to stare up at the sky. "It's beautiful, isn't it? My pa used to tell me that when good people die they go up into heaven and become a star." She looked at Clay. "Do you believe that?"

Clay smiled slightly. The girl was so guileless. "I suppose it's possible."

"But you don't believe it." Christina walked over and sat by the fountain. "You're lucky to live in a place like this. It's so pretty."

Clay walked over and sat next to Christina. "It's nice enough but you get used to it. After awhile it's just like any other place."

"I'd never get used to this place." Christina took a deep breath. "Even the air smells sweet."

Clay shook his head, amazed at Christina's enthusiasm "You never answered my question."

"What question?"

"Why're you with Shadow Hawk?"

"He's my friend. I wanted to help him find Aissa."

"That's all he is to you?"

"Why?" Christina asked, her voice sharp.

"Just wondering."

Christina laughed. "Just what do you want to know, Clay?"

Clay hesitated. She was direct. "I want to know if you're in love with him, if you two will be leaving together."

"Oh," Christina muttered, looking back up at the sky. "No, I'm not in love with him. And no, we won't be leaving together. We'll be leaving with Aissa."

There was no mistaking the anger in Christina's voice. "I'm sorry, I didn't mean to insult you." Clay apologized.

"You didn't insult me." Christina stood up. "I think it's pretty clear to everyone that you're in love with Aissa and you want her to stay here. But I'm telling you, she loves

Shadow Hawk."

Clay stood up next to her. "If she loves him so much, why does she want to stay here?"

Christina laughed. "You're arrogant, and you're not very smart. The only reason she wants to stay here is because she doesn't want to be a burden to her father or Shadow Hawk. If she stays with you, you'll be miserable after a time."

Christina started to walk away, but Clay reached out and grabbed her arm. "Wait," he said, his voice harder than he had intended.

Christina shrugged free of Clay's grasp. "I appreciate your kindness to me, but I don't need to stay here. I can leave right now if I have to."

Clay held his hands up in mock defeat. "Sorry, I didn't mean to hurt you."

"What do you want then?"

"I guess I just wanted to find out what kind of man Shadow Hawk is."

Christina was silent for a moment. "He's the best man I've ever known. He saved my life and took me to Aissa and her father. All of them are like family to me. But Shadow Hawk," she said his name softly, "he's special. He's good and honorable."

"You make him sound like a saint," Clay said dryly.

"And you sound jealous, Mr. Montrose," Christina replied with obvious glee.

"I'm not jealous. I'm just tired of hearing about him."

"Well, you better get used to it. Aissa loves him and that will never change." Christina's boot heels clattered against the stone as she crossed it and went into the house.

Clay smiled. He liked that girl. He thought about what she had said, and he knew it was true. Aissa loved Shadow Hawk and that wasn't going to change. Clay sighed, wondering why he didn't just encourage Aissa to go. It would be easier for them all if he did.

Shadow Hawk ran his fingers along the edge of the paw print, straightened up, glanced at Clay, then squinted into the rising sun. "We're close. These tracks aren't more than an hour old."

"That's about what I figured," Clay answered as Shadow Hawk swung back onto the paint.

Shadow Hawk forced himself to remain silent, as he had been ever since they had left the ranch. Clay's bravado grated on his nerves. The man's fear was obvious. Shadow Hawk felt sorry for him. Clay was not a coward but the memories of his childhood and his brother's death still overwhelmed him. As he had several times before, Shadow Hawk tried to imagine what it would have been like to have a father cruel enough to blame him for a brother's death, but it was impossible. His own father had been incapable of such a thing.

Shadow Hawk led the way, knowing that Clay was grateful even as he resented it. Shadow Hawk wanted nothing more than to find the cat and be finished with the hunt. The tension between him and Clay was bad and could only worsen. Whether or not Christina decided to go with him, Shadow Hawk was going to leave.

The land became rockier as they followed the fresh trail down into a stand of oaks. Shadow Hawk tried to quiet the paint as the stallion became more and more nervous. The smell of the cat was stronger now, and the paint was too intelligent an animal not to sense the danger in the low-hanging limbs of the oaks. Shadow Hawk smiled. Impatience was never a good hunting companion.

They rode slowly, carefully scanning the broad branches of the oaks for the cat. The sun was up now and the tracks were fresh, leading them through the trees. Something was wrong with the cat or it wouldn't be away from the safety of the hills. It needed the easy kill of domestic animals. Either it had killed again, or it was going to kill again.

Shadow Hawk pulled back on the paint's reins, holding him steady. The paint nickered nervously and Clay's horse echoed the sound. Both of the horses sensed that the cat was near. Shadow Hawk slowly eased his rifle into a ready position. He looked over at Clay and saw that he had done the same.

The tracks led them to a narrow draw, overhung with oaks. If Shadow Hawk had been alone, he would have waited for the cat to show itself but that could take hours, sometimes days. Sliding off the paint, he tied him loosely to some oak brush. Clay dismounted beside him, tense and silent. Shadow Hawk started up the draw, every muscle in his body tensed. There was no bird song, no rustling of lizards in the brush. Everything was still and quiet.

Bright spatters of blood on the oak leaves caught Shadow Hawk's eye. He glanced back. Clay had not seen the blood. Shadow Hawk watched him for a moment. There were beads of sweat on his forehead, and he was gripping his rifle so tightly his knuckles were white. Shadow Hawk scanned the brush in front of them. He saw the outline of the cat about a hundred feet ahead of them, its head down, feeding on a fresh kill. Before Clay could see the cat, Shadow Hawk brought his rifle up and fired. The cat's screams terrified the horses. Shadow Hawk could hear their hooves on the rocks below him.

Before the echoes of the shot died, Shadow Hawk knew that he had been too impatient. The cat was not dead. In a fury of pain and confusion, the animal turned and faced him. Shadow Hawk tried to aim as steadily as he could and pulled the trigger. Nothing happened. The cat crept toward him. The gore of its kill smeared across its face. Shadow Hawk backed up, his trigger finger working frantically to no effect. The cat gathered its weight to leap. Shadow Hawk shouted for Clay, as he turned the rifle in his hands gripping the barrel to use it as a club. The cat came forward. Shadow Hawk knew that it would be completely unpredictable, maddened by pain and fear. Still, cats were less likely to charge someone who faced them bravely instead of running. So he forced himself to stare into the animal's eyes.

Without warning, the lion leapt. Shadow Hawk swung his rifle and felt the force of the blow numb his hands an instant before he felt the fiery pain of the cat's claws raking down his shoulder and back. As he was slammed backward, Shadow Hawk heard the sound of a rifle shot and darkness closed in around him.

Shadow Hawk fought against the weight of the cat on top of him. Abruptly, the weight lifted and Clay's voice seeped into his consciousness.

"Don't fight. It's dead."

Shadow Hawk let Clay help him to his feet, then stood leaning on him, waiting until his vision cleared. The searing pain in his back and shoulder was almost more than he could master but he fought to remain conscious.

"You're bleeding bad." Clay tore Shadow Hawk's shirt and slid the tattered cloth carefully over his wounds. Using his own shirt, he made a crude but tight bandage. "That'll stop the worst of it for awhile." He glanced down the draw. "I'm afraid the horses are gone."

Shadow Hawk shook his head. The paint would still be there. He had seen many battles and hunts. He would have torn his reins free but would not have run.

"Whether they're there or not, we have to get you back somehow. Lean on me."

Shadow Hawk shrugged off Clay's hands and began to walk. Step by painful step he made his way back down the path. He was furious with Clay for having been so slow to react, but he was more furious with himself. He had been taught from boyhood that the hunt was no place for impatience or for the distractions of pride or rivalry. He had given Clay his word and had only wanted to make the kill cleanly and quickly so that he could leave this place. His own pride had prevented him from even considering the possibility that he might miss the cat. And now he was paying the price.

"No horses," Clay said. "Looks like we walk. You up to it?"

Shadow Hawk looked into Clay's face. Behind the cocky expression, the paleness of Clay's skin still lingered. More than anything, the man was relieved that it was all over. He had faced the remembered enemy of his childhood. The cat was dead.

"I can't carry you, but I can help you walk since the horses aren't here," Clay said, grasping Shadow Hawk's forearm.

"The Comanches," Shadow Hawk said between clenched teeth, "know how to train a horse." Refusing to wince and pulling away from Clay's grasp, Shadow Hawk took a deep breath and whistled. There was an immediate answering whinny. Although it hurt him to turn, he shot Clay a glance, enjoying the astonishment on the white man's face. Shadow Hawk started off again, walking with difficulty, following the path. As soon as they were out from beneath the overhanging limbs, he saw the paint and stopped. The powerful animal came toward them. Shadow Hawk fought the haze of pain and forced himself to smile. "I will not leave you, white man. I will ride slowly so that you can keep up." Clay nodded and Shadow Hawk saw laughter in his eyes.

"That is a fine stallion. I just want to see how you're going to get up on him."

Trying to conceal what he was doing, Shadow Hawk took a step toward the paint, glancing frantically for a rock outcropping he could use to mount. He might manage to get on without losing consciousness from the pain, but he would almost certainly start the bleeding again.

"Might be easier if you just let me give you a leg up."

Shadow Hawk looked at Clay. The shadow that had haunted the white man's eyes all morning was gone. Some of the scars from his brother's death had disappeared. "If you are as brave as your sister, you can ride with me. The stallion can easily carry two men."

Shadow Hawk stepped forward to catch hold of the paint's reins. For a moment, he let himself lean against the animal. Clay laced his fingers together and Shadow Hawk stepped into the stirrup formed by his hands. Clay lifted him steadily and smoothly and Shadow Hawk was grateful. As he swung his leg across the stallion's back, Shadow Hawk tangled his left hand in the stallion's mane to steady himself against the wave of pain that washed through him.

"Thank you for saving my life," Shadow Hawk said when Clay was mounted behind him. Clay didn't answer and Shadow Hawk had not expected him to. He knew Clay was feeling many things. He was freed from some of the burden of his brother's death, but at the same time, he had to be wondering why it was his destiny to save a stranger when he had been unable to save the brother he loved.

The motion of the stallion's gait brought Shadow Hawk fresh pain. He admitted to himself that he would not be leaving in the morning or anytime soon. He was badly hurt.

Christina was worried. She had been sitting in the courtyard staring through the doorway for hours. When she heard the hoofbeats, she assumed that one of the cowhands had ridden up to the house to ask Bradford a question. Then she heard Clay talking. She couldn't make out the words but the odd urgent tone of his voice brought her to her feet. She ran to the edge of the courtyard then stumbled to a stop. Clay was helping Shadow Hawk dismount. She could see a blood-stained cloth wrapped around his torso.

Clay looked up and saw her. "Christina, get my mother."

Christina whirled and ran shouting Dorothea's name. The older woman met her halfway on the stairs, and Christina stammered out that Shadow Hawk was hurt. Together they ran to help Clay bring Shadow Hawk inside.

"Keep your voices down," Dorothea cautioned them as they started up the stairs. "Aissa was half-crazy with pain from another headache but she's sleeping now." Dorothea glanced sharply at Clay. "If she hears he's been hurt, she'll try to get up."

Shadow Hawk leaned heavily on Clay and Christina, giving up all pretense that he could climb the stairs alone. Dorothea ran ahead and turned down the linens in Shadow Hawk's room.

"You need to lie down on your stomach so I can wash the wounds," Christina said, taking charge. "Mrs. Montrose, we're going to need boiled water and something I can use for bandages." Dorothea nodded and left.

Shadow Hawk eased himself into a kneeling position on the bed. Then with Clay's help, he managed to lie down on his left side, his face contorted with pain. Finally, with Clay and Christina supporting his weight, he slowly rolled onto his stomach. Breathing hard, he lay still, his eyes closed.

Christina held out her hand for Clay's knife and cut away the bloodied bandages. Clay started to speak and she shook her head to silence him. If Shadow Hawk didn't already know how bad the wounds were, it might do more harm than good to hear Clay say it. She glanced at

Shadow Hawk's back again and bit her lip. The wounds were deep and probably dirty, especially if the cat had been feeding. Christina had seen one of her uncles die from lockjaw, a long and painful way to die.

Dorothea appeared in the doorway, carrying an enamel basin full of steaming water and strips of white cloth. Clay went to help her. "I'm going to wash the wounds but then I want to make a poultice," Christina said looking at Clay. "Find that bag Shadow Hawk carries."

"In my bedding," Shadow Hawk said without raising his head.

Clay searched for the medicine bag and Christina steeled herself and set the basin beside the bed. She poured some of the water into Shadow Hawk's washbasin and set it beside the larger one. She bent close so that Clay and Dorothea could not hear what she said. "This is going to hurt, but I don't want you getting cat fever."

"Just do it, Christina." Shadow Hawk opened his eyes, then closed them again.

Christina looked at Dorothea and Clay. "It might be best if you left."

Clay handed her Shadow Hawk's medicine pouch. "Are you sure you don't need help?"

Christina shook her head and knelt on the floor next to Shadow Hawk. She felt Dorothea's hand on her shoulder.

"If you need help, you call. We'll hear you."

Christina nodded absently and wet the cloths in the basin. She took a deep breath then wiped quickly and carefully at the wounds. As she worked, a wave of despair washed through her. It was even worse than she had thought. Trying desperately to remember everything that her mother had taught her, Christina cleaned the wounds, pressing the ragged edges of flesh together. She prepared a poultice, using some of Shadow Hawk's medicine and put it in a clean cloth and applied it to the wounds. Then she stood back, uncertain. Shadow Hawk had flinched several times but had not spoken nor had he opened his eyes. Tentatively, she bent down and kissed the side of his face. He still didn't move.

Christina straightened up and stared at him a moment, involuntarily backing toward the door. She was frightened and needed to talk to someone who cared about Shadow Hawk as much as she did. She was going to tell Aissa.

Chapter Fourteen

Aissa was running across the meadow. The wildflowers were beautiful this spring. She lifted her skirt and skipped through the tall, wild grass. She had never seen the sky look so blue.

"Aissa."

She stopped. The voice was close and insistent.

"Aissa." She opened her eyes and the meadow darkened and then disappeared. It had just been a dream.

"Aissa, it's Christina. I have something to tell you."

Aissa tried to still the pounding in her temples and to ignore the sparkles of light that flashed in her dark world.

"Let me help you sit."

Aissa held onto Christina's arm as she struggled to sit. "What? Just tell me."

"It's Shadow Hawk. He's been hurt."

She gripped Christina's arm tightly. "What do you mean he's been hurt?" Then she remembered. He and Clay had gone hunting for the mountain lion. "How badly?" As Christina described what had happened, Aissa fought to keep her emotions under control. "I want to go to him."

"You can't do him any good now. He's resting. But I knew he'd want you to know."

"Do you think he'll be all right?"

Christina took Aissa's hand. "I don't know. I'm scared,

too. The moment that Shadow Hawk wakes up, I'll come get you. You rest now."

"Take me to him, Christina."

"Aissa—"

"If you don't take me, I'll go myself. I just want to be with him."

"All right," Christina said, helping her up.

"Dorothea gave me a robe. It's on the back of the door."

Christina helped Aissa into the robe then led her carefully down the hall and across the landing. Whispering so they wouldn't disturb Shadow Hawk, Christina settled Aissa in a rocking chair with a blanket across her lap.

Aissa caught Christina's hands as she smoothed the blanket. "Thank you. I had to be here."

"I know," Christina replied. "If you reach out your right hand, straight out, you'll touch him."

"Where are his wounds?"

"The worst ones are on his shoulder and side. Just reach straight out. You'll touch his face." Christina kissed Aissa on the cheek and left the room, closing the door behind her. Aissa leaned forward, listening for the sound of Shadow Hawk's breathing. It was low and rasping; it frightened her. She reached out her hand, then stopped, afraid that she might touch his wound. Again she listened, concentrating on the sound of his breathing, and she let the sound guide her hand to his face. She touched his cheek, then ran her hand up to his hair, stroking it gently. "I love you," she said softly, then leaned back in the chair and closed her eyes. She wanted to dream again, and in her dream, she wanted to be with Shadow Hawk.

After Christina washed up, she went outside and sat in the courtyard. After a few minutes she grew restless and walked aimlessly down the stone path toward the barn. The hands were busy working with the horses, the smithy was pounding out new shoes, and Jeb was barking out orders to one of the men. When Jeb saw her, he waved her over.

"How's he doing, missy?"

Christina shrugged, suddenly feeling very tired. "He's pretty bad. That cat cut him real good."

"Heard you did just fine taking care of him."

"Who told you that?"

"Clayton. He said you were real strong."

"How's the mare?" Christina asked.

"She's still pretty gimpy, but I think she'll make it. You going to see her?"

"I think so."

"You want some company?"

"No, thanks, Jeb." Christina smiled weakly, hoping he would understand. She walked away from him, threading her way through the corrals, ignoring the hands that tried to catch her eye. She passed through the wide doorway at the front of the barn and walked down the aisle until she came to the mare's stall. The mare stood bravely, her head up, but her wounds looked terrible. Christina could see her trembling. Jeb had said the mare would make it. Christina hoped that Shadow Hawk would do the same.

Suddenly, Christina couldn't stand the smell of blood a second longer. She left the barn and walked out past the corrals. She climbed up on the wooden fence that separated the stable yard from one of the pastures and sat, looking out at the grazing horses and cattle. She felt strange, and she felt alone. Tears coursed down her cheeks, and she wiped them away angrily. She loved Shadow Hawk, and she loved Aissa. She just wanted them to be all right. She wanted them to be together.

"I've been looking for you."

Christina heard Clay's voice but refused to look at him.

"Are you all right? I know that must've been hard for you back there."

Christina's heart raced. She jumped down from the

fence and stood to face Clay. "You'll never know how hard it was for me."

"I'm sorry, I—"

"He didn't have to go with you, you know. He only did it because your father was so hard on you."

"Christina, listen—"

"No, you listen," she shouted angrily. "Why are you doing this to them? They love each other. Let Aissa go."

Clay's face darkened with anger. "I'm not holding her here, Christina. She's free to leave."

"No, not as long as you keep her dependent on you."

"Anything else you want to say?"

"Yes." Christina's eyes narrowed. "How did Shadow Hawk get hurt? I've hunted with him. He's too smart to get hurt." Christina watched Clay. He shrugged his shoulders and leaned back against the fence.

"I'm not quite sure how it happened. I was behind him. I think he saw the cat and shot but only wounded it. When he tried to fire again, the rifle jammed, and the cat attacked him."

"And where were you all of this time?" Christina demanded.

"I was coming up the draw behind him." Clay shook his head, staring ahead. "It all happened so quickly. I saw him try to fire the rifle again and then nothing came out. Then the cat was on him. I aimed my rifle and fired." Clay shook his head. "I should've fired sooner. I think I froze for a few seconds."

"At least you did fire." Christina leaned back against the fence next to Clay. "Why was Shadow Hawk leading? This is your land. You know it better than he does."

Clay looked at Christina, shaking his head. "I let him take the lead. I think he knew I was afraid."

"Afraid of what? The cat?"

Clay sighed, closing his eyes for a moment and then opening them again. "You haven't heard about my brother and me? I'm surprised my father hasn't told you."

"I just heard that he got killed by a mountain lion when you and he were hunting together."

"My father thinks it was my fault that my brother died. Maybe he's right, maybe I should've done something more to save him."

"You were just a boy, weren't you?"

"Yes."

"What more could you have done?" Christina touched Clay's arm. Her voice was softer when she spoke. "I know what you're feeling. I was hiding underneath our wagon when my parents were murdered. I still wonder if I could've done something to save them."

"Well, we're quite a pair, aren't we?" Clay smiled at Christina.

Christina looked at Clay's brown eyes and his blond hair; for the first time she realized he was truly handsome. And when he smiled, it changed his face completely. He looked almost like a boy. "I'm sorry. I guess I was a little too hard on you."

"It's all right, I probably deserved it."

Christina turned around and leaned her arms on the fence, staring into the pasture. "Shadow Hawk can't die." Her voice trembled as she spoke, and she felt Clay's hand pat her back reassuringly.

"He won't die, Christina."

Christina looked at Clay. "You don't know much about cats, do you?"

"What do you mean?"

Christina shrugged. "Means they carry all sorts of diseases. Had the cat just killed something?"

"Yes."

"Then whatever was on his claws is now in Shadow Hawk's wounds. He could get real sick from that, maybe even die."

Clay tried to smile at her. "Well, you'll just have to

make sure that doesn't happen."

"I only know what my mother taught me, Clay, and that's not a whole lot. I'm scared." She looked at him, her eyes filling with tears. He stepped toward her and took her in his arms.

"It's all right, Christina. Shadow Hawk is strong. He won't die."

Christina nodded, resting her head on Clay's chest, praying that what he said was true.

Shadow Hawk tried to turn but stopped, the pain coursing through him. He felt hot and his throat was dry. He turned his head to the right, looking for some water. Instead, he saw Aissa sitting in a rocking chair. She was asleep, her long, blond hair falling over her shoulders and breasts, her head tilted to one side. He closed his eyes a moment, trying to gather the strength to get up. He moved his legs to the edge of the bed, and tried to stand, but a loud moan escaped his lips.

"Shadow Hawk?" Aissa was sitting up, reaching out toward the bed.

Shadow Hawk lay back down, unable to get up. "Can you get me some water, Aissa?"

"Yes. Just tell me where it is."

"Stand up. Now, move to your right about six steps. If you reach out you'll feel the stand. The pitcher is on it."

"Is there a glass?"

"No, just bring the pitcher." Shadow Hawk watched as Aissa followed his directions, never stumbling as she brought the pitcher to the bed. She knelt next to him and he raised his head. "I'm going to have to sit up. I don't know how I'll do it."

"I'll help you," Aissa said calmly. "Just tell me what to do."

Shadow Hawk reached out and put his hand on Aissa's

shoulder. "Just let me use you to hold on to. I'll do the rest." With his left arm, he pushed himself up, while swinging his legs over the edge of the bed. It felt as if his shoulder and back were on fire as he sat up. He fell forward, leaning on Aissa for support. He rested his head on her shoulder, feeling her arm go around him.

"You're burning up," Aissa said. Gently, she freed her right hand so she could pick up the pitcher from the floor. "Here, drink some of this."

Shadow Hawk raised his head, steadying the pitcher with his hand as he drank. He drank until he was sated then pushed it away. "That's enough." Aissa put the pitcher back on the floor. Shadow Hawk looked at her again, touching her face. "I love you, Aissa," he said softly, his voice barely audible. "I have no home without you." He closed his eyes and leaned on Aissa again.

"Shadow Hawk, you have a fever. Would any of your medicines help?"

"I want to hold you," Shadow Hawk said, pulling her to him. Suddenly, the pain seemed to vanish; nothing seemed to matter but the two of them. He felt Aissa gently pushing him away.

"I want you to lie back down. I'm going to make some tea and bring it back to you. Tell me where your medicine pouch is."

Shadow Hawk shook his head, fighting Aissa. "I don't want to lie down."

"Where is the pouch, Shadow Hawk?" Aissa demanded, her voice insistent.

Shadow Hawk opened his eyes. "It's on the table by the bed. To the right of you."

"Good, now lie down."

"Aissa—"

"Listen to me!" Aissa's voice was sharp. "You're very sick. You have a fever."

Shadow Hawk smiled. "You're worried about me."

"Yes, I'm worried about you. Now, lie down."

Shadow Hawk eased himself onto his left side, still holding onto Aissa. "You're beautiful."

"I'm going to leave you for awhile. Don't try to get up."

Shadow Hawk watched Aissa as she picked up the pouch and carefully made her way across the room and out the door. He wanted to say something to her, but he was suddenly too tired. He closed his eyes. He was thirsty again, and the pain had come back. He tried to clear his head, to make sense of his thoughts, but he could not. His body ached and burned. The only thing that mattered to him right now was sleep.

Aissa made her way down the stairs and to the kitchen, as if she had been able to see. "Elaina?" she called out, as soon as she entered the kitchen.

"*Señorita,* what are you doing up? You should be in bed."

"I want you to boil some water and put some of this medicine into it. Do you understand me?"

"*Sí,* but—"

"Where is Christina? I need her help."

"I do not know."

"Please, Elaina, I must find her."

"I did see her go outside."

"Can you help me find her? Please." Aissa heard Elaina bark some orders in Spanish to her helper, then she took Aissa's hand and led her through the side door of the kitchen and took her around into the courtyard.

"We are coming to the steps. Be careful. *Madre de Dios!*"

"What is it?"

"You are dressed only in your robe, *señorita*. You should not be seen by any of the hands."

"I don't care, Elaina. I need to find Christina."

"Aye," Elaina muttered, taking Aissa's hand.

"Where does she go during the day, do you know?"

"Usually she is back there, in the courtyard. She likes it there."

"She also likes animals. Maybe she's by the corrals or the barn."

"If the patron sees me leading you around dressed like this. . . ." Elaina continued to mutter something in Spanish.

"Don't worry, Elaina. I'll make sure Mr. Montrose doesn't do anything."

They walked on, Elaina's plump hand firmly on Aissa's arm. Elaina's steady stream of Spanish stopped suddenly. "There she is with *Señor* Clay."

"Christina!" Aissa yelled, not caring what anyone thought if they saw or heard her. She turned to Elaina. "Can you see her? Did she hear me?"

"*Sí*, I think everyone on the ranch heard you, *señorita*."

Aissa smiled and squeezed Elaina's hand. "Thank you, Elaina. You can go back now. Christina can take me back to the house. Get the tea made."

"*Sí, señorita*."

Aissa waited for only a few minutes before she heard the sound of footsteps. Two people. She felt a hand on her arm.

"Are you all right, Aissa?" Christina asked frantically.

"I need your help, Christina. Let's get back to the house in a hurry. I want you to make sure Elaina made some tea for Shadow Hawk."

"He has a fever," Christina said flatly.

Clay stepped forward. "You shouldn't be out here, Aissa. You could've fallen again."

"I don't care, Clay," Aissa said brusquely. "I want to go back to the house." Aissa took hold of Christina's hand, and they hurried across the yard and up the steps to the courtyard. Aissa started up the staircase but Clay grabbed her arm.

"Are you all right?" Clay asked.

"No, I'm not all right. I'm worried about Shadow Hawk. He has a fever," Aissa said impatiently.

"He'll be all right, Aissa."

"How do you know? What if it kills him?" Her tone was so frantic-sounding it surprised even her. "I'm sorry, Clay."

"It's all right, Aissa. I know you love him."

"I don't know what I'll do if something happens to him. . . ." Aissa took a deep breath. "I've made a decision, Clay. As soon as Shadow Hawk recovers, I'm going home."

"And if he doesn't recover?"

"Don't say that, please."

"What if he doesn't recover, Aissa?"

"Then I'm still going home. I can't stay here any longer. I need to be with my father." Aissa reached out and touched Clay's arm. "I'm sorry. I never meant to hurt you."

"You were always honest with me. You have nothing to feel bad about. Come on, I'll take you upstairs."

When they were halfway up the staircase, Aissa heard Christina's footsteps behind them.

"I have the tea," Christina said, catching up with them.

At the top of the stairs, Aissa stopped. "Clay?"

"Yes."

"Thank you for everything, I mean that."

"Why don't you come with us, Clay? We might need your help to lift him up," Christina said, smiling at Clay.

Aissa held onto Christina's hand as they went into Shadow Hawk's room. Christina led her to the bed, and Aissa knelt next to it. She reached out and touched Shadow Hawk's face. "He's burning with fever, Christina. We have to get him to drink the tea."

"I can bring the doctor back out here," Clay offered.

"No, he wouldn't want to see a doctor. Just give him the tea, please."

"All right. Clay, help me get him up," Christina said.

Aissa stayed close to the bed and listened as Clay and Christina maneuvered Shadow Hawk to a sitting position. When Shadow Hawk didn't speak, Aissa was frightened. "Is he awake? We have to wake him up."

"Come on, Shadow Hawk," Christina urged, "it's time to wake up. Come on."

"You're too gentle," Clay said, slapping Shadow Hawk's cheek.

"Clay!" Christina shouted, grabbing Clay's hand. "Don't hit him."

"Look, he's waking up," Clay said.

Aissa leaned forward. "Shadow Hawk," she said gently. "Can you hear me?"

"Aissa."

Aissa felt Shadow Hawk move on the bed. "You need to drink this."

"Water."

"You can have some water after you drink this," Christina said, putting the cup to his mouth. "Drink."

"I hate this tea. My grandmother made it for her enemies."

Aissa smiled in spite of her fear. "Just drink it."

When Shadow Hawk was finished, Christina poured some water into the cup and let him drink. "You have to keep drinking until your fever breaks."

"Leave me alone, Christina."

"If you don't drink it, I'll pour it down your throat," Clay threatened.

Shadow Hawk barely lifted his head, beads of sweat dripping down his face. "You are here to taunt me, white man. Why didn't you just let me die out there?"

"Aissa would never have forgiven me if I had let you die. Besides, I wanted you to owe me." Clay grinned at Christina.

Shadow Hawk shook his head. "I am being punished."

"You need to lie back down," Christina said. She and Clay helped Shadow Hawk onto his left side. Christina pulled the rocking chair close to the bed. "The chair is behind you, Aissa. Sit down. We don't need you to get sick again."

"How are the headaches?" Clay asked.

"No headaches right now. I'm fine, thank you." Aissa was tempted to tell Clay about the flashes of light she'd been seeing but decided against it.

"I'll be back to check on you both later and I'll bring some more tea."

"Thank you, Christina." Aissa heard Christina and Clay as they left the room, and she put her head back against the chair. She heard Shadow Hawk's steady breathing and knew that he was already asleep. She closed her eyes and she rubbed them. She was so tired. She wanted to dream. She needed to hope that everything would be all right.

Clay and Christina went into the study. Clay poured himself a whiskey and downed it. He poured another and then turned and held the glass up to the portrait of his brother. "Here's to you, Russell. I'm sorry I couldn't save you, but I have to get on with my life." Clay drank the glass, slamming it down on the desk. He started to pour another, but Christina put her hand on his arm.

"What're you doing?"

"I think it's pretty obvious what I'm doing" Clay poured another glass but Christina took it from his hand. He looked at her, astonished. "Christina—"

"What's the matter with you? Are you upset because Aissa is with Shadow Hawk? You knew from the start that she loved him."

"Leave me alone. You're a bothersome woman."

"Good," Christina said, taking his arm and leading him to the sofa. "Sit down, Clay. You've had a long day."

"Don't treat me like a child."

"What is it?"

Clay was silent, staring at the portrait of his brother. "I feel responsible. If I'd shot sooner, Shadow Hawk wouldn't be hurt."

"And if Shadow Hawk had taken better aim, maybe he wouldn't have been hurt. Did you ever think of that?" Christina pulled Clay down on the couch next to her. "It's over. You can't do anything about it now."

"Why're you being so nice? I thought you didn't like me."

Christina shrugged. "Maybe I've changed my mind."

Clay reached up and pushed a strand of hair from Christina's face. He knew the whiskey was making him bolder than he would've been otherwise. "What would make you do that?"

"I thought about it. You could've let Shadow Hawk die out there and no one would've known what happened. But, you saved his life."

"My father won't see it that way."

"You know what happened out there, Clay. That's all that matters."

Clay looked at Christina's sweet face with the freckles sprayed across her small nose, and he suddenly found her quite charming. "You think so?"

"Yes, I think so. You can stand up to your father. It's about time, don't you think?"

"I've never had a problem standing up to him, I've just never stayed around long enough to give him the chance to knock me back down."

"Well, this time you're not going to run away. You're going to face him."

"Why do you care?"

"Because you have a chance to be close to your father again. I'll never have that chance. Don't throw it away, Clay."

Clay saw the sadness in Christina's eyes. "I'm sorry. I know you must miss your parents."

"Sometimes I miss them so much, I don't know what to do." Christina looked around her. "They worked so hard all of their lives. They never saw a home like yours, never even got to stay in a nice place."

"Then they'd be happy you're with people who care about you." He wanted to touch her but was afraid she'd pull away.

"I can't stay with Shadow Hawk and Aissa forever. They have their own lives."

"Then stay here." Clay was surprised when he said the words and surprised that he meant them. "We have plenty of room. Rayna would welcome someone she could talk to besides my mother and father."

"And what about you, Clay?" Christina asked, her eyes sparkling.

"I guess I'd like it if you stayed here, too." Clay touched Christina's cheek. "I'm not the best man in the world. I drink and I gamble."

"I didn't ask you to marry me, did I?"

Clay laughed. "I do like you, and I'd like it if you stayed here."

"We'll see. Right now I think I'd like you to kiss me."

Clay stared at her, taken aback by her honesty and her beauty. He leaned close to her, pressing his mouth to hers, feeling her soft lips yield to his.

"Am I interrupting anything?"

Clay jerked away from Christina at the sound of Rayna's voice. "No, we were just talking."

"Yes, I could tell you were in deep conversation." Rayna smiled slightly. "I just got back from town. Mother said Shadow Hawk was hurt. What happened?"

"The cat attacked him."

Rayna's face went pale. "How, Clay? Weren't you there?"

"Yes, Rayna, I was there," Clay said angrily, standing up and walking to the desk. "I didn't make the cat attack him. I did what I could." Clay's hands started to shake as he poured himself another drink.

Rayna walked to him, taking the decanter from his hands. "I'm sorry. You know I didn't mean it that way."

"He saved Shadow Hawk's life," Christina said, crossing the room to stand by them. "If Clay hadn't been there, Shadow Hawk would be dead."

"Is he hurt badly?" Rayna asked.

"He was clawed along his right side and shoulder. The wounds are pretty deep," Clay said, looking down at Christina. She had moved to stand next to him.

"I cleaned out the wounds, but he's real feverish right now," Christina said.

"Shouldn't someone be with him?"

"Aissa is with him," Clay said, his voice calmer.

"Can I see him?"

"I don't see why not," Christina said. "Aissa could probably use the company."

Rayna nodded to Christina, then walked to her brother and kissed him on the cheek. "I'm glad you were there."

Clay watched Rayna as she left the room. He loved her. She'd grown up to be a fine person. He felt Christina's hand on his arm and he looked at her. She was willing to stick up for him, too; he'd never had any woman but Rayna do that for him. Without speaking, he pulled Christina into his arms and hugged her fiercely.

Ray Grimes stepped silently into the room, a hunting knife held in front of him. He walked toward Shadow Hawk, looked at him for a second, then put the knife to his throat, slashing it from ear to ear. Blood soaked the bed. Then he walked toward Aissa. She was sleeping in the chair, her head back, her throat exposed. Ray stood over her and smiled. He had waited for this for a long time and now that time had come. He had finally gotten the Apache and now he was going to get Aissa. He pressed the point of the blade into Aissa's throat and she felt the searing pain. She tried to scream, but nothing would come out. She felt helpless as the knife dug into the flesh of her throat, and she felt her life drain away. She screamed a silent scream.

Aissa sat up, striking out at the image in her own mind, a stifled scream actually coming from her throat. She gasped for air, feeling as if she would suffocate. Half-awake, she touched her throat, reality slowly taking over. There was no blood. It had only been a nightmare. She sat back in the chair, trembling. She was all right. After a few moments, when the pounding of her heart had lessened, she sat up to check on Shadow Hawk. A blinding pain went through her head. She closed her eyes and lowered her head, pressing the heels of her hands into her eyes. Little specks of colored light illuminated the darkness. When the pain passed, she opened her eyes. The room was bathed in a soft, yellow light. Aissa looked slowly around. She could see the outlines of the bed, the door, the window. She raised her hands; she was even able to see her fingers.

"My God," she said softly, kneeling close to the bed. She looked at Shadow Hawk. The details of his face were blurred, but she could see his dark hair and his sun-bronzed skin against the white linens. She rested her cheek on his. He was still burning with fever.

Suddenly, her eyes ached again. Slowly, she stood up, the pain overwhelming. She was afraid to move. She sank back down into the chair, afraid to hope, closing her eyes against the beautiful, soothing light that was quickly fading.

A moment later Aissa opened her eyes and stifled a cry of despair. The darkness had come back.

* * *

Shadow Hawk fought the fever for two nights and two days, lapsing in and out of consciousness. Sometimes he remembered seeing Aissa, being forced to drink the tea; other times he couldn't remember anything. He dreamed constantly. Once he even dreamed his father talked to him.

"You must wake up, Shadow," he said, his voice seeming to come from everywhere.

"I am too tired, Father," he had said.

"You must fight your tiredness. If you do not wake up, you will soon be with me in the land beyond. You have yet to live your life, Shadow. You cannot come with me yet."

Shadow Hawk had tried to speak to his father again, but he was gone. He dreamed of his cousins, his uncle, his brother, and his mother. He even dreamed of Ocha, his grandmother, and thought he saw her sitting by a pot cooking some of her foul-smelling medicine.

"Drink the tea, Grandson," she had said in the dream. "Draw on your own strength."

Shadow Hawk felt as if he were so deep in his dreams he would never come out, but then he would hear Aissa's voice. He would fight his way back, to see her, to touch her. The morning of the third day, Shadow Hawk opened his eyes. The room was quiet and still. Aissa was sleeping in the chair. He lifted himself, slowly managing to sit up. The ice and fire of his fever had abated. The pain wasn't as great. Shadow Hawk pulled in a deep breath. He was thirsty. He reached down for the pitcher that Aissa had left beside the bed, trying not to aggravate his wounds. He drank until the pitcher was empty and set it back on the floor. Then he looked at Aissa. Her hair was tousled, and there were dark circles underneath her eyes. Her hands were folded in her lap. He reached out and touched them and she opened her eyes. Her eyes had always taken his breath away and they were still beautiful, but now their beauty made him sad. He squeezed her hands.

"Shadow Hawk?" Her voice was soft and low.

Gently, with his left hand, he pulled her toward him until she got out of the chair and knelt beside the bed, her head against his chest. He put his arm around her and rested his chin on the top of her head. "You should go to bed," he said, stroking her hair.

She reached up and touched his face. "Your fever has broken. I was so worried."

"I'm all right now." He held her again, kissing the top of her hair. "I want you to go back to your room, Aissa. You need to sleep."

Aissa looked up at him. "I want to be with you."

"Go now." Shadow Hawk tried to stand but couldn't.

"You shouldn't be trying to move yet."

"Either you go back to your room, or I'll get up and take you there."

"All right." Aissa leaned against his chest. "Can we talk later?"

"Yes, we have a lot to talk about." He kissed her again then gently pushed her away. "Be careful, the chair is right behind you. Hold my hand." Shadow Hawk gave Aissa his hand and helped her to her feet, directing her to the door. He watched her as she slowly felt her way out of the room. She was finding her strength.

Shadow Hawk heard Aissa's door close, and he relaxed on the bed. He was still a long way from being well, but he could tell he had beaten the fever. All he needed now was to rest.

Shadow Hawk heard Bradford's booming voice on the stairway and prepared himself for a visit from the older man. When Bradford entered the room, Clay and Rayna were with him.

"So, you're up." Bradford walked to the bed, looking closely at Shadow Hawk's wounds. "Looks like you'll survive."

Shadow Hawk nodded his head. "I'm going to live, Bradford." He smiled at Rayna as she walked toward him.

"How're you feeling?" she asked.

"I am better, thank you."

"I came in to see you a few times, we all did, but you were delirious."

"Aissa never left your side. She took good care of you," Clay said.

Shadow Hawk glanced at Clay. "I sent her back to her room to get some sleep. Has she had any headaches?"

"I don't know. She hasn't said much to anyone. Christina might know. She's been staying in Aissa's room."

"Where is Christina?" Shadow Hawk asked.

"She's helping my mother," Rayna said. "Can I get you anything?"

"No, Rayna. I'm fine."

Bradford sat on the foot of the bed and cleared his throat. "So tell me, boy. What happened? I thought you were a good tracker."

"I am a good tracker," Shadow Hawk said impatiently, moving the pillows, trying to find a comfortable position. "I found the cat, didn't I?" He looked at Clay and thought he saw him smile.

But Bradford wasn't smiling. "More like he found you. Clay's told me his version, now I want to hear yours. What the hell happened?"

"We followed the cat's tracks up into a draw. He was feeding on his kill. I shot but only wounded him."

"Made him mad," Bradford said, nodding.

"When I tried to fire again, the rifle jammed and he attacked me."

Bradford shook his head. "I still don't understand. Where was Clay?"

Shadow Hawk glanced quickly at Clay before he answered. "He was behind me."

"Why was he behind you?" Bradford demanded, then he turned to Clay. "It was your hunt, why were you letting him lead?"

"He's the better tracker."

"Damn you, Clay," Bradford shouted. "Why didn't you tell me he was leading?"

"You didn't ask." Clay's voice was almost devoid of emotion; he'd been waiting for this.

"It doesn't matter, Bradford," Shadow Hawk said.

"It does matter. I told him to get the cat, not you."

"And I went along to help him. I said I was a tracker and I took the lead. He did not suggest it."

"But he didn't try to talk you out of it either." Bradford shook his head. "And what about when your rifle jammed, where was Clay?"

"I already told you, he was behind me."

"Exactly. Why wasn't he next to you?"

"I'm right here in the room, Pa. Why don't you ask me?" His voice was cold and strained.

Bradford turned to Clay. "All right. Why were you behind Shadow Hawk?"

Clay was staring at his father like a man who wants the talking to stop and the fight to start. "I was behind him because I was scared. Is that what you wanted to hear?"

Rayna walked to her father, taking his arm. "Pa, it's over. Just let it end."

He shook her off. "It's not over, it'll never be over. Your brother almost got another person killed because of his cowardice" Bradford stood to face his son. "Isn't that right, Clay?"

Clay was breathing hard. "You tell me, Pa. You're the one with all the answers."

"I know exactly what happened up there. Shadow Hawk tracked the cat, he tried to kill the cat alone, and when his gun jammed, you froze. Just like you froze when Russell got killed."

"You're right, Pa. You're always right." Clay's voice was cold again. He started for the door.

"Wait," Shadow Hawk said, struggling to sit up. "Don't leave, Clay."

Clay turned and glared at Shadow Hawk. "It won't matter what you say."

"The truth always matters." Shadow Hawk looked at Bradford. "I don't understand your hatred of your own son, Montrose." Shadow Hawk glanced at Clay. "Your son did nothing wrong. It was not his fault that I was attacked, it was my fault. In my haste to make the kill and leave here, I was too anxious. I was not cautious as I had been taught from the time I was a boy. I shot the cat but I did not take true aim, so he attacked me. Clay shot him as soon as he could. If he had frozen, I would now be dead." Shadow Hawk looked at Clay and saw the gratitude in his eyes.

"He should've been leading."

"Why? Did you want him to find the cat first, Montrose? Did you want him to be the one who got hurt?"

"No, I—"

"You have taken me, a Comanche, into your home, and you treat me better than you do your own flesh and blood. You do not deserve this family, Montrose."

"Don't talk to me of things you know nothing about," Bradford said angrily.

"Did you hear what I said?" Shadow Hawk demanded. He ignored the pain from his wounds and sat up straighter, forcing Bradford to meet his eyes. "I told you that your son did nothing wrong. He saved my life. I was the one who made the mistake, not he."

Bradford started to speak but Rayna went to him, again taking his arm. "Listen to him, Pa. Clay is the only son you have. He didn't kill Russell. He loved Russell.

Don't you remember how close they were?"

Bradford's eyes betrayed his grief as he looked at Clay. "I remember everything," he said, his voice uneven. "I remember thinking that someday I would give this ranch to both of my sons."

"Well, you have one son to give it to, and he's alive."

Bradford looked at Clay and seemed for a moment as if he was about to speak, then shook his head and walked out of the room.

Shadow Hawk collapsed against the pillows. "I'm sorry. I thought he would listen."

"It's not your fault. Thanks for trying. You didn't have to say anything."

"Yes, I did. I was thinking only of killing the cat and getting away from here."

"From me you mean."

"I didn't want to see you and Aissa together anymore."

"I don't think you have to worry about that. She's already made it real clear she's going home with you." Clay shrugged. "I knew she was never in love with me." He walked to the door. "I think I'll go on into town. I could use a drink right now."

"Clay, please don't," Rayna begged him.

"Don't worry about me, Sis. I'll be fine." Without another word, Clay turned and left the room.

Rayna walked to the bed and plumped the pillows behind Shadow Hawk. "He won't be fine. I'm worried about him."

"He's a good man, Rayna. He'll find his own way."

"All he wants is my father's forgiveness. That's not asking much."

"I don't think your father knows how to forgive, Rayna. His heart is barren."

"I know," Rayna said sadly, sitting down in the rocking chair. "I'm glad you're feeling better."

Shadow Hawk smiled gratefully. "As soon as I'm well,

I'm going to take Aissa and go home."

Rayna nodded. "I'm glad. It's time."

"What will you do? Stay here until you grow old?"

"You're trying to insult me, aren't you?" Rayna's eyes twinkled defiantly.

"You're too smart and capable to take care of your parents all of your life, Rayna."

"So, you think I need a man?"

"I didn't say that. Why don't you make your own life away from here?"

Rayna shrugged. "Maybe I will." She plumped the pillows again. "I think Christina is going to stay here when you leave."

Shadow Hawk looked puzzled. "Christina? Why would she stay here?"

"She and Clay are becoming close. Maybe they're even falling in love."

"Christina and Clay?" Shadow Hawk shook his head. "She has said nothing to me."

"She wouldn't. She probably doesn't think you approve."

"He was just in love with Aissa, how could he be in love with Christina?"

Rayna smiled. "See, you don't approve."

"When have they had the time to get to know each other?"

"They've had plenty of time. You haven't seen that much of Christina since you've been here. Your mind has been on Aissa."

Shadow Hawk shook his head, grinning. "You're a hard woman, Rayna."

"Is that good or bad?"

Shadow Hawk looked at her, pretending to have no ready answer. "Strength is always good." He leaned his head back against the pillows, positioning himself so he was leaning mostly on his left side.

"You look tired. I'll visit again later." Rayna stood up.

"Thank you for defending Clay."

"I didn't defend him, I told the truth."

Rayna smiled. "I'm going to miss you." She kissed him on the cheek. "But while you're here in bed, I may ride the paint!"

"Rayna!" Shadow Hawk yelled after her as she sashayed out of the room. Shadow Hawk shook his head and grinned.

Shadow Hawk closed his eyes. He was tired and his wounds ached, but he felt better than he had in a long time. God, how he loved Aissa. Soon they would be going home. Finally, nothing stood in the way of their happiness.

Chapter Fifteen

The man at the bar shoved some coins toward the bartender. "Gimme the bottle," he said, looking around the room. "He in here yet?"

The bartender handed the man a bottle and glass and nodded toward a table. "He's sitting over there. You got lucky, haven't seen him in here in awhile."

"What's he drinking?"

"Same as you."

The cowboy nodded, picked up the glass and bottle and headed toward the table. "Mind if I join you?" he said to the man at the table.

The man picked up his glass, stared at the contents, then downed it quickly. "I don't care." He poured himself another glass.

The cowboy sat down and poured himself a glass of whiskey. "Been on the trail a long time. Trying to find myself a job. You wouldn't happen to know of any around here, would you?"

"Depends on what you're looking for." He slid his glass in a slow circle on the rough, wooden table.

"I can do anything. Bein' a cowhand is all I know."

"You might not be working with cows or horses. You might just be mending fences."

"Doesn't matter. I wouldn't mind staying in one place for awhile." The cowboy drank his glass and poured another.

"Truth is, my woman just left me for another man. I need to get my mind off her."

"Know what you mean?"

"My name's Pete. What's yours?"

"The name's Clay. Clay Montrose."

The cowboy nodded. "So, you think you know of somebody who'll hire me?"

Clay finished the bottle. "Yeah, I might hire you if you share that bottle of yours with me."

"Sure thing,' the cowboy said, filling Clay's glass. "You're sure drownin' your troubles, friend."

"Yep," Clay said, leaning forward and staring into the glass.

"Woman trouble with you, too, friend? I recognize the signs."

Clay looked at the cowboy. "She never really loved me anyway." He shrugged. "But she was a beauty. Never saw anyone like her before."

"Tell me about her," the cowboy said, filling Clay's glass again.

"Tall, blond, with the most beautiful blue eyes you ever saw. Break your heart just to look at her."

"Sounds like it," the cowboy agreed, nodding his head. "My woman wasn't that good-looking, but she was real good at other things, if you know what I mean."

Clay shook his head. "I never had the satisfaction myself."

The cowboy poured another drink for Clay and himself. "She up and leave you for somebody else?"

"Not yet."

"What do you mean?"

Clay swirled the whiskey in his glass. "She's still staying at my pa's ranch, but she's in love with somebody else."

"So you have to watch them together?"

Clay nodded. "Yeah."

"Then you really are hurting." The cowboy leaned forward with a conspiratorial grin. "I have an idea. Why don't we each get ourselves a woman and head on upstairs? I can't think of a better way to forget one woman than with another one."

Clay looked up, considered it for a minute, then nodded his head slowly. "Why not?" He finished the drink and stood up, knocking over the chair.

"I'll follow you," the cowboy said, picking up the bottle and their glasses. He nodded surreptitiously to a man in a black hat and his companion, who had a long scar across one cheek. The two men were sitting at a nearby table. Then the cowboy made a show of looking over the saloon girls. "You," he pointed to a redhead who was wearing a bright green dress that pulled tightly across her breasts. "Bring a friend and follow us upstairs."

Clay and the cowboy waited on the second-floor landing. A few minutes later, the redhead and a tall, slender brunette came up the stairs. As they neared the top, the redhead pulled a room key from her bodice, and Clay and the cowboy followed the women down the hall, then into a room. Clay collapsed on the bed and the cowboy sat in a chair, pouring them a drink.

"Here you go, friend," he said, handing Clay a glass.

Clay accepted, sipping at the whiskey as the brunette sat next to him on the bed. The cowboy watched as Clay set his glass on the nightstand and lay back. The brunette leaned forward, talking in a low voice. Whatever she said made Clay smile, and the brunette kissed him. After a moment, she began to unbutton his shirt and Clay closed his eyes. The cowboy glanced at the redhead and found her watching him with a puzzled expression on her face. He put a finger to his lips and backed toward the door as the brunette put Clay's hand on her breast. The cowboy opened the door and stood back. The man with the scarred face came inside quickly, followed by the man in the black hat. They crossed the room before Clay had time to react. One pulled the brunette off the bed, the other one punched Clay in the face.

"Don't hurt him too bad," the cowboy said.

The man with the scarred cheek glanced at him and nodded curtly. He hit Clay in the face twice more then straightened up. Clay didn't move. The cowboy nodded in satisfaction then pulled a roll of bills from his pocket.

"Here's your regular price," he said to the redhead. "And a little more for keeping quiet." The redhead thumbed through the money quickly, counting it as her friend looked over her shoulder. They nodded to each other and then at the cowboy. A second later, they were gone.

The cowboy pulled out more money and handed it to the man in the black hat. "Tie him up real good. Make sure he's not gonna go anywhere for awhile." The cowboy left the room and went downstairs. The redhead smiled as he crossed the saloon but he didn't even notice her. His business was finished. He mounted up and rode out of town to the camp. Grimes would be real grateful to hear what he had to tell him.

Ray Grimes watched from the safety of the trees as his men went toward the bunkhouse. After almost half an hour had passed without anyone firing a shot, he knew that his plan had worked. As soon as he got the sign from one of the men that they had Montrose's hands under guard, Grimes and his men went to the walled courtyard. One of the men roped a corner post and quickly scaled the wall. He braced himself against the wall with his feet as another man threw up a heavy blanket to cover the glass. The man placed the coarse cover on the glass and quickly stepped over it, holding onto the rope as he climbed down the inside courtyard wall. He went to the courtyard doors, removed the heavy wooden slide bar, and let in Grimes and his men.

Grimes motioned for one of the men to lead the way into the house, and he and five others followed. He was sure that he wouldn't need more men. But if there was trouble, three shots in quick succession would bring his other men up from the bunkhouse.

The man who had climbed the wall stepped forward. He took a long, thin knife from a sheath strapped to his ankle.

Ray stood back and watched with admiration as the man slid the blade into the crack between the double doors. A moment later, the latch had been sprung and the men were inside. With quick gestures, Grimes sent two men into the kitchen and two others in the opposite direction through the arched doorway to the dining room. The remaining two men walked with him to the staircase that went upstairs. They waited, guns drawn, until the others returned. When the men reassured Ray that the downstairs was empty, he started up the stairs. There were lamps in niches along the wall and all of them had been extinguished for the night. Ray paused a moment. He could hear the sounds of heavy snoring somewhere off to his right. On an impulse, he turned away from it, crossed the landing, and entered the hallway on the left side of the stairs. Again he hesitated, listening. He pointed to Will, a short stocky man, and then to Johnnie, a wild-eyed kid he'd picked up in Santa Fe.

"The rest of you wait here," he whispered.

Grimes went to the first room and motioned Johnnie to go in ahead of him. Johnnie flattened himself against the wall beside the door. Then, gun drawn, he pushed the door inward. There was no sound from within the room. Johnnie inched forward, cautiously, slipping into the room. A moment later, he gave the all-clear signal. Grimes went through the doorway and looked at the still-sleeping figure in the bed. He stepped forward. It was an older woman, probably Montrose's wife. In one swift motion, he put his hand over her mouth and jerked her into a sitting position. She tried to scream, but he clamped his hand so tightly over her mouth that she could not. He could feel her trembling.

"Johnnie, light the lamp. Will, you close the door."

Grimes leaned close to the woman's ear. "You try to scream again, you're a dead woman. Understand?"

Dorothea nodded and he took his hand from her mouth, drawing his gun. "Do what I say and I won't kill you," Grimes said, the gun close to her temple. She nodded frantically. "How many other people in the house?"

Dorothea hesitated and he cocked the gun. "Five," she answered, her voice trembling.

"How many men?"

"Two, my husband and a guest."

"Where are they?"

Dorothea glanced at the men who stood behind Grimes. "On the other side of the landing. My husband is in the room at the east end. A guest is staying in the middle. That's all, there's no one else here."

"What about on this side?"

"My daughter is in the next room, and two guests are in the last room."

"Where is Aissa Gerard?"

A look of shock crossed Dorothea's features. "What do you want with her?"

"It's none of your business. Which room is she in?"

"She's in the last room."

"What color hair does the other woman have?"

Dorothea hesitated momentarily but answered. "Brown."

Grimes turned to Will. "Take the woman with the brown hair and put her in the middle room with this lady's daughter. Do it as quietly as you can. Make sure they don't go anywhere." Then Grimes looked at Johnnie. "Go tell the others to tie up the two men on the other side of the hall. When you're done, get back here and keep an eye on this one."

"What about the blond woman, boss?" Will asked.

"I'll take care of her myself," Grimes said, his voice cold.

"What are you going to do? Aissa can't hurt you," Dorothea's eyes filled with tears.

"Shut up," Ray commanded.

"Please, don't harm her. She's blind!" Dorothea cried out.

Ray put his hand over Dorothea's mouth, smothering her cry. "What did you say? And don't yell again."

Dorothea nodded. "Aissa is blind. She can't see a thing."

"You're sure?"

"Yes."

Ray nodded and smiled. "I can't believe this," he said, pacing impatiently around the room until Johnnie returned.

"It's done, boss. Will says the blond woman never woke up."

Grimes looked at Dorothea, the gun held in front of her eyes. "Keep your mouth shut if you want your family to be all right." He nodded to Johnnie as he left the room.

Grimes walked down the hall to the last room. He almost felt like laughing out loud. This was better than anything he could've imagined. He opened the door and walked across the room. He could see Aissa in the bed. He turned up the lamp and looked at her. God, she was beautiful. If she had only come to him of her own free will, all of this could have been avoided. He put his hand over her mouth and sat on the bed. "Hello, Aissa."

Aissa murmured in her sleep and then struggled, pulling at Grimes's hand. Her eyes were open and she seemed to be looking at him, but he knew she couldn't see a thing.

"Did you actually think you'd get away from me?" He watched her face as she recognized his voice. She was terrified. He sat down on the bed and roughly pulled Aissa into his arms, his hand still over her mouth. "I came here to make you suffer a little before I killed you, but it looks like you've already had a pretty rough time. Tell me, what's it like to be blind, Aissa?" Grimes held onto her as she fought to get away. "It's not going to do you any good to struggle, Aissa. I have my men in the house; everyone is under guard. And don't think you'll get help from the hands. I have guards at the bunkhouse." Grimes uncovered her mouth. "So, what do we do now?"

"I hate you!" Aissa said, striking out but missing him.

"You are pathetic, Aissa. At least before you were able to put up a good fight."

"I wish I had killed you when I had the chance."

"You can thank your Apache lover for that. How is he, anyway? Been a long time since you've seen him, hasn't it?"

Aissa suddenly stopped struggling. "What're you going to do, Ray?"

"I'm going to kill you, and then I'm going to find Shadow Hawk and kill him."

"What about the others? They haven't done anything to you."

"I'll decide about them later. If you're nice to me, maybe I'll let them live."

"How did you find me?"

"Aissa, you really are losing your touch. I suspected you were with Montrose, but I wasn't sure. So, I waited until he came into town and I asked him. It was that simple."

"Clay told you I was here?"

"Surprised? Haven't you learned that everyone has their price, Aissa?"

"I can't believe Clay would've told you anything."

"You don't know him very well, do you?" Ray stood up. "Let's go see if my men have everyone tied up. Then I'll decide what I'm going to do."

"No!" Aissa protested, pulling at Ray's arm.

"What's the matter? Are you that scared?"

"Please, Ray, if you're going to kill me, just do it here. Leave the others out of it."

"Why are you so suddenly concerned about the others?" Ray jerked Aissa to her feet. "What aren't you telling me, Aissa?"

"Nothing."

"Well, I guess I'll start with that old woman. She's so scared right now it won't take much to finish her off. Or maybe I'll just take her daughter in there and kill her in front of the old lady."

"No!" Aissa pleaded.

"Then tell me what you're hiding."

Aissa lowered her head in defeat. "Shadow Hawk is here."

"Where? Which room?"

"The middle room across the hall."

Ray shook his head. "So, the Apache couldn't stay away. I

should've known."

"Leave him alone, Ray. Do what you want with me but leave him alone."

"That's touching, Aissa. Really." Ray took Aissa's arm and forced her down the hall, across the landing, to the other side of the house. Twice she twisted free but both times he caught her again, laughing at her clumsiness. He walked into Shadow Hawk's room, holding Aissa in front of him. Shadow Hawk was sitting up, leaning to one side. One guard was by the bed, another by the door. Ray pushed Aissa toward the bed, one of her arms held behind her.

"You're not looking too good, Shadow Hawk." Shadow Hawk winced as he tried to move. "Isn't it amazing how things turn out? Look at this, both of you here in one house. And it's even better than that—you're wounded and Aissa is blind."

"Let her go, Grimes. She's suffered enough."

"Do you think I care?" Ray asked, his voice loud. "As far as I'm concerned, she hasn't even begun to suffer." Ray pulled Aissa back against him, locking one arm around her neck, running the other hand over her breasts. "She still feels real good."

Shadow Hawk lunged forward but the guard next to the bed shoved him back with the barrel of his rifle. "Let her go," Shadow Hawk said. "Take me."

"I will, but first I'm going to have some fun with Aissa." He turned Aissa around to face him. "Aren't we going to have some fun together?" Ray pulled her close and looked into her sightless blue eyes. Surely, she would give up now.

"I hate you," she said angrily, then she spit in his face.

"You little bitch!" Ray shouted, slapping her hard. He held her so she wouldn't fall, and he hit her again. "I'm going to break you, Aissa."

"Never."

"You don't think so?" Ray grabbed her and pulled her toward the bed. "Turn him over," he commanded and the guard shoved Shadow Hawk onto his stomach. Shadow

Hawk didn't cry out. "Hold her," Ray commanded, shoving Aissa toward the guard. Ray pulled out his knife and cut the bandages from Shadow Hawk's wounds. "These cuts look pretty bad." Ray walked to the man at the door and spoke to him quietly. When he turned back, Ray saw Aissa listening intently to the guard's footsteps. "He'll be back in just a minute. He's doing an errand for me."

"No matter what he does, don't give in to him, Aissa," Shadow Hawk said, trying to lift his head. "Do you hear me?"

"Shut up!" Ray said and the guard pushed Shadow Hawk back down on the mattress. Ray glanced at Aissa; the color had gone out of her face. He wished she could see what he was going to do, but maybe it would be worse for her to imagine what he was doing as she listened to Shadow Hawk's screams. The guard came back into the room and handed Ray a small container. Ray walked to the bed.

"Here's what I'm going to do, Aissa. I'm holding a small pot of salt in my hand. I'm going to pour it all over your lover's wounds and then I'm going to rub it in. I won't stop until you beg me to."

"Don't listen to him, Aissa," Shadow Hawk pleaded.

"Ray, don't. Please," Aissa said, struggling to get free of the guard's hold.

Ray got close to the bed. "You're going to have to do better than that, Aissa. I hear this is an old Apache custom, rubbing salt in the wounds of your enemy." Ray took some of the salt between his fingers and dropped it into the wound on Shadow Hawk's shoulder. Shadow Hawk grabbed onto the bed, burying his face in the pillow. "You'd be real proud, Aissa. Old Shadow Hawk hasn't uttered a sound yet. He's trying to be real brave. But that's not going to last long." Ray took some more of the salt and dropped it into the gashes on Shadow Hawk's back, then he took one of the bandages and pressed the salt into the wound. Shadow Hawk moaned into the pillow.

"For God's sake, Ray, don't do this. Please."

"There's only one way to stop me, Aissa."

"No!" Shadow Hawk turned his head. "Don't give in to him, Aissa. Promise me."

"I can't," Aissa said, her voice breaking as she spoke.

"Well, I guess one more time might do it," Ray said, dropping some more salt into the gashes on Shadow Hawk's back. He took the bandage and began to rub the salt around. This time, Shadow Hawk's entire body went rigid and sweat broke out across his shoulders. Shadow Hawk wasn't completely able to muffle his pained moan.

"Did you hear that, Aissa? That Apache of yours is not as strong as I thought. Next time I could break him."

"All right," Aissa said, barely able to stand.

"What's that? I didn't hear you?"

"I'll do whatever you want me to do."

"Willingly?" Ray asked, his tone almost cheerful.

"Yes," Aissa replied.

"Good." Ray said, pouring the rest of the salt onto Shadow Hawk's back and throwing the bowl across the room. "Let her go," he said to his man. "Come to me, Aissa."

"Aissa, don't," Shadow Hawk pleaded, his voice full of pain as he strained to look at her.

"I can't see you. I don't know where you are."

"I'm over here. Come on," Ray urged, watching in fascination as Aissa felt her way along the foot of the bed and then put her arms out in front of her until she touched him. Ray held onto her as he spoke. "Turn the Apache over. I want him to see this." Ray took Aissa's arm and led her to the foot of the bed so they were directly in front of Shadow Hawk. "Hey, Apache. Open your eyes." Ray waited until Shadow Hawk looked up at them. Ray reached around in front of Aissa, unbuttoning her nightgown. Slowly, he pulled it over her shoulders and let it glide down her body until it fell to the floor. Aissa stood naked, unable to hide her shame. Tears streaked down her face. "So, what do you think Apache? Have you ever seen a woman that looks as good as this one?"

Shadow Hawk lunged toward the foot of the bed, but the two guards shoved him back, one hitting him in the jaw with the butt of his rifle. "I'll kill you, Grimes!" Shadow Hawk shouted.

The guard lifted the rifle to hit Shadow Hawk again, but Ray shook his head. "Don't knock him out. I want him to be awake for all of this." Ray pulled Aissa back against him and ran his hands over her breasts and down her stomach to her thighs. Aissa didn't fight, she didn't even struggle. She stood still and silent. "How's it gonna make you feel when I take your woman right in front of you?" Ray demanded, his hands sliding over Aissa.

"Aissa!" Shadow Hawk cried out her name, and Ray felt Aissa tremble at the pain in his voice.

"You better get used to it, Shadow Hawk. Cause it's just beginning." Ray forced Aissa to the floor next to the bed. "It's gonna be a shame to have to kill her, Shadow Hawk. She's such a beauty." Ray looked at Shadow Hawk. The Apache was a blank mask of rage, and he was straining against the guard who held him. He looked at the man standing by the door. "Help Karl hold him." Ray forced Aissa's legs apart and knelt between them. "I've been waiting for this for a long time, Aissa."

"You can't do it, Ray," Aissa said between clenched teeth. "You've never been able to."

"Shut up!" Ray said, hitting Aissa across the face.

"That's why you kept me drugged when we were married. You didn't want me to know that you aren't capable of loving a woman."

"You bitch." Ray hit Aissa again, this time bloodying her nose and mouth. "I should kill you right now."

"Do it," Aissa urged him.

Ray sat back, fumbling at his pants. "I don't think so." He looked back at his men. "Come here, Karl. Would you like to show this little lady a good time?" Ray stood up, watching as the large man walked toward him.

"You sure, boss?"

"I'm quite sure. She's all yours."

The man smiled a toothless grin. He stood over Aissa and began unbuckling his pants. As he began to kneel between Aissa's legs, she shoved a foot up and kicked him in the groin, sending him sprawling sideways. She tried to squirm away but the man grabbed her hair, forcing her back down.

"You better watch out for her, Karl. She's a tough one."

"I've never met a woman who was too tough for me." Karl shoved Aissa's legs apart, holding both her wrists with one hand above her head. "You're gonna know what it's like to have a real man," he muttered, leaning forward. Aissa struggled but Karl pressed his heavy body onto hers, pinning her to the floor.

"You going to wait all day, Karl?" Ray asked, a smile on his face, his gun trained on Shadow Hawk. "What do you think, Apache? You having any fun?" Ray laughed as Shadow Hawk tried once more to move forward and the guard shoved him back.

Just then, two gunshots rang out in another part of the house, and Ray's smile faded. "Get up, Karl. Quickly." Ray went to the door, glancing back at Shadow Hawk. "Get out there and see what happened." As Karl shouldered past him, Ray looked at the other guard. "Keep an eye on the Apache and the girl, Mort."

Ray tentatively walked into the hall. A guard stood in the doorway to Bradford's room.

"What is it, boss?"

"Don't know, Abe. Stay there until I tell you different. Keep your gun ready." Slowly, Ray backed up to the door of Shadow Hawk's room, waiting. He turned. Shadow Hawk was still sitting in the same place on the bed. Aissa had put on her nightgown. She stood at the foot of the bed, her arms crossed protectively across her body. Mort stood with his rifle raised, aimed at Shadow Hawk's head.

Ray turned back and looked down the hall, listening intently. What was happening on the other side of the house? Then more gunshots rang out and Ray backed into Shadow Hawk's room. Something had gone wrong.

Rayna watched the guards intently, never taking her eyes from them. She and Christina were forced to stand against the wall while the two guards were sitting. One was in a chair; the other, on the bed. Rayna was waiting for a chance. She slept with a pistol under her pillow. She knew if she could just get onto the bed, she might be able to get the gun.

She looked at the man who was sitting on the bed and she smiled seductively, tossing her curly blond hair back over her shoulder. "I'm awfully tired," she said in a low voice. "Do you suppose I could sit down for a bit?"

The guard shrugged his shoulders awkwardly and glanced at his companion. "I don't see why not," he said, motioning Rayna toward him. "But don't try anything."

"What am I going to do?" Rayna asked innocently, ignoring the astonished look Christina shot her as she went to the bed. She sat on the edge and then inched her way back against the headboard, allowing her nightgown to ease up over her bare legs. She leaned toward the guard and whispered, "I don't suppose you and I could be alone for awhile?" She arched her back as she reached up to push her hair from her face.

"Hey, Henry, take that girl into another room so the little lady and I can be alone for awhile."

"I don't think you're supposed to do that."

"Shut up, Henry, and get the hell out."

Rayna ignored Christina as the guard took her out of the room and closed the door. Rayna smiled and looked at the guard.

"My father never lets me go into town. I feel like a prisoner here." She lay back against the pillows, stretching her hands up over her head.

The guard stood up, unbuttoning his shirt and loosening his gun belt. He dropped them to the floor and then began to unbutton his pants. Rayna slipped her hands under the pillow and searched for the gun. When she felt the cold metal, she grasped it firmly and pulled back the hammer. As the man bent to step out of his pants, Rayna pulled the pistol out from under the pillow and sat up. "Don't move," she said, her voice hard.

The man straightened up and saw the gun. He lunged for his own pistol. Rayna never hesitated. She pulled the trigger and the man fell limply forward. She got up and ran across the room, standing behind the door. Within seconds, the other guard rushed into the room. He ran to the body of his friend then, a second too late, realized his mistake. But it was too late. Rayna pulled the trigger before he managed to raise his gun.

Rayna picked up both of the rifles and hid the men's pistols under her mattress. Then she went out, closing the door behind her. She went silently down the hall to her mother's room. The door was open and Rayna could hear the man inside telling her mother and Christina to keep quiet.

Rayna quietly laid the rifles on the hall floor. She flattened herself against the wall beside the doorjamb, holding her pistol against her chest. After a moment, she peeked inside her mother's room. The guard stood in the center, her mother and Christina were on the bed behind him. One quick shot, Rayna thought. She took a deep breath, stood up straight, and came around the edge of the doorway, her pistol held in front of her. She looked at the man for a fleeting moment before she squeezed off two quick shots. The man fell. Rayna got the rifles from the hall and shut the door. Christina had already picked up the guard's rifle and was holding it.

"Shoot anyone who comes in, Christina. Mother, you get over here behind us," she said, motioning to the door.

"Give me a gun, Rayna. I can shoot if I have to."

Rayna looked at her mother, nodded, and handed her her pistol. Rayna took one of the rifles and went back behind the door.

"I wondered what you were doing," Christina whispered.

"I want a man, Christina, but not that badly." Rayna smiled as Christina covered her mouth to keep from laughing. "Someone's coming," Rayna whispered. She could hear one of the men go into her room and call out some names, then she heard his footsteps as they came to her mother's door.

"You in there, Johnnie?"

Rayna held her finger on the trigger of the rifle, waiting for the man to enter the room. After only seconds, she heard his footsteps go back across the landing. "He's gone."

"What're we going to do?" Dorothea asked, trying hard to keep the fear from her voice.

"You're going to hide, Mother. I don't want you involved in this."

"I will not hide. I'm no coward."

"I know that, Mother," Rayna said gently, "but I want you out of the way. I want you under the bed until this is over."

"I will not get underneath that bed, Rayna," Dorothea said indignantly.

"How about the wardrobe, Mrs. Montrose?" Christina asked, gently leading Dorothea to the closet. "Rayna's right. It really would be much safer for you in here." Christina opened the door, moved some of the clothes aside, and helped Dorothea inside.

"I don't much like this," Dorothea muttered.

"It's best, Mother. Please." Rayna kissed her mother on the cheek and closed the door to the wardrobe. She looked at Christina.

"What now?" Christina asked.

"I don't know. I don't know how many more men are in the house."

"Should we try and go for help?"

"I don't know if there are men outside. The hands

must've heard the shots, but none of them have come up to the house. I wish I knew where Clay was."

"So do I," Christina said.

"Well, I guess there's not much else we can do for now but wait."

Clay opened his eyes and tried to lift his head, but it throbbed so badly that he sank back down on the bed. Nausea washed through him. He tried to turn over, and slowly realized he couldn't move—his hands were tied to the headboard of the bed. "What the hell?" he muttered to himself as he tried to free his hands. Then it came back to him. The ride into town, the whiskey, the talk with the stranger, the girls. The stranger . . . who was he? Clay couldn't remember much after the two men had come into the room but he knew this much—the stranger had set him up and he had fallen for it like a fool.

Clay struggled at the ropes that bound him until his wrists felt raw, but finally the ropes loosened enough for him to slip his hands out. He sat up, wincing. His head felt as heavy as a brick, and it pounded like a smithy's hammer. He stood up and walked unsteadily to the small table that held the washbasin. He poured some water into it from the pitcher, washed his face, then took the pitcher and poured the water over his head. He put on his hat and looked around for his holster; it was nowhere around. He patted his pockets. They hadn't taken his money. Clay stood still, trying to make sense out of what had happened. He had almost a hundred dollars in his pockets, but they hadn't bothered to rob him. Why had the cowboy arranged all this? Clay rubbed his head. If he hadn't been so damned eager to forget his father's accusations and the fact that Aissa would never love him. . . .

Clay suddenly remembered that the cowboy had asked him questions about Aissa. There was only one man Clay knew of who would go to this much trouble to find out where she was. Ray Grimes!

Clay tried the door, but it was locked. He walked to the window, lifted it up, then climbed out and dropped to the ground. He went to the hitching rail. His horse was gone, but there were two others; one had a rifle scabbard tied to the saddle with a Winchester in it. Clay untied the horse, led him down the street, then mounted up and rode out of town toward the ranch.

Clay rode hard, urging the horse faster. If anything happened to his family or Aissa, it would be his fault. He had to get there to help them.

Karl ran back into the room. "Henry and Will are dead." He was obviously unnerved, his voice shaky.

"What about Johnnie?" Ray asked evenly.

Karl swallowed. "Don't know. He didn't answer."

"What do you mean he didn't answer?"

"The door was shut and I wasn't about to walk in there and get myself shot."

"You idiot," Ray shouted. He paced around the room, furious. Things were beginning to fall apart but he'd be damned if he'd give up now. He glanced at Aissa and Shadow Hawk. He was tempted to kill them both now, but he hated to let them off that easy.

"Keep your gun on these two, Mort." Ray started for the door then froze in his tracks. Clay Montrose was leaning against the doorway, one thumb hooked through his belt loop, the other loosely holding a rifle. Ray raised his gun. "What the hell are you doing here?"

"I live here, Ray. Remember?" Clay walked slowly forward.

"Don't come any closer."

"Look, I just want what's mine. You owe me some money, remember?"

"What?" Ray shook his head. What kind of game was Clay playing?

"Money. You owe me money from Mexico. I admit I

didn't kill her but blinding her was pretty damn good, I thought."

"Clay."

Ray turned and looked at Aissa as she spoke Clay's name.

Clay walked over to her and reached out and touched her cheek. "You sure are pretty, you know that. I am going to miss you." He pulled her to him and kissed her as she struggled against him, her confusion obvious. Clay released her, then he shoved her back into Ray's arms. "Look, Grimes, I just want my three thousand dollars."

"What about your old man? From what I hear, he's rich."

"Yeah, and he's not leaving a dime of it to me." Clay shrugged his shoulders. "Look, Grimes, I did what you asked. So she's not dead, but at least she's suffered. And now you get the pleasure of killing her yourself." He looked past Ray to Shadow Hawk. "I hope you're going to kill him, too."

"Why?"

"Because I hate the bastard," Clay said, walking toward the bed. He stood next to it and then leaned down, his face close to Shadow Hawk's. He whispered something and mockingly plumped up the pillows. Shadow Hawk reached for him, trying to grab him, but Clay easily pushed him away.

"You bastard," Shadow Hawk said, his voice low.

"Maybe, but at least I'll be alive to talk about it," Clay said, laughing.

"I'll find you, Clay," Shadow Hawk shouted. "I'll kill you."

"You won't be around to do anything." Clay walked back to Ray. "So what about my money?"

"I don't have it on me."

"If you're stalling, Grimes, I'll kill you myself right here." Clay lifted his rifle.

"I'm not stalling. You think I carry three thousand dollars around with me. I'll have to wire my bank. I can have it here in a day."

Clay shook his head. "That's not good enough. I want to get the hell out of this place."

"What about your family?"

"My family?" Clay laughed harshly. "I don't have a family." He raised the rifle again. "The money, Grimes."

"I have some on me but not much," Ray said quickly.

"Look, Grimes, either you give me the money or I take things into my own hands."

"What does that mean?" Ray asked.

Clay reached for Aissa, locking his arm around her neck. "I'll kill her right now and then I'll kill him. And you'll be next."

"Calm down," Ray said, his eyes darting back and forth between Clay and the two guards. "I'll give you your damned money as soon as we're done here."

Clay released Aissa. "I'll wait outside. Let me know when you're finished." He stopped. "My mother and sister haven't done anything. Leave them alone. But my father," Clay walked toward the door, "I don't really give a damn about him."

"Wait," Ray said, going up to Clay. "Your sister has herself holed up in one of the rooms with some guns. She's already killed a couple of my men. Do you think you could get her out of there?"

"Why do you need her to come out anyway? It's these two you want. Just let her stay in there. She can't hurt you as long as she's pinned down in the room."

Ray nodded. "You're right. And your father's no threat, he's tied up like a Christmas goose."

"Where is he?"

"Next door."

"Let me take care of him."

Ray raised his eyebrows. "You serious?"

"Deadly," Clay replied, turning and leaving the room. He walked down the hallway, almost afraid to breathe. Grimes wanted to believe that everyone was as cold as he was.

Maybe this was going to work. He knocked on the door. "Let me in," Clay said.

"Who're you?"

"I'm Clay. Ray said I could come in."

The guard slowly opened the door and looked out. Pointing his rifle at Clay, he shouted down the hallway. "You tell this guy he can come in here, Ray?"

Ray stuck his head out of the doorway. "Let him in, Abe."

Abe nodded and Clay stepped inside the room. His father was tied to his desk chair. Clay walked forward, standing in front of his father. "Well, Pa, looks like things got a little out of hand."

Bradford leaned forward, pulling against the ropes that held him. "Are you a part of this? I swear to God, Clay, if you're a part of this, I'll kill you."

"I don't think so, Pa." Clay raised the rifle and leveled it at his father's head. "How does it feel, Pa? You scared?"

Bradford closed his eyes. "You'll rot in hell for this."

"I'm already in hell, Pa," Clay said angrily.

"You gonna shoot your own father?" Abe asked, clearly astonished.

"He's a bastard. He deserves it," Clay said, his voice cold.

"Yeah, but your own father," Abe said, standing next to Clay.

"Wouldn't you?" Clay glanced at his father.

Abe shook his head. "No. I've done lots of things I ain't proud of but I'd never shoot my own father." As he spoke, Abe slid his pistol back into his holster.

Clay's eyes locked with Abe's. "Neither would I." As realization dawned in the man's eyes, it was too late. Clay had swung the rifle like a club, hitting Abe in the face. The blow knocked him backwards; before he could recover, Clay swung again. Clay caught the man as he fell, laying him down gently. Then he went to the door and closed it. He leaned against it for a moment, breathing hard. His father was staring at him.

"I thought—"

"You really thought I was going to shoot you, Pa?" Clay said, walking across the room. He knelt, untying the rope that bound his father's hands. He handed him Abe's pistol then untied his legs from the chair. "I've been mad at you most of my life, but I never wanted you dead." Clay stood up. "More than I can say for you."

"I never wanted you dead, Clay," Bradford said, shoving the pistol into his waistband. He followed Clay to the door.

Before he opened it, Clay glanced back at his father. "You let me know a number of times that you wished it had been me instead of Russell who had died. You can't deny that." Clay opened the door a crack.

"Clay—"

"Never mind," Clay said quietly. "We have to figure out how to get Aissa and Shadow Hawk out of there."

"What about Rayna and your mother? Are they all right?"

Clay shook his head. "All I know is what Grimes told me. He said Rayna was holed up in one of the rooms. He also said a couple of his men were dead."

"What's this all about, Clay?"

"Just a blackguard bent on revenge, Pa, and he wants to make sure that Aissa and Shadow Hawk both die."

"How many men does he have in there?"

"Two besides him. But he has men in the bunkhouses, too. They had to have heard the shooting, and it's only a matter of time before somebody comes to look. We have to get Grimes quick if we can."

"He thinks you're on his side."

Clay managed to smile. "I told him I was coming in here to kill you, Pa."

"Well then," Bradford said, "maybe you better do what you said you'd do."

Shadow Hawk gripped the knife that Clay had slipped under the pillow. He was waiting for the moment when the guard came close enough for him to use it. One of the men was a couple feet to his left, Grimes and the other guard were by the door. Aissa was standing between the foot of the bed and the door, still hugging herself, swaying slightly on her feet. Shadow Hawk tried to think of every way imaginable to get the two guards and Grimes, but he knew it was impossible. Even if he were not hurt, his chances would have been slim.

Underneath the pillow, Shadow Hawk moved the knife from his left hand to his right. He groaned, turning onto his right side. He slid the knife down the length of his body until he could conceal it under his leg. Ignoring the pain, he gripped the edge of the bed with his hand, trying to sit up straighter. Just then, two shots rang out from Bradford's room.

"My God," Aissa muttered, backing up a few steps.

"What's the matter, Aissa, didn't you think he had it in him?" Ray nodded in satisfaction.

"He couldn't have shot his own father," Aissa said, shaking her head. "He wouldn't do that."

"I think he just did," Ray chuckled.

Shadow Hawk watched as Aissa stumbled backward toward the bed. The guard to his left was looking at Grimes, the other was looking out into the hall. Without hesitation, Shadow Hawk willed himself to stand. With lightning quick movement, he stabbed the guard in the side, grabbing the man's rifle from him as he started to fall.

"Get down, Aissa!" he yelled. He aimed at the other guard and fired, hitting the man in the chest. Grimes stood motionless for a moment, then lunged toward the door. Shadow Hawk fired again. He heard Grimes grunt as the bullet knocked him against the wall, but it wasn't enough to stop him. Shadow Hawk watched helplessly as Grimes staggered out the door. Shadow Hawk followed as quickly as he could, unable to ignore his own pain further. When he looked out into the hallway, Grimes was gone. The only one there was Clay.

"Grimes is gone," Shadow Hawk yelled, gripping the door frame.

"I'll look for him," Clay said, running down the hall.

Shadow Hawk turned around. Aissa was on her knees, her hands covering her face. Slowly, he walked to her. "Take my hand, Aissa," he said gently. When she hesitated, he bent slightly, pain searing across his side and back. Still sobbing, Aissa groped for Shadow Hawk's hand until she found it.

"I'm sorry," she said. Her voice was quivering. "I feel so helpless."

"Don't, Aissa," Shadow Hawk said, leading her to the bed. He sat down heavily. "I need you to clean my wounds. I have to wash the salt out."

"Of course," Aissa said, letting go of his hand. She started across the room.

"Stop," Shadow Hawk said. "Not that way. It's more to your right."

Aissa stopped. She took a deep breath and let it out. "I can't help you," she said, shaking her head. "I can't even walk across this room."

"Yes, you can. You did it before."

"I can't do it now, Shadow Hawk. I can't."

Shadow Hawk watched Aissa as she stood, her shoulders rounded, her head buried in her hands. He wanted to help her but couldn't. He prayed that she would find her own strength.

He looked up when he heard Christina's voice in the hallway. She came running into the room, rifle in hand. Rayna followed close behind.

"Are you two all right?" Christina asked.

He nodded. "What about you?"

"How do I look?" Christina asked, smiling. "Clay went after Grimes. He thinks you wounded him. He found blood on the stairs." Christina looked over at Aissa. "Are you all right, Aissa?"

"I'm fine but Shadow Hawk needs your help."

"Aissa—" Shadow Hawk's voice was weighted with pain. "Christina can help you better than I can. At least she can see."

"Why don't I take you back to your room, Aissa?" Rayna said, walking to Aissa and taking her arm.

"What's the matter with her?" Christina asked, watching as Aissa left the room with Rayna.

"She's frightened. Grimes and one of his men almost. . . ." Shadow Hawk thought about Grimes for a moment and his eyes turned storm gray.

"But they didn't, did they?"

"No." Shadow Hawk stared at the empty doorway. "There's something else, Christina."

"What?" Christina put down the rifle and sat on the edge of the bed. "You're scaring me, Shadow Hawk."

"I'm beginning to think that Clay is better for her. She seemed to accept her blindness when she was with him. With me, it's different."

"Of course, it's different. She's always loved you."

"She wants it to be the way it used to be. When she's with me, she remembers when she used to be able to see. She doesn't know any other way with Clay."

"Listen to me," Christina said, taking Shadow Hawk's hand. "Aissa loves you. She loves you more than anything in this world."

"That may not be enough, Christina," Shadow Hawk said, laying his head back against the pillow.

"I'll clean your wounds, then I'll check on Aissa. Everything will be all right. You'll see."

Shadow Hawk turned onto his stomach and closed his eyes. He felt as if he could sleep for days. Aissa was suffering, and Grimes had escaped once again. It seemed as if they'd never be free of him.

He grimaced as Christina began to clean his wounds. "How long will it be before I can travel?"

"It's going to be awhile," Christina answered, then drew in a quick breath. "My God, what did he do to you?"

"Salt." Shadow Hawk could only manage the single word.

Christina stood up quickly and got the heavy pitcher. A moment later, Shadow Hawk felt the indescribable relief as she poured water over his back and shoulder. As Christina worked, Shadow Hawk let his mind drift. When she finally finished, he opened his eyes. His wounds still stung slightly, but he felt better.

"We need to get out of here, Christina. We need to get Aissa back home."

"Shadow Hawk," Christina said hesitantly. "I won't be going back with you."

"What do you mean?"

"I'm going to be staying here."

"What?" Shadow Hawk started to protest but stopped himself. Rayna had told him that Clay and Christina had gotten close. "Did Clay ask you to stay?"

"I know what you're thinking, but he does care for me."

"He would be crazy if he didn't," Shadow Hawk said, smiling slightly. "Do you love him, Christina?"

"I think so. I don't know, I've never been in love." Christina lowered her eyes and then looked up, a slight blush touching her cheeks. "I thought I was in love with you."

"But you're not."

"No. I love you like a brother, not like. . . ."

"Not like you love Clay."

Christina nodded. "I guess I do love him. I know I want to be with him, and I know he makes me feel real special."

"Good." Shadow Hawk struggled onto his side, then sat up. He pulled Christina toward him, hugging her with his good arm. "I'm happy for you, Christina. You will always be like a sister to me."

Christina smiled and kissed Shadow Hawk on the cheek. "Aissa is very strong, you know. Be patient with her and love her. She needs your love."

Shadow Hawk touched Christina's cheek. "Go find Clay. I'm fine now."

"I'll visit you later."

Shadow Hawk sank back into the pillows as he watched Christina leave the room. He closed his eyes and allowed himself to relax. He thought for a long time until it became quite clear what he had to do. He had to take Aissa to see his grandmother. Maybe Ocha could help Aissa live with the pain and loneliness she felt in her dark world, for Ocha had felt it for most of her life. Perhaps Ocha could reach her in a way that he could not.

Ray wound the bandanna around his arm, tying the ends with his teeth. The bullet was still in his arm and was still bleeding. He'd have to find somebody to get it out.

When he had escaped the house, he had made it to his horse; without saying a word to his men, he had mounted up and rode off. He rode for most of the night, making sure he wasn't being followed. He stopped only to tend to his arm. He was tired and the arm was beginning to throb, but he rode on. As soon as he got the arm fixed, he would ride west because he knew that's where Aissa and Shadow Hawk were headed. There was only one thing on his mind—killing them. He couldn't rest until he had finished the job.

Chapter Sixteen

Almost a month had passed since Ray Grimes had tried to kill Shadow Hawk and Aissa. The ordeal had had a strange effect on everyone. It had somehow brought Bradford and Dorothea closer. He had never seen his wife so indignant over anything in his life, and he was pleased to see that she had handled herself so well. Clay and Christina were in love. They couldn't hide it any longer, and his family was pleased. They adored Christina.

Aissa and Shadow Hawk had not been so lucky. Although they still planned to return to her ranch as soon as Shadow Hawk was completely healed, there was a strain between them. Aissa was afraid of depending on Shadow Hawk, and he still wasn't sure how far he should push her toward her own independence. He had not yet told her he was planning to take her to see his grandmother. Deep inside he was hoping that Ocha would be the flame to light Aissa's way.

And then there was Clay and Bradford. After Clay had chased Ray Grimes and found that he had gotten away, he and his father had rounded up the rest of Grimes's men and held them for the sheriff. They had worked well together, and it had surprised and pleased them both. Bradford hadn't actually thanked Clay for saving his life, but he was thanking him in other ways—by asking for his opinion on ranch matters, by welcoming Christina into the family, and by offering to give Clay and Christina five hundred acres of their own land.

This morning, as they did every morning, Aissa and Christina were taking a walk. They had become so close, and Aissa dreaded the time when she and Shadow Hawk were to leave.

"I want you to be here when Clay and I get married." Christina held onto Aissa's arm, and they walked along the stream.

"Have you talked about when that might be?"

"Not really." Christina stopped, picking a flower and handing it to Aissa. "I just know I love him."

"I'm happy for you, Christina." Aissa felt the petals of the flower.

"I just wish my folks could see how well things turned out."

"I'm sure they're watching."

"You think so?"

"Yes." Aissa twirled the flower in her fingers. "There are times I miss my mother still, but I talk to her anyway. I honestly believe she can hear me."

"You sound like an Indian when you talk like that," Christina said.

"Like a Comanche maybe, not an Apache. They're afraid to even talk about their dead. They speak of them as the ones who have 'gone away.' "

"Tell me about Shadow Hawk's grandmother. He speaks of her all the time."

"Ocha?" Aissa smiled and stopped walking. "Ocha is wonderful. She helped me in so many ways when I was a captive. She is blind but sees and understands more than most people."

"What about you and Shadow Hawk?" Christina asked, sitting down on the bank of the stream and guiding Aissa to sit next to her.

"I don't know, Christina," Aissa said, crumbling the flower and dropping it to the ground.

"He loves you so much, Aissa. Why do you make it so hard for him to love you?"

"You know why."

"Because you're blind? When will you understand that it doesn't matter to him? He loves you."

"But it will change. After awhile he'll come to resent me and my dependency."

"He's not like that. Shadow Hawk is a good man."

"I know that, Christina."

Christina patted Aissa's shoulder. "I'm sorry. Why am I telling you about Shadow Hawk?"

"Because you love him."

"I wouldn't be alive and I wouldn't have the happiness I have now, if it weren't for you two. I just want you both to be happy."

"You shouldn't be spending your time worrying about us."

"Aissa—"

Aissa shook her head. "No more, Christina. This is your time. I want you to be happy. Don't worry about us. We'll be fine." Aissa leaned forward and asked suddenly, "What does Rayna look like?"

"Rayna? She's small and pretty, kind of delicate-looking. But she's a real strong person. Why?"

"I just wondered. Shadow Hawk and she have become good friends."

"That doesn't bother you, does it? Cause it doesn't mean a thing. I know, I've seen them together."

Aissa smiled. "I'm not worried, I just wondered."

"You wondered for a reason. What is it?"

Aissa shrugged. "I wondered if he'd be happy with a woman like Rayna."

"How could you say such a thing?"

"Rayna is everything I am not, Christina. She is

bright and capable. She's a good horsewoman and—"

"She can see," Christina said simply. "I thought I knew you, Aissa."

"What do you mean?"

"I didn't realize you were such a coward."

"I'm not a coward," Aissa said, trying to sound sure of herself.

"Yes, you are. You'd rather give Shadow Hawk to another woman than fight for him."

"I simply asked what Rayna looked like, Christina."

"And all those things you said she was, you are, too."

"I was before."

"Did your blindness take away your ability to think or feel?"

"Of course not, but there are so many other things I don't do well anymore."

"When are you going to realize that it doesn't matter how well you do things? It only matters that you try," Christina said in an exasperated tone. "For a smart woman, you don't think very well sometimes."

"That's why I have you," Aissa said gently, reaching out for Christina's hand.

Christina shook her head and hugged Aissa. "I love you. You're like a sister to me. I just want you to be happy."

"I know," Aissa said.

"Come on," Christina said, standing up and waiting until Aissa was on her feet. "How about wading in the lake?"

Aissa hesitated then smiled. "Sounds good."

They followed the stream until it widened into a small lake. Some cattle and horses were grazing nearby, some were drinking along the far side.

"We're here," Christina said.

"I know. I can smell the water."

Christina lifted her nose into the air. "I can't smell it."

"That's because you can see it. Tell me what it looks like."

Christina looked around. "It's pretty big and the water's a dark blue. There are some reeds growing along this end and some of them are real tall. You can still see parts of the old beaver dam and where Bradford's men built the dike. On the other side, there're lots of cattle and horses." Christina laughed. "And two colts are chasing each other around."

"Well, I'm ready for a swim." Aissa sat down and took off her boots and stockings, then unbuttoned her dress. She stood up when she was finished. "Are you done?"

"Just about," Christina answered, dropping her dress onto the ground. "What if some of the hands are around?"

"I can't see them so they don't exist," Aissa said with a grin. "Besides, we have our slips on."

"All right, let's go." Christina took Aissa's hand as they waded into the cool water of the lake. "How does it feel?"

"It feels wonderful," Aissa said, letting go of Christina's hand and wading out until the water touched her thighs and was deep enough for her to swim. She pushed off the bottom and glided along the water, feeling weightless. She swam with long strokes, as if she didn't have a care in the world.

Aissa recalled the time in the Apache camp when she had been bathing in the stream. She had stepped onto the bank and Shadow Hawk was there. He had taken her into the woods and had made love to her for the first time. It was unlike anything she had ever experienced in her life. She wanted him to make love to her again.

"Aissa! You're out there pretty deep." Christina's voice sounded uneasy.

Aissa turned over and floated on her back. "Come on out, Christina. It'll do you good."

"I don't know. I think you should come back in."

"I may never come in." Aissa kicked her feet and continued to float, her head arched back so she could feel the sun on her face. She smiled when she thought of the times she and her father had ridden to the lake and jumped in on a hot day.

"Aissa, I can't touch bottom!" Christina's voice sounded shrill. "I don't know how to swim."

Immediately, Aissa rolled onto her stomach and began to tread water. "Keep talking, Christina."

"I can't," Christina gasped.

"Say something, damn it!" Aissa screamed.

"Aissa, I'm. . . ."

Aissa could barely make out Christina's garbled words. Aissa treaded water quietly, trying to orient herself. She didn't know which way she had swum out; she didn't know where Christina was. She started to panic, afraid she wouldn't be able to save Christina. But she forced herself to listen. She waited until she was sure she was facing the sound of Christina's frantic splashes. Then she began to swim. After ten or twelve strokes, she was afraid she had veered in the wrong direction. But then her outstretched fingers touched Christina's arm.

"It's all right. I have you," Aissa said calmly as Christina struggled against her. "Don't fight me, Christina, or we'll both drown. Just relax."

Aissa turned Christina onto her back, hooking an arm underneath her chin. Aissa turned on her side and began stroking with her left arm, while she held onto Christina with her right. Aissa heard the high-pitched whinny of a colt and headed for it, praying that she wasn't striking out across the entire width of the lake. Her arms felt heavy and her legs were tiring before she touched the muddy bottom. When she was sure she could stand up, she pulled Christina to her. "You can stand up now," she said gently, releasing Christina but still holding onto her arm. "Are you all right?"

"I think so," Christina answered quietly. "I was just so scared."

"I know. Come on." Aissa took Christina's hand and followed the sound of the water lapping against the shore. She led Christina through the mud and reeds up the bank. They both collapsed on the warm, dry dirt.

"You saved my life," Christina murmured.

"You could've saved yourself if I wasn't there."

"No, I couldn't have. I never learned how to swim, and I was always too scared to learn."

She reached out and touched Christina. "Why didn't you tell me?"

"Because you were being so brave going out there swimming, I thought I should be brave, too. Besides, you made it look so easy."

Aissa sat up. "There's no shame in admitting you can't do something, Christina."

"I think I told you that earlier, didn't I?"

Aissa smiled. "Yes, you did."

"And you can still do some things real well, can't you?"

"I suppose I can."

"Our clothes are on the other side of the lake, you know."

Aissa shrugged her shoulders. "Are they?" Aissa turned her head. "Is someone coming?" Aissa heard Christina stand up quickly.

"Yes. How did you know?"

"I can hear the horse."

"I'll run to the other side and get our clothes."

Aissa reached out for Christina. "No, you can't leave me here. What if it's one of the hands?"

"I'll hurry back. Promise."

Aissa pulled her knees into her chest and pulled the slip over them. She wrapped her arms around her knees, trying to hide herself as best she could. She heard the horse drop back into a trot and slow to a walk, then the rider dismounted. She knew immediately from the light footfall that it was Shadow Hawk. She shook her head. Christina was playing matchmaker.

"Aissa, are you all right?" Shadow Hawk walked up to her.

"I'm fine. Christina and I went for a swim. We left our clothes on the other side of the lake."

"It's not a very good idea to swim out in the open dressed like that."

Aissa sat up, squaring her shoulders. "What do you suggest? I swim fully dressed?"

"No, I suggest you take a man with you next time. Haven't you learned your lesson?"

"Not every man is like Ray Grimes."

"No, but some are." Shadow Hawk sat down next to her. "I'd like to leave tomorrow."

"Tomorrow?" Aissa felt her stomach tighten. "I thought you said we'd leave in a few days."

"I want to go home, Aissa. Don't you?"

"But I thought it was still hard for you to ride."

"I'm well enough."

Aissa sighed but didn't answer.

"Don't you want to leave, Aissa?"

"I feel safe here."

"Because of Clay?"

"No, because no one expects anything of me. You and my father will expect me to be like I used to be."

"Is that so bad?"

"It is when I can't see. There are so many things I won't be able to do. I won't even be able to work in my garden."

"I'll help you. So will your father."

"It won't be the same. You know it won't."

"Christina is coming. We'll talk later," Shadow Hawk said, greeting Christina as she approached with the bundle of clothes and shoes. "Do you think it's wise for two women to swim alone out here?"

"Probably not," Christina said, handing Aissa her dress and boots.

Shadow Hawk gripped Christina's shoulder and turned her to face him. "Christina, you should be looking out for her. What if someone came? She wouldn't know."

Christina shrugged and sat down. "And what if I had almost drowned, just think what might've happened."

Shadow Hawk nodded. "That's right."

"Sit down, Shadow Hawk," Christina ordered, "you're beginning to sound like Clay. You act like Aissa can't do a thing for herself." Christina angrily jerked her dress down over her head and reached for her stockings. "I did almost drown out there, you know. Aissa saved my life."

Aissa hid a smile and turned away to step into her dress. She pulled it up over her hips and slipped her arms into the sleeves. As she shrugged it up over her shoulders, she was sure she could feel Shadow Hawk staring at her. She sat down, patting the ground until she found her shoes. Christina had rolled up her stockings and put them inside.

"How were you able to save her? Was she close?" Shadow Hawk demanded.

"I didn't know where she was. I thought she could swim. When I knew she was in trouble, I listened for her." Aissa pulled on one boot and then another.

"I was scared to death, I can tell you that," Christina said. "But Aissa was real calm. In fact, I thought she was going to club me over the head once she got to me."

Aissa laughed. "You shouldn't fight the person who's trying to save you from drowning, Christina."

"This is not funny," Shadow Hawk said harshly. "You both could've drowned out there."

"But we didn't," Aissa said firmly. "You're the one who keeps telling me I can do things well if I let myself."

"I wasn't talking about going swimming in the middle of a lake with someone who can't swim."

"She didn't know I couldn't swim. I never told her." Christina stood up, brushing out the skirt of her dress. "If you two don't mind, I'm going to head on back to the house. I don't want to interfere with your arguing."

Shadow Hawk shook his head and laughed.

"Tell me," Aissa prompted.

"You should see her face. She looks different. Her eyes sparkle and her cheeks are flushed. The sadness in her eyes is gone. She has the face of a woman in love."

"I'm so happy for her. I'll miss her."

"We'll all miss Christina."

Aissa stood up. "Could you guide me back to the ranch?"

"Do you plan to walk?"

"Yes."

"Why don't you ride with me?"

"I thought Rayna was the only one you took riding on the paint."

Shadow Hawk leaned close to Aissa. "Is that jealousy I hear in your voice?"

"I'm not jealous," Aissa protested, turning her head away.

"Aissa," Shadow Hawk said, taking Aissa's chin in his hand. "I don't love Rayna. She's my friend, just as Clay is your friend. I love you. I want you. I want you to be my wife."

Aissa felt Shadow Hawk's mouth on hers and she kissed him back, feeling the passion that was there. She leaned her head on his chest. "I'm still so scared sometimes."

"I'll help you, I promise you. Just as you'll help me."

"I can't resist you. I never could."

"I don't want you to resist me," Shadow Hawk said, kissing her lightly. "Come on, we should be getting back.

You need to get out of those wet things." He picked Aissa up in his arms.

"I can walk."

"I'm putting you on the paint. Put your hands out."

Aissa reached out and felt the stallion as Shadow Hawk lifted her on to its back. She held the reins and patted the paint's neck as Shadow Hawk swung up behind her. Shadow Hawk's arms went around her and she leaned back against him. It felt good to be in his arms again. She felt as if she could stay there forever.

"That was a wonderful dinner, Mrs. Montrose," Christina said. They were all gathered in Bradford's study after dinner that night.

Clay went up to Christina and put his arm around her shoulders. "I think it's time you called my mother Dorothea. Pretty soon she's going to be your mother-in-law."

"Yes, please do call me Dorothea."

"I'll try," Christina agreed.

Aissa, Shadow Hawk, and Rayna were standing near the fireplace, and Bradford was pouring drinks and putting them on a tray. When he was finished, he walked to the others. "I want you all to take a glass. I have a toast to make." Bradford cleared his throat. "I want to make my first toast to Christina and Clay. May they have many years of happiness together."

"And lots of children," Rayna added.

Everyone smiled and sipped at their glasses.

"Actually I have more than one toast to make," Bradford said, still holding out his glass. "Here's to the lovely Aissa. Thank you for saving Christina's life today. You are a marvel, my dear."

Aissa smiled broadly. "Thank you, Bradford."

Bradford nodded and looked at Clay again. "I don't quite know how to start this next toast. I know I've been rough on you, Clay. Hell, I've been more than rough on you, I've been a bastard to you." Bradford took a deep breath and continued, "I'm not sure why I've blamed you for Russell's death all of this time. Maybe it's because I really blamed myself. I never should've allowed you two out there to hunt that cat. See, it was easier for me to blame you, that way I didn't have to hate myself.

"I drove you to do all of the things you did, I know that, and I don't blame you if you hate me. I haven't been much of a father to you or to Rayna." Bradford looked at his daughter. "I know all the work you've put into this ranch, Rayna. You've been my right arm. A man couldn't ask for better children than I've got." Bradford hesitated, looking from Clay to Rayna. "I guess I just want to say that I love you both and you deserve more from me. So, to begin with, I've changed my will. If something should happen to me, the ranch goes to both of you. It'll be divided evenly between you. I trust you'll both take care of your mother."

"Pa. . . ." Clay started to speak but his voice broke. Rayna walked to Clay and took his arm.

"I'm not through yet." Bradford walked to the wall that held Russell's portrait. "I loved Russell. He was a good boy, but he wasn't perfect. You were right, Rayna, when you said he just didn't have a chance to grow up and make mistakes. He's been between me and the rest of you for far too long." Bradford reached up and took the heavy portrait from the wall, setting it on the floor. "I was thinking I could use a portrait of my children who are with me right now." Bradford held out his glass to toast but his hand was shaking.

Rayna walked to him and without hesitation, she hugged him tightly. "Thank you, Pa. That's the best gift you could've given us."

Clay still stood with Christina, not moving.

"I understand it'll take you some time to learn to forgive me, Clay," Bradford said, his voice tight with emotion.

Clay handed his glass to Christina and walked to his father. "There's been enough hate in this family to last us all a lifetime." Clay embraced his father and Bradford nodded, fighting back tears.

Christina walked to Aissa and Shadow Hawk. "Doesn't that make you want to go home and see Ben?"

Aissa quickly wiped the tears from her eyes. She nodded. "We're leaving tomorrow, Christina."

"Tomorrow? But I thought you weren't leaving for a few days."

"It's time," Aissa said confidently. "It's time for me to go home."

Aissa was sure she would never get used to riding this way. Since she couldn't guide her own horse, Shadow Hawk held the reins. Every time her horse crossed broken ground, or stepped over a rocky patch, it startled her. As much as she hated to admit it, it frightened her. She had become so accustomed to the polished wood floors and the cool smooth walls of the Montrose house that the slightest jar confused her.

Aissa lifted her face and pulled in a determined breath. She ran her hands over the gear tied to her saddle. Shadow Hawk had insisted on packing her things in the same order every time they broke camp. She could find the little porcelain teapot that Rayna had given her as a farewell present as quickly as she could find strips of rawhide in case she had to repair her bridle.

She hesitated when she touched the smooth stock of the rifle Shadow Hawk had given her. Every evening after they had made camp, Shadow Hawk made her practice shooting. He threw rocks into the brush and she aimed and fired, reacting as quickly as she could. He said she was getting better, but she knew that she would never be a match for anyone who seriously wanted to harm her.

An image continually arose in Aissa's mind. She remembered Ray Grimes's face, twisted into ugliness by his cruelty, the cold amusement in his eyes as his men dragged her father away. What would she do if Ray followed her home? What could she do? Her father would die to protect her, she knew that. And so would Shadow Hawk. It would be insanity, she realized, for her to go home and endanger the lives of the people she loved most dearly. Maybe they could all go to Flora's ranch, or even somewhere farther west. But even as Aissa thought it, she knew it wouldn't work. Her father would never leave the land her mother had loved so much. And Shadow Hawk could never live so far from his people.

"Do you hear it?"

Aissa's thoughts were broken by Shadow Hawk's voice. She straightened in her saddle. She could hear bird song, the wind, and something else. . . . It was a more musical whisper than the wind. "A stream," she said, turning her face toward Shadow Hawk.

"How far?"

Aissa frowned. He rarely praised her. He was so different to her than Clay would've been, different even than her father would be. Of all the people she knew, Shadow Hawk would insist that she learn to stand on her own two feet. She cocked her head to one side and listened for a moment. "The stream is a few hundred feet in front and to the left."

"You're getting lazy, Aissa. If you were by yourself, you would've ridden right into the water. It's only about a hundred feet in front of us."

Aissa grimaced, trying to keep her composure. He acted as if everything was a test. "I don't know how many feet it is. Why does it matter?"

"It matters because you must learn to depend on yourself more."

Aissa jerked the reins from Shadow Hawk's hands. "I didn't depend on anyone else when I saved Christina from drowning, but you said I shouldn't have been there."

Shadow Hawk pulled up on the stallion. "I was worried for you."

"But I saved Christina by myself."

"Aissa, I know more than anyone how capable you are."

"Then why do you keep badgering me like this? I'm tired of it."

"Do you want to give Ray Grimes one more chance at taking your life?"

Aissa started to reply but stopped. She could hear the fear in Shadow Hawk's voice, and she could hear the love. "I understand what you're trying to do, Shadow Hawk, but no matter how hard you try to teach me things, I still won't be able to see. If Ray Grimes decides to come after me, there's not a thing I can do about it."

"But there might be. You're becoming capable of 'seeing' with your ears, Aissa. Do you remember the times at the ranch or in the Apache camp when I would sneak up on you and you would get angry with me because it startled you? I can't do that now. You know my footsteps. You can hear me."

Aissa thought about it. Shadow Hawk was right. She had learned to depend on her ears as if they had become her eyes. She was now aware of almost every sound around her. "How would I defend myself against Ray? It's not possible."

"Either your father or I will be with you most of the time. But if you are alone, you'll have the rifle. You can hear him if he's on a horse or on foot. You know how to shoot at sounds. You have to know how to defend yourself, Aissa."

"I know," Aissa responded softly. "I just wonder if it will ever be over with Grimes. I think he lives to torment me." She felt Shadow Hawk's comforting hand on hers.

"Grimes won't live forever, Aissa. Soon his time will come."

Aissa nodded, handing the reins back to Shadow Hawk. As much as she wanted to see Shadow Hawk's face once again, she wanted to see Ray Grimes's face more. Just once. For a long time she'd been glad she hadn't killed him when she had the chance. Now, though, it seemed like killing him was the only way she'd be free of him.

Shadow Hawk led Aissa's horse up the narrow mountain trail. The junipers and pinon pines threatened to overtake the path, but Shadow Hawk managed to find a way through them. This was a new camp, different from the one he had grown up in. He hadn't yet told Aissa that he was taking her to his people, but he knew she was suspicious. He had looked back many times and seen her moving her head around, trying to hear the new sounds, trying to smell the new smells.

"Where are we?" Aissa asked suddenly. "Where are we going, Shadow Hawk?"

"We're heading into the mountains," Shadow Hawk replied.

"Wait. Why are we going into the mountains?"

Shadow Hawk pulled up on his horse, turning around to face Aissa. "We're going to be with my people for awhile."

"Your people? What about my father?"

"Gerard will understand."

"I don't understand. You've been telling me for a long time now that I'm not being fair to my father. So why are you taking me to your people?"

"I think it would be good for you."

"Don't make decisions for me just because I can't see," Aissa said angrily.

"I'm sorry, Aissa. I didn't do this to upset you."

"Tell me why you did it then."

"I thought it would be good for you to be with Ocha. She could tell you many things about the darkness. You, yourself, said she walks as if she sees." Shadow Hawk watched Aissa, unsure of what she would say. She was quiet for a time, closing her eyes.

"Why didn't you just tell me?"

"I didn't think you would want to go back to my people. I know you have bad memories of your time there."

"But I care for Ocha. She was good to me. You should've been honest with me."

"Perhaps I wasn't honest because I know I was the cause of your unhappiness in the Apache camp."

"You weren't responsible for everything that happened to me, Shadow Hawk. You know that."

"But I can't excuse or forgive myself for what I did do to you."

"I've forgiven you. That's what matters."

"Aissa—"

Aissa held up her hand. "No, I think you're right. It would be good for me to spend some time with Ocha before I return home."

"All right. But when you're ready to leave, we'll go," Shadow Hawk added.

Shadow Hawk touched his heels to the paint's side and guided him up the rocky trail. He knew this camp would be similar to the other; both were high in the mountains, accessible only by a narrow, rocky trail. The forest created a shelter and camouflage for the camp, allowing them to see without being seen.

Shadow Hawk breathed in the pungent odor of the pine trees, recalling the first time he had come to the Apache land, remembering how overwhelmed he had been by his new people. In some ways this would be like that first time. He had not seen his family in months and had only been to the camp for a short time to take his mother back home. Now he would have time to visit with her and Brave Heart, and to catch up on everything that had happened from Gitano. It would be good to be with them again.

He glanced back at Aissa. He wondered if he was doing the right thing by bringing her here. Maybe he should've let her make the decision.

"Do you hear that?" Aissa asked.

Shadow Hawk frowned slightly. "Hear what?"

Aissa smiled. "So, I've surpassed the teacher. Don't you hear the wind in the pine trees? There is no more beautiful sound."

Shadow Hawk turned his head. He could reach out and touch the pine trees they were so close, yet he hadn't noticed the sound of the wind blowing through them. "I confess, I heard nothing."

"Then you also didn't hear the voices from up above."

"There were no voices," Shadow Hawk said adamantly, looking high above them. "You are imagining things." He pressed his heels into the paint again. But before they had gone far, he pulled up abruptly. High above them, at the edge of the trees, he could see three Apache. How had Aissa heard them?

"I was right, wasn't I?" Aissa asked.

Shadow Hawk nodded his head. "You were right." He knew that the men had been watching them all along.

"I remember when you had keen senses, Shadow Hawk. What has happened to you?"

Shadow Hawk smiled. He hadn't heard that playful tone in Aissa's voice in a long time. "You were right. I will not say it again." Shadow Hawk urged the paint up the trail until it leveled out into a semi-flat meadow. Like the other camp, the horses grazed here and the camp itself was up above. Shadow Hawk reined in and dismounted, helping Aissa down from her horse. He greeted the men who stood guard and led Aissa up the uneven path through the thick branches of the pine trees and into the camp. Hide lodges and wickiups were set up in no particular order around the clearing. The shouts and laughter of children rang out immediately. Shadow Hawk smiled as he watched one little girl chase a boy with a stick.

"Something smells wonderful," Aissa said, breathing deeply.

"Fresh roasted meat," Shadow Hawk said. "Deer."

"I'm hungry," Aissa said.

"So am I." Shadow Hawk led Aissa through the camp, greeting people he knew, smiling at others he recognized. When he saw his mother, she was carrying a bundle of firewood. She smiled when she saw him, dropped the wood, and walked briskly forward.

"You are not too old for me to embrace you," Broken Moon said, hugging her son.

"It is good to see you, Mother. You look good."

"As do you." Broken Moon looked at Aissa, taking her hands in hers. "It pleases me to see you again, child. You are as lovely as I remember."

"Thank you, Broken Moon."

"We're hungry, Mother. Do you have food to feed us?"

"Come," Broken Moon said, leading Shadow Hawk and Aissa to her lodge. "Sit," she ordered as she quickly filled some bowls from a pot that hung over the fire. "There is fresh meat in the stew."

Shadow Hawk took one of the bowls from his mother, placing it firmly in Aissa's hands. He saw the curious look Broken Moon gave him. "Aissa cannot see, Mother."

"I would not have known," Broken Moon said simply. "Do you have pain, Aissa?"

"Only sometimes."

"It surprises me to see you, Shadow," Broken Moon said, sitting down in front of her son and Aissa. "I thought you were going to live in the white man's lodge."

"It is a long story, Mother. I will tell you all of it later. Now I want to eat and rest."

"You will never rest once Gitano finds out you are here. He will want to know everything you have done since he last saw you."

Shadow Hawk smiled. "How is my cousin?"

"He is in love, or so he says." Broken Moon leaned forward. "But I think he likes the girl because her father owns so many horses."

"Who is she?"

"She is Red Wing. Do you remember her?"

Shadow Hawk nodded. "Gitano never liked her. Something must have changed."

"Horses," Broken Moon said in disgust. "Are you thirsty, Aissa?" Without waiting, Broken Moon handed Aissa a cup of water.

"Thank you, Broken Moon."

"Will you stay for awhile, Shadow?"

"For a short while, Mother. I thought it would be good for Aissa to visit with Grandmother."

Broken Moon nodded. "Yes, my mother could be of great help to you, Aissa. But perhaps you should rest now. Come," Broken Moon said, taking the emptied bowl and cup from Aissa. "I will lead you into the lodge. You look tired."

"Yes, I am." Aissa stood and turned toward Shadow Hawk. "I will see you later?"

"I will be here." Shadow Hawk finished his stew and [illegible] the bowl down, waiting for his mother. When she c[illegible] back out, she sat close to him, her voice barely ab[illegible]e a whisper:

"Tell me you did nothing to harm her, Shadow."

Shadow Hawk looked into his mother's eyes. "I did nothing, Mother. While I was looking for you and Brave Heart, Aissa was kidnapped. She was also taken to a mining camp. She was injured during a cave-in."

"You loved her even while you were married to Paloma."

Shadow Hawk nodded without hesitation.

"Why don't you marry her then?"

"I want to marry her, but she is not so eager."

"Why, because of the past?"

"No, because she cannot see. She thinks she will be a burden to me."

"Will she?"

Shadow Hawk looked sharply at his mother. "How can you say such a thing, Mother?"

"I am only asking you to be honest with yourself and her. This girl does not deserve to be hurt yet again."

Shadow Hawk nodded. "There will be times when it will be difficult for both of us, but I cannot imagine my life without Aissa, Mother. I love her."

Broken Moon touched her son's hand. "This pleases me. She is strong. She will do well."

"Yes, I know."

"Is it true, or are the gods deceiving me?"

Shadow Hawk and Broken Moon looked up when they heard Gitano's loud voice as he walked toward them.

"I told you it would not take him long to find you," Broken Moon said, picking up the bowls.

Gitano stopped in front of Shadow Hawk. "So, it is true, Shadow Hawk is back from the white world. Tell me, Cousin, what stroke of good fortune brings you to us?"

Shadow Hawk smiled. "I missed you, Gitano. What else?"

Gitano looked around. "Where is Aissa? I heard she was with you."

"She is resting." Shadow Hawk stood up and kissed his mother on the cheek. "I will return later. I think it would be more restful for Aissa if Gitano and I went for a walk."

Broken Moon nodded, her mouth curling in a smile. "Yes, I agree."

"My father wishes to see you," Gitano said to Shadow Hawk as they left Broken Moon's lodge. "And of course Brave Heart will want to welcome his brother."

"Where is my little brother?"

"He is hunting with Teroz."

Shadow Hawk stopped. "Brave Heart and Teroz are hunting together? I cannot believe it."

"Many things have changed since you were last here, Cousin." Gitano led Shadow Hawk through the camp until they reached the forest of pine trees. Gitano ducked and led Shadow Hawk underneath a dense tangle of branches until they stood on a precipice, looking down on the steep trail that Shadow Hawk had just traveled.

"I thought we were going to see Ataza."

"My father can wait. I thought we could talk first." Gitano walked along the rocky edge as if he were a mountain goat, never missing a step. Shadow Hawk shook his head in wonder, still marveling at Gitano's agility. They walked along the edge, sometimes holding onto pine branches, until Gitano stopped. "Here, this is my favorite place. It is not quite as good as the boulder stairway in our old camp, but it is peaceful." Gitano sat down.

Shadow Hawk looked at the place Gitano had chosen. There was barely enough room for both of them to sit and one misstep would send either or both of them tumbling over the side. Yet Gitano sat as if he were on perfectly flat ground. "Perhaps you could have chosen a higher place, one that is more difficult to reach, Gitano," Shadow Hawk said, as he managed to perch next to his cousin.

"It is good to see you have not lost your sense of humor, Shadow. So, tell me what it is like to live in the white man's world? Is it strange living in that wood lodge?"

"I haven't been living there, Gitano."

"Where have you been?"

"It's a long story."

Gitano stretched his arms above his head. "I have all day. I have nothing else to do."

Shadow Hawk didn't want to tell the story again but knew he would have to; Gitano wouldn't leave him alone until he knew what had happened. Shadow Hawk shrugged his shoulders and began talking. He told Gitano everything that had occurred over the last few months. When he was through, he sat quietly, listening to the sound of the wind blowing through the pine trees.

"I am sorry, Cousin," Gitano said, his voice sincere. "I am sorry for Aissa."

"I hope Ocha can help her."

"Grandmother will help her. She will teach her to see as she sees."

Shadow Hawk nodded, trying to take hope in what Gitano had said. "Cousin, tell me about Red Wing."

"Red Wing?"

"Do not act so innocent, Gitano. Mother told me you are in love with her."

"In love? Ha!" Gitano shook his head. "I will never be in love with any woman."

"That's what I told my mother."

"Do not get me wrong, Cousin, Red Wing is nice enough. She is even pretty."

"And her father has many horses, I have heard."

"My aunt has been talking too much."

"Is it true? Are you going to marry Red Wing?"

"No, and I do not need her father's horses. I have horses of my own," Gitano said indignantly.

"It is cruel to deceive her if you have no feelings for her, Gitano. Perhaps there is another who would court her sincerely."

"She is interested in no other."

Shadow Hawk suppressed a smile. "Perhaps not now, but she will not wait forever."

"What is this? Why do you wish to marry me off? I am still young."

"You are a man, Gitano, or so I have always thought." Shadow Hawk regarded his cousin thoughtfully. "What is this fear you possess about marriage?"

"I have no fear but I have seen many men get married and I have seen them change. They become like small boys again, fooling their wives as they once deceived their mothers. I will not have a woman try to make me ashamed because I have gambled with my friends or drunk too much *tizwin.*" Gitano shook his head. "I will not be like that."

Shadow Hawk held up his hands. "I will not argue with you, Cousin." He shifted on the narrow ledge, pretending to be deep in thought. "Years ago I saw Red Wing swimming with the other girls. Tell me, does she still have those long legs and the beautiful—"

"Enough! I admit there are a few reasons a man might want to marry Red Wing."

Shadow Hawk nodded thoughtfully. "And as I recall, she is a sweet-natured girl, always smiling and singing."

Gitano shot him a look but did not answer.

"And her baskets—"

"You have been so long in the white man's world you are beginning to think like a woman. You sound like the old women, matchmaking around a winter fire. Or perhaps," Gitano added, raising his eyebrows, "I should begin to court Aissa since you are so interested in Red Wing's baskets."

Shadow Hawk could no longer keep a straight face. "I have missed you, Gitano. There were many times when I needed your laughter."

"Tell me really, Shadow, how is Aissa?"

"I would only admit it to you, Cousin, but I am frightened for her."

"Does it not scare you, too?"

Shadow Hawk shook his head emphatically. "I can live with Aissa's blindness. It is she who cannot."

Gitano stared out over the land.

Shadow Hawk recognized his cousin's intense expression and the silence which accompanied it. Since they had been boys, Gitano had always fallen into deep thought in the middle of their conversations. Shadow Hawk knew better than to disturb him. Shadow Hawk leaned back, settling himself, enjoying the warmth of the afternoon sun. After a long time, Gitano turned and faced him.

"Tell me something, Shadow Hawk," he said in an uncharacteristically tentative voice. "When were you sure of your true feelings for Aissa?"

Shadow Hawk tried not to smile. He loved Gitano and did not want to anger him, but he had the answer now to his questions. Red Wing's legs were still long, and she still had beautiful eyes.

Chapter Seventeen

Aissa was frightened and she was angry. Shadow Hawk would not let her hold his arm as they walked, insisting that she rely on the sound of his footsteps. Around her, the sounds of the camp swirled and echoed. The shouts of children; the short, sharp bark of a startled dog; then from behind her, muffled giggling.

Aissa felt herself flush, then she shivered, even though the morning sun was warm. Were they laughing at her? Everything seemed so strange, just as it had so long ago when she'd been a captive in this camp. And Shadow Hawk didn't seem to care. He wanted her to be as independent and self-sufficient as Ocha was, but Aissa didn't think it was fair that he expect so much of her. Ocha had been raised in the mountains. It was easier for her.

Aissa remembered how the old woman had walked through the camp, her head high and her unseeing eyes seeming to focus on everything. Ocha was able to find healing plants by following the scent of their leaves. She had helped many people in the tribe when their hearts were troubled. Ocha was content with her life, even happy.

But it was different for Aissa. She remembered the first time she had opened her eyes and seen blackness; she had wanted to die. Had Ocha ever felt that? Aissa still wondered if her life would ever be worth living. Would she ever feel the contentment that Ocha seemed to feel?

"Here," Shadow Hawk said, taking her arm. "The path narrows and there are trees on both sides." The reassuring warmth of his hand was gone almost as quickly as it had come.

Aissa cocked her head to one side. The sound of the wind blowing through the pines was louder here. That meant that the land dropped away on the windward side. Ocha had always set her lodge apart from the others. The old woman liked it that way. Ocha even seemed to enjoy the stories that the young ones told about her. Even Teroz had believed them, had been sure she was a witch.

"This way." Shadow Hawk's touch came again. This time turning her abruptly uphill. Aissa stumbled slightly. There were small, sharp-edged stones scattered on the path. They bruised her feet through the thin leather soles of the moccasins that Broken Moon had given her. Terrified for a second that she would fall, she involuntarily reached for Shadow Hawk. He allowed her an instant of contact then gently lifted her hand from his shoulder and led the way again. Aissa forced herself to walk more quickly. For Shadow Hawk, Ocha and herself, she was going to try.

She could hear Ocha singing as they got closer to the lodge. She listened to Shadow Hawk's soft footfall, stopping when she heard him stop.

"Who is it?" Ocha called out in Spanish. Aissa shook her head. The old woman was expecting them or she would have spoken Apache. Aissa heard the rustling of soft leather as Ocha opened the lodge flap. "Ah, it is you, Shadow."

Aissa could hear the warmth in her voice as well as the amusement. Even people who knew Ocha well were often startled by her ability to recognize them before they spoke.

"I have brought someone with me, Grandmother."

Aissa took a tentative step forward.

"It pleases me that you are here, girl. How has my grandson been treating you?"

Aissa smiled. "He treats me well, Ocha."

"Broken Moon told me of your misfortune, girl. Now you will have to listen to what I say."

Aissa could imagine Ocha's weathered face creasing around her youthful smile. "It seems I am a prisoner again, Ocha."

"But no one keeps you in this prison but you," Ocha said gently. "Leave us, Shadow, and do not come back until the evening meal."

Aissa was startled at the soft kiss Shadow Hawk placed on her forehead. An instant later, she heard him walk away.

"Come inside, girl."

Aissa reached out, groping for the lodge flap, ducking so low that she was bent almost double.

"The door," Ocha said dryly, "was not made for those who cannot see, but neither is anything in this world. You will learn."

Aissa stood up straight inside the lodge, afraid to walk forward, afraid of stumbling into the cook fire. She could smell the thin wisps of acrid smoke that meant the small fire was burning brightly. She could also smell the tangled, pungent scents of Ocha's herbs. She remembered clearly the inside of Ocha's lodge. There were bundles of drying plants hung from the lodge poles and intricate baskets stacked behind the sleeping robes. The baskets were filled with yet more plants, as well as dried bark and roots.

"Come sit by me."

Aissa hesitated.

"The deerskin that covers the floor ends two steps before the firepit. Remember, too, that the firepit is in the center of the lodge, in a straight line from the door."

Aissa waited for Ocha to say more, but the old woman fell silent. For an instant, Aissa wanted to scream at her but the impulse quickly passed. Ocha, like Shadow Hawk, wanted only for Aissa to be as independent as possible. Still, this was frightening. If she walked too close to the fire, there would be no one to see her begin to fall or to catch her if she did. She slid her right foot forward, feeling the deerskin through the thin leather soles of the moccasins. She extended her right hand until she felt the stiff leather of the lodge wall. Following its curve, she moved forward slowly, extremely aware of the heat from the cook fire. She took a few more steps, feeling the heat behind her now.

"I'm here, girl."

Aissa reluctantly took her hand away from the lodge wall and walked toward the sound of Ocha's voice.

"Sit."

Aissa lowered herself cautiously onto a thick sleeping robe. She ran her hand over the soft fur, suddenly flooded with memories of her time in the Apache camp. She had been frightened many times, but she had never felt as helpless as she felt now.

"I can feel your fear, girl."

"Don't I have a right to be afraid, Ocha?"

"Yes, you have the right to be afraid."

Aissa waited for Ocha to say something more, but she was silent.

"Tell me about the accident."

Aissa sat with her hands clenched tightly in her lap. "I was in a mine, much like the one Broken Moon was in. I was inside and there was a cave-in."

"That is all?"

"Yes."

"What did you hear?"

Aissa hesitated, trying to get past the fear of remembering. "I was coming back out of the mine. I was feeling good, almost happy. I knew that a friend and I were soon going to escape. Then I heard a sound, almost like thunder, and everything began to fall around me." Aissa felt drops of sweat roll down her face. "I ran but not for long. Something hit me in the head and I fell. I remember that it was so hard to breathe, I thought I was going to suffocate. Dust filled the tunnel, and I could feel it inside my lungs when I breathed."

"When did you first know that you were blind?"

"I think I knew in the tunnel. I was hit by a heavy wooden beam. I opened my eyes and tried to move. I couldn't see anything. I just thought it was the darkness in the tunnel. I thought the cave-in had knocked down all of the lanterns."

"And when you awoke later?"

"I was terrified. I couldn't stop crying. My head ached terribly and I kept thinking I was dreaming. But it wasn't a dream, it was a nightmare." Aissa's voice rose sharply.

"Calm yourself, girl. You are safe here."

Aissa breathed in the many smells of the lodge and started to relax in spite of her fear.

"Tell me about the darkness," Ocha repeated.

"I hate it," Aissa replied, tears filling her eyes. "I can feel the warmth of the sun, but I can't see its light. I can hear the sound of a hawk screech overhead, but I can't see it against the blue sky. There is no beauty in this dark world, Ocha." Aissa's voice trembled, and she didn't try to stop the tears. She could feel Ocha's warm and comforting touch on her hand.

"There are many who can see but still they find no beauty in their world, Aissa."

Aissa wanted to cry out, to say it wasn't true, but there were people like that in the world. Ray Grimes was one of them. "I see light sometimes, or maybe I just dream that I do," she said suddenly.

"Describe this light."

"At first I would get headaches and then I would see little sparkles of light. Then one day I was able to see the outlines of things."

"Did this last for long?"

Aissa shook her head. "No."

"Has it happened again?"

"Yes, on the trip here, it happened several times. What does it mean, Ocha? Am I just imagining it?"

"Perhaps it is your imagination, or perhaps your eyes are trying to see again."

"Is it possible?"

"Anything is possible, girl."

"I am too afraid to believe it."

"It would be wise to learn the ways of the sightless world. Your eyes may never heal, girl. But if they do, it will be a wonderful, unexpected gift."

"Did you ever wish that your sight would return, Ocha? Were you ever frightened?"

"Ah, girl," Ocha responded in an amused tone, "I wished for my sight to return every day. People spoke of my courage, but they did not know of my fear. I wanted nothing more than to see the faces of my husband and children. And the fear was my constant companion for a long time."

"How did you learn to live with it?"

"I did not learn to live with it. I sent it away."

"I don't understand."

"Fear is something you feel, just like happiness or sadness. If you choose to be happy, you will be happy. If you choose to be sad, you will be sad. If you choose to be fearful, you will be fearful. I finally grew tired of being fearful and I simply bid the fear goodbye."

Aissa tilted her head slightly. "But aren't you ever afraid anymore?"

"Oh, I am afraid of many things. I am afraid that I will not be able to cure one of my people, I am afraid for my grandchildren and children if they are in danger. I am afraid that the white man will one day find our people. But the darkness, I no longer fear that."

Aissa was silent. How could she ever learn to be like Ocha? How could she ever learn to accept her blindness? "It saddens me that you have never been able to look upon the faces of your children and grandchildren."

"But I have, girl." Ocha reached out, slowly running her weathered fingers over Aissa's face. "Just as I have seen yours. You have a fine face, lovely and delicate, with soft skin. Your chin is strong and your cheekbones are high. And you smile often." Ocha took her hand away.

"How did you know that?"

"I can feel the lines. It is not so difficult."

"Tell me about Shadow Hawk," Aissa demanded gently.

"You are the one who has looked upon his face."

"Please," Aissa insisted.

"Shadow Hawk has a strong face. His eyes are set wide apart, his nose is straight. It is a face that people like to look upon because they see something honest and good."

Aissa nodded to herself. "Yes, you have seen him. His eyes are dark blue and they grow even darker when he is angry."

"You love my grandson very much, do you not?"

"Yes," Aissa responded without hesitation.

"Then you must learn to go on with your life, girl. You cannot dwell on your own pain."

"It's hard, Ocha. I want so much to see again."

"But you are learning to see in truer ways."

"What do you mean, Ocha?"

"When you were sighted and you met someone for the first time, did you not already form an idea of what the person was like by the way he or she looked?"

Aissa shook her head. "I don't think so."

"Think about it, Aissa. You were frightened of Teroz."

"I had reason to be afraid of Teroz."

"But as your friendship grew, did he not begin to look different to you?"

Aissa thought about the last time she had seen Teroz at her father's ranch. He hadn't frightened her in the least. He no longer looked hard and cruel.

"We, who do not have sight, have somewhat of an advantage, girl."

"An advantage?"

"Yes, when we meet someone, we do not know if they are pretty or homely, if they have scars or if their skin is clear. We know only what our ears and our hearts tell us. Our eyes do not even tell us if a person's skin is white or dark. We know only what a person is like inside."

"You make it sound so easy, Ocha," Aissa said.

"Life is never easy, girl, even if you have sight."

Aissa nodded, realizing there were no simple answers. Ocha could not just give her a special tea and help her see again. Aissa would have to learn how to accept her blindness and then learn how to live with it.

Ocha left Aissa at the edge of the trees. "You can find your own way back to Broken Moon's lodge," she had said and disappeared.

Aissa stood still, unable to move. None of the sounds were familiar to her, and she was afraid to take even a tentative step forward. The only way she would find her way back through the camp would be if she stumbled and fell and made a fool of herself. She couldn't suffer that humiliation.

She held out a hand in front of her; there was nothing. She moved it around. There were branches on both sides of her. She tried to remember. Once she left the trees, she would bear to the right and that would take her back through camp. But how would she find Broken Moon's lodge? How would she avoid tripping over campfires, dogs, and children? She kicked at the ground, once again angry at Shadow Hawk for bringing her here and wanting her to do something she didn't want to do. She heard a sound and lifted her head, concentrating. Footsteps. They were not Shadow Hawk's footsteps but they belonged to a man, not a woman.

"Who is it?" Aissa asked in broken Apache. The footsteps stopped, and Aissa could feel the man close to her. "What do you want?" Aissa felt a hand on her hair and she jerked away, stumbling backward.

"Do not be afraid, Aissa. It is only I, Gitano."

At the sound of Gitano's voice, Aissa relaxed, almost wanting to cry. "Why didn't you tell me it was you?"

"I am sorry. I did not mean to frighten you."

"It doesn't matter."

"Why are you standing here?"

Aissa was quiet. She didn't want to admit to Gitano that she couldn't find her way back to Broken Moon's lodge.

"I thought we were friends, white woman. I remember a time when we talked of many things."

Aissa nodded. Gitano had been a good friend to her. "Will you give me your hand, Gitano?" She felt his hand touch hers and she squeezed it tightly. "I need a friend, Gitano," she said, her voice catching as she spoke. Suddenly the fear threatened to consume her again and she felt the panic build in her. She felt Gitano take his hand from hers. An instant later, she felt the weight of his arm around her shoulders. She let him lead her as she tried desperately to fight her panic and fear. When he tripped, Aissa held onto his arm.

"It is all right. We are at my lodge. Sit."

Aissa sat down, tucking her legs beneath her. She crossed her arms in front of her chest and rocked nervously back and forth. There was something strange about Gitano's lodge. What was it? She moved her head around and tried to listen and then she realized what it was: it was quiet here. There were no camp sounds. "Where is your lodge, Gitano? It is not in the camp."

"That is good, you are learning. Drink this." Gitano handed Aissa a clay bowl. "I am like my grandmother. I like to be away from the others. As much as I like to talk, I also like to be alone."

Aissa sipped from the bowl and recognized the sweet taste of the mint tea that Ocha had often made for her. "Thank you, Gitano."

"It is only tea."

"You know that's not what I mean." Aissa set the bowl on the ground beside her. "I'm sorry."

"I have seen your fear before, Aissa. I do not think less of you because of it."

Tears filled Aissa's eyes as she recalled how Gitano had gone against Shadow Hawk and taken her from the Apache camp and helped her to escape. "I feel like such a coward."

"Why, because you do not attempt to walk through camp alone? I am surprised my cousin and grandmother would make you. I think they ask too much of you too soon."

"They are only trying to help me."

"And I am only trying to help you."

Aissa smiled, reaching around for the bowl and lifting it to her lips again. "Why is it you are not married, Gitano? You would make a fine husband."

"Ah, do not say such a thing to me, white woman. You insult me when you speak of such things."

"So, you don't want people to know that you are truly a kind man, is that it?"

"It is best to let people wonder."

"Why?"

"Because that is the way I want it."

Aissa set her bowl down. "All right, I won't tell anyone

that you're a kind man. I wouldn't want to ruin your reputation."

"I see time has not dulled your sharp tongue."

"Some things do not change, Gitano. Like you."

"That is enough, white woman. I am not so kind as you think. I have done things that I am not proud of, that are not so honorable."

"We have all done things we are not proud of, Gitano." Aissa smiled when she heard Gitano make an impatient sound.

"You make me uneasy with this talk. You remind me of Ocha. So, do you not want to know of the others in the camp?"

"Yes, tell me. How are Teroz and Paloma, and Brave Heart and Singing Bird? How is your father?"

"My father is the same; he is much too wise for one man. I am afraid he will take it with him when he passes to the other side and leave none of his wisdom for me."

"You are already wise in your own way, Gitano."

"Not wise enough," Gitano said seriously, then continued. "Brave Heart and Singing Bird are still very much in love. They cannot bear to be apart from each other. And Teroz and Paloma have a daughter. Her name is Morning Sun."

"Teroz and Paloma must be very proud."

Gitano sighed, shaking his head. "I cannot believe I am saying this, but Teroz is a different man. He is a good husband to Paloma. He began to change when you were his captive. That is when we all began to see a different side to Teroz."

"There was always goodness in Teroz. Your own sister saw it long before anyone else."

"Yes, many times I heard Singing Bird telling me that Teroz was good but I would not listen. I was determined to hate him."

"What about you, Gitano? Is there a woman that you love?"

"Me, love a woman? Never."

"I can hear the lie in your voice."

"I am not lying. There is no woman."

"If you say so."

"I say so," Gitano said stubbornly. "Besides, she is afraid of me."

"This woman you do not love, who does not exist, is afraid of you?"

"You are sly, just like my grandmother."

"I am a woman, Gitano. Even if I can't see, I can hear. You have feelings for this woman."

"Yes," he said softly.

"Why is she afraid of you?"

"I do not know. Can you imagine anyone being afraid of me?"

"No," Aissa said, laughing for the first time.

"You wound me with your laugh, white woman," Gitano said in jest.

"I'm sorry, Gitano, it's just that there are many more men who are much more frightening than you. Have you done something to scare this woman?"

"No, I have done nothing. Singing Bird says she is afraid of my words."

Aissa tried not to laugh. "Oh, you mean you talk too much."

"I do not need this," Gitano said impatiently. "I should just leave you here to find your own way back."

"You wouldn't do that. I know you, Gitano. Tell me truthfully and it will go no farther, do you have feelings for this woman?" Aissa waited for Gitano's response, but it was not forthcoming. She heard the wind blow through the pine trees and the sound soothed her. Not far away, she heard men's voices as they walked by. She also heard Gitano as he moved around. "What is it, Gitano? Have I made you uncomfortable by asking you this question?"

"You have always made me feel uncomfortable, white woman. Even when you could see."

Aissa didn't understand what he meant. For a moment, she was hurt by his words. "Please explain, Gitano."

"It does not matter."

"Gitano, listen to me. When Teroz brought me here, you were kind to me from the beginning. You talked to me and you were my friend. And when Shadow Hawk took me from Teroz and treated me so badly, you were still my friend. You risked your friendship with Shadow Hawk to help me escape from your camp. I will never forget that. Please forgive me if I have intruded into places where I do not belong." Aissa started to get up, but she felt Gitano's hand on hers.

"Sit," he commanded. "I like you, Aissa. I like you very much. You are a good, honest woman. You taught many of us that not all white people are the enemy."

"Then what is it, Gitano? I hear such sadness in your voice."

"It is my father," Gitano said simply. "He is dying."

Aissa was stunned. Ataza had been such a strength to his people, she couldn't imagine that anything could harm him. She had not known him well, but he had always treated her with great respect. "I am sorry, Gitano. I did not know."

"Most do not know. Only my grandmother, my mother, and Broken Moon."

"What happened? Was he injured in some way?"

"No, it is a sickness, one that even Ocha cannot cure." Gitano sighed deeply. "My heart is so heavy, Aissa. My father is such a wise man, a good man, how is it possible that he can be struck down by such a thing?"

"I don't know, Gitano."

"I could understand if he had been killed while fighting. That, at least, would be honorable. But this sickness has no honor. It will leave my father without his pride."

"Ataza will always have his pride, Gitano. No sickness can take that away from him."

"He does not want me to tell Miho."

"Where is Miho?"

"He is back with his wife and her family, but he should be here with our father."

"Don't go against your father's wishes, Gitano. You must be his source of strength now."

"I have fear, too, Aissa. I worry about the time when my father has gone over to the other side, to the time when the white man will find us and hunt us down. Already, we have to move our camp more often. Our life as we know it will soon be gone."

Aissa remained silent, remembering the times when she had heard the townspeople talk about hunting down the Apache.

"But I will not run from the whites. I will fight them."

"Gitano" Aissa said gently, reaching out for his hand. "There is also honor in living, in passing on what you know to your children and their children. If you and the others are killed, then no one can teach them the Apache ways." Aissa felt Gitano's hand grasp hers tightly, then pull away.

"Come, we grow too serious. It is time to take you back to Broken Moon's lodge."

Aissa held onto Gitano's hand as she stood up. She tugged at his arm when he started to walk away. "Thank you for being my friend, Gitano." Aissa wrapped her arms around him and hugged him. Unlike the first time she had hugged him, he did not pull away.

Ben saw Flora and Joe ride up into the yard. He was sitting on the porch, drinking a cup of coffee and stood up when they dismounted. "What brings you two out here?"

"We need to talk, Ben. Inside," Joe said.
"Why, it's nice out here."
"Don't argue with him, Ben," Flora said, taking his arm and leading him inside the house.
"What's this all about?"
Joe closed the door, looked out the window and turned around. "Someone saw Ray Grimes."
"Grimes? Around here? Why don't you find him and bring him in, Joe?"
"I can't, Ben. I don't know where he's hiding."
"He's the one who kidnapped Aissa. I know it."
"Then, I'm keeping a lookout, but you need to do something for me."
"What?"
"I need for you to leave the ranch."
"Are you crazy? I can't leave here. If Aissa comes back—"
"If Aissa comes back she'll find you," Flora said gently. "She knows she can come to me or Joe."
"You'll be safer if you stay with Flora, Ben. If you're out here I can't protect you."
"I don't need your protection," Ben said angrily. "I can handle Grimes."
"Just like you handled him the time he burned you out?" Flora said angrily. "Ben, listen to me, if anything happens to you, I'll never forgive myself. And what if Aissa comes back and you're dead? It'll break her heart."
"I don't know if she's coming back."
"She's coming back, you know she is. You know she's alive."
Ben nodded, thinking about the letter that Shadow Hawk had written him. He had explained everything in it and had begged him to be patient with Aissa. Silently, he thanked Shadow Hawk again.
"Ben, Grimes obviously knows that Aissa is alive and he's waiting for her. You're just a target if you stay here."

"What if Aissa comes back when I'm gone?"
"Shadow Hawk will be with her. He's not going to let anything happen to her."
"What about the house? If I'm not here, Grimes is liable to set it afire."
"I'll stay here, Ben, if you don't mind."
"Are you sure that's safe, Joe?"
"Grimes isn't after me, he's after Aissa."
"Please, Ben," Flora implored, putting her arm through Ben's. "I care about you. I don't want anything else to happen to you."
"All right, all right," Ben relented. "I'll stay with Flora. But I want to know the minute you see Aissa or you catch Grimes."

Grimes squatted down behind some rocks and hid until the rider went past. He lifted his head slightly to look. He recognized the horse. What was the deputy doing out here on Gerard's land? Grimes shook his head. He forgot, the deputy was now the sheriff. He turned around and sat down, leaning against the rocks and stretching his legs out in front of him. He rubbed his left shoulder. It hadn't healed well from the gunshot. It still gave him trouble. He couldn't even straighten it out completely.

He'd been waiting around for weeks now, knowing that Aissa would eventually return home, but she hadn't. Neither she nor the Apache had returned to the ranch. In fact, he hadn't even seen Gerard lately. What was going on?

He turned around and looked back over the rocks. The horse was out of sight now, but he knew it or another would be back later. The deputy was keeping watch over the old man. Grimes shrugged his shoulders. He could wait. In fact, the longer it took, the more he knew he'd enjoy seeing the look on Aissa's face when he got her for the last time. And there would be no mistakes this time. He would take her to the lake, shoot her, and throw her body into the water. And if Gerard and Shadow Hawk got in the way, they would die, too. After he killed Aissa, he would take back his land. No one would ever deprive him of what was rightfully his again.

"Why have you not been to see me, Nephew? You have been in camp for a day."

Shadow Hawk looked at Ataza. They were sitting inside his lodge. Ataza sat with his back straight and his arms at his sides. His face was full of caring when he looked at Shadow Hawk. Shadow Hawk recalled the first time he had seen him on the trail leading up to the other camp. Shadow Hawk had never seen another Apache besides his mother, and he had been astounded at Ataza's strength and speed. But he had been more impressed with Ataza's wisdom. Ataza had treated him like a son when Shadow Hawk most missed his own father.

"I am sorry, Uncle. Yesterday we arrived and I visited with my mother, Brave Heart, and Gitano. By the time I was going to visit you, my mother told me to wait until today."

"It is no wonder if you visited with Gitano last," Ataza said dryly.

"Yes, my cousin has not lost his way with words."

Ataza laughed. "Gitano has his own wisdom, but he would have everyone believe otherwise. I believe he would make a good leader. He shows all of the qualities that are needed."

"I agree, Uncle. Gitano likes to play the clown, but he is responsible when it is necessary."

"Good, I was hoping you would agree with me."

"Why?" Shadow Hawk asked, suddenly uncomfortable with Ataza's words.

Ataza's dark eyes held Shadow Hawk's for a moment before he answered. "I am dying, Shadow, and I want Gitano to lead our people."

"Uncle," Shadow Hawk stammered. "But you look healthy. What is it?"

"It is a sickness that eats away at me."

"Can my grandmother help you?"

"No one can help me, Shadow. I have accepted it."

"But you cannot, Uncle," Shadow Hawk protested.

"It is all right, Nephew. I have had a good life. I regret nothing. I only worry about my family and my people."

Shadow Hawk nodded, realizing that there was no arguing with his uncle. "Gitano would be a capable leader. I would trust my family with him."

"You help make my decision easy, Shadow. Thank you. Now, tell me about you."

"You have heard about Aissa?"

"Yes, I am sorry."

"I will make a life with her, no matter how much she protests."

"And she does protest?"

"Yes, she thinks she will not be a good wife because she cannot see."

"So, you brought her to my mother to teach her the many ways of the sightless world."

"Yes."

"That is good. Ocha cares very much for her." Ataza fell silent, breathing as though he had just walked uphill. "When I am gone, will you check on our people, make sure they are doing well?"

"Of course, Uncle."

Ataza nodded. "I am tired, Shadow. I must rest. Come visit me again tomorrow."

"Yes, Uncle," Shadow Hawk said, as he stood up and walked to the door of the lodge. He turned to say something to Ataza, but his uncle was already lying down on his side. Shadow Hawk left the lodge, his heart heavy. He could not imagine this world without Ataza.

Aissa sat up, her head throbbing. The headache had come again, this time worse than ever. She pressed her hands against her temples, trying to blot out the pain. She wanted to cry out Ocha's name, to ask her for help, but she didn't want to wake her. This pain frightened Aissa beyond all else.

"What is it, girl?" Ocha asked, her voice low and comforting.

Ocha had decided that it would be best if Aissa moved in to her lodge, and now Aissa was glad that she was there. "It is the pain in my head, Ocha. It grows worse."

"Relax, girl. Do not fight it."

Aissa could hear Ocha moving around, but she didn't know what she was doing. Aissa pushed her robe aside. The strange dots of light began to dance in front of her eyes, and Aissa thought she could see the light from the fire. "I feel as if there's a devil inside my head," she said. "And he plays games with me."

"What games does he play, girl?" Ocha asked, coming to sit by Aissa.

"He lets me see bits and pieces of light, and then he takes them away so I am in darkness again."

"Drink this. It will take away your pain."

Aissa took the bowl from Ocha and quickly drank the bitter contents; she would do anything to be free of the pain. "Why is this happening, Ocha?"

"I don't know, girl. But you must not fight it. That will only make the pain worse."

Aissa nodded, trying to relax. She heard Ocha as she began to chant softly, and Aissa lay back down, feeling sleepy in spite of the pain. She closed her eyes, still seeing the light dancing around in her head. But soon it didn't matter; soon she was asleep.

When Aissa awoke the next morning, she slowly moved her head around. There was no pain. She sat up; the pain was gone but so was the light.

"How do you feel this morning?" Ocha asked.

"I am better, thank you. My head does not even hurt."

"Good. And the light, do you still see the light?"

"No, I see no light, Ocha. I think it was my imagination."

"Perhaps," Ocha said. "Drink some of this."

"What is this you have me drink everyday?"

"It contains many herbs and roots. It will make you strong."

"I am already strong."

"Drink it," Ocha ordered.

Aissa drank the bowl and set it down. "What are we doing today? I am anxious to go outside. I don't like staying in here."

"This is good. I will take you to the place where I search for many of my healing plants."

"I didn't say I wanted to dig for roots, Ocha," Aissa said dryly, amusement in her voice.

"I see your tongue grows sharper everyday."

"I'm sorry. I didn't mean to offend you."

"You did not offend me. It is good to see your spirit."

"What is it you gave me to drink last night, Ocha? I feel better than I have felt in a long time."

"It is a special mixture, one that assures peace of mind."

"May I say something, Ocha? Something personal."

"Anything, girl."

"I am sorry about Ataza."

"You know about my son?"

"Gitano told me."

"It saddens me greatly but I know there is nothing I can do about it. So I will make his days as comfortable as possible. Are you ready to go outside now?"

"Yes," Aissa responded, sorry she had brought up Ataza's name. She could hear the sadness in Ocha's voice. She heard the lodge door and turned.

"Are you coming or not, girl? I have many things to do today."

"I am coming." Aissa hurried to the door, counting her steps along the way. When she stepped outside, she listened for Ocha's footsteps but heard nothing. "Are you here, Ocha?"

"I am beside you, girl. Why did you not hear me?"

Aissa shook her head. "I don't know."

"Think."

"I guess I was afraid you had left me, and I was listening for the sounds of your footsteps, not your silence."

"That is good." Ocha took Aissa's hand. "We will walk along a stone-covered path and turn to the left. I want you to pay attention. Tell me of the things you hear along the way."

Aissa held onto Ocha's hand as they walked. She heard the sound of her feet crunching on the small stones. She heard the annoying sounds of crows flying overhead, their caws echoing back and forth. There was the ever-present sound of the wind blowing through the pine branches, and the sound of horses whinnying from the pasture below. When Ocha stopped suddenly, Aissa almost ran into her.

"Tell me of the things you heard," Ocha demanded.

Aissa told Ocha.

"Good, that is good. But did you not hear the grasshoppers as they rubbed their legs together? There is no more distinct sound."

Of course Aissa had heard them, but it was such a familiar sound, she had almost ignored it. That was what Ocha was trying to teach her: she must ignore no sound, no matter how familiar.

"There is a hill here. It is not too steep. Feel your way slowly with each step."

Aissa felt uneasy. She didn't like walking on anything but flat ground unless she was being led. She recalled the way Ocha had trampled through the woods and crossed the stream in search of her roots and healing plants. Aissa shook her head in wonder, unable to understand how she could so confidently find her way.

"Are you coming, girl?"

"Yes," Aissa said, putting one tentative foot in front of the other. Now she wished she had accepted Shadow Hawk's offer of a walking stick. She listened for Ocha's soft footfall as she walked up the hill and Aissa followed her, knowing that Ocha would not lead her into danger.

"We are almost there," Ocha said.

Aissa stopped when she could no longer hear Ocha's footsteps. "Is this the place, Ocha?"

"This is it, girl. Bend down. Can you not feel many plants growing around your feet?"

Aissa reached out her hands, feeling the leaves of the plants.

"There are many different ones here." Ocha was next to Aissa. "Feel this. Tell me the shape of the leaf."

Aissa ran her fingers over the rough plant. "It has three distinct points and it has a rough texture. The stalk feels fuzzy."

"Very good. We use this plant for pains in the stomach. Now, tell me about this one." Ocha held onto the leaf until Aissa touched it.

"It is smooth and round and it grows on a vine. It has small berries."

"We take these berries and crush them. They are very useful for aches in the head. The leaves can be made into a tea that will aid in sleeping. It is what I gave you last night."

"How do you know all this without seeing, Ocha? What if you pick a poisonous plant and you make someone very sick?"

"I try every one of my medicines on myself. So, if someone is to be poisoned, it will be me first."

Aissa smiled, amazed at the old woman's spirit.

"And this one," Ocha said pressing a smooth, broad leaf into Aissa's hand. Ocha's voice was soft, almost singsong, as she recited the virtues of these smooth-leaved plants. Aissa knelt in the dirt, trying to listen. Would she ever learn to walk in the woods like Ocha could? Aissa shivered. It was frightening to be here, even though she loved and trusted Ocha. If something happened, who would help them? She wasn't even sure how far they had come from Ocha's lodge. Would anyone hear them if they had to call for help? She remembered the first time she had seen the vast mountain range that these Apache called home. The peaks were enormous, massive beyond imagining.

The wind sighed in the pine trees. Ocha's voice went on, describing the scent of the plants' spring bloom. Aissa tried to listen, but her attention was distracted by her own fear.

"Will you listen, girl?" Ocha's voice was no longer a murmur. It was suddenly sharp and stern. "You are not listening to me at all."

"I'm afraid out here," Aissa admitted. She heard the rustling of the old woman's beaded skirt.

"Run then, run from your fear." The stern voice had softened a little and came from above. Aissa stood up.

Run? She felt like laughing or like crying, but in a crazy way Ocha was right. That was exactly what she wanted to do; to run like a deer, leaping, digging at the earth with her feet until she had left everything behind. No, not everything. Just her blindness.

"I hate it, Ocha." The words came from Aissa's heart, from a place deep inside. "I hate not being able to see. I hate it." Aissa wanted to cry, but her eyes remained stubbornly dry. Finally, she quieted.

The old woman remained silent for a long time. Then she spoke quietly. "But you are blind. If you hate your blindness, you are hating yourself and the Spirit that made you as you are. That is foolish, girl."

Aissa pulled at the cloth of her skirt, unable to stop imagining the threatening mountains she knew loomed above them. "But it's so easy to get lost, Ocha. It's so easy to—"

"You will not get lost with me. I know how to return to my lodge. I often go much farther than this in search of my herbs."

Ocha sounded offended. Aissa tried to calm herself. "I know you can find your way. And I was listening, Ocha. You said that the leaves are good for fever and that the flower is good for cleansing the blood."

"So I did. And what does it prove, that you can tell me what I said."

"It proves I was listening."

Ocha made a disgusted sound deep in her throat. "With your ears perhaps. Not with your heart. You will forget this by the time you awaken in the morning."

"No, I won't." Aissa found herself smiling, remembering how Ocha loved to argue like this. She remembered Ocha's face, too, the sunburst of wrinkles that surrounded the old woman's amazingly clear, seemingly focused eyes. Ocha's hands were slim and strong, and her erect posture belied her age.

"You are ready then to go on?"

Aissa nodded, then felt ridiculous. Ocha couldn't see her anymore than she could see Ocha. How strange it was to be with someone else who was blind, too. And yet, Ocha almost never needed anyone to guide her. "How do you find your way around so well, Ocha?"

"As I told you, girl, by learning not to be afraid."

"I was better at Clay's ranch, the place I stayed before Shadow Hawk found me."

"So I understand. You were taken care of. That is well enough for a time, but it must end. There was a woman, when I was a child, who had a baby whose feet were bent backwards."

Aissa held still, grateful that Ocha's story would distract her from the unsettling feeling of the looming mountains.

"The baby's feet were turned inward, like so." Ocha took Aissa's wrist and angled her hand until it almost hurt. "The child could barely walk. That woman, her name was Oak Maiden, never let the child want anything for more than an instant before she leapt to bring it. Food, the beaded moccasins she had spent so much time making, the baby's doll, anything the child wanted her mother ran to get."

Aissa pulled her hand away, suddenly less grateful for the story. "I know what you're going to say, Ocha, and I—"

"Perhaps not," Ocha cut her off. "The child was merry and she grew up enchanting men with her lovely face and her sweet need of their help. She did learn to make baskets and to sew very well."

Aissa was confused. "What then? Did she ever marry?"

"Yes, she did marry."

Aissa waited for Ocha to go on, but the old woman stubbornly remained silent.

"Well? What happened?"

"One day her husband found her inside their lodge, dead. She had done it herself."

Aissa caught her breath.

"She could not be happy." Ocha reached again for Aissa's hand, and once she found it, she squeezed it tightly. "She slept each night with her husband, yes. But also with her fear."

Aissa nodded to herself and smiled. "I may have to hear that story more than once, Ocha."

"No," the old woman reassured her. "Not you. You learn quickly. When you listen."

Aissa smiled then found herself laughing aloud.

"All the feelings will follow fear. Joy, anger, all of them follow like fish escaping a basket trap," Ocha advised.

Aissa reached out tentatively until she found Ocha's sleeve, then her shoulder, and her face. She ran her fingers over Ocha's leathery skin, the way Ocha had once explored her own face. "But I will never be like you," Aissa said. "I will never be as good as you are, as needed by other people."

Ocha did not answer immediately. Aissa wondered if she had gotten angry again. Then Ocha spoke, "Do you smell it?"

Aissa was startled. "Smell what? Is there a flower I'm supposed to notice or something, or. . . ." Aissa trailed off, realizing that Ocha was no longer bantering. Aissa drew in a deep breath, concentrating. There was a faint odor of campfire smoke, but that was normal.

"It's not the camp," Ocha said slowly. "The breeze is wrong for that. This smoke comes from the mountains."

Aissa felt a sudden tightening in her stomach. Fire? The scent of wood smoke seemed stronger suddenly, burning her lungs. She turned, aimless, wanting to run again, but completely lost. "Which way? Which way do we go?"

"Give me your hand." Aissa reached out, groping, until the strong, bony fingers gripped hers. Ocha started off, walking slowly. Or perhaps, Aissa thought, it just seemed slow because she wanted so much to run again.

"Hurry," Aissa spoke her thought. Ocha squeezed her hand and quickened her step. The land leveled after a few minutes and Ocha stopped. In the sudden silence, without the sounds of their skirts brushing through the grass and their footsteps Aissa could hear something. A roar, muted and ominous. The fire? How close? Oh, God, how close?

"We will not be able to make it back to the camp,"

Ocha said evenly.

Aissa found herself pressing the back of her hand into her own teeth so hard that it hurt. Furious with her panic, she jerked her hand away. "Where then?"

Ocha squeezed Aissa's hand. "Think."

"Not now, don't test me like that," Aissa screamed. "Just get us—"

"Think," Ocha repeated, unmovable as stone.

"Back to your lodge? But it's so far. I. . . . The creek, we crossed a creek. That's where we should go."

Ocha patted her hand and led her forward again. Aissa felt her fear ebb, then swell again when a sharp crackling sound rose above the dull roar.

"Don't listen to the enemy's voice," Ocha said. "Listen to the voice of our friend. The creek is not far now. I can hear it. But we must go faster."

Aissa tried to keep calm as Ocha led her along at a striding walk. Ocha went so fast that Aissa couldn't keep herself from walking with her free hand extended, trying to protect herself from the brush that slapped at her arms and face. They started downhill.

"Hear it?" Ocha asked abruptly.

Aissa tried, but their footsteps, her own ragged breathing, and the rumble of the distant fire drowned out the sound of the creek. Suddenly she felt the old woman stumble. An instant later, they were both sprawled in the grass. Aissa sat up, scrambling to her feet, her head aching fiercely. She touched her temple. A large bump was rising under the skin. She hadn't even felt the blow.

"Ocha?"

The old woman didn't answer. Aissa dropped back down, groping in a frantic circle until she felt Ocha's moccasined foot, then her shoulders, and her face.

"Ocha?"

Aissa raised the old woman. She was limp. Frantically, hands shaking, Aissa found Ocha's lips, and felt the tiny flutter of breath. She searched Ocha's face, grimacing when a sticky warmth touched her fingers. Forcing herself to breathe slowly, she felt the cut. It wasn't too bad, a short, deep gash. But the impact had been enough to knock Ocha out. Aissa lowered the old woman gently and felt the ground around them. The rock outcropping jutted up less than six inches. But it had been enough, combined with their fear, their hurry, and their blindness.

"Help me," Aissa demanded, tipping her head back and raising her face to the sky. Her temple throbbed so intensely that she had to fight the urge to lie down, to just rest until the pain passed, to let the fire find them. A dozen streaks of light raced across the blackness of her vision. Aissa tried to ignore them. The smell of smoke was stronger every second. She couldn't pass out now, or sit here like a scared rabbit. She had to get Ocha and herself to the cool safety of the creek.

She stood up slowly, trying to hear the gurgling of the water. The roaring of the fire was close enough that she could feel the unnatural warmness of the air, but still she thought she could hear the sound of water. Aissa lifted Ocha, surprised at the smallness of the old woman's bones and her slight weight. She stood swaying, uncertain. She took a few steps, sliding her feet carefully forward, then a few more.

Aissa could hear the water now. She shifted direction slightly, praying silently that she would not blunder into an embankment, a steep drop-off that would send them both plunging downward. The smoke was thicker now, burning her lungs and her eyes. Aissa stopped and freed one hand long enough to rub at her eyes. The flickering was getting worse, taunting her with unreal shapes and shifting light. She started forward again, still too afraid to go faster, still timidly shuffling her feet along the ground with each slow step.

The roaring of the fire suddenly exploded, and Aissa

staggered involuntarily, flinching away from the heat and light. Light, she thought distractedly, turning her head. It is brighter on that side. I can see the light of the fire. She turned away from the light, still doggedly following the downslope, still walking without lifting her feet more than a few inches with each step. Ocha's head lolled, and Aissa stopped to hitch the old woman higher in her arms. Then she started off again. The gurgling of the water was close now, and the ruddy light of the fire suffused her vision.

A root caught at Aissa's foot and she stumbled, catching her balance at the same moment she felt cool water flood her moccasin. She sank into the creek gratefully, feeling the heat of the fire on her face. She positioned Ocha carefully, cradling her head so that only her face was above the water. In that moment, the world exploded into an orange and yellow hell. Aissa squinted against her tears and the throbbing pain in her temple.

For a long time, Aissa could only watch, fascinated, afraid even to form the thought in her mind. "I can see," she whispered finally. The flames ate through a limb and it crashed to earth, sending out a shower of sparks—beautiful and evil. Aissa tore her gaze from the fire to look at Ocha's face, wincing at the sight of the ugly cut on her cheek. As the fire crashed and thundered around them, Aissa bathed the cut. At least the bleeding had stopped.

The roaring of the fire intensified until Aissa had to raise her eyes. She watched again as the trees groaned and died in the heat. She wet the skin of her face and Ocha's, finally tearing cloth from her skirt to cover Ocha's whole head. After an eternity, her lungs aching, she heard something besides the rumbling ferocity of the fire.

She heard Shadow Hawk calling her name. For the first time, she realized what being able to see would mean. It would mean more than her independence and the end of her fear. It would mean that she would be able to see his face, to see the love in his eyes again. She heard him call her name once more and she cried out, answering him. Then, because she knew they were safe, she began to cry.

Aissa looked back toward the mountain. The charred stumps would scar it for a lifetime. But none of the people had been hurt. The fire had stopped short of the camp. Only Ocha talked of her injury. She wore her scar proudly, a visible mark of her pride in Aissa's bravery. Aissa smiled as she imagined Ocha talking to a young woman who was too afraid to live her life. This time the story would start out, "I knew a young woman who lost her sight." She glanced up to see Shadow Hawk's face. His eyes were dark with sorrow, and Aissa knew that he was thinking about Ataza and what would happen to their people when he died. Shadow Hawk had faith in Gitano, but Aissa knew that he felt his place was at Gitano's side, helping.

"We'll go back," she said decisively.

"Ataza would not want me to go back." He was silent a moment. "It is time for Gitano to stand alone."

Aissa saw the darkness in his eyes and wanted to make him smile. "I know when we will have to go back."

"What do you mean?"

"I know that you couldn't resist bragging to your cousin."

"Bragging about what?"

Aissa tilted her head, smiling. "We will have children one day, won't we?"

Shadow Hawk nodded, the sorrow slowly lifting from his eyes. "Will we?"

"Of course, we will," Aissa chided him. "And you will be like a strutting rooster."

Shadow Hawk laughed. "You know who will be the strutting rooster?"

Aissa smiled and nodded. "My father."

Shadow Hawk nodded again. "I have missed Gerard. It will be good to see him."

Aissa smiled, thinking about her father. Shadow Hawk had told her about the letter he had written, so at least her father knew she was alive. It would be heaven to kiss him, and it would be heaven to sleep in the beautiful home they had all built together. Aissa leaned forward and dug her heels into her horse's sides, urging it into a gallop. The paint broke into a run, startling Shadow Hawk. Aissa shot him a mischievous grin, and he let her take the lead, thundering down the trail toward home.

Chapter Eighteen

Aissa looked at herself in the white gown that Flora had sewn for her. It was beautiful. The gown had long sleeves with lace cuffs and delicate pearl buttons. A lace bodice set off the shimmering satin of the gown, and the waist was cinched tightly and gathered in a sash in the back. Flora had pulled Aissa's long, golden hair into a loose knot on her head, leaving soft tendrils falling around her face and neck. She wore her mother's gold locket and a pair of pearl earrings that Flora had given her.

"You are the most charming bride I've ever seen in my life," Flora enthused, straightening out the skirt of the dress. "Are you nervous?"

"No," Aissa said smiling. "I've waited for this for a long time."

"You'll need a veil. Why didn't we think of that? Damn!"

"It's all right, Flora. I don't need a veil. I have this." Aissa opened a drawer of her armoire and unwrapped a packet of yellowed paper. "My mother wore this when she married my father. I'd like to wear it." She put the white lace over her head and adjusted it so that it fell just so on each side.

"It's lovely," Flora said. "It's perfect, in fact."

"Thank you, Flora. Is the minister here yet?"

"Yes, he's downstairs."

Aissa took a deep breath. "And the others? They're here?"

"They're here." Flora shook her head. "I have to say, this is going to be the strangest wedding I'll ever be witness to."

Aissa smiled and kissed Flora on the cheek. "Thank you for everything you've done, Flora. You've taken such good care of my father, I don't know what he would've done without you."

"I like taking care of your father." Flora walked around Aissa once more, checking to make sure everything was right. "You are beautiful, Aissa. Just be happy."

"I will," Aissa said, squeezing Flora's hand.

"You want some time alone?"

"If you don't mind." Aissa took a deep breath and walked to the window as Flora left the room. She could see Joe standing out in the yard talking to her father. Tears filled her eyes when she thought of her father and the look on his face when they had gotten home. He had cried openly and held her tightly. They had stayed up and talked most of the night.

She and Shadow Hawk had only been back at the ranch two days when he had asked her to marry him. She felt the queasiness in her stomach again, and she leaned against the wall, closing her eyes. For a long time, she had been afraid that she would have another headache and would lose her sight again. But it hadn't happened. And now she knew that it wouldn't. She still had her sight and the dizzy spells and nausea were nothing to worry about. She smiled. She knew she was going to have Shadow Hawk's child. She put her hand on her stomach and closed her eyes, forcing the tears away. She didn't want to cry now. She was so happy for the first time in a long time.

Aissa took a deep breath and walked to the door. She went to the top of the stairs where her father was waiting for her. She smiled broadly when she saw him and went into his waiting arms.

"You're lovely," Ben said, his voice trembling with emotion.

"Thank you, Father." Aissa reached up and wiped the tears from his cheeks. "These are tears of happiness I hope."

"Of course they are. I couldn't imagine a better man for you than Shadow Hawk. I have no doubts anymore."

"Thank you," Aissa said, hugging her father. "Well, I'm ready if you are."

"I'm more than ready."

"What does that mean?"

Ben shrugged. "Nothing."

"What've you been up to?"

"Just had a drink with the groom, that's all. He needed it to relax."

"He needed it?"

"Aissa, never mind, we have guests waiting."

Aissa took Ben's arm as they descended the staircase and walked through the house. She hesitated on the porch, searching the yard for Shadow Hawk. "Where is he?" she asked, more to herself than to her father.

"He's here. Come on."

Aissa gripped her father's arm tightly as they went down the porch stairs and walked to the garden. Joe and Flora stood by the oak tree next to the minister. Aissa smiled at them and then looked over at Shadow Hawk's family. Gitano stood, dressed in new, beaded buckskins, his arm around Ocha. Next to them were Broken Moon and Brave Heart. Broken Moon's lovely, dignified face was composed and joyous. Aissa smiled at them, but reserved her biggest smile for Gitano. She felt as if she were going to cry and realized quite suddenly how much she thought of Ocha and Gitano as family.

"Ah, here's the bride," the minister said.

"But where's the groom?" Joe asked, looking around.

Gitano stepped forward. "If he does not show, I would be willing to marry the woman."

Everyone laughed.

Aissa let go of Ben's arm and reached out to hug Gitano. "Thank you for being here," she said softly, kissing him on the cheek, "and for talking them into coming." She gestured toward Broken Moon and Brave Heart, knowing how much it meant to Shadow Hawk to have them here. Gitano nodded.

Aissa walked to Ocha. "I know this wasn't an easy trip for you to make, Ocha. I don't know how to thank you."

"I do not need your thanks, girl. Just marry my grandson."

Aissa and the others laughed again.

"Where is he anyway?" Ocha asked.

"I am here."

Aissa turned at the sound of Shadow Hawk's voice, stunned into silence by the intensity of his gaze. He walked slowly forward, as if measuring each step, never taking his eyes from Aissa's. He was dressed in near-white buckskins, worked and reworked until they were softened and sewn to perfection. Beads were sewn on the front of the shirt, depicting the outline of a hawk in flight. He made barely a sound in his newly sewn moccasins as he walked toward her. Aissa thought Shadow Hawk looked magnificent.

"You are ready to marry me?" he asked, his blue-gray eyes staring into hers.

"Yes," Aissa replied without hesitation.

The minister read a passage on marriage from the Bible and then he turned to Shadow Hawk. Aissa had asked the minister to keep the ceremony short, only to ask one question. "Will you take this woman to be your wife?"

"Yes," Shadow Hawk answered, a slight smile playing at the corners of his mouth.

"And you, Aissa, will you take this man to be your husband?"

"Yes," she answered, smiling back at Shadow Hawk.

"Do you have the ring?" the minister asked.

Shadow Hawk took the thin gold band from Ben and placed it on Aissa's finger. He listened to the minister's words and repeated them. "I, Shadow Hawk, take you, Aissa, to be my wife."

The minister hesitated, looked at Aissa and Shadow Hawk, then put their hands together. "With the power vested in me, I now pronounce you man and wife. You may kiss your bride."

Shadow Hawk looked at the minister and shook his head. "Not yet." He nodded to Gitano. Gitano led Ocha to them. She reached out and took their hands, holding one in each of hers.

"Do you love this woman, Shadow Hawk?"

"Yes, Grandmother."

"Will you be a good husband to her?"

"Yes."

"Will you comfort her when she is sad or when she is ill?"

"Yes."

"Will you help her raise your children?"

Shadow Hawk looked at Aissa and nodded. "Yes."

"And you, Aissa, do you love Shadow Hawk?"

"Yes, Ocha. I do."

"Will you be a good wife to him? Will you care for him at all times?"

"Yes, I will."

"Will you bear his children and help them to grow strong and wise?"

"Yes," Aissa said smiling.

"I stand between the two of you, and I feel the love you have for each other flow through me. It is a strong love, the kind of love that cannot be broken. You must let this love serve you in times of hardship."

Aissa looked up at Shadow Hawk, seeing his eyes soften and grow lighter as he looked at her.

"You must remember that along with love comes understanding. Do not take your love for granted." Ocha took their hands and put them together. "Do not let anyone or anything come between you." Ocha reached around her neck and took off two turquoise and silver necklaces. "Lean forward, Aissa." Ocha put one of the necklaces around Aissa's neck. "Now, you, Shadow," she said gently, lifting the other to place it around his neck. "Let these gifts remind you of the love you have created for yourselves and for those around you. Let the love you feel for each other remain unbroken." Ocha raised Aissa's and Shadow Hawk's hands to the sky and she chanted in Apache. Then she said simply, "You are married."

Aissa turned to Shadow Hawk. He stepped close to her and took her face in his hands, kissing her softly. "I love you," he said just loud enough for her to hear.

"What is happening?" Ocha asked impatiently.

"They are kissing, Grandmother," Gitano said.

"I am thirsty," Ocha said.

Shadow Hawk released Aissa, smiling and shaking his head. "She wants to speak with you alone," he whispered in Aissa's ear.

"Come, I'll get you something to drink." Aissa led Ocha out of the garden to the table in front of the house that was set up with food and drink. She poured Ocha a glass of lemonade and handed it to her.

Ocha sipped at it, grimaced slightly, then continued drinking. "You whites have strange tastes."

"Thank you, Ocha," Aissa said, ignoring Ocha's insult. "I feel truly married now."

"I care for you, girl. You saved my life."

"Just as you saved mine," Aissa said, kissing her on the cheek.

"Is there food?" Ocha asked.

Aissa laughed. "Yes, there is food but you probably won't like it." Aissa filled a plate for Ocha and led her to the porch to eat.

"I am well. Go find your husband."

"I'll be back to check on you," Aissa said.

"I do not need you to check on me," Ocha replied impatiently.

Aissa shook her head and was met by Gitano at the bottom of the stairs

"She likes you," he said with a broad grin.

"I'm glad she's not one of my enemies."

"Her enemies," he said, looking up at Ocha, "she turns into crows."

Aissa started to laugh but thought about all of the crows that flew above the Apache camp. She glanced quickly at Ocha then walked toward the table and poured herself a glass of lemonade.

"You all right?" Ben asked, standing beside her.

"I don't know when I've been happier, Father," she said, setting the glass down.

"Do you know how much I love you, Aissa?" Ben asked, gently holding his daughter in front of him.

"Yes," Aissa replied, seeing the joy in her father's eyes.

Ben nodded. "I wanted to give you a big party, you know, one with lots of people."

"These are the only people who matter to me, Father." Aissa kissed him on the cheek. She looked across to the oak where Shadow Hawk stood talking with his mother and younger brother. Broken Moon was clearly uncomfortable at this white man's ceremony, but Aissa also knew how much she loved her son and that nothing would've prevented her from coming. Brave Heart was looking around eagerly, taking in everything with wide eyes. Flora stepped toward Broken Moon, offering her a plate of food. Shadow Hawk glanced up and his eyes met Aissa's. She smiled as Shadow Hawk walked up to her. "Hello," she said, her eyes full of love.

"Hello, my wife," Shadow Hawk said gently, putting his arm around Aissa's waist. He looked at Ben. "Thank you, Gerard, for allowing me to marry your daughter."

"I somehow think you would've done it anyway."

Shadow Hawk shrugged and glanced at Aissa. "Yes, I probably would have. But you know what your blessing means to both of us."

"I know you'll take good care of her; you always have. And I don't think there's a man on the face of the earth who could love a woman more than you love her. So, just be happy, both of you." He held out his hand and Shadow Hawk shook it. "Now, I think it's time Flora and I started moving things inside."

Aissa looked at Shadow Hawk, but before she could say anything Joe walked up to them.

"I want to congratulate you both."

"Thank you, Joe," Aissa said, taking his hand in both of hers. "And thank you for looking after my father while I was away."

"It's all right, Aissa. I like your pa." Joe looked at Shadow Hawk. "Don't leave Aissa alone out here just in case Grimes is still around."

"I won't leave her alone," Shadow Hawk said, shaking Joe's hand.

"So, you're a married man now," Gitano said, walking up and slapping Shadow Hawk on the back. "Soon your wife will be after you to help her with the work, and she will grow fat and ugly. You will wonder what has become of your beautiful Aissa."

Shadow Hawk laughed. "I am not worried, Gitano. Visit with my wife while I go talk to Grandmother."

Aissa looked at Gitano, shaking her head. "I have a lot to say to you," she said, pulling him away from the others.

"What do you mean? You always talk in puzzles, white woman."

"Gitano, listen to me," Aissa said, holding his eyes with her own. "Thank you for being my friend and thank you for being here on my wedding day. I can't tell you how much it means to me." Aissa looked at the handsome young man who stood before her, knowing that he faced so much danger and hardship. She hated the injustice in the world that made it so. She took his hand and kissed it gently. "If I could have had a brother, I would have wanted him to be like you."

Gitano looked at Aissa, his dark eyes clouded with emotion. Slowly, he wrapped his arms around Aissa, a gesture she knew he found strange and foreign. He held her for a moment then nodded his head. "Enough of this, go to your husband."

Aissa smiled and walked to the porch. When Shadow Hawk saw her, he put his arm around her waist.

"I was just telling Grandmother that we are grateful she made such a long trip."

"Stop!" Ocha said impatiently, holding up her hand. "You insult me with such words. You are my grandson. I should be at your wedding." Ocha stood up, banging her walking stick on the porch floor. "Where is Gitano? I am ready to leave."

"I am here, Grandmother."

"You do not have to go, Grandmother. There is plenty of room here," Shadow Hawk said.

"I could not sleep in a white man's lodge."

"But it will soon be dark, Grandmother," Gitano added.

"It is always dark to me, Gitano. It makes no difference."

Gitano shrugged his shoulders and led Ocha down the stairs. "Your horse is over here."

"Wait, where is the white man? I wish to speak to him."

"I will lead you to him."

Aissa looked up at Shadow Hawk and saw him smiling at his mother and brother as they approached. Shadow Hawk playfully jabbed his brother in the stomach.

"I still cannot believe you are the same frightened little boy who tried to defend me against Red Arrow."

"Me, a frightened little boy?" Brave Heart shook his head. "Never."

Shadow Hawk grinned and embraced his brother. "Take care of Singing Bird, she is a good woman."

"Yes, I know." Brave Heart looked at Aissa. "I wish you

well, Aissa. It is plain for everyone to see how much my brother loves you."

"Thank you, Brave Heart."

"Go now," Broken Moon ordered her adopted son. "I want to say good bye to Shadow." Broken Moon looked up at Shadow Hawk, reaching up to run her hand over his cheek. "I did not expect you to grow so tall. Your father would have been pleased that you turned into such a fine man." Aissa started to walk away but Broken Moon took her arm. "Please, stay. You are my son's wife now." Broken Moon looked at them both. "It seems my mother leaves me little to say." She smiled sadly. "Hold tightly to each other."

Shadow Hawk pulled his mother to him, hugging her fiercely.

Aissa watched them. Broken Moon was so small that the top of her head fit beneath Shadow Hawk's chin. They held one another without speaking and after a moment, they began to sway slightly, almost as if they were dancing to music that no one else could hear. Aissa could see tears forming in Shadow Hawk's eyes when he finally released his mother and stepped back. Without another word, Broken Moon walked toward the horses.

Aissa took Shadow Hawk's hand, leading him toward Ocha and her father.

"And your wife also grew these flowers?" Ocha asked.

Ben smiled over Ocha's shoulder as Aissa and Shadow Hawk approached. "Yes, my wife loved her garden as much as Aissa does."

"It is time, Grandmother," Gitano prodded gently.

"Of course, just when I was beginning to enjoy good conversation with the white man." Ocha reached out, touching Ben's arm. "You have a fine daughter, white man. She is strong and possesses much courage. Thank you for allowing me to be here today."

"It was my pleasure," Ben replied. "I'll walk you to your horse."

Gitano smiled as he watched Ben lead Ocha. "I thought I was good with words, but I think your father is better, Aissa. Look at the way he calms my grandmother."

"Gerard is a sly one," Shadow Hawk agreed.

Aissa walked between Shadow Hawk and Gitano as they walked to the horses. Gitano hesitated before mounting. "I wish you both much happiness and many children."

"Thank you, Gitano," Aissa said, kissing him on the cheek once more.

"I wish I could go back with you, Cousin."

Gitano shook his head. "Your place is here, with your wife."

"If you need me for anything, send a messenger."

"I will. Do not worry so, Shadow."

Shadow Hawk placed a hand on Gitano's shoulder. "You will be a good leader to your people, Gitano. You will make your father proud."

"I will try."

"Tell Ataza. . . ." Shadow Hawk searched for the words. "Tell Ataza that he was my father. Tell him that I will never forget all of the things that he taught me. Tell him that my heart is full from the love he bestowed on me."

"I will tell him," Gitano said. "Do not be so troubled, Shadow. My father is at peace." Gitano looked around for Ocha. She had not mounted her horse and was still talking to Ben. "Are you ready, Grandmother?"

"No, I want to speak to Aissa and Shadow Hawk." Ocha held out her hands. "Each of you give me your hand," she said. "Never let yourselves forget how much you love each other at this moment."

Shadow Hawk kissed Ocha on the cheek. "Thank you, Grandmother, for everything you have taught me. I will miss you."

"You will see me soon enough when you bring me your son."

Without thinking, Aissa put her hand to her stomach.

Was it possible that Ocha knew about the child? She felt Ocha's hand squeeze tightly around hers.

"You have done well for yourself, girl. You have true courage and I believe you possess the soul of an Apache."

Aissa smiled. "Thank you, Ocha."

"Take care of yourself. You have others to think about now."

Aissa stood still, stunned by Ocha's words. She leaned close to the old woman's ear and whispered. "You know, don't you?"

Ocha nodded and whispered, "I know but it is up to you to tell your husband."

Aissa wrapped her arms around the old woman's thin frame and hugged her. "Thank you for everything."

"It is time to go," Ocha said, immediately dismissing Aissa. "Where are you, Gitano?"

"I am here, Grandmother." Gitano helped Ocha onto her horse and walked to his. "It will be a long ride home," he said to Shadow Hawk and Aissa.

"I heard what you said, Gitano," Ocha spoke in a harsh voice.

"I know, Grandmother," Gitano said, shaking his head as he mounted up. "Goodbye, Cousin. Take care of your beautiful wife, or some handsome Apache brave will one day ride in here and steal her away from you." He took Ocha's reins in his hand, flashed one last grin at the assembled group, and rode off.

Aissa stood, holding onto Shadow Hawk's arm, watching until Shadow Hawk's family was no longer in sight.

"Ben, help Joe move this table," Flora ordered.

Aissa turned around. Flora had already cleared the table and taken everything inside. Ben and Joe carried the table to the side of the house and Flora stood on the porch, purse over her arm, shawl draped around her shoulders.

"You ready, Ben?"

"I think so."

"You're not leaving already, are you?" Aissa asked.

"We have things to do, darlin'. And so do you," Flora said, her eyes twinkling.

"I'll be moseying myself," Joe said. "You two come by if you're in town."

Aissa watched as he walked to his horse. "Thank you, Joe." She turned when she heard her father and Flora come down the porch steps. "Are you sure you two have to go?"

"I think you two deserve some time alone," Ben said. "Why don't you two come into town tomorrow night and I'll buy us all dinner?"

"Oh no, you won't," Flora said. "If they're coming into town, I'll cook. I'm a better cook than Bessie is anyway." Flora hugged Aissa. "I'm happy for you, Aissa. I'm happy for you both."

"Thank you, Flora."

"I'll be waiting over by the buggy, Ben."

Ben looked at Shadow Hawk and Aissa. "You two look real fine together. Like a picture."

"Father—"

Ben held up his hand. "I love you, Aissa." He looked at Shadow Hawk. "Make her happy."

"I will try, Gerard."

Ben shook his head. "Well, I'd best go now. Don't forget about dinner tomorrow night."

"We won't," Aissa said, stepping forward into the circle of her father's arms. She stayed for a moment, remembering how safe she'd always felt there. Then she felt him gently push her away. "I love you, Father." She kissed him on both cheeks and saw the tears in his eyes. She held onto Shadow Hawk as Ben and Flora drove away, and then she turned and looked up at him. It had been a long time since they'd been together. And she had never wanted him more than she wanted him at this moment.

"What is it?" Shadow Hawk asked, concern in his voice.

Without speaking, Aissa reached up and wrapped her

arms around Shadow Hawk's neck, kissing him softly at first, then more passionately. "Make love to me," she whispered, her mouth close to his. Without answering, Shadow Hawk picked her up in his arms went into the house, closing the door behind them. He carried her upstairs and into the room that they would now share. Aissa eased herself down until her toes touched the floor, her body close to Shadow Hawk's. She untied the belt around his waist and lifted the buckskin shirt over his head, dropping it to the floor. Shadow Hawk sat down and tried to pull Aissa with him but she backed away, unbuttoning her boots and rolling her stockings down her long legs. As Shadow Hawk watched, she pulled her dress over her head and stepped out of her undergarments. Then she stepped forward, sliding her slip up to her waist.

Shadow Hawk wrapped his arms around Aissa, pressing his face into her belly, leaving a trail of kisses on her flushed skin until he found the center of her passion. He dropped to his knees and Aissa tangled her fingers in his hair, throwing her head back. She bit her lip, trying to control her love cries. He kissed her again, like she had never been kissed before, and she began to move against him. Shadow Hawk had loved her in many ways but nothing had prepared her for the heat and overwhelming desire she now felt. The intensity was almost frightening, and she tried to move away but Shadow Hawk held her against him and she found herself being swept by a tide of sensations she had never before experienced. Her breath came faster and faster until she could only arch her back and let the thundering waves engulf her. Shadow Hawk held her until the tremors subsided.

Shadow Hawk stood up and Aissa leaned against him, still filled with love. She wanted to give him as much pleasure as he had given her. With trembling fingers, she unlaced his buckskins, pushing him gently back onto the bed. Kneeling, she pulled off his moccasins then slid his pants down over his lean hips. He reached out to pull her down beside him but she straddled him instead, moving sensuously against him. Reaching down, he guided himself inside her and Aissa gloried in his closeness and his desire. He took over the rhythm that she had begun. Moving faster and faster, Aissa felt the depth of his love for her. Shadow Hawk thrust himself more deeply into her. When he cried out her name, she felt her own soft explosion and she collapsed onto his chest. For a long time they lay together in happy exhaustion. Shadow Hawk reached down to push her hair back from her face.

Aissa looked up at him, her eyes filling with tears of joy. After all they had endured, all the times they had been separated by fate, the future was finally theirs. All of their happiness was ahead of them.

Even after Ray saw the lights go out at the Gerard ranch, he waited for a long time until he was sure Shadow Hawk and Aissa were asleep. He had watched them during the day, had seen the people in the yard, and had seen them all leave. Now it was time to do what he should've done a long time ago.

He guided his horse down the slope and into the pasture, stopping before he reached the stable yard. He thought about Aissa and about how miserable she had made his life. Involuntarily, he rubbed his shoulder. Thanks to her, he'd probably never have full use of his arm again.

He stepped quietly onto the porch and touched the front door, knowing it would be barred. But to his surprise, the door opened easily, squeaking slightly as he closed it behind him. This had been too easy, he thought. He took his gun out of its holster and held it in front of him. Tonight he would make sure she never interfered with him again. He started toward the stairs then froze. There were footsteps on the floorboards above his head. As he listened, the footsteps paused, then started again coming down the stairs.

Ray quickly backed behind the cupboard that stood in the kitchen, his gun held ready. He heard the footsteps as the person crossed the room to the kitchen. Whoever it was, was coming closer. Abruptly, the footsteps stopped. A moment later, Ray heard the scraping sound of a match being struck and the yellowish light of a lantern illuminated the kitchen. Ray pressed himself back against the wall, waiting. The footsteps came closer. The lantern cast a shadow on the wall, the silhouette of the Apache.

Shadow Hawk walked closer to the cupboard. As he reached up to open it, Ray stepped around behind him and clubbed him on the back of the head with his pistol. Shadow Hawk staggered, falling to his knees, and Ray hit him again. Ray stepped back quickly as Shadow Hawk lunged sideways and sprawled, unconscious on the floor. For a moment, Ray stood still, his gun pointed at Shadow Hawk. Then he walked toward him, nudging him with the toe of his boot, then kicking him. Shadow Hawk didn't move. Ray nodded in satisfaction. Maybe later he would let Aissa watch him kill the Apache. He turned and headed toward the stairs.

Aissa opened her eyes, smiling as she remembered the lovemaking that she and Shadow Hawk had shared. She reached out to touch him but he wasn't there. She heard a noise down in the kitchen and smiled. Neither one of them had eaten at their wedding. She was hungry, too. Drowsy, she sank back against her pillow, waiting for his footsteps on the stairs. She wasn't sure whether or not she had dozed off, but when she had awakened again, Shadow Hawk had not returned.

Aissa got up and straightened her slip. It was a warm night and she didn't want to take the time to get dressed. She started across the room but before she could call out Shadow Hawk's name, the sound of footsteps on the stairway made her stop in confusion. She had learned to listen well to all sounds when she was blind; now in the darkness, she listened. She knew Shadow Hawk's footsteps and these were not his; he made little or no sound. Whoever was coming up the stairs was trying hard not to make any noise. But the footsteps were heavy; the sound of a man who was wearing boots.

She turned and went to the nightstand next to the bed. She opened the drawer and took out the pistol her father had bought her for protection a long time ago. She unhinged the cylinder, quickly pushed bullets into the chambers, then clicked it shut. As the footsteps neared she hurried to stand behind the open door. The steps stopped short of the door. The amber glow of a lantern filled the doorway. She flattened herself against the wall, trying to still the shaking of her hands.

"No use fighting it, Aissa. You knew I'd find you." Aissa closed her eyes at the sound of Ray's voice, fighting the fear that threatened to overcome her. She remained silent and still against the wall.

"You can't fight me, Aissa. There aren't too many places you can hide. I've got the advantage. I can see, you can't."

Slowly and quietly, Aissa lowered the gun until she was holding it with one hand behind her back. Although Ray didn't know it, she had the advantage. He still thought she was blind, and she didn't intend to let him think otherwise. The steps and the light came closer. Ray was standing in the doorway.

"I know you're in here somewhere, Aissa. If you want me to look for you, I will. We can make a game out of it if you like."

From behind the door, Aissa could see Ray as he walked into the room, lantern in one hand, gun in the other, then he was inside. Suddenly, he yanked the door away from her. She kept the gun behind her back.

"Did you think you could hide from me?" Ray asked, taking Aissa's arm and jerking her forward.

Aissa looked past Ray, trying to appear as if she were still blind. "Get out of here. Leave me alone."

"I'll never leave you alone, Aissa. Don't you know that." Ray set the lantern down and pulled Aissa to him, crushing her against his chest. He held the barrel of the gun up to her head and ran it through her hair. "You are one of the prettiest women I've ever seen, you know that. You could've avoided all this trouble if you'd just been willing to marry me in the first place."

"I hate you," Aissa said, struggling against Ray, trying to keep the gun hidden in the folds of her slip.

"I don't care if you hate me. In fact, I like it." Ray pressed his mouth to Aissa's but she pulled away. Ray took her face and held it, forcing her to accept his kisses. "I figured we could have a good time before . . . well, you know."

"Where's Shadow Hawk?"

Ray forced Aissa toward the bed. "Your lover won't be helping you anymore, Aissa. He's dead."

"No!" Aissa screamed, struggling to get away from Ray, to put enough distance between them so she could raise the gun and shoot. Ray pushed her onto the bed. The gun was in her right hand, pinned underneath her by Ray's weight. Aissa fought frantically but Ray only laughed, holding her down, forcing his tongue into her mouth. When she bit him, he laughed, a deep, ugly laugh. Aissa remembered that Ray was the kind of man who grew more excited when a woman struggled. Aissa forced herself to let all of her muscles go slack. When she felt him slide her slip up her thighs, she didn't move or utter a sound. She felt his hands on her thighs and on her belly but still didn't move. She stared at the ceiling, praying for the strength she would need. She arched her back, sliding the gun a little at a time, working to free it, even as Ray continued to move his hands over her body.

"What's wrong, Aissa? You don't seem so brave." Ray straddled Aissa and got up to his knees. He dropped the gun on the bed. As he fumbled with his belt, Aissa eased her pistol from underneath her back and brought it to her side.

"Get off me, Ray," she pleaded.

"I don't think so. Not this time," Ray said, his hands shaking with desire.

"Get off." Aissa's voice was hard as she cocked the pistol and held it to Ray's head. When Ray hesitated, Aissa pressed the barrel to his temple. "I'll kill you if I have to." When Ray rolled to the side, Aissa stood up, careful to keep the gun trained on him. "Get on the floor."

"What?"

Aissa clenched her teeth and squeezed the trigger. A bullet went into the bed next to Ray. He scrambled onto the floor, lying on his stomach. Aissa walked around the other side of the bed and picked up Ray's gun. She threw it through the open window and heard it hit the dirt.

"You can see."

"Yes, I can see. It's over, Ray."

"It'll never be over, Aissa. Not until one of us is dead," Ray said angrily. "You'd better kill me now cause if you don't, you know I'll be back."

Aissa held the gun in front of her. She pointed it at Ray's back but her hand began to shake. She couldn't shoot a man in cold blood, no matter what he'd done to her. "I'm taking you into town. You're going to jail."

Ray laughed loudly, looking up at Aissa. "I'm not going to jail. How're you going to get me there all alone?"

Aissa stood, trying to control the shaking in her hands. Ray was right, she couldn't get him into town alone.

"You thinking about the Apache? Too bad, he can't help you. He isn't going to wake up until day after tomorrow."

Shadow Hawk! Did that mean he was alive or was Ray lying? What if he was lying downstairs bleeding to death? She had to think of a way to help him.

"What's wrong, Aissa? I don't think I killed him, but

you won't know unless you go look, will you?"

Aissa tried to think. How could she go find Shadow Hawk without letting Ray go?

"What you really need," Ray said, his voice cold, "is a piece of rope. But then how would you tie me up without laying the gun down."

"Shut up!" Aissa started to step backward but Ray lunged forward. She felt his iron-like grip on her ankle. He pulled her forward until she lost her balance, but she held onto her gun as she hit the floor. Ray threw himself onto her, his hands at her throat. Aissa stared, transfixed, at the hatred that twisted Ray's face into ugliness. She gasped for air, realizing that he had left her no choice. She raised the gun to Ray's chest and pulled the trigger. Ray looked at her in astonishment, raising his hands to cover the wound in his chest. Then his head fell to one side. Ray Grimes was dead.

Aissa dropped the gun on the floor, realizing for the first time that she was crying. She stood up, trembling. She stared at Ray a second longer, then picked up the lantern and hurried down the stairs. Shadow Hawk was lying on the floor by the cupboard. His head was bleeding but he was breathing steadily. She wet a cloth and wiped his face. "Shadow Hawk," she said his name. She began to cry again and rested her face against his. "Please be all right." She lay next to him on the floor, her head on his chest, her arms around him. "I love you," she sobbed, closing her eyes.

"Aissa."

Aissa heard his voice in her dream. In her dream, everything was safe and fine.

"Aissa."

She opened her eyes, squinting at the sunlight that showered the room. She looked up at Shadow Hawk. His eyes were open. "You're awake?" She sat up, touching his face. "You're all right?"

"I think so," Shadow Hawk said, struggling to sit up. "What happened?"

"Ray was here. He was waiting for you when you came downstairs. He knocked you out and came for me."

"Where is he?"

"He's dead," Aissa said, lowering her eyes. "I shot him."

Shadow Hawk pulled Aissa into his arms. "I'm sorry. I shouldn't have been so careless."

"You can't always be there to protect me."

Shadow Hawk stroked Aissa's hair. "But I want to protect you."

She pulled away, touching his face. "When I was blind, you made me realize that I had to depend on myself. It's the same now that I can see."

"So, you don't need me anymore?"

Aissa smiled. "I will always need you."

Shadow Hawk rubbed his head. "And it seems I will always need you to protect me."

Aissa kissed Shadow Hawk. "I've loved you from the moment I saw you in the loft. I knew you would never hurt me."

"But I did hurt you, Aissa," Shadow Hawk said, brushing her cheek with the back of his hand.

"You didn't mean to, I know that. You helped me when I needed you, and you helped to make me strong."

Shadow Hawk put his arms around Aissa, holding her against his chest. "When I first saw the white girl with the eyes the color of the sky and the hair like new corn, I knew I would love her. I just didn't know how much. I want everyone to know the love I feel for you."

"Even your people?"

"Especially my people."

Aissa sat up, a sly expression on her face. "Well, you can show them all how much you love the white woman when we go back there."

"We won't be going there for awhile."

"Yes, we will." Aissa took Shadow Hawk's hand and put it on her stomach. "Your son is alive in here and will be born before the winter. That will be a good time to visit your people."

"My son?" Shadow Hawk's eyes narrowed as he looked at Aissa. Gently, he ran his hand over her belly.

"Soon I will grow big and round," Aissa said, smiling.

"I will look forward to it." Shadow Hawk held Aissa to him. "It will not be easy for our son, Aissa."

She looked at him, her eyes filled with love. "It hasn't been easy for us either, but it has been worth it, hasn't it?"

"Yes, it has been worth it."

Aissa closed her eyes as Shadow Hawk kissed her, and she felt his mouth press gently against hers and his arms hold her tightly. This was where she wanted to be. There was no other place for her but here in the shelter of Shadow Hawk's arms, surrounded by his love. This was home.